AN EPIC
OF HONOR

ELIZABETH OF CHESTER

None frightened the fiery Elizabeth, neither man nor beast. Yet she ached with a burning passion she could neither control nor forget.

ROGER, EARL OF HERESFORD

No stranger to women and the manly words and caresses that softened their hearts, he found in Elizabeth a woman not easily tamed. He was determined to bend her to his will with love . . . despite royal intrigue, epic battles, and a mounting turbulence of sexual tensions heightened by the great conflicts of England's history.

HENRY OF ANJOU

A central figure in the tumultuous course of events, he inspired both devotion and rebellion. Though only 18, he strove and schemed with kingly fervor . . . to stop at nothing until he had ascended the throne of England.

A passionate and troubled quest
set against the rich tapestry of English history
in chivalry's most treacherous era.

ROBERTA GELLIS

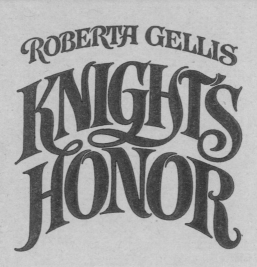

KNIGHT'S HONOR

AVON
PUBLISHERS OF BARD, CAMELOT, DISCUS, EQUINOX AND FLARE BOOKS

AVON BOOKS
A division of
The Hearst Corporation
959 Eighth Avenue
New York, New York 10019

First Avon Printing, June, 1976

AVON TRADEMARK REG. U.S. PAT. OFF. AND
FOREIGN COUNTRIES, REGISTERED TRADEMARK—
MARCA REGISTRADA, HECHO EN CHICAGO, U.S.A.

Printed in the U.S.A.

To FELECIE
who so patiently read
and so patiently listened.

IRISH SEA

IRELAND

St. George's Channel

WALES

Chester

Painscastle

Hereford

SEVERN

Cheltenham
Gloucester

Dursley
Bristol

Bath
Devi

Bruton

Ilminster

Bridport

Seaton

BRISTOL CHANNEL

N
W   E
S

Miles

0   50

map by palacios

ockbridge
Tuxford
Lincoln
Nottingham
Corby
Oundle
L A N D
Norwich
urford
Bampton
Oxford
Faringdon
Shrivenham
LONDON
Henley
THAMES
Wallingford
Hungerford
ownton
Arundel
ENGLISH CHANNEL
FRANCE
NORMANDY

AUTHOR'S NOTE

BECAUSE OF THE LENGTH OF TIME which separates us from the period of this novel and the very limited literateness of the period written about, it is very difficult to write a perfectly accurate historical novel. The principal character of this book, Roger, Earl of Hereford, did exist, and the military activities in which he engaged in the company of Henry of Anjou, later to become Henry II of England, are historical facts. Most of the information regarding the actual events comes from the *Gesta Stephani*,[1] one of the few chronicles written in England during the period of the reign of Stephen of Blois and the best source of information about it. Unfortunately, like most chronicles—and, indeed, like most purely historical material except direct biography—the *Gesta* makes virtually no reference to the personalities or appearances of the characters mentioned, all being called, according, probably, to the author's feelings, brave and energetic or barbarous and wicked. Equally, no mention is made of the personal affairs of the individual. Under these circumstances, and within the limits of making no alteration in any truly historical event or personality, the author has considered herself free to invent a suitable wife, character, and family for her hero.

Where any historical information is available about the characters mentioned in the book, it has been followed faithfully. About the hero of the book, the *Gesta* has only to say, "Roger Miles's son then succeeded him as Earl of Hereford, a young man but distinguished for exceptional prowess."[2] William, Duke of Gloucester is briefly char-

[1] *Gesta Stephani* (*Deeds of Stephen*), K. R. Potter, ed. and trans., Thomas Nelson and Sons, Ltd., London, 1955, pp. 139–48.
[2] *Ibid.*, p. 106.

acterized as "a man already advanced in years but effem-
inate and more devoted to amorous intrigue than war."[3]
And the Earl of Chester was said to have "devoted himself
wholly to the cunning devices of his accustomed bad
faith."[4]

Henry of Anjou's personality and appearance are treated much more fully in several other works, *De Nugis
Curialium* of Walter Map, the *Epistolae* of Bernard of
Clairvaux, and *De Principis Instructione* by Giraldus
Cambriensus, to name the most important. Within the
limits of disagreements among these authors themselves,
an accurate reproduction of his person and character has
been attempted.

The author has taken some liberty in marrying Hereford
to a daughter of Chester (who may never have existed),
but the long and faithful association between those two
houses may indeed betoken some close blood ties between
them. Another liberty has been taken in introducing Hereford's private feud with de Caldoet and with Peverel, Constable of Nottingham (for which there is no historical
evidence whatsoever, although the inital event—the poisoning of Chester's vassals—did take place) into the book. No
disruption of the actual historical events is caused by this
intrusion of fiction into fact, however, and such events were
common enough in the terribly disrupted period of Stephen's reign. Certain characters aside from those already
mentioned, are purely fictional—the entire Gaunt family and
Alan of Evesham, for example, and they are introduced
solely for the purpose of the plot and character contrast.

For the rest of the material of the book, descriptions of
food, clothing and armor, of dwelling places and forms of
amusement, of methods of warfare and siege engines, as
well as for the more important concept of homage and the
attitudes regarding duty, honor, and personal relationships, the author has been as accurate as possible within
the range of about one hundred years. As a final explanation for the well-informed reader who may be somewhat
surprised to read of a baron of the twelfth century crying

[3] *Gesta Stephani (Deeds of Stephen)*, K. R. Potter, ed. and trans.,
Thomas Nelson and Sons, Ltd., London, 1955, pp. 139–40.
[4] *Ibid.*, p. 128.

out for peace and feel that this is a false note for the period, the following points must be made. It is to be understood, firstly, that the barons who desire peace mean peace as we know it today; that is, a condition of many minor wars and no major ones—except that the area in which the wars take place is small rather than global. Secondly, the condition to which England was reduced during the reign of Stephen was so pitiable that even men who considered war as a pleasant if rather rough sport began to look for a king who would have some measure of control over the barony. According to *The Peterborough Chronicle*, under the year 1137:

> ... then (they) perceived that he (Stephen) was a mild man and soft and good, and did no justice, then they did all atrocities. They had done him homage and sworn oaths; but no man held his troth. They were all perjured and their honor worthless, for every lord made castles and held against him and filled the land full of castles. They oppressed the miserable people of the land very much with castle works. When the castles were made they filled them with devils and evil men. Then the took the men, those whom they believed had any goods, both by nights and by days, men and women, and cast them in prison to get gold and silver, and tortured them with indescribable pains, for never were martyrs so tortured as they were ...

A long passage follows in which the individual types of torture used are described, and then the commentator continues:

> I cannot nor may I tell all the horrors nor all the pain that they caused the miserable people of this land and that lasted the 19 winters while Stephen was king, and ever it was worse and worse. They imposed forced payments on towns at all times and called it protection for the miserable people. When they understood they had no more to give, then they

burned all the towns so that you might travel a full
day's travel and you might never find a man living in
a town nor land tilled . . .[5]

Under such conditions it is understandable that even a
warlike man who considered fighting with his neighbor his
right and his chief form of amusement might crave at least
a temporary cessation of hostilities, especially when it is
considered that there was no industrialization and all
wealth came from the agricultural products of the land.

---

[5] *The Peterborough Chronicle*, under the year 1137. Translation by
the author.

CHAPTER 1

THE PALE SUN of late November, cold and white, giving light without warmth, turned the narrow strip of beach into a scintillating ribbon, beautiful but uninviting. The frothy breakers before the bow of the small ship had lost their summer look of soft lace and glittered with hard sparks like ice. Roger of Hereford removed his leather gauntlets sewn with steel and tucked them under his arm so that he could blow on his fingers. He repressed a shudder at the thought that he would have to get down into that water in a few minutes to wade ashore; he could see the party waiting for him clearly now. But the wetting would bring him home—home to England. It had been a long time.

The young man who looked across the narrowing band of water to the shore was dressed in the latest fashion for a man of war in 1149. Over the hauberk, which was a continuous garment of double-and triple-linked metal rings that covered him completely from the hood for his head to his knees, he wore a peacock-blue surcoat lavishly embroidered down the front and around the cuffs and hem with golden leaves. The surcoat, which fell nearly to his ankles, hid the fact that the hauberk was split from hip to hem to permit him to sit astride a horse. Through the splits, when the surcoat blew open, one could see the white wool tunic that protected his body somewhat from the gall of the steel. Leather shoes, soft and pliable to make foothold and stirrup hold more secure, were cut low and exposed brilliant red chausses which did service as both stockings and underpants, cross-gartered to make them fit smoothly with the same peacock blue as the robe.

One would have thought that such a combination of

1

brilliance would have obscured the wearer, but Roger of Hereford could wear anything. So far in his life, for he had just passed his twenty-second year, no amount of exposure had been able to affect the perfect whiteness of his complexion, untroubled as yet with much growth of beard. Unlike most of his contemporaries, his face was unmarked by scars of war. This was not due to lack of fighting experience but to good fortune, almost as if Fortuna herself could not bear to mar that great beauty. Fine brows, sufficiently darker than his yellow-gold hair to lend character to his face, arched smoothly above large, almond-shaped eyes of a particularly changeable shade of blue. Thought, sorrow, or passion could make them almost black; anger and laughter could make them the blue of a hot coal flame; and they could burn with an almost white incandescence when their owner's spirit was lifted to enthusiasm. The straight, sharply modeled nose might have been a trifle short for perfection, but no one could cavil at the mouth which had the ideal classical contour, even to the faint smiling upturn at the corners.

To say that the young Earl of Hereford was unconscious of these beauties was untrue; he used them, particularly on women, rather ruthlessly to gain his ends. However it was true that he was not vain, merely accepting the gift of personal beauty as he accepted the fact of his important social position and substantial wealth. Certainly at the moment he would have bartered every scrap of his good looks for the assurance that the enterprise he was setting out upon would have a successful conclusion. This enterprise was no less than treason, although Roger of Hereford called it by other names, for Hereford had returned to England to take part in a rebellion which would wrest the crown of England from Stephen of Blois and set it upon Henry of Anjou's head.

On the shore, a few moments later, Lord Hereford set his jaws to keep his teeth from chattering and reached impatiently for his long indigo-blue cloak lined with the finest squirrel pelts, the silvery-gray vair. He had just about succeeded in controlling his shivering when the group on the beach reached him.

"Greetings, Roger. How was your trip?"

"Very calm, very cold. For all that you wrote to watch for trouble, we did not sight another ship in the entire passage. They were waiting for larger game, I suppose, or your informant was shying at shadows. How goes it with you, your grace?"

The Duke of Gaunt removed a gauntlet to extend a hand to be kissed. He was an old man now, having passed threescore years, but was still hard and vigorous, his eyes keen and clear, and his mouth, though sunken with toothlessness, held firm and hard.

"I will tell you on the way. Mount up. My aged bones feel the cold."

At a lifted hand, five extra horses were moved forward for Hereford, his three squires, and his body servant, and they got under way for a nearby keep belonging to the friendly Duke of Devonshire.

"The news of importance I will keep until we can sit and drink to it in comfort. For the rest, it is quickly told. We are all well."

"I thought to see Lord Storm here to greet me, Is he still so tied to the Lady Leah's skirts that he could not tear himself away?"

Gaunt laughed coarsely. "Ay and nay. He still thinks that if she sheds a tear or he misses a night in her bed the heavens will fall, but he does his duty properly. I must say to my daughter-in-law's credit that she interferes in no way with that. Cain is in Scotland, and has been these four months. We look for him any day at home now. He went to confirm the plans for the knighting of Henry of Anjou according to what you last wrote us about that, and he was delayed to help stave off more Norse incursions. By God, you would think those devils could not feel the cold the way they continue to fight in the dead of winter."

"And will he ride north with us again in the spring to the knighting?"

"That I cannot answer, Hereford. It depends on many things. Ah, here we are. Let us get warm and comfortable and I will tell you what I can."

They clattered over the drawbridge of the moated keep, the two destriers' iron-shod hoofs ringing sharply, the unshod palfreys making a duller echo. Under the portcullis they rode, Hereford keeping his eyes straight ahead with a slight effort. Although he gave no evidence of it at all, he could not totally repress the inner qualm that riding under that heavy iron gate with its sharp pointed base gave him. Once the portcullis of a keep he had previously thought was friendly had come down. It had missed him so nearly that it tore the surcoat from his back and split his horse in two, giving evidence of what his fate might have been. This one stayed put, however, screaming and groaning its way down to rest position only after they were well inside. One flight up on the outside, Hereford's shoes, frozen hard, crackled and caught on the rough-hewn wooden boards. Then through the dark turrent entrance and out into the great hall lit by the windows in their deep embrasures and the two great blazes of fire, one at each end.

Both men shed their furred cloaks but remained at a respectable distance from the fire because the heat, although pleasant in one respect, was agonizing as their chilblained hands and feet thawed out. They were too accustomed to this form of discomfort, however, to comment upon it, and as soon as servants had brought hot spiced wine to drink, Hereford spoke a trifle impatiently.

"Well, my lord, now that we are private, what news? What word you sent to France was so ambiguous that we could not make head nor tail of it. I was hard put to keep Henry quiet—harder since I must admit that I was not overhappy myself."

"What did you want me to say? You know how everything has gone against us. Robert of Gloucester died two months after you left England, and with him the organized resistance in the south died. In the beginning we had some hope that William might come into his own with both his father and his brother Philip gone. He did win that brilliant battle at Castle Cary against Henry de Tracy, as you heard, but that hope did not live long." The old man spat contemptuously on the floor. "He found the effort too great. He is back among his women, his boys, his perfumes, and his jewels."

"No surprise to me. I never liked that family for all your trust in them, your grace. I grant you Robert was a great man, but the sons—and William was worst of all. A man who could stomach the de Caldoets as vassals—"

"Nay, Roger, do not put that upon him. Hugh was hanged and Ralph driven out as soon as an excuse could be found to be rid of them. No man may drive a vassal off his land without reason, no matter how foul that vassal is, and you know it. Philip was all right too. A man cannot help dying. Besides, this discussion is neither here nor there. If Gloucester is done, they are done. William, I must say, has not turned against us. He will do what he can in the old way; he only will not fight. The troops of Gloucester lie still for want of a leader. I was almost tempted to tell Cain—I even approached him on leading them—but you know how he is about his oath of homage. He will keep it to the letter, and before I forced him to something so much against his heart and will, I bethought me that there was one among us almost as well suited to the task and who had never given a personal oath of fealty to King Stephen."

"Who? Who would the troops of Gloucester obey besides yourself or Lord Storm? Chester is no man for a task with a steady purpose; Lincoln would use them only for personal gain; Norfolk—"

"What of Hereford?"

"Me?" The one word exploded out of the young man and was followed by a dead silence.

Gaunt rubbed his itching, burning hands against each other wishing vaguely that he was at home, where his daughter-in-law would hasten to make him comfortable. He pulled his mind back to the work in hand, his keen eyes following the young earl who had turned his back and paced away. Would he jump at it, Gaunt wondered? Hereford was so young, and this was a tremendous responsibility. Then Gaunt's eyes narrowed; it was not Hereford who was young, it was he who was old. Hereford had been earl since sixteen, when his father had died in a hunting accident in 1143. He had later won his right to his position by staying alive and free at the disastrous battle of Faringdon. Hereford had won his name as a fighting man there too, helping to hold the walls as long as practical and, when the men of the castle decided to surrender, he and a small band of faithful troops had hacked their way through the entire opposing army so that he might bring his name at least out of that catastrophe uncaptured and unransomed. Nonetheless, Gaunt mistrusted Hereford's ability to maintain a fixed purpose over a long period, for his eyes, old in the experience of men, saw something haunted behind the usual madcap gaiety of his young friend.

Hereford was returning, his eyes dark and his fine brows drawn together in a worried frown. "My lord Duke, I cannot do it."

Gaunt prevented his mouth from dropping open with an effort and allowed an expression of contempt to creep over his usually wooden face. "Does that mean you are afraid to undertake the work, that you are incapable of doing so, or that you are unwilling to do so?"

Flushing bright red and biting at his mouth, Hereford swallowed hard. He had learned most painfully to repress the hot retorts that rose to his lips. "It means exactly what I said, no more, no less. I cannot undertake that burden." Hereford threw out an appealing hand. "Nay, Lord Gaunt do not torture me. You know I would give the eyes out of my head and the soul out of my body to lead that force, but my lands cannot support the charges of such an army, I would be beggared and they would be starving in one short moon, and you know how that would end. They would take to raiding and I—I would be one more outlaw baron tearing the body of the land that gave him birth for no purpose. Storm might do it if you allowed him to draw on your purse as well as his own, but I—" he swallowed his disappointment—"I cannot do it."

Gaunt's face cleared as though by magic, and he began to laugh. "The boy grows into a man and considers before he leaps. Well done, Roger. But what sort of people have you been consorting with who would ask you to bear the burden of leading an army and in addition expect you to pay the costs of the force."

Hereford's eyes came alive with excitement. "People!" He gesticulated an impatient dismissal of the dealings he had had in the past two years. "But who—?"

"William of Gloucester is perfectly willing to bear the

major cost so long as he is awarded the major portion of the spoils. To a limited extent Cain and I will help—not with the revenues from our own lands, that is not consistent with our oath to Stephen, and although I have come very close of late to being forsworn, I will not yet go so far. But Cain has three wardships now and what we do with the income from those lands, so long as it is to the eventual benefit of the child, is our own affair. if you provide for those men you yourself bring, no more will be asked of you—except to win the battles you engage in."

Forgotten were chilblained feet, cold, and discomfort. Roger of Hereford, poised in the quivering alertness so characteristic of him, laughed without merriment. "At least you may be sure I will not be there to be reproached if I do not. A man who does not win when given a chance deserves to die."

Shaking his head, Gaunt replied, "I should not have said that. You will not always be a free agent, you know, Hereford. This early action will be part of a larger plan and there will be times when it will be necessary to take a calculated defeat."

"A larger plan? What plan can there be but to defeat Stephen and wrest the throne from him?"

Gaunt raised a hand. "Curb your tongue, Roger. Servants are not deaf-mutes. Can you not see they are setting up for dinner?"

"Are we not safe here? Devonshire is surely with us."

"Ay and nay. Personally yes, but he has great interests and wide connections. Anyway it is never safe to trust another man's servants and not too safe to trust your own with everything. Just lower your voice and watch carefully for any man who lingers overlong in our vicinity."

"Very well," Hereford replied impatiently, but in a much lower tone, "but what plan? Are we not to seat Henry on the throne?"

"Ay, in the long run, but to depose Stephen is not enough. All we will have is the same trouble over again except that we of the west will fight for the king and the south and east against him. That is senseless."

"I suppose worse might happen to Stephen than deposition."

"So you kill him. Eustace is a man now and has showed himself a fine fighter. Maud is no weaker or stupider than two years since. There is even a second son approaching manhood, and Constance may well give Eustace an heir. Will you slay them all?"

"If needful."

"Nay, Roger, your words are hard but I know you well. I might bring myself to it, but you and even my own son could not. The women would weep and thereby save themselves, and neither of you could bring yourselves to touch a hair on a babe's head. Men are soft these days."

Lord Hereford moved restlessly, kicking pettishly at a stool nearby. "Then what do we do, wait longer? Two long years have already—"

"No. Would I ask you to lead Gloucester's army if we planned to do nothing but wait? in the spring we will begin what was planned long ago. You will prick Stephen here, Hugh Bigod will raise Norfolk against him, Arundel in the south, King David in the north. Between this and that, he will have neither rest nor peace, and all our efforts together will be bent on taking Eustace."

"Eustace? Why not Stephen?"

"Because Stephen is the king. You know he is a brave man, no fear for himself could make him renounce the throne and, even if we could force him to do so, or if we stooped to infamy and killed him, Eustace might suceed him. Stephen, however, is brave only for himself. He is a man first and a king later—and that is why he is of no worth as a king. If we take the son and threaten him with that—the cub is precious to him as I have seen myself—then I think we will have him. Between the pain of constant fighting, rushing now north, now south, now east, now west, and the agony of losing that child, dearer than life to him, I think he will be glad to give us the crown for Henry and return to Blois. We will pay him well to leave us in peace. It will be worth his while. The rest will be up to Henry.

Gaunt sighed suddenly, remembering he was tired. He was always tired now, even in the morning when he woke from a good night's sleep. Damn Stephen and burn him. If only the plague would take the entire family, Gaunt thought with half his mind, he could lie down and rest. Threescore years and one was too old for these hard times. That was an age for peace, for sitting by the fire and watching your grandchildren—although he had only one. The other half of the duke's brain considered Hereford who had not yet replied to his reasoning.

The young man had walked toward the immense fire and held his hands out toward it, unconscious of the pain the heat caused him. The Duke of Gaunt's proposal had thrown him off balance and he had accepted it on the crest of an imaginative wave of enthusiasm in which he had envisioned himself at the head of Gloucester's armies sweeping Henry to the throne. The subsequent conversation had brought him back to earth with a thud, but Roger of Hereford, in the stage of flux between early manhood and full maturity, knew that he was still too excited to think clearly.

"Perhaps you are right," he said slowly. "I do not know. I cannot think just now. You and that son of yours could always talk rings around me. I only know that I like direct action best. These elaborate plans fall by their own weight, and so many men involved in separate action tend to think, each one, that his own merit is slighted. Such things often come to naught."

"You need not answer now. There is time enough. You should settle all personal matters first, Roger. It is not well to start a war with a divided mind. Some time before February we must all meet. If we can agree, then you should be ready to join Gloucester's forces by February. You will need at least a month to get to know your men, and I hope we can go into action after the early thaws and planting of March."

"Good. I have personal matters to settle, it is true. If this affair had been urgent I could have set them aside a little longer, but—"

"Lady Elizabeth grows restless, eh?" Gaunt looked at Hereford who had blushed faintly and laughed. "You must be something very special. I had not thought that one could wait at all for anything."

Hereford moved away restlessly again. He had learned to control his expression, but the curse of his fair complexion was that his blood wrote his emotion in his face without his permission for all to see. The best he could do was to turn his back and hope the color would subside before he needed to face his companion.

"It is not so much that as my lands. Of course my mother sent me word of how matters went, and I know Storm defended them well, but I would like to see with my own eyes what heart the land has. My men-at-arms too must come to know me again."

Gaunt laughed again and drew Hereford toward the table where dinner was laid. "Yes, yes, I know. There are reasons and reasons, and none of them ever is a woman. So it is with my own son also. That being the case and since I see that you feel there is no need for haste at all in the matter of Lady Elizabeth, perhaps we had better go right after we eat. If we can make Ilminster tonight, we may catch Gloucester at Bath tomorrow and possibly settle the manner in which you may draw funds for support of the men. Once that is securely agreed and provision that cannot be readily revoked made, all else will follow easily. You may then devote yourself to collecting Elizabeth of Chester's dowry and person with a mind undistracted by minor matters such as affairs of state."

Several days later in the magnificent solar of Chester Castle, Lady Elizabeth sat staring into the fire with her hands idle in her lap. The room was otherwise empty, but if anyone had seen her it would have been apparent that some decision of momentous weight was being considered, for Lady Elizabeth was never idle. In a sense she was not even idle now, or at least she was not quiet, although she appeared so. In spite of the fact that her head with its two lustrous black plaits, thick as a strong man's wrist, rested against the carved lions and lilies of the chair back, a tension emanated from her that gave an almost palpable effect in the room.

A log snapped, and golden-amber flame shot up anew. Elizabeth turned her face slightly from the fire and slowly closed and reopened her dazzled and dazzling eyes. The light played on the soft roundness of her cheek showing her skin to be a smooth olive against which the long curled lashes of her eyes looked almost blue rather than black. Elizabeth Chester was a strikingly beautiful woman, her nose short and fine, her mouth naturally red and generous, but beyond every other beauty it was said that she could turn men to stone with her eyes. Certainly those eyes were startling enough to stop short in mid-sentence anyone who did not know her, for they were not the soft dark brown or light blue or gray that ordinarily went with her dark complexion. As though lit from within, Elizabeth of Chester's eyes glowed with the same golden-amber as the flames leaping in the hearth. They could become hard and cold as topaz, those eyes, but they were always so clear and bright that a man felt as if he could look right into her soul through them.

Even her present trouble could not cloud their limpidity, and Elizabeth was deeply troubled. Almost a year ago her father had told her that he had received a proposal for her in marriage from the Earl of Hereford and that he had accepted it. The Earl of Chester had spoken glibly, defensively, and at great length, expecting the worst, but Elizabeth had raised no protest, and Chester had allowed his voice to fade away while he examined his daughter's lovely face. She is pleased, he thought, pleased. Ten, twenty, fifty, he could not even remember how many negotiations had been started, and all had come to nothing. Some Chester himself had turned down as unsuitable because, unlike many men, he loved his daughter devotedly and would not sell her where he thought she would not be happy. Some he had urged upon her with every form of pressure he could devise, but Elizabeth was no ordinary meek woman of the time. She laughed in his face when he commanded her; she cursed him when he beat her; she spat at him when he threatened to starve her. In the end she had always won, for she could make his life a hell on earth.

When Elizabeth was upset, no clothes were washed or mended, few meals were served and those so poorly cooked they were inedible, and day and night she railed, her venomous tongue picking out and lacerating every sore spot on her father's conscience. For the past five years Chester had refrained from argument. He had mentioned any proposal and accepted her negative without question. Only in part, however, was this acquiescence due to Elizabeth's behavior; mostly it was because Chester found his daughter increasingly useful to him in political affairs. Now it seemed that that usefulness was at an end. He had broken with King Stephen, and Queen Maud had dismissed Elizabeth from her retinue of ladies. Court circles were closed to her and she could no longer bring her father information or advice. Hereford had every qualificatian for a good husband; he was young—younger than Elizabeth if it came to that—handsome, rich, brave, and heart and soul with Chester's cause. The lands Elizabeth had inherited from her mother lay closer to Hereford's domains than to Chester's, some of the castles to be ceded as Elizabeth's dowry being right on the border of Hereford's estates. Best of all, Elizabeth knew Lord Hereford well and liked him. Chester had gambled, accepted Hereford's offer, presented his acceptance as a *fait accompli*, and the gamble had paid off.

At that time Elizabeth had been almost as pleased as her father. The year before the proposal was tendered she had, as a matter of fact, laid snares to entrap Lord Hereford and had been chagrined because, although plainly interested in her person, the young earl loudly proclaimed that he would not marry. When, therefore, after a year of absence Hereford had written to her father offering very generous terms for her, she had been filled with triumph at her victory. Now she was not at all sure that she wanted the spoils of that victory, but it was too late to retreat.

Elizabeth of Chester had many faults, but dishonesty with herself was not one of them. This idle hour before the fire had been spent in an earnest inquiry into why she was so unhappy about Hereford's return. She knew that she liked him, indeed found him more attractive than any other man she had ever met; they laughed about the same things, enjoyed the same rough sports and unrefined jests. He was rich—at least as rich as her father—not that it mattered, for she believed she could have had Lord Storm if she desired wealth. He would not be harsh to her; no man as soft to his mother and sisters as Lord Hereford would be really brutal to his wife. What then? He was young, handsome, more than handsome, beautiful in a way that stirred her blood, virile—. Elizabeth stopped her thoughts and closed her tawny eyes. Ay, she thought, there lies the pin in the cloth. Take it out and look at it. All of Roger of Hereford she would welcome gladly into her life—his fighting skill, his laughter, his principles— all but his passion. Her knees trembled and she put her hands on them to stop the motion while a dark blush which gave her complexion a fascinating violet-hued rosiness covered her face and throat. It was true that her revulsion at the thought of complete physical contact had been a small part of her previous rejections, but it had never been the major reason. It was different with Roger anyway; she was not icily revolted or flatly indifferent; she hated Roger's passion because she responded to it. Every time he touched her she was driven so wild that she wanted to scream and strike, yet when he was near she could not resist placing every temptation in his way to make him touch her.

A year, how little she had thought of him in that year. She had spent much more time considering how to make him offer for her than in considering their relationship once he had done so.

"So here you are, Elizabeth. I have sent all over the castle for you. I thought you would like to read Roger's letter."

"Thank you, Father. I had one from the same courier."

Elizabeth took the letter, nonetheless and started to read, a skill only a few women had then. Her mind, however, was more occupied with the difference between her father's appearance and her memory of Hereford's than with the written message. Both men had blue eyes, but Chester's were pale, without intensity, and often shifted. In a sense Chester's face was nobler, with its high, broad forehead and long, high-bridged nose, but the forcefulness of her father's upper face was denied by the soft, almost loose lips and the chin which receded slightly. Even the white puckered scar along the jawbone could not lend decisiveness to that chin, while Roger's jaw line promised that, for all his laughter and good humor, he would be a bad man to cross. Elizabeth handed back the sheet of parchment.

"He is certainly no great correspondent. The words and phrases might have been copied one from the other. All he can think to say, apparently, is that he will be here in two weeks' time and is in great haste to be betrothed. Great haste! He managed to wait a year without the least sign of impatience. What makes him so hot to grasp his prize now?"

"That is no way to talk, Elizabeth. It was the thought of a considerate man to write to you separately. As you know, there was no need for him to let you know his plans at all."

"There is no contract made," Elizabeth retorted hotly, "only a promise without witnesses. I may still decide to withdraw myself as unwilling."

Chester narrowed his eyes. "You! You have no voice in this matter. It is too late now to seek excuses to deny your word. I will make that contract with Hereford no matter what you do or say. There is no need to make contract here. I can easily ride to Hereford Castle to do it. And I will bring you to the church door for your marriage even if I must drag you screaming and cursing every foot of the way, even if I must beat you unconscious and make the replies for you. A fine sight that will be for those who know you, a fine laughingstock you will make of yourself."

"You would not treat me so. You threaten often, but you would not." Elizabeth was not sure this time, however, because her father's voice held a certain note, and her own voice trembled a little. She knew her father. He was weak and changeable, but sometimes unbelievably stubborn and there was not time enough left now to wear him down.

"I swear to you by the True God, by His Holy Mother, and by all the blessed saints that I will marry you to Roger of Hereford though all hell should bar the way. What ails you, Elizabeth? You have passed four and twenty summers. You are already too old for any but a widower or a madman like Hereford to desire. Where will you find another offer like this one? What single fault can you find in Roger of Hereford?"

"You will drag me to the church!" Elizabeth spat, her eyes blazing like a vicious cat's as she cleverly avoided her father's questions and stabbed at what she knew would hurt him most. "You could not summon strength enough to make a toad obey you. You will run weeping to Roger and offer him more money. He, indeed, might drag me all unwilling for a high enough price. If he got enough money, he would think he could win this accursed war single-handed." She gasped a moment, then caught her breath. "Do not tremble so, I will make no protest, but not through fear of you. I have given my promise and I will keep it. I know it is too late to retract."

Chester, who had started to flush at his daughter's words, suddenly began to laugh instead. "So that is where the steel galls, eh? Nay, my pretty, you need not fear that Hereford covets your dower. You know what offers he made. He would have taken you empty-handed, I think, had I insisted that was the only way." Chester came up to Elizabeth and attempted to stroke her hair but she pulled angrily away. "Come, child, the boy only did his duty. He could come no sooner. His honor is engaged with Henry of Anjou's cause and he is young and cleaves greatly to his given word."

"Ay. At least that I will gain from a change of masters. I need not fear that he will be forsworn with every breath of rumor that blows."

That really hurt. Chester cast one reproachful glance at his daughter and turned to leave. He was a weak man and often broke his word, but he was no coward and was driven first one way and then another by ambition and dreams of glory, not by fear. His daughter's insinuation that he was attempting to avoid danger truly distressed him because he felt that if she believed that of him everyone else also would. Elizabeth had not meant to go so far; she fully returned her father's affection, and, although she was by no means averse to tormenting him to get her way, he had not meant to hurt him needlessly.

"Father, wait," Elizabeth cried, running after him. "I did not mean that. Oh, my accursed tongue! You know I did not mean it. I have always agreed with you in what you have done. If you have been at fault, have I not been so too?" Chester stopped, and Elizabeth curtsied deep before him and kissed his hand. "Dear Papa, forgive me. I do not know what ails me. I am so cross I hardly know how to bear myself."

Chester raised her and caressed her fondly. "It may be that you do not know what troubles you, but I do. You will not believe me, Elizabeth, for you have long resisted marriage, but think on what I say. You have waited too long for a man of your own and children of your own. You have had my children by your stepmother, curse the woman, to care for, that is true, and you think you have filled your heart with them. Perhaps you have, but you cannot so fulfill your body." He patted her shoulder as she turned her face away. "It is the body calling for its rights and the mind denying that call which distresses you."

"It is not true," Elizabeth murmured, her nostrils pinched with the violent suppression of her emotion.

"You are an honest girl, Liza, love," Chester said, kissing her again. "Think on it. Make not such haste to deny. It is no shame to acknowledge the body's needs, even if the priests sometimes tell us it is a sin to satisfy them."

CHAPTER 2

LORD HEREFORD lifted his head slightly to call "come" to a
sound at the door. He did not turn to see who entered because there was no need to do so; he was at home, in his
own bedroom in the manor house of Hereford Castle, totally safe, totally relaxed, totally lapped in luxury. The
room was far different from the stuffy or dank wall cham-
bers of a keep. It was a section partitioned off from the
main hall of the manor house which had been built within
the walls of the old keep and had been furnished by his
father and mother for their own private use with unbeliev-
able luxury. The floor before the hearth of the huge fireplace where flames leapt and wood crackled, instead of
being strewn with rushes, was covered with two great car-
pets brought back from the East by a crusader and won
as booty by Miles of Hereford. Their originally blatant
colors had been mellowed by time and use to softer but
still glowing hues of red and blue touched with gold. On
either side of the fireplace hung great tapestries worked by
the Dowager Countess of Hereford. They were beautiful,
but their purpose was not solely decorative, for they were
hung to reflect heat and keep out the chill of the stone
walls. It was impossible to make out the subjects clearly
because the room was rather dim although it was full
morning, the shutters of the large windows being drawn
to keep out the cold. To the left of the door stood the
huge curtained bed, and Lady Hereford glanced at it
briefly with a faint look of distaste as she approached her
son.

"I have a letter for you, Roger, from Lord Chester."

"Mamma!" Hereford exclaimed. He smoothed the troubled frown from his face and got to his feet, extending one

hand and using the other to pull his robe closed. Lady Hereford twitched the robe aside.

"Let me look at you."

Obligingly, with a faint smile, Lord Hereford slipped off what he was wearing and allowed his mother to examine him.

"That is an ugly scar, child," she commented, touching a red, angry mark that ran halfway round his right thigh.

"Yes. I was fighting with Henry in Normandy and had no time to let it heal. I tell you, I was lame for six months with it, but it mended as all wounds do eventually."

"As they all do unless you die of them. I wish you would have more sense, Roger. This letter came last night," the countess said, reverting to her reason for intruding upon him once she was satisfied that he needed no care. "The messenger said it was not urgent, and, under the circumstances," Lady Hereford again glanced briefly at the curtained bed with obvious displeasure on her face this time, "I felt it would keep until morning."

Hereford laughed at the look and walked with his swift, nervous stride to fling back the curtains, showing the empty bed. He returned just as quickly to shrug on his robe again and take the letter.

"She is gone. Sit down, Mamma, and do not look so black at me. I am not so very wicked, after all."

"No, Roger, you are not. You are a good son and, I think, a good man. Your father would have been proud of you." She stopped to look at the fire for a moment. Her husband had been dead for six years, but she still missed him, for they had been an affectionate couple, very happy in their marriage. Her son had been good to her; he had allowed her to choose to remain a widow and had protected her from molestation in that state. He could have forced her into marriage and obtained a good bride price for her, since her dower estates were large and at that time she had still been capable of childbearing. "Nonetheless, Roger," she continued firmly, putting those thoughts aside, "I would like to know what you plan to do with those women."

"What women?" her son asked, his brows knitted over Chester's letter. He had gained much facility in reading and writing over the two years he had spent with Henry of Anjou, for that young man was an inveterate scribbler and message sender.

"Your whores."

"Oh—marry them off, I suppose, and in all haste too." Hereford's eyes gleamed with mischief. "It is as well you mentioned it. You had better see about that, Mamma, and do your best to please the girls, if that is possible. Lord! What Elizabeth would say if they were still about when she came."

"And the children?"

Roger's mouth hardened, and the laughter disappeared from his eyes. "She may say what she likes about them. They are only two daughters, after all, and I will not cast my girls out or permit them to sink to the level of serfdom."

"You are right, of course; they are of your blood, but Elizabeth is of hasty temper. When she is mistress here, it is possible that she may not be overkind to your bastards. Also, child, there is the question of myself and your sisters. Have you given any thought to what arrangements you wish to make about us?"

"No, I have not, Mamma," Roger laughed, "but I am sure you have. I have had a few other things to think about."

"It might be best," the countess said slowly and regretfully, "if we all moved to my dower castle." Lady Hereford did not wish to go. She loved this house and had been very happy in it, but she also did not wish to become her daughter-in-law's handmaiden. Nor, knowing herself, did she think it would be possible for her docilely to give the management of the keep and estates into Lady Elizabeth's hands. No doubt they were capable hands; Elizabeth had run her father's house with commendable efficiency, but no two women did things in exactly the same way, and Lady Hereford knew that she would be constantly fretted if Elizabeth changed her methods.

That sobered Lord Hereford instantly. "No, I had not thought of it, but I see that I must." His memories of Elizabeth were not terribly clear, but he remembered enough to know that she and his mother would clash. "I am not sure, Mamma, but certainly that need not be done at once. For a while, at least, I will keep her with me, when there is no fighting, and we are likely to do much traveling. That would mean that you would have to return here to care for the place while I was away since I have no castellan here. Also, we live in a settled way and Elizabeth will have to learn who is who and what their duties are. Stay, at least in the beginning. Later we will see how things go." Hereford smiled suddenly and mischievously again. "Besides, I should miss you, and I would never feel truly at home if my sisters did not plague my life out with their insanities."

"I wonder where you get this habit of putting everything off till tomorrow? Everything except fighting, that is. Your father never did so, and I certainly do not." She paused to look at her son, who had sunk luxuriously into his chair again and opened his robe so that he could feel the heat of the fire on his skin. "Are you going to dress and look at the demesne lands or do you intend to sit in front of the fire all day?"

"I am a good, obedient son," he replied gravely, but with dancing eyes, and straightened up at once. "So meek am I that I will do your bidding straightaway." The countess shook her head at that nonsense. A more considerate but less obedient son would be hard to find. She rose, looking rather cross, and Roger came up to her, hugged her quickly, and kissed her cheeks. "I swear I liked the Lady Elizabeth best of all the women I know because she always spoke to me and looked at me just so sharply as you do."

Instead of smiling in reply, Lady Hereford looked even more troubled. It was one thing to scold and criticize Roger herself, but she could not pretend that it would give her any pleasure to see another woman do so. Roger was the most precious of her children, her eldest son, born after the disappointment at the birth of three daughters. She had two other sons and two younger daughters, but none was as dear as this first male child. She helped Hereford to dress automatically and went to the hall to summon his chief squire to help him arm. Then she started for her own quarters but stopped halfway and returned.

"Roger, how long do you plan to stay with us?"

"I meant to stay two weeks when I came—did I not tell you yesterday? But now—I think perhaps I had better ride to Chester as soon as possible and come back to check the estates. Not that there is need, for I am sure you cared for my interests well, but I would like to see with my own eyes how matters go and perhaps take some promising young men into service."

"You have had bad news from Lord Chester then?"

"No—" Hereford replied frowning slightly, "not bad news. Something a trifle disturbing."

"You will not permit Chester to drag you into trouble again, will you?"

That brought a wry smile. "No, Mother. I am more like to drag him into trouble this time, not that he will need much urging. It is not that. Lady Elizabeth—"

"Is that she-devil making difficulties again?" Lady Hereford could have bitten her tongue as soon as the words slipped out. She had no desire to let her son know how little she approved of his contact. Had he been in England and mentioned it, she would have attempted to dissuade him from contracting a marriage which, she felt, would make him unhappy. He had not consulted her, however, and now it was too late to retract the offer, even if Roger was willing to do so.

"That is no way to speak of the woman who is as good as my wife. Do not do so again."

Lady Hereford scarcely recognized the blue eyes that fixed her own, so hard had they become. Normally they held nothing but laughter or affection when she saw them.

"I am sorry, Roger."

"It is naught." But his expression did not soften. "Lady Elizabeth is apparently distressed by the idea that her dowry is more important to me than her person. This may be true for most marriages, but I will tell you plainly, Mother, so that you too will not be mistaken—that is not true for this one." It was really partly true, but Hereford wished to impress his mother with his attachment for Elizabeth in the hope that it would give her caution in dealing with the girl.

"No," Lady Hereford faltered, "of course not. She is a

very beautiful woman, and good, and clever. I have no word to say against her except that her temper is a little hasty. But I did not mean to talk about Lady Elizabeth. If you go so soon there are two matters which I must mention now."

"Yes?"

"Anne is sixteen now and should have been married already. The sooner we can fulfill her contract, the better. Also, you should be thinking about a husband for Catherine. She will be thirteen in the spring."

"Very well. Go ahead and begin preparations for Anne's wedding. As soon as I know myself, I will tell you what date will be most convenient to me—and, of course, to Lincoln. I will write and ask him when Rannulf will be ready to take her. Is there something else? Surely you do not expect me to pick a suitable man for Catherine out of the air. I must think about it."

"The other matter can wait. You are too angry now to listen with patience."

Hereford had walked away to stare into the fire, but now he returned, brow smoothed and lips faintly curved. "Not really. It is true that Lady Elizabeth does not have a gentle disposition. I do not know why it should enrage me to have you make the point, but it does. There, I am recovered. You had better ask what you want because Sir John is riding over to join me at dinner. I believe he would like me to foster his son. That is not important one way or the other, but he will talk and talk, and that will give us little time because I think I will leave in the morning."

"Well then, your brother Walter—"

"Good God, what trouble is he in now?"

"None yet, but I have no control over him at all. He was perfectly all right until he learned that you were planning to return. Then he took up with a band of out-and-out robbers, and he is coming very close to hanging. I cannot think why he should be so outrageous. You have always been most generous to him and he lacks for nothing."

"He will lack his head if I lay my hands on him," Hereford flashed, crimson with rage. "I have no time to bother with him, but tell him for me, Mamma, that if he blackens our name any more with his lawlessness I will hunt him down like the criminal he is and see that he has no further opportunity to offend Heaven or me with his actions."

A stool crashed as Hereford booted it across the room. Lady Hereford stood quietly, hands folded, eyes on the floor. She hardly knew whether Roger was dearer when he was filled with laughter and teasing or when he raged, so like his father that her heart ached anew. This rage did not frighten her, she was accustomed to Roger's hot temper. She was only frightened when he turned to ice and she could not recognize her son.

"I have borne enough from him. I will bear no more. I will—"

"This is nothing to the point, Roger." The countess interrupted sharply with the privilege of a mother. "You may be as angry as you please, but you know that that will only make Walter worse. Do stop shouting and think of something practical or the family will have worse shame than a robber baron to bear—it will have a member on the gibbet."

"I tell you, I—" Hereford stopped suddenly. His color faded slowly to normal as he stood staring into space, and he put a hand up to pull gently on the lobe of one ear. "Tell him instead to stop being foolish and to meet me here after Epiphany. I will have work for him of just the kind he likes. He shall have rich booty and, in addition, will bring honor instead of dishonor to his name."

"You would not have me set a trap for him, Roger? He is my son too, though you are dearer."

"Do you think I have changed so much, Mother? Nay, I speak the honest truth. I did not tell you, for it cannot matter to you, but I met with Gaunt and Gloucester when I first came from France and I have large plans." He smiled at her widening eyes. "Do not trouble your head over these things. They are not a woman's affair—at least, not an ordinary woman's," he added, thinking of Elizabeth, "but Walter may well be useful to me and satisfy his craving for power at the same time."

Lord Hereford's party topped a small rise, and Roger looked with relief at the gray stone towers of Castle Chester. He had been so anxious to make good time that they had ridden far into the night and camped in the open, and Lord Hereford, as well as his men was nearly frozen. A raised hand brought Sir Alan of Evesham to his side.

"Ride ahead and let Lord Chester know we are but a few minutes behind you. If he is not within, you had better ask for the Lady Elizabeth."

"Yes, my lord. Shall I ask for quarters for the men?"

"Yes. I will not send them back in this weather." Lord Hereford smiled. "Fair frozen, are you not, Alan?"

"Ay, my lord. That we are, and not used to it any more either. But it is good even to be frozen with you in the lead again. I do not say that Lord Storm was neglectful in guarding your lands, for he was most zealous in keeping them quiet, but I for one am sick of the same dull patrolling, and he is a man of sour temper to work for."

"Never mind, Alan. You will see hot enough action and in strange places plenty soon now. I am not given to idleness."

"That you are not, I warrant my head on it, my lord."

The Earl of Chester was not at home; he was out hunting, for it was a sport he was violently addicted to and neither cold nor wet could dissuade him from the chase. Elizabeth, greeting Alan with courtesy, for he was well-born, though a younger son and therefore employed as Hereford's master-at-arms, concealed the mixed emotions his news aroused in her. After making him comfortable with hot wine and a place by the fire in the great hall, she hurried off to arrange for quartering Hereford's men. Arms and food stores would have to be shifted from the ground floor of the donjon to other places in the keep, the arms to some tower room, the food to sheds in the bailey. The hearth, Elizabeth said, looking with disfavor at the accumulated filth in it, would need to be swept clean at once and a large fire lighted. The banks of the Dee were frozen, but she ordered a group of male serfs out to gather what fresh rushes could be found. Others were to be brought from storage in an outhouse, mixed with dried marjoram and rosemary, and spread on the floor. She sent a page for the head cook and gave orders that another pig was to be slaughtered and another side of venison taken from the salted meats to be added to the dinner meats.

"First he said he is coming in two weeks and four days later he is here," she grumbled, suppressing a little thrill of excitement. "I swear that he does it to be contrary, give trouble, and catch me unprepared. The meats have not been hung and cannot be roasted," she said to the cook a little breathlessly. "You will have to boil them well first to soften them and then bake them on the open coals to give them some taste. Remember to put in plenty of pepper. If you have not enough, I will give you more. Use all the broken meats for pasties, and be sure that ten at least are made for the high table. Doubtless his lordship will wish to hunt with my father tomorrow and they will need to break their fast with more than bread and wine."

"Yes, my lady, but—"

"But what?" Elizabeth said, turning furiously on her servant. "Am I the cook here or you? Can you do nothing without my help? Shall I come and stir your pots?"

"No, my lady," the man replied meekly, backing away. It was not unknown for her ladyship to use her nails when she was in this temper. "I only wish to say that there is no time to bake extra bread and we are short because tomorrow is baking day."

"Idiot! Send to the alehouse and take all they have. Send also to the village and scour the huts. You should get a loaf or half a loaf from each. If they have none it will do them no harm, fighting men must eat first. Yes, yes," she said sharply, turning on the page who had come to tell her that Lord Hereford had arrived, "I am coming."

Damn the man, she thought, tears rising to her eyes as she smoothed her hair with her hands, pinched her cheeks, and bit her lips, he must needs arrange it so that the first time he sees me in two years I am dressed like a slattern and all unkempt. Neither of course was true. Elizabeth was most particular about her appearance, even in private. What she meant was that she was not perfumed and bejeweled as she would be in full court dress, as Roger had always seen her previously. It did not occur to Elizabeth to wonder why she should care how she looked if she was truly unwilling to awaken Hereford's passion, nor why her breath should catch when she saw his rather slight form poised before the fire in conversation with Alan of Evesham. His cloak had been cast aside and his mail hood pushed back, his gold hair vying in brilliance with the embroidery of his surcoat. Elizabeth checked her footsteps and deliberately advanced more slowly, struggling also to control her breathing, which seemed to have gone a little out of order. Alan touched his master's arm and Hereford turned quickly, leaving his sentence unfinished. He started to come toward her and then stopped.

"My God," he breathed softly, "I had forgotten how beautiful you are. No man could trust his memory for that. I kept telling myself that I exaggerated, but in fact you are lovelier than anything I dreamed."

Elizabeth stopped too, clasping her hands together to stop them from trembling. "What a graceful remark! Did you spend your entire ride here planning the words, my lord?"

That broke Hereford's reverent mood and he came forward again swiftly, laughing. "I might count on you, Lady Elizabeth, to depress my pretensions and puncture my vanity. Nonetheless, I swear that it was you alone that brought forth the praise. I had no such sweet words in mind at all. I could think of nothing the entire way but how cold I was and what a fool a man must be to love a country with such a climate."

"Then perhaps you should have stayed where you were well satisfied. What should you return in such haste for? Is there anything of value here that you feel cannot wait forever?"

Hereford took her hands in his; she attempted to pull them away, but his grip tightened painfully and she desisted.

"You hands are like ice, my dear, and you are trembling. What is the matter?"

"I am cold, my lord. That is all the matter. What do you expect when you descend on us thus without warning and I must go into that freezing barracks below to see it made comfortable for your men."

"I am sorry if I have made trouble, Lady Elizabeth, but I—" his blue eyes had been darkening steadily as his glance swept over her, and his expression was frankly covetous. "I just felt that my lands might wait."

Elizabeth freed herself with a desperate jerk and walked to the hearth. She was sorry a moment later because she could not stop shaking and in the heat of the blaze she could scarcely blame it on cold. The men around the fire withdrew a little as Hereford followed her, to allow them some privacy. He stood a trifle behind and to the right of her as she watched the flames but made no attempt to touch her.

"For one thing, Elizabeth, I came back for you."

"My manners are too good, my lord, to laugh in a guest's face, but I have seldom had them put to such a test as they suffer just now."

Hereford was puzzled in spite of Chester's warning. Women often said they were angry with him in his absence, but a few soft, flattering words and a few glances of open admiration ordinarily brought them quickly to heel. This time when both words and looks were not mere flattery but totally sincere and should therefore have worked even better, having the ring of truth, the lady did not respond. Every sentence seemed to make her angrier.

"I do not lie, Elizabeth—you permit me to address you so?"

She shrugged. "How can I stop you? You will, no doubt, do as you please."

"In all truth I suppose I will, but I will always try to please you too. I have often blamed myself that I did not offer for you before I left for France, then I could have taken you with me. I thought of it, but everything was so hurried and at odds, and my situation so precarious—I could not ask a woman like yourself to share so uncertain a future."

"You brought yourself to it in the end, however. Are you sure it was your situation and not my father's that restrained you?" Scorn was thick in her voice, making her words slow and heavy. "In all truth! In all truth he was then in prison. Did you not wish to be sure that he would still have lands to give you before you committed yourself?"

Hereford blushed hotly. "By God, you know how to prick a man where it will hurt."

Elizabeth turned on him with eyes like coals. "Why should it hurt if it be not the truth? I have no fault to find with your desires to increase your estates, my lord, it only sickens me that you overlay them with honeyed talk of my beauty. If she held my lands or some of greater value, no doubt you would take a cow to wife."

The earl opened his mouth and clamped it shut again. The cold fire of his eyes met and held her burning glance; once more he opened his mouth and shut it, this time with lips bitten together into a thin line. Then his color lessened and his expression softened. "I will not quarrel with you, Elizabeth. If you can really believe that of me, I have no wonder that you are angry." He spoke sadly, and to a certain extent he was sad, but he was also determined to have Elizabeth and her dowry. If blatant admiration would not soften her, perhaps reason would. It was true that Elizabeth was no ordinary woman, and by now it was plain that his usual approach would have to be modified to deal with her.

"What do you want me to do? Do you wish me to tell your father that I will take you without a dowry? I am even willing to do that, as far as I am concerned, but think what will be said of your father, that he sent his daughter penniless from his house—or yourself, that you came like a beggar maid to me. Who will you hurt in the end but your own children? Your lands, as you well know, can never belong to me. They will be a livelihood for your second son or dowry for your daughters."

The amber eyes grew quieter, long black lashes dropping finally in a vain attempt to hide their remorseful expression. Hereford half put out a hand to take her arm and, as he saw her stiffen slightly, dropped it. His light voice was a little husky as he tried to drive home his point.

"Your lands can mean nothing to the Earl of Hereford, Elizabeth, but you, yourself, can—nay do—mean much to Roger."

Elizabeth turned away. "You have not had much of a welcome, my lord, I am sorry. I cannot tell you why I am so cross, but my father can warrant my words that you have not been the only sufferer. Perhaps I should go out and come in again. I might behave better on a second entrance. I have a sour disposition and a bitter tongue. You should consider well whether you wish to take such a shrew into your home."

An expression of satisfaction, quickly veiled, came into Roger of Hereford's face. "Nay, my lady, do not missay yourself. Your temper is hasty and your tongue sharp—I have felt both before—but there is no sourness in your disposition. You have ever been quick to forgive an honest blunder and I know you do not cleave to your wrath. If I desired a mawkish milksop for a wife, I could have chosen from a hundred wellborn and well-bred girls."

"Ah," Elizabeth cried spinning round, "you can say nothing against my birth so you say you think I am not well-bred." But now her eyes were alight with laughter and a slight flush gave that delicious violet overmantling to her cheeks.

Hereford hastily dropped his eyes to hide their avidity. He had her gentled now and he did not wish that any emotion of his should unsettle her again. "Well," he drawled, stepping back a little to give her room for movement. If he infuriated her enough to make her swing at him, he wanted space to dodge. "Not everyone greets their guests, not even humble suitors, by telling them that they have caused inconvenience. It is a new experience for me, at least, and by virtue of that must have some interest."

This time he had guessed right, however; although Elizabeth's flush deepened, she laughed. "Lord Hereford, you are a beast. How dare you trample a woman already overthrown. Is that true knightly conduct?"

"No, my lady," he replied meekly, but with twitching lips, "but then, you know, I am no knight."

"That is nonsense, Roger," Elizabeth said, forgetting her assumed formality in her surprise. "What do you mean you are no knight?"

"Just what I say." He laughed at her shocked expression. "You know a man sometimes swears fealty at his knighting ceremony, and in a case such as mine where the only man of fit rank to knight me would be the king, it would be customary to do so. I did not wish to swear to Stephen—therefore I have not yet been knighted. Ergo, I am no knight." His face sobered. "I have never broken an oath I made, Elizabeth, I pray that no force will ever be strong enough to make me do so."

"That I readily believe. I have always admired that in you."

She had a look of frustration as she spoke which told volumes about what her pride had suffered through her father's political vacillations. Her love for him could triumph over her shame enough to allow her to stand by Chester in all his twistings and turnings, but she felt the shame bitterly all the same. Quite suddenly Hereford's past knowledge of her strength, her ambition, and her pride was reawakened from a dim memory of something unusual to a reality of something magnificent, something even more remarkable than her quite astonishing beauty.

"Sit down with me, Elizabeth," he burst out. "I have something very serious to say to you." He hesitated uncomfortably because he knew Elizabeth's devotion to her father and he wished to avoid infuriating her by criticizing Chester and yet to induce her not to transmit what he was about to say to him. "I did not write to your father because—because—"

"Because my father is often not very wise and is sometimes too talkative. Say what you wish, Roger."

"Well then, Gaunt met me at Seaton and proposed—I hardly know just how to put this, but I suppose it is best to speak plainly. I am no hand, you know, at talking around a subject."

"If you are going to speak plainly, we may be safer in my solar. Come up with me. Are you hungry? Dinner will be a little late."

"We broke our fast in the field, and not too liberally. I was anxious to get here in good time so we rode half the night. If you have something to hand, it would be welcome."

"Go up, then, Roger, you know the way. I will just tell the maids to bring you some cold meat."

Two chairs faced each other in the solar before the fireplace, high-backed, in a wood deep-carved with stylized lions and fleurs-de-lis, smooth as satin and dark with continual polishing. The cushions were of a bright blue sarsenet, embroidered by Elizabeth's skilled fingers in the same stylized pattern as the chair carvings. The room was lighter than the great hall because the walls of the keep were thinner on this third floor, and, behind the heavy screens which separated Elizabeth's quarters from the sleeping and working area of the other women, voices and the soft sounds of female activity came faintly. Hereford paced restlessly, his thoughts divided between the fierce awakening of his passion for Elizabeth and the problem of whether or not to include Chester in his political plans. He started nervously as Elizabeth allowed the door to slam and spun on his heels, hand on his sword hilt.

"You remind me of Lord Storm when you do that, although I cannot think of two men more different in looks and disposition."

Hereford smiled a little sheepishly. "Sorry. I have been under arms so constantly these past two years that I find it hard to remember when I am with friends."

"Were you not among friends in France?"

"Friends? To whom is the Empress Matilda a friend? Henry is loyal enough, but sometimes I think he too looks over his shoulder when he is among his mother's adherents. The woman is—is like a ravening beast. Even Geoffrey the Fair cannot live with her, and you would not think that anything a woman could do would disturb him. She hated me, moreover, because I preached caution to her son."

Elizabeth came up close and took him persuasively by the arm. In her interest in what he had to say, she had completely forgotten his reasons for being there. "Come and sit down. I can hardly imagine you preaching caution, even to a madman, and Henry, from what I have heard, is not without sense."

"No. He is wise far beyond his years. Young as he is, I believe he can whip the curs of this land to heel. Nonetheless, he is young and sometimes his spirit chafes at this continual delay. He would be king and try his wings."

"He is a far cry from king and not like to see that state soon—if ever. When Gloucester died, the driving force behind the rebellion crumpled. You cannot have failed to hear."

"That is what I wished to speak to you about. You are no ordinary woman, Elizabeth, and I feel that, being as you are, you have a right to know what I plan to do. If I succeed—if I succeed my name will stand next to the king's at the head of the council. But if I fail, I will be ruined." Roger's eyes flickered, their blue incandescent. "When I offered for you, I did not know this was coming."

Elizabeth had not yet taken the seat opposite his. Her hand, which was still on his arm, tightened as her muscles contracted involuntarily, but she did not move away when she consciously relaxed her grip. What was coming? Was Chester's daughter not worthy of the honors Roger of Hereford expected to reap? He had turned his face under her fixed stare and she could feel the knotted muscles of his arm quiver.

"I want you, Elizabeth," he said, his voice suddenly choked with sincerity because a sense of power seemed to flow through him from her touch. "I want you as I have never wanted another woman in my life, with my head as well as with my body." Hereford stopped on a deep drawn breath, grinding his teeth in his effort to retain at least the external appearance of control. "But I have no longer the right to hold you to the promise your father gave. Wait—let me speak. It is never easy for me to find words, and now I am so—. There is no sense in my broaching this matter to your father. He is not only ambitious but incurably optimistic, and would see only the glory; he would not see—would not permit himself to see—the degradation to which I might drag you. He would say at once that you must hold to your promise. By my faith, Elizabeth, I did not think of this when I came here, but when I saw you again, so lovely as you are, so—so more than a woman only—. Can I bring you all unknowing the chance of being an outlaw's wife, of being hunted from keep to keep, or, worse yet, being a landless fighting man's lady, dependent upon some foreign lord's bounty? My heart fails me, Elizabeth. You are used to so much more, to being like a queen in your own castle. I know well in what honor your father holds you. You cannot be forced like some mindless maid into a pit of your husband's digging. You must be permitted to think on this matter and decide for yourself."

She was staring at him, suspended between wondering whether he simply wanted to be rid of her, for Chester's daughter might well be an encumbrance if he was planning complicated political maneuvers, or whether he spoke the plain truth.

"I—it is not fair to urge you, Elizabeth, but I have told you only the worst that might be. You may trust me to do all a man can do to avoid that eventuality. I will sell my life full dear before I come to that. I only ask you that in weighing these things in your mind you add to the scale the fact that I—" he closed his eyes and swallowed. It was unnatural for him to appeal to a woman for any but sexual favors. "I want you—nay, more—I need you."

A log burst in the fire sending sparks flying. Elizabeth tightened her lax grip on Hereford's arm. He could have made no appeal that was surer of winning her. A reflection on her courage was to Elizabeth like a deep-driven spur in a horse's side, and the open recognition of her ability to think and reason was a tentative guarantee that Hereford did not plan to use her as a brood mare, obliterating her from his mind between conceptions.

"I am not afraid of disgrace. I have suffered that before. Dishonor I need not fear as your wife, I know. But you have not told me what this is all about. How can I answer when I do not know what I must face?"

Hereford raised his eyes to her, and Elizabeth's heart checked its beat and then began to pound. Written plainly on his face was the reason it was necessary for her to answer without previous explanation. He might or might not ask for her counsel, but it was necessary to him that she have blind faith, not perhaps in what he was about to do, but in him personally. But but she had no time to think about whether she did have faith in him, and her personal fear struggled with her smothered desire for him, effectually blocking her ability to think at all.

Roger cleared his throat and looked away; the rigidly straight back sagged a little. Had he mistaken the softness he thought he saw at times in Elizabeth's face? Was she all Chester, so ambitious that she had to know if the goal was great enough before she would take the risk? More important, did she care so little for him that the goal and not his need was the essential fact? He ran a hand through his hair, impatiently pushing the blond curls off his forehead. Gaunt—"

"Wait, Roger." The flat tone of his voice, usually so vibrant with some emotion, hurried her into speech. She had no idea what she was going to say, and the words, when she heard them, surprised her more than they did him. "I thought I had answered you, but I realize that you may not have understood. No consideration of future trouble could make me void my promise. If you still want me—you may have forgotten what Elizabeth of Chester really is, for it is long ago that you offered for me—I am yours for the taking—"

She was about to add that she wished to understand the situation in order to consider whether Chester's daughter would be more hindrance than help and whether, with that consideration in mind, it would be best to go ahead with their marriage, delay, or break the contract entirely. She never had the chance to say another word, however. Roger was on his feet and her words were smothered by his embrace. He reacted at once, thanking her for her faith in the way he knew best how to thank a woman, with physical caresses, not realizing until hours later that she had not offered him her faith, only exhibited her proud determination to keep her word.

Elizabeth was a powerful woman, but her strength was like a child's compared with his and in his excitement he did not realize that she was fighting to be free. In fact, she did not fight him long; her mind could control her body only for the first few seconds. When Roger freed her lips she was so dazed by the impact of his passion that she made no protest as he drew her with him to the chair and pulled her onto his lap. He kissed her again, her throat, her ears, the corners of her mouth. His hands made no attempt to restrain her but caressed her breasts and thighs; and now she could not have moved even if she had wanted to because her limbs were trembling so that they could not support her. The greatest effort her pride was capable of was to keep her passive. Her longing to reply to his kisses, to touch his body as he touched her, made her sob, but something in the back of her mind cried that if she yielded she would be lost.

Women were chattel. Like horses or dogs they belonged to the men who were their masters. Their dual purpose in life was to provide these masters with creature comforts—food, clothing, sexual satisfaction—and to bear them children, men-children to be their heirs, females to sell for a bride price and to make alliance between houses by a mixing of blood. In her father's house Elizabeth had risen above this state for, although she was an excellent housewife, she was also Chester's most important confidante and adviser. There was no wife that Elizabeth knew of, except Queen Maud, whose husband was a fool, who enjoyed both a satisfactory marriage and independence, and she unconsciously associated sexual yielding with loss of the freedom of thought and action she had achieved. The conflict between the terror of losing that independence, so dear to her, so hardly won, and the violent pressure of her desires was robbing her of her senses.

"Please, Roger, oh please," she sobbed, not knowing herself whether she was pleading with him to stop or to take her then and there and end her agony.

Her pleading stopped his caresses, and Hereford drew back to look at her so that he could judge what she meant by it. Elizabeth's eyes were closed, but their lids quivered, and her pallor was so deep that it gave a greenish cast to her complexion which even the rosy firelight could not counteract. His passion was quenched by his concern for her.

"Elizabeth." He was holding her gently now, supporting her so that her head rested against his upper arm, her face turned up to his. "Elizabeth, I would not hurt you for the world. What is it?"

"Let me go, please let me go."

"I will not hold you against your will, but see how you are trembling. Are you ill? Shall I call your women?"

"No," she cried, biting her lips to restrain her tears. She would die before she would allow the other women to see her in such a state.

"Gently, gently. Only tell me what you want me to do, and I will try."

Elizabeth was silent, struggling with herself. She wanted to tell him to kiss her again. Instead, she whispered, "Go away. Leave me in peace."

She made no effort to get off his lap, however, and Hereford was confused. Had she been another man's wife, such behavior would have been an open invitation to him to take further liberties, but she was promised to him. There was no need for pretense of this kind to save her face, and besides, her pallor and distress were beyond pretense. But the wildest leap of Hereford's imagination could not have offered him an answer to the problem because to him there was none. Women did not crave independence because they did not think of it and were not capable of it—so much he accepted, as all men did, as an article of faith. However, he did not class Elizabeth as "a woman" and was prepared to allow her to continue to act as she did with her father. Indeed, her pride and strength were what he found stimulating, for beautiful women, although not perhaps always as beautiful as Elizabeth, were a commonplace in his life.

"If that is what you desire, I will go, of course, but how far am I to go and for how long? Do you mean that you are upset now and want a little time to recover, or do you mean that you do not desire to be my wife?"

"I have promised," she said softly, and there was something in her voice that certainly was not gladness.

"What is it about me that offends you?" There was an edge to Hereford's voice; his pride was hurt.

Elizabeth recognized the tone. One push more and he would be willing to withdraw his offer; she would be free. He put her off his knees gently and stood looking at her. Her eyes were so wide that they seemed nearly starting from her head, tears trembling in the corners but unshed. Again what she said had little relevance to her conscious thoughts. It was as if her tongue had a life of its own and was not under her control.

"Oh, Roger, have pity on me. I am afraid. I have never been so afraid of anything in my whole life as I am of you."

He melted like the rare morning frost of April which disappears the moment the sun touches it. "Of me?" Elizabeth sank into the chair and he went down on one knee with the graceful motion of a man trained to physical activity all his life. "I would not harm a hair on your head, and I would kill anyone who even looked crosswise at you. Of all men on earth you have the least to fear from me."

"I am not afraid that you will hurt me," she whispered.

"Then what?" He kissed her hands and she began to tremble again. A faint glimmer of an idea illuminated Roger's mind, but it left him even more puzzled. Elizabeth had always been rather bold in her dealings with men; Hereford could distinctly remember times when her advances to him had been so open that he was rather embarrassed and a little disgusted. Now he wondered if that boldness was not bravado, as a frightened man will boast of his prowess before battle to reassure himself. But a man had to fight and Elizabeth did not have to deal with men—or did she? A girl so beautiful, so dowered, and modestly behaved in addition would have been snatched up in childhood. Perhaps her boldness had protected her well from what she feared.

"Nay," he said, very gently, "you need not answer. I will press you no further. If you like I will go and let you rest, but if you can bear it, I would like to tell you what I started to say when we first came up here." He had risen and walked out of her range of vision so that she jumped and cried out faintly when he stroked her hair. "I can see that you are really in no state to hear me, but once your father returns we will not be able to speak freely."

"I am all right," Elizabeth replied, pressing her hands to her cheeks. "I can listen."

"Good. Listen then. Gaunt and I had not been together half an hour when he proposed—straight out—that I should lead the forces of Gloucester and reorganize the rebellion."

Elizabeth had been slouched in her chair, her face turned away from the fire to keep it in shadow. Now she jerked upright and turned very quickly to face Hereford. This was greater news than she had expected.

"But what of Gloucester?"

"We, Gaunt and I, met him the next day in Bath. Ah, here is that food you promised me. I never heard the maid bring it in." Neither had Elizabeth, and she spared half a thought wondering whether the woman had seen and heard anything which should not be spread all over the keep. Her attention, however, was now focused on Roger with great intensity, and the maid was only a vague unease at the back of her mind. "I cannot understand that—I hardly like to call him a man. I tell you, Elizabeth, he nearly flirted with me." That made the girl laugh, and their eyes met briefly with understanding before Hereford, not feeling safe when their glances locked, walked away to pour wine. "Well, that is neither here nor there, but I swear I wish you could have seen him. He turned the rings on his fingers and looked up at me under his lashes—faugh! Yet Gaunt told me he bore himself like a man before Castle Cary and turned a very shaky thing into a decisive victory."

"Yes, yes, Roger. I know William well and have seen and, indeed, borne most of his tricks and ways. But what did he say about his army? For someone who says he does not talk around a subject, you seem to be having great trouble in keeping to it."

"That was all a piece—does a maid lead an army? He was not only willing, he was urgent with me to take his mercenaries under my command."

"Then you agreed?"

"Of course, do you think I could turn away from such an opportunity? I am not alone in this—"

"Roger, you cannot have thought. Even if my father were to help you and you had my revenues to add to your own, you could never support—"

Smiling, Hereford could not resist caressing her with his eyes. She was quick as a man—quicker than he had been—to add it up and come out with the right answer. "Do you take me for a fool, Elizabeth?" It was better just now to sound indignant; if he began to praise, he would also begin to kiss. "The matter of supporting the men was easily settled—I will give you the details of that another time, but Gloucester will continue to pay them through my hands, and—"

"Gloucester does this for what reason? To honor his father's memory? Nonsense, he hated Robert's guts. Because he loves you? Roger, I do not like this. William is not that kind of man."

Hereford still smiled, but now there was a wry twist to his lips. "I do not trust him either, but it is not so bad as that. He has good reason for his generosity. He takes one half of the noble's share of the booty—when there is booty."

"One half!" Elizabeth shrieked, starting out of the chair. "You did not agree to that! It is your blood that will be spilled while he sits safe lapped in scent and silken cloth. A tenth above his costs is ample reward for his exertion."

"Now, now, Elizabeth, he does more than that. You know he is our ear at court. Moreover he takes no small risk in trusting his men to my leadership. What if I turn against him? What if I fail?"

"What if the sun did not rise tomorrow?" she retorted hotly. "He risks nothing, and you know it, Roger. Your word is better than his gold. And if you fail, what would it cost him? A year's revenues from chests already overflowing with gold? You will belike lie dead in the field—" her voice faltered as the sense of her words penetrated and she pushed back her heavy hair. Hereford paused with his wine goblet halfway to his mouth, very curious as to what her reaction would be, but he was not rewarded with anything of note for she recovered at once.

"I suppose," Elizabeth continued, a little less angrily, "that Gaunt and Storm take the other half and you have the glory remaining."

Hereford laughed in the middle of his drink, spluttered, and choked. "I say, Elizabeth, do not make me laugh when I am drinking. You should know the Gaunts better than that—and me too. They requested only that their costs be returned if possible, and that Henry, when he comes to the throne, should grant such favor as is consonant with their help to Storm's wards. Gaunt insists, and in a way it is true enough, that they are doing nothing and deserve no reward."

"Then they are as great fools as you—hark, the dogs. My father is returning."

"Hereford," Chester cried and started forward across the hall almost at a run, "by God, I am glad to see you."

The men embraced warmly, for although Chester was the elder by many years, their relationship was that of equals, and Hereford was not given to a display of formal ceremony.

"It is good to have you here, my boy—nay, my son—and I speak the truth of my heart when I saw I am not prouder or fonder of my own blood."

"Now that," Hereford said, detaching himself from Chester but maintaining an affectionate grip on one hand, and turning to Elizabeth, "is the way a man should be greeted."

"Do not tease me, Roger," Elizabeth replied sharply, but smiling. "I will give you as good as I get."

"Do I not know it! All your daughter could say to me in greeting was that I made extra work for her. I tell you, if I was cold when I came in, she soon warmed me well with the back of her tongue."

"Roger!"

"Elizabeth!" He mocked her tone.

Chester smothered a smile. He had done well to write to Hereford and had done well to be absent when the boy arrived. "Well, Roger, you are better off than I am. I have been offered nothing to warm me—not even angry words."

"Alas," Elizabeth cried in mock dismay, "I am abandoned by all." She went to kiss her father and then with a brief curtsy left the men to themselves as she crossed the hall to order hot wine and more torches, for the daylight was fading.

"How comes it that you are not disarmed, Hereford? Was Elizabeth really in such a rage when you came that she would not attend you or do you fear treachery in my house?"

"All jesting aside, that daughter of yours is hot at hand, Rannulf, but that nor the other is why I am still armed. I had something to settle with her pertaining to our marriage and we both forgot. Truly, I have scarcely shed my mail for a day these two years so that I hardly know that I bear it."

Chester's pale blue eyes shifted around the room and

returned to the earl. "So the rumors I heard were true? You are joining Gloucester's forces?"

"By the eyes and ears of Christ," Hereford burst out, "from whom did you hear? The matter was decided scarcely a week since—"

"Calm yourself, Roger, I hear most things. Is it true then? I am glad. What do you plan?"

Hereford pulled gently at his right ear and ran his knuckles down along his jaw. "I need a shave," he commented with mild surprise, and then as he saw the look on Chester's face, "Sorry, I was not avoiding your question, I was thinking of Elizabeth. There really is nothing to avoid because, as yet, aside from some vague discussion with Gaunt about general matters, there are no plans. Gaunt felt, and I agreed with him, that I had better settle my private affairs first. It is too cold to fight anyway just now."

"Chester narrowed his eyes. "Do you mean to tell me, Roger, that things were left hanging like that?"

"Just so." Hereford rubbed the back of his neck where the mail came above the folded hood of the tunic and irritated his skin. Chester was going to be difficult to deal with. However unreliable the man was, he was no fool at all. "I swear," Roger continued, keeping to the literal if not the exact truth, "that no further definite plan was made. Gaunt was anxious to get home—he is getting old and tires easily, and Storm, as you no doubt know, is in Scotland. Gloucester," he made a moue of distaste, "did not seem to be interested, and I myself was a little distracted by other matters."

"You have changed, Roger."

"What do you mean? I am older and I have seen some new things, but I do not think I am different from what I was."

"You swear, eh?" Chester watched the young man's face narrowly although he took only quick glances at it now and again. "I have no doubt that what you say is true, if you swear it, but I fear you tell the same kind of truth that Storm does when he swears—half the truth with the important parts left out."

Hereford flushed, for the remark had hit home. "What

more do you want me to say? I suppose that you could guess without my telling you that I expect to hear from the others so that we can meet to plan in the future. You have changed too if you now need every little thing to be explained."

"I need very little explained. I have good eyes and good ears, but I did not think to need to use pincers to get information from my son-in-law."

"What information do you want?" Hereford asked irritably, his voice now so loud that Elizabeth checked in the middle of the instructions she was giving and hurried back to them. "I have told you everything I know myself that you had not already heard. Do you want me to make up tales for you?"

"You have avoided mentioning Henry and what befell in France, as though the topics were sacred."

Elizabeth drew breath to speak, but caught the flicker of relief on Hereford's face and just stood listening.

"Oh, Henry," he shrugged, "there is nothing to tell."

"You have grown very cool since I last heard from you. What happened?"

"Cool toward Henry, you mean? No, not at all, but he has no part in the immediate future and my mind has been so taken up with—. He will come when it is safe for him to do so, and we will be knighted together by David of Scotland. I can do homage to him then as the heir to England with perfect propriety since Stephen has not yet openly repudiated the arrangement that Henry should succeed him. That is neat, I think. I do homage to England without pledging my honor to Stephen."

The look of relief had been caught by Chester as easily as by his daughter, even though it had been quickly hidden. Nor did the slip Hereford make about his thoughts being on some immediate action go unnoticed, but Chester was too clever to press the young man when his temper was plainly on edge. He would have opportunity to discover all he wanted to know in the next few days, he thought, believing that Hereford was still too transparent and honest to be a good keeper of secrets. Chester, however, knew nothing of the training his friend had undergone in the last two years; he was closer to right when he said Hereford had changed. He took the goblet of wine Elizabeth was holding out to him and drank, seeking a new approach.

"Do you still think Henry is the man for us? He is young. Will he be able to hold the barons of England together?"

"Hold them?" Hereford laughed. "He is likely to mash them together if they do not behave. By God's bright eyes, Rannulf, it is a man! It is a man such as we have not seen in this country since the first Henry died. Yet in all, perhaps, he is better still for, though he has the old king's fierceness and determination, he has his father's disposition. He is free completely of his mother's and grandfather's sourness. You never saw a man easier of laughter, nor more willing to laugh and talk. It is as well that I am no great talker in little things because that one's tongue is never still. You should see him. He talks in French and writes in Latin at the same time. Ay, and like as not, the other eye is on another letter or set of accounts."

"Then the young king is perfect?"

"Nay, I did not say that. Some faults he has, being a man, but they are not such as make a bad king. He has a temper—he will say anything and do anything in a rage— but the heat cools as fast as it rises, and, when cool, he is just. Also, and this he takes, without doubt, from his mother, he is close-fisted as a usurer. He does not ask for much, but what he gets and what is his, he holds hard. This matter is something we must talk over well, Father, and not carelessly or in haste. Do you be very certain you know what is yours and what more you wish to have of him before he comes. Then write it all down—and many copies also so that if one be lost there will be others—one grant for what is yours already, another for what you desire. When he comes, make him sign before you promise your aid—sign every copy and take one for himself—you understand?"

"I understand well, Roger, thank you for the warning. But should I not approach him now to prove my good intentions?"

"No. Join him when you are needed and make your bargain. He will hold to that much, but if you think that anything will influence Henry beyond that bargain, you are mistaken. I know that one—friend or foe, he will ever be a king first. I tell you that if I did not care for the well-doing of the land as a whole more than for my personal profit I would have none of him. There is more to be had out of Stephen. As a man I love Henry, and he me, I believe, but he would see me hung or in hell for that matter, for a breach of his command as quickly as he would so treat his most ardent enemy."

"But, Roger—" Elizabeth interjected.

"Do not 'but, Roger' me," he said with sudden bitterness, turning on her. "He will bring us peace—peace to marry, and breed, and die. Do you think, Elizabeth, that I look forward with pleasure to rising from my wedding bed to make war, to knowing that even if you conceive a child of me it is like as not that I will lie cold in the field before I ever see it? As long as Stephen is our king, every man's hand will be set against every other's for a word of insult or a strip of land. Who is there to judge between the barons? Who can say them nay? I am no coward. I do not mind fighting for my right and my king to protect my lands, but I wish to accomplish something. I do not wish to lay down my arms one night to have to pick them up in the morning to fight the same battle over again. I wish to be able to swear a clean oath with a clear mind, not to think of disgusting artifices to avoid doing my duty. It is my duty to fight *for* the king of this country, not to make rebellion against him. Do you think I am not sick inside when I think of what lies before me, and sicker when I remember what lies in the past." He shook free of the hold Chester had taken on him. "Let me be. Let me go and wash the filth from me, if I can. I can talk no more."

CHAPTER 3

THREE DAYS HAD PASSED LAZILY. It had begun to snow the night Hereford had arrived, and, although Chester and his son-in-law-to-be had hunted the next day the sport was poor and dangerous. William Beauchamp's mount had fallen in a hidden hollow, throwing his rider and breaking his own foreleg. After that they had killed the stag they were coursing, but reasoned that it was too dangerous to continue and returned to the relative warmth of the keep. Confined within, the gentlemen had idled away their days playing chess and gambling or drinking hot spiced wine and listening to Elizabeth sing and play the lute.

The marriage contract had been signed, Elizabeth joining the discussion and arguing various points with such heat and success that the clerics who were writing the document and witnessing it had often stared at both men involved with blank amazement. Since Hereford and Chester seemed to take her behavior as a matter of course, as often deferring to her opinion as contesting it, they had made no comment, but when the contract was signed, the Bishop of Chester had read her a long sermon on her unmaidenly and unmannerly conduct. Whether this had an effect, which was unlikely as the bishop had been lecturing Elizabeth with no visible result for years, or some other matter preyed on her mind, neither Hereford nor Chester could decide. In any case, Elizabeth was very subdued and peace descended upon the house.

Midmorning of the fourth day brought a half-frozen courier, the perspiration of exhaustion nearly congealed on his face, with letters sent on from Hereford Castle. Roger opened the bag and first extracted the note in his mother's

45

hand. Laughing as he read, he passed it on to Chester, remarking that she had gotten along fine without him for two years when she knew he was inaccessible but now could not live a day without his presence. Two other letters were perused in silence, the first brought only a mild look of consideration to his face, but the second brought a steadily darkening expression. Elizabeth watched her betrothed with silent concern, unwilling to question him before her father, but Chester was not so nice."

"Well, what is it, Roger? What makes you look so black?"

"I have sufficient cause," Hereford snarled. "Here, read this." He passed along the second letter, which Chester saw bore the royal seal. Elizabeth looked anxiously from one man to another as her father's brows also contracted with anger and Hereford, catching her eye, motioned impatiently that she too might read.

Chester passed her the parchment to finish since she had been reading over his shoulder but he looked at Hereford. "How did Stephen know you were back? How dare he address you in such terms?"

"How dare he?" Hereford nearly choked with the rage which had been rising steadily as he considered what he had read. "Because he is safe behind his walls." He sprang to his feet, nearly weeping with frustration. "Oh, God, I will make him eat those words. I will send him back his 'legitimate offspring' piece by piece—first his ears, then his eyes—" He struck the chessboard between himself and Chester a blow that brought blood to his knuckles and sent the pieces flying all over the room.

The bishop, just entering, hurried across to the raging man. "Gently, my son. How often have I said that this is a game of the devil's invention. See how it makes enemies of father and son."

Hereford strode off across the hall, incapable of reply, pounding his fist into his open palm. Chester too was in no mood for a discussion with the man of God and turned away angrily. It was left to Elizabeth to enlighten him.

"It was not the game, Father." Her eyes flashed, bold and yellow as a she-wolf's. "See, only the way our king—may the Lord smite him for his presumption—takes upon himself authority over the Church of God." Elizabeth was angry, but as her pride was less than the men's her rage was less overwhelming and she saw a way to turn this threatened setback to an advantage. "Look," she cried, handing the bishop the letter, "see how he sets his authority higher than God's. He forbids Lord Hereford and myself to marry. My father has granted his consent; the Church acknowledges that we are outside the bonds of consanguinity and through your sacred hands has given its consent, and I am willing. Is not wedlock a sacrament of the Church? How dare King Stephen interfere in a sacrament of God?"

"My daughter, let me read," the bishop protested, but Elizabeth's aim was already accomplished. The prelate, as jealous of his rights as any temporal lord, had been predisposed, by her introduction to think of Stephen's prohibition as an infringement of his spiritual authority. He passed lightly over the point that Stephen was Hereford's overlord—although this was not technically true because Hereford had never done homage to him—and therefore did have a right to forbid the marriage, and moved on to consideration of a matter that was clearly within his realm.

"This is nonsense. If you are not consanguinous and are married by an ordained priest, neither of you having a previous spouse living, your children must be legitimate and must inherit your lands. No king can deny that right to a man's children—he cannot even deny it to the children of a serf, so how much less right must he have over the children of a free lord of the land. Perhaps for other causes," he hedged, thinking that possibly he had gone too far, "a king may sequester estates, but not on the grounds of legitimacy if you are properly married."

"Yes," Elizabeth said, her bosom heaving, "but what priest would have courage to marry us in the face of this prohibition?"

Chester shifted his eyes from the bishop's face so that he could hide his recognition of the trap his daughter had set. The Bishop of Chester was notorious for literally taking up arms to defend his rights in a most unpriestly fashion and for boasting of his courage and prowess.

"I will marry you myself," the priest said with determination, neatly snared by Elizabeth's net.

"But we are to be married at Hereford, and within a few weeks," Elizabeth said appealingly, "and I know the Bishop of Hereford will be afraid."

"That old woman is afraid of his own shadow. So much the better. It would be a shame if a beautiful lady like yourself and a lusty young man like Lord Hereford were to be joined by those feeble and trembling hands. I will come to Hereford and if that sniveling dotard objects—I will see to him."

"Thank you, my lord," Elizabeth murmured, dropping a deep curtsy and kissing the prelate's hand. "You have lightened my heart and reassured my conviction that courage is not lacking in a good priest to do God's will. Now I must go and see if I can quiet his lordship before he does someone some hurt in his rage."

Hereford was standing before the second large hearth in the hall, the male retainers and women servants having scattered into colder areas to be away from his wrath. The women, watching Elizabeth approach, nudged each other and commented on her lack of fear. "She," one maid remarked bitterly, having felt Elizabeth's hand that morning, "she fears nothing—man, beast, or devil. She is Satan's daughter, not Chester's, and the fires of hell burn within her."

"Let me be, Elizabeth," Hereford said in the same strangled voice before she could speak, "I am in no temper to have speech with anyone, even you."

There was a new type of respect in Elizabeth's face as she looked at her betrothed. The Hereford she knew did not have this type of control over himself; that young man would have beaten his servants, destroyed the furniture, possibly even have armed and galloped off to call his vassals to make war.

"If it will ease your heart to beat me, Roger, you are perfectly welcome to do so, but I have already found a way to turn that addlepate's blow from us."

"His blow! Who cares for that. If I could not force the Bishop of Hereford to marry us—and I do not doubt that light persuasion would make him willing enough—there is always the house chaplain who will do my bidding." He ground his teeth and began to tremble, crimsoning again. "It is the insult. How dare he write in those terms of command! The—"

Elizabeth raised her brows and smothered a smile as she listened to five minutes of the most elaborate obscenity that even she had ever heard. Some of the terms were so picturesque and surprising that they made her eyes open and once she spluttered a little. Finally, however, even Hereford's invention ran out and he subsided, gasping.

"That was lovely, Roger," she said calmly, "but cannot you see that you are directing it against the wrong man?"

Shock quieted Hereford, and he turned to face her. "What does that mean?"

"Have you ever known Stephen to speak or write in such terms to anyone. He is God's greatest fool, but even you must admit that he is gentle and conciliating to a fault, unless he is thrown into a great rage."

"So he is in a rage—do you think I am blessed with the calm of heavenly harmony just now?"

"Yes, but why is he in a rage? Roger, be quiet and try to think."

"I do not need to think. What is there to think about. He knows I am here and what I am here for—is that not sufficient?"

"How can he know? That you are here, doubtless he has heard. Maud has spies everywhere and you have not tried to hide yourself, but your business with Gaunt and Gloucester, who knows of that except ourselves? I do not suppose you made plans such as those at the top of your lungs in the main hall. Besides, even if he knew of your plans, why express his anger by forbidding our marriage? Are there not more direct ways?"

Hereford frowned thoughtfully. "You are right there. Besides, even if someone did overhear Gaunt and myself, there would not have been time. This letter must have been written only a day or so after I arrived. What the devil does this mean?"

"It means that there is someone close to the king who does not wish us to marry and join our houses."

"Ridiculous. I have been your father's ally for years, and I am not changeable in that way."

"No. But as a simple ally you would not be likely to intervene in his private quarrels, whereas as his son-in-law you would, since his sons are so young. Another thing, there can be no doubt that if anything should befall my father you would become the guardian of his sons once we are married."

"Very well, all that is true, but I still cannot see what this has to do with our marriage. Why should Stephen care about any of those things. Granted he does not love Chester, but he is not a covetous man and does not desire his vassals' lands. Possibly it might be feared that my coming would involve your father in political affairs again, but it would do so whether we married or not."

"That is what I have been telling you. Of himself Stephen would not care if we married ten times over. Someone has deliberately enraged him and fixed the idea that our marriage would be a danger to him in his mind. It is the marriage itself, not a military alliance which Peverel wishes to prevent."

"Peverel! The Constable of Nottingham? He is your father's cousin, is he not?"

"Yes, may he die a leper." Elizabeth flushed suddenly with remembered rage and shame. "You may not know that when my father was taken two years ago, he was committed to Peverel's care. I believe Stephen meant well. The Earl of Chester has many enemies at court and Stephen chose a man whom he thought was at once loyal to him and fond of my father. Peverel entertained him nobly—so nobly that his three companions died of poison and my father was sick unto death for a month."

"You cannot mean that!"

"Mean it? Ask Lord Storm if the Earl of Chester could sit a horse when he was released from prison. I nursed him, who should know better?"

"I never heard a word of this. Why did Chester make no complaint?"

"To whom should he complain?" Elizabeth nearly shrieked, her eyes filling with tears of fury. "Is there a just man in Stephen's court who would carry the tale against such a favorite as Peverel? Could my father personally approach the king who had sworn to cut him to pieces?"

Hereford was physically sick with disgust. Two years of involvement in the intrigues of the Empress Matilda's court had not been sufficient to harden him to the subtler forms of treachery. He was a perfectly direct individual, prone to avenge insult or injury with a blow, quick to anger, and slow to forgive, but forgiving when he did with complete sincerity. He had never borne a tale for the purpose of discrediting anyone and could never bring himself to tell a direct lie, except to women for obvious reasons. It was terribly difficult for him to conceive of a nobleman behaving in the manner Elizabeth had described. Instinctively he sought for excuses.

"It must be a mistake. Peverel could have no reason for such an action. You should not carry such tales, Elizabeth. It may have—"

"Are you saying that I lie? I have many faults, but that is not one of them. Of what did my father's companions die, vomiting and foaming at the mouth, minutes after they drank wine sent to them by our dear cousin? Oh, Roger, you know it is true. Your face is a perfect match for that green gown you are wearing. If you would but stop thinking that all men are like yourself and consider the facts, Peverel's purpose would be clear enough. My father's sons are children; his brother, who is not even a full blood brother, the Earl of Lincoln, is an avowed rebel; there is no member of the family other than Peverel who has the king's ear. Who then would the king name as guardian for Chester's lands and children? Lincoln might fight, but he has troubles enough of his own. Think of the power the man would wield with the lands and men of Chester at his back."

Hereford was silenced for a moment. "I still do not see why he should wish to stop our marriage," he replied sullenly after a while. "Soon I too will be an avowed rebel. Where is the difference between myself and Lincoln."

"But Peverel does not know that! He would think that you returned only to fulfill your contract—some men do such things, you know." There was a bitter undertone to Elizabeth's voice, but Hereford was totally preoccupied

with his own still smoldering anger and the problem of
Lord Peverel and did not notice.

"What does your father say to this?"

Elizabeth raised her eyes heavenward in exasperation.
"The good Lord give me patience! He probably has not
yet thought of it. Like you he is too busy being furious to
think at all. I cannot imagine why rage turns men into idiots."

"Because," Hereford snapped nastily, "it makes women
who ordinarily are idiots so wise." He started to walk back
to where Chester and the bishop were still talking about
the arrangements for the wedding ceremony, and Elizabeth caught his arm.

"Just a minute, Roger, I have something to tell you."

"Well, come and tell your father too. This is as much
his affair as mine, according to what you say."

"No. I do not want him to know this."

"Why?"

Elizabeth dropped her eyes. "I have kept it from him so
long—in the beginning because I was afraid, and later
because there was hatred enough between my father and
his cousin and I was no longer afraid."

"Well?" Hereford's tone was still cold. It was not Elizabeth's fault that her cousin was a treacherous cur, but his
resentment carried over.

"When I was a child my father and Peverel were allied,
and Peverel was often here at Chester. He—" Elizabeth
turned her face away. "He attempted me. He tore my
clothes and handled me—" Hereford made a sound of re-
gurgitation and stepped back as if she had suddenly
grown repulsive. "Do you think I welcomed that? Oh,
God, how I hate men," she faltered. Hereford could not
swallow or speak and spat to clear his mouth. At that,
Elizabeth turned to look him full in the face, her eyes defensive, cold, and angry. "I would not have said anything,
I assure you, except that I won free of him then, and
later, more than once, I defended myself in such a way
that he hates me. I think he would do anything to have
me subject to him. You are betrothed to me, Roger, and I
have warned you. If I am less in your eyes because of it, I
cannot help it."

Head high, she left the hall, abandoning Hereford to his struggle with his revulsion. It did not take him long to clear Elizabeth of any connection with it, however, and he caught up with her at the door to her solar.

"Elizabeth!" He had her in his arms before the bitter words on her tongue could find release and he pulled her inside with him and kicked the door shut with his heel. "Do not say it. Whatever you were going to say, I have well deserved it, but do not. Just let me hold you." He pressed her close, stroked her hair; her cheek was forced against his neck and she could feel the quickened pulse and his uneven breathing. Slowly the rigidity of her body relaxed and she dropped her head until her forehead rested on his shoulder.

There was a chest near the door to which Hereford drew her, and he seated her next to him without releasing her. His eyes were black with a steady abiding fury that boded Peverel no good in the future, and his mind was so occupied with calculating how many men and how much time it would take to destroy Nottingham Castle and its lord that he had nearly forgotten Elizabeth.

"Roger," she said faintly.

"Hush, Elizabeth." He tightened his grip. "I am in no temper for talk."

"But I cannot bear it. The way he looked at me—all my life men have looked at me like that. Even you—the way a rutting boar looks at a sow—"

Hereford's breath caught. Even if he had formulated the difference between his feeling for Elizabeth and that called forth in other men by her voluptuous beauty, he would not have known the words with which to explain. He could do no more for her than to caress her gently. Eventually she turned her face into his breast and began to cry despairingly. Hereford was wrenched with a pain which made him set his jaw; the sensation had nothing in common with the combined pity and exasperation that stirred him when his mother or sisters wept, it was a pure agony comparable only to what he had felt when his father died.

"Stop, Elizabeth," he said with desperate sincerity when he could bring himself to speak at all, "you are killing me.

Tell me what you want me to do, and I will do it. Do you want to be free of me? Shall I leave everything I have come for and go back to France? On Crusade? Do you want me dead, Elizabeth? That could be easily arranged—"

She covered his mouth with her hand, shuddering. Triumph, shame, and her own suppressed and rejected passion, awakened only to be denied whenever Roger touched her, boiled together until she was beside herself. She tore loose from his hold and ran across the room to her bed. Hidden by the curtains, she gave free, if silent, reign to her emotions for a few minutes. It was hopeless, she thought, misled by Roger's silence into thinking that he did not understand her. Free of her initial burst of despair, however, she was first soothed and flattered by the extremities to which Roger seemed willing to go to please her, and then alarmed. He, no more than she, should be forced into an action not sanctioned by his own will and conscience. She wiped her face and bit her knuckles until she had regained some measure of self-control and then peered out of the curtains almost fearfully. Hereford had risen to his feet but made no attempt to follow her. He was standing indecisively near the door, plainly unsure of whether to go or stay.

"I am sorry, Roger," she said with commendable calm, coming forward. "I cannot think what overcame me. You know it is not my habit to weep for nothing, and that was all so long ago." She could only pretend that she wept in memory of her past shame and terror since it was impossible to explain her present conflicts. His face did not relax and her voice faltered a little. "I should not have told you. I see now it was stupid, for he did me no real harm, but at the time I was so angry because you did not seem to believe Peverel's treachery to my father. I wanted you to know what sort of a man he was. He is an evil man." In spite of herself she shuddered.

"Well," Hereford replied with deadly quietness, "he will not be much longer, I hope. Let God be his judge. I will dispatch him to his just reward shortly."

Hereford at last relaxed enough to sigh heavily. He realized that his hands had been clenched into fists so hard and for so long that his fingers were numb and he forced them open and flexed them. "Praise God he is a king's man," he said, his face twisting into a grimace he thought was a smile, "the way I feel just now I do not believe that my loyalty to any cause could—" he choked. "The incestuous—" Elizabeth looked away. "Forgive me, Elizabeth. I will not speak of it again." He drew a deep breath and made an attempt to sound more natural. "Everything falls at the wrong time. My other letter was from Gaunt to say that he has heard from Lord Storm and expects to see him early next week. He asked that I come to Painscastle. He thought, of course, that I was at Hereford which is scarce more than a day's ride, even in this weather, and that he was giving me sufficient warning, but now with the time the news has taken to come to me and the distance—I will have to leave early tomorrow to be there in time."

"I see." Elizabeth straightened her back. "And when will you return?"

"Not at all, I am afraid. My mother urgently desires me at home and I have no idea how long Gaunt will keep me or what he wants. But you will be leaving for Hereford yourself in a few weeks' time. I will see you there."

"I have never known you to be so quick to respond to your mother's word before, Roger. Are you sure you do not return because you truly feel I am too sullied to be Lady Hereford now?"

"Elizabeth, you are not reasonable. It will take me three to five days' hard riding to Painscastle in this weather. Would you have me ride all the way back here only to start out at once for Hereford which is so close to the Gaunt lands?"

"Of course not. I would not expect you to put yourself out in any way for me."

"Elizabeth!" Hereford exclaimed, torn between his present irritation and his memory of her recent distress. His memory won. "If you desire it, of course I will come back. Mayhap, instead, you would like to come with me. You know Lady Leah and she would be happy to welcome you, even without invitation, I am sure."

"I would like that." She laughed a trifle shakily. "I need diversion. I will tell my father, and—oh, Roger, I cannot."

"Why?"

"Because," Elizabeth said, putting out both hands to him and smiling with a genuine warmth for the first time since he had been back, "I do not propose to come like a beggar maid to you. Do you realize that my wedding gown is not yet finished, nor a thousand other things which are necessary? Moreover, you had better not return. Somehow nothing is done when you are here and the last day or two will be the worst of all for hurry."

Glancing at her uncertainly, Hereford thought that women often said one thing and meant another. With Elizabeth he did not seem to be able to guess what was under the words. He replied finally with caution. "You must decide. I would like to have you, but will not urge you. If you change your mind, you can come at the last moment, or—if you want me, Elizabeth, write and I will make the best haste I may to return."

"You are kind, Roger, but you always are, and I count upon it. I have been unreasonable—but there, I always am." She smiled, unwilling to show how shaken she still was. "Go down and settle what you must with my father and the bishop—I never told you but he has offered to come to Hereford to marry us. I will not come. I—I want to be alone for a while."

Passing southward through the valley of the Dee soon after sunrise the next morning, Roger of Hereford could not be distracted from his fatigue and ill temper even by the beauty of the scene. Like most landowners dependent upon agriculture for his livelihood, he usually noticed the weather without seeing the landscape, but just now he was thinking of a military campaign and was forced to consider the terrain. He had been trying to compare the land formation around the Dee with his vague memory of that of the Trent, which he had passed through once going to Nottingham, when the glittering loveliness surrounding him impinged upon his consciousness. The alders and aspens drooping above the river were hung with necklaces and bracelets of icicles which dropped, now and again, as the light wind caused branch to rub against branch, into the water below with a tinkling splash. Blackberry and thorn were draped and blanketed into fantastic shapes which should have been dazzlingly white but were now delicately rosy where touched by the rising sun.

In some places where the rosy glow was reflected into bluish shadow, the snow even gained a certain vague violet hue that recalled to his mind Elizabeth's dusky blush. Hereford shifted his reins from one frozen hand to the other which he had been warming beneath his cloak and restlessly hitched his shield further back over his shoulder. He had parted amicably enough with Elizabeth, but there had been no return of the momentary flash of warmth to her manner. She had been alternately sharp and depressed throughout dinner and the evening which followed, and, although she had been courteous in her farewells, Hereford was sure that she was glad he was going. What was he to do with her? How could he deal with a woman who took admiration as an insult? He was ready to admit that Elizabeth was more than a body which could give him pleasure. If she had not been, he would not have offered to marry her. After all, he could take pleasure with almost any woman in the kingdom; there were very few who would refuse Roger of Hereford. Why could she not understand, or why did she deliberately misunderstand?

He began to damn her fretfully and stopped the thought. Even as an expression of his temporary annoyance he did not wish to curse Elizabeth. For a while he sought for words to explain what he felt, thinking he would write to her, but there were none that did not include or reflect his sexual attraction, and he thrust the problem away with a bitter sense of frustration. Everything was wrong, everything. He had known Elizabeth would be difficult, that she would scold and drive him, but he had never had the faintest suspicion that she might not care for him or even that she might accept him because she was growing older and "a woman must marry either a man or Christ" and still emotionally reject all that went with marriage. He had no joy even in this journey. How ardently he had looked forward when he was in France to the time when he would return, even to the period of war which would precede seating Henry on the throne. Hereford experienced a horrible sinking sensation and swallowed to still the fluttering of his stomach. In

France, if he had known of the offer that had been made to him, he would have been delirious with joy. What was wrong with him?

"My lord."

Alan of Evesham's voice called Hereford out of the pit into which he was steadily sinking.

"What is it?" he grated furiously, angry even at the relief he experienced in being drawn from his unpleasant thoughts.

"The baggage animals are falling behind, my lord. You are setting too hard a pace for them."

"Very well." Hereford reined in his horse and made an irritable gesture which dismissed his master-at-arms. He had been unconscious of steadily increasing the pace under the pressure of his unhappiness, as if he could outrun it.

Alan shrugged and dropped back to ride with William Beauchamp. "Two years abroad seem to have embittered his lordship. He has changed a great deal."

Beauchamp laughed softly. "Not two years abroad, Alan, two weeks at home. Actually, I suspect, two minutes in Lady Elizabeth's company could do more to sour his temper than twenty years of exile."

Evesham raised his eyes to heaven expressively. "God help us."

"Ay. They do nothing but fight like cat and dog. I can see why any man would want her on first seeing, but his lordship has known her all his life. You would think he would have more sense. I do not suppose it is the woman, really. I think he looks to bind Chester to him by some stronger bond than an oath."

"He will surely gain that by taking the Lady Elizabeth. Lord Chester positively dotes on the girl. Mayhap if he were not so doting, his lordship would have an easier time of it. You are right though, there is something in the wind that smells of rough hunting. If it be rough enough, it would be needful to bind Chester securely. He wavers every time the scent changes; he cannot hold to the straight trail."

"And he can always drive the woman out to her dower castle when the need is past or her father dead. Even if she bears him nothing, he has his brothers to follow him. Walter is nothing but trouble, but Miles is said to be a promising child."

Alan of Evesham looked with surprise at William. "You have been with him nearly four years, how can you say that? I came with him at Faringdon—I too would have rather died there than yielded—and I knew what a man he was even at sixteen. Yet when I saw his softness to his mother and his sisters, I nearly left him again before I did him homage, thinking that the one act might have been childish bravado or had drained his courage. Soon enough when he was well of his wounds and I of mine we went to fight again and I saw that he was split in two parts. With men he is one way, good-humored but not soft. With women—they can make him jump through a hoop like a whipped dog. Lady Elizabeth may spoil his temper, but we will suffer for it, not she."

"His mother and sisters are one thing. It is true that he melts like snow in summer for a drop of water in their eyes—and mayhap it is no bad thing. He lives in a house of laughter. Those women run to meet him, and fawn on him, and pet him—are they ever sad? Ever too tired to sing to him, play for him, sew for him, make sport for him? Now I think on it, Alan, you have a point. He was not so happy or even-tempered as he used to be, in France. I had grown used to his new ways and forgot that in the old days in England he never stopped laughing."

"Ay. He needs the coddling. Some men are like that, and I do not deny that it is a happy house—but what possesses him, Beauchamp, being as he is, even for Chester's alliance, to take a shrew to wife? He will never cast her out, only grow sourer and sourer."

"I am not so sure. That was what I was about to say. He is so with the women of his own blood, but with the others—. He may speak soft words, but when he is bored or annoyed, that is the end. Tears avail nothing, nor anything else either."

"Blast the man, what ails him?" Evesham exclaimed, as a shout and a squeal made him turn and he saw one of the baggage animals founder, "Ride up, Beauchamp, and tell him to slow down again. Let him bite your head off for once, I will go and see about the animal."

Hereford, however, had also heard the shout. He had a good leader's faculty of being aware of any disturbance in his troop no matter how occupied he was with his personal affairs, and he had stopped and begun to return prepared to fight when he saw the cause of the excitement.

"Who is in charge of those animals?" he snapped at Beauchamp when the younger man came up. "Why can they not keep them steady?"

"You are riding too fast, my lord," William replied stolidly. "That cattle cannot keep up with your destrier in this soft snow."

"If the men paid more attention to where the beasts set their hoofs and less to their talk, there would be less trouble. You tell them that if another animal falls I will have their skins for it—and yours too."

"As you say, my lord."

"You are carrying my lance in a damned funny way, William. Is that what I taught you?"

"I am sorry, my lord. I hurt my wrist in that fall I took. I will correct it."

"Young fool! Give it here, I will carry it myself. Did you think to have it bound up? How badly are you hurt? Let me see."

"It is nothing. I can use the hand, but the lance is heavy."

"As you like. Keep it warm or it will stiffen, and you may have a use for it sooner than you expect. If you cannot wield your sword when I need you, I will have a few warmer things than 'young fool' to call you."

William Beauchamp, as wellborn as Hereford and in no need of his favor for a livelihood, lost his temper. A squire owed even his life to the man who taught him his trade in arms in exchange for service, but he did not need, in William's opinion, to accept insults. "When I have first failed you, you will have a right to speak to me in that manner. If I no longer—"

"Hold your tongue, William. I am responsible to your father for you. How would I ever be able to explain a crippled sword arm to him? Now take care of that wrist; put no strain on it, and when we get to Painscastle let Lady Leah see to it."

Beauchamp dropped back, fuming, and it was Evesham's turn to laugh. "Heated you a bit, did he?"

"It must be more than the woman, Evesham, even that she-devil of Chester's could not bring him to this state."

William Beauchamp was perfectly right, for Hereford, capable of holding only one serious idea at a time in his head, had almost forgotten Elizabeth's existence. He was trying to find the cause for his feeling of predestined failure and had reviewed his meetings with Gaunt and Gloucester from every aspect. It was hopeless. Everything about the plans he had formulated to present to the others appealed to him. He would attack the king's strongholds in March, just after the early thaw had passed enough to allow the ground to harden. This would doubtless draw Stephen out of London away from Maud's advice and the information about rebel movements supplied by her spy system. Hugh Bigod would attack, if they could bring him to agree at the proposed meeting, a week or two later so that Eustace would be drawn to the northeast. Henry should then be able to land secretly and safely in April with the king and Eustace far too occupied in defending their lives and property to concern themselves with his movements. Then he and Henry would ride north, picking up Chester and his army on the way. That would permit Hereford to leave almost all of his own command behind to continue the diversionary action.

The end of April or beginning of May should find them in Scotland where they could lend David some help either in beating back the Norse or in attacking Stephen's northern allies. These actions, particularly if they were successful—and about that Hereford felt perfectly confident—would proclaim to all England Henry's presence and prowess as a leader and warrior, and promise an alliance with David which would stop the sporadic fighting in the north if Henry became king. The culmination of this activity, once sufficient notice of it had been gained—and word of that would come from Gloucester and Gaunt—would come with Henry accepting knighthood from King David.

That would make him an English knight, knighted on English rather than French soil.

Fresh from his knighting, Henry, with Hereford, Chester, and David, if possible, would make a feint at York which would, they hoped, draw Stephen northward while he sent Eustace into Gloucestershire to continue the fight there. Leaving Chester and David to occupy Stephen, Henry and Hereford would hurry south to engage with Eustace. If they could take him prisoner then their primary objective would be gained and negotiations with Stephen could proceed.

The whole plan, precluding some unforeseeable catastrophe, was nearly perfect and, provided they were better men, almost certain to succeed. If Eustace came north instead of Stephen, it would be even simpler, for Henry and Hereford would save themselves a grueling trip south, or, if he remained to fight Hugh Bigod, they could all move east to attack him in force. They had sufficient men, money was not wanting, and the allies were bound together with a combination of blood ties for Chester and himself, deep-seated honor and long-standing enmity to Stephen on the part of Gaunt, Bigod, and Hereford, and hope of great gain for Gloucester as well as all the others. The whole should have given Hereford the uplift of complete confidence instead of the continued and increasing sensation of foredoomed failure, as if in punishment for something, which he suffered.

The great brown destrier stumbled, and Hereford, jerked from his thoughts again, pulled up his horse's head and steadied him with caressing hands and words. The Dee had curved westward already; they would soon have to ford it and would doubtless find some town at the ford where they could stop to eat, warm themselves, and rest their mounts. Hereford glanced at the sun.

"Alan."

"My lord?"

"Send some men forward to the ford of the Dee to arrange for food and fire for the men and fodder for the beasts. Buy if you can—I do not wish to enrage the Welsh—use force only if you must. Wait, take my lance a moment. I have letters here from Chester and Gaunt. If there is a keep or manor house there, one seal or the other will bring us courteous treatment."

"Yes, my lord."

"Come back when you are done, I wish to speak to you."

The twenty chosen men spurred their mounts forward eagerly. They had wondered, considering the pace that Hereford was setting, whether they would be allowed to stop at all, and were most eager to see his lordship comfortably installed so that they might have the longest rest possible. Alan exchanged glances with William and rode forward again.

"How long have you been my master-at-arms, Alan?"

Evesham raised his brows. Normally Lord Hereford's memory was excellent and he wondered what such a question could preface. "Six years—a little more or less."

"You rode with me out of Faringdon and saw me take this there." Hereford touched his chest lightly where his clothing hid a scar that ran from nipple to navel. "Have you ever had cause to doubt my courage?"

"No." Alan answered flatly, startled by the similarity of Hereford's thoughts to his own such a short time before. Then, wondering if his master's sharp ears had picked up the conversation, he covered himself. "Once when we newly came together and I saw how soft you were to your womenfolk, I did wonder, but now I know the two things are separate."

"You have been a true man to me, Alan, and you are your own master. I have a great task before me, and a bitter and dangerous one. If I were sure of success, there would be no need to say this, but I have a great foreboding of evil. I would release you from your homage to me."

"My God!" Evensham exclaimed, "how have I failed you? How have I displeased you that you must cast me out?"

Hereford laughed without humor or relief. "On the contrary, it is because you have done neither that I wish to release you. Nay, Alan, I would not send you succorless into the world. I would arrange a new position for you before we part. Gaunt is growing old, he would doubtless be glad to have you on my word, or Lord Storm—he has a young son who will need a tutor in arms. If you like them not, I have connections in England and in France where you might be better suited."

"But Beauchamp and the others stay with you. What cause have you to doubt my loyalty?"

"William, Harry, and Patric are not their own masters and have nothing to say to this. I have written to their fathers that my state is precarious and left it to their wisdom to withdraw their sons or bid them continue to serve me." Hereford laughed again. "Your loyalty is not in question, Alan, but your safety is."

"I have not displeased you, you do not doubt my loyalty, yet I am not offered the same choice as the others. Why? You talk about my safety as if I were an old woman. Have I never fought back to back with you in a place as near hopeless as could be? Speak your meaning plain, my lord, for I am a plain man."

"I too, Alan, but I can speak no plainer. What you say is true. I have led you without consideration into many places where you risked your neck. Still, that was different. I always felt all would be well if we but bore ourselves like men. Now—I do not know."

"You may say what you like about coming evil, but I do not take it kindly that you treat me like a child. I am old enough, ten years older than you are—to know what I must face and decide for myself. I am too proud to take your charity, my lord. I have given you good service; if that no longer contents you, cast me out, but if I have done no wrong give me leave to know my own good and ask for my own freedom."

Hereford stared dully at the snow-covered track that snaked away before him. "I can tell you nothing," he said slowly, "except that I go in the near future either to glory or to defeat and disgrace—and my heart misgives me of the outcome. Your protest is just, however. You are no child and the choice should be yours. Think on it and let me know. There is no hurry."

"I need no time. I came with you out of Faringdon because I preferred death to yielding. I have served you six years and found you a man after my own heart." Alan smiled wryly. "In this country and these times, disgrace can be more honorable sometimes than great favor. You are not the mother of my husband, yet will I say unto you 'Whither thou goest, I will go.' "

For a while Hereford made no reply, and Evesham waited impatiently. He had bared his heart in those few words more than he had ever done so before. Hereford was less sensitive to men than to women, and he did not recognize that Alan of Evesham was very like himself. Bred to regard honor and his given oath as more important than life, he expected to serve one master only until that master died.

At last Hereford sighed, but when he turned to Evesham his most mischievous smile curled his lips and lit his eyes. "Well, that will teach me in the future to try to save my friends from themselves. If I had held my tongue, perhaps you would have seen how the straws lay in the wind and asked for your freedom. Now you will be constrained by your overweening pride to cling to me. Let us hope—since you have become so eager to speak in old saws—that your pride goeth not before my fall."

Painscastle, the home of the Duke of Gaunt and his son, Lord Storm, had always given Hereford a most uneasy feeling. It was a hard, ugly keep, old and scarred as its owner by hundreds of assaults, set high on a barren hill. In the early evening of winter it looked colder and more desolate than ever, the cleared, untilled slopes before it a sad contrast to the neat village that clustered at the foot of the hill. Hereford marveled anew, passing through that village, at the relative fearlessness and content of the serfs on Gaunt's land. He knew they were well guarded and well treated because Gaunt had a crazy theory that satisfied and fearless men worked harder. Hereford shrugged and dismissed the problem; his own serfs were reasonably well off because he was a good-humored man, just and not grasping, but he was not going to make a fetish of caring for those animals, as if they were his children, as Gaunt did. It was true, Hereford thought, that he preferred his serfs to be comfortable and not starving, but that was because he valued his own comfort. Gaunt and Storm, on the other hand, never seemed to know whether they were comfortable or not, and part of the reason Hereford disliked visiting them was that they also did not care whether their guests were comfortable or not. Painscastle was as barren and ugly within as without.

When he was across the drawbridge and inside the bailey, Hereford received several minor shocks. The first was the excellent order of the bailey, the outhouses and cooking areas in that courtyard between the inner and outer walls of the keep clean and in perfect repair, the clear space free of refuse and scavenging animals. Hereford heard the animals, but they were either confined to pens or kept out of the portion of the bailey most often used by those who lived in the castle. The second was that he was greeted not by Gaunt or Storm but by a sandy-haired, middle-aged man of pleasant countenance and graceful manners who looked only very vaguely familiar.

"I do not suppose you recall me, Lord Hereford, but I am Harry Beaufort. Please come in and warm yourself. This is terrible weather we are having. I do not remember such a bitter winter in my whole life."

Hereford dismounted stiffly, feeling for the ground with caution because his feet were so cold they were numb. He took Sir Harry's proffered arm gladly. "Has Storm been delayed again?"

"No, my lord, we arrived yesterday, which is why I am so busy offering you sympathy. I too was nearly frozen."

Hereford was just about to ask where the men of the keep were when he entered the great hall and stood stock-still, speechless. The last time he had seen the great hall at Painscastle it had been a shambles. Rats had fought the dogs and cats for the refuse on the floor; the fire was choked in its own ash; light was supplied by smoking, resinous torches, so ill-made that they stank and caused the eyes to smart. Surely this room was not the same. The rushes on the floor looked almost fresh and gave off their own faint sweet scent. With this odor was mingled not the usual spice odors but lavender; Hereford had a swift memory of the fact that Lord Storm's young bride loved lavender, her clothing and hair being permeated with that scent. Two lymers, Storm's special pets, nosed through the rushes for bones and stale bread, but they were the only animals present, both cats and rats were gone. The fires were clear red and the torches clear yellow, both giving light and heat without smoke or soot.

"Will you come and sit down here, Lord Hereford," Beaufort said, touching his arm and leading the way through the huge, high-raftered room. "Lord Gaunt will not go and sit in Lady Leah's solar—he says he is too old to be coddled and that men do not belong in the women's quarters—so she arranged this part of the room for him. At first he pretended to be angry and would not sit here, but she rules him now as easily as the other."

There could be no doubt that a woman had arranged that part of the hall. The rushes were swept back and held by thin, shaven logs so that a rug, as fine as those in Hereford's own room, could be spread before the hearth. Facing each other at an angle away from the fire were two well-carved chairs cushioned in dark crimson. The lowbacked one was pushed back from an embroidery frame as if a woman had leapt to her feet in haste, but Beaufort invited Hereford to take the high-backed chair with a gesture and sat in Leah's chair himself.

"I am grateful for your kind welcome, Beaufort, but where are Lord Gaunt and Lord Storm?"

"The Duke has gone to a nearby village to sit in judgment on some local disputes. Lord Storm is here."

"Here? Where? Am I not a sufficiently important guest to have the lord of the manor welcome me?"

Beaufort laughed easily. "You are most eagerly looked for, my lord, but nothing is as important as that." He glanced upward in the direction of the women's rooms in a manner that could not be mistaken, and Hereford could not avoid laughing too. His further comment was interrupted by a low voice from the stair entrance.

"Roger! I am glad at heart to see you."

Hereford looked toward the giant of a man who had paused to speak before he limped forward painfully again. The dark eyes smiled under lids heavy now with sensuality and the lips were softer than Hereford remembered them, the whole face smooth with satiety. Only the limp and the two scars, one carving a cheek from brow to lip, the other a deep groove across the forehead, were completely the same. Even Lord Storm's manner of dressing had changed. The old homespun gown which Hereford remembered so well had been replaced by a magnificent crimson velvet affair, embroidered and bejeweled. Hereford was hurt with the sense of loss that any change, even for the better, in a dear, familiar object brings.

"For God's sake, do you do nothing but lie with that woman day and night?"

Lord Storm stopped again and opened his eyes wide, too lulled with his physical satisfaction to take offense. "Ah, Roger, but I am newly returned to a pleasure ever new." He came forward again as quickly as he could and enveloped the slighter man in a bear hug which would have crushed Hereford's ribs had they been crushable. "Why missay me when you have laid plans to furnish yourself with the same provisions? Never mind, Roger, you may be as cross as you like after a ride like that—I love you in spite of yourself."

"Curse you," Hereford replied, laughing, "you have broken every bone in my body. How many times do I have to tell you that you are too big for playful affection."

"Ay, I see I have damaged your fair frailty. By my faith, Roger, you are beautiful. I forget every time until I see you again. Mayhap I should tell Leah to stay above. The shock of a face like yours after close contact with mine might be too much for her."

Hereford blushed faintly. He was accustomed to compliments from women, and men like Gloucester, but when they came from Storm he was slightly embarrassed. "Still trying to veil your wife, I see. You have not changed a mil's worth for all your grand looks nor for living in this grand manner."

"That is Leah's work. It matters little enough to me how I look or live. It is good to see you again, Roger. I have missed you. Life has been so dull since I have not had to pull you out of scrapes that I have been reduced to chasing the Norse up in Scotland." Beaufort had quietly effaced himself and Lord Storm took the vacated chair. "Setting our jests aside, however, my father tells me that you have accepted Gloucester's proposal."

"Yes."

Storm lifted his head and frowned slightly. "What is it, Roger? You sound—not cold and tired—as if you were not satisfied or happy."

"I do not know," Hereford said, turning away. "I do not know. I only know my heart is as cold and heavy in my breast as a lump of iron."

"Why? I thought to see you bursting with excitement and enthusiasm. If you have no lust for this task, I am sorry. It was I who proposed your right to it above all others. I did not mean to do you an ill turn, Roger. I thought I was urging what you yourself would desire."

"You were right. When your father mentioned the matter I was—I was beside myself with joy, but as I thought of it—"

"What mislikes you in it? Nothing is settled yet. Indeed, that is why my father asked you to come, so that we might set our minds to work together. If there is something you wish amended, speak out."

"I have done nothing but think of it. A hundred times— a thousand—I have gone over and over the outline of action I will propose. Nothing is wrong. To me it seems that it cannot fail if we all do our parts—yet—"

Storm studied his friend with knitted brows, his large hands, their even brown marred by the white scars of many battles, picking restlessly at the jewels of his robe. "Could it be other matters, Roger?" he asked a little hesitantly, "Elizabeth—"

"Why does everyone pick on Elizabeth? May I not be distressed for any other cause?" Hereford burst out furiously. "Is your woman alone perfect?"

"Gently, gently. I like Elizabeth Chester well, and you know it. I do not do her injustice because she would not suit me. Every man desires a different kind of woman. I only seek to know why you are uneasy."

"If I could put my hand on the hurt, I could salve it myself." Hereford was on his feet, so tormented with frustration at this inexplicable and totally new sense of futility that he could have screamed. "I tell you, I do not know. I only know that all will come to naught. Men will die and crops will burn and keeps will fall, and all for nothing—nothing."

Lord Storm's face had been darkening steadily, not with contempt or rage but as if a feeling he had long suppressed was gaining ground. He said nothing, but his hand went up to finger the scar by his mouth. Hereford, breathing as if he had been running, played nervously with the bright threads of the material on the embroidery frame.

"Don't mess Leah's work, Roger," Storm said absently, his mind plainly elsewhere, and then as Hereford took no notice he spoke urgently. "You have sworn no oath to do this thing. Do not. Tell my father you want none of it. Marry Elizabeth and sit on your lands and breed children. Do not drive yourself to what you have no stomach for."

Hereford dropped the yarn which he had now tangled hopelessly and turned slowly. "Are you making jest of me?"

"You know I am not. I should have kept my tongue between my teeth. Half I believed you would welcome the chance, it is true, but half I urged you upon the others for selfish reasons. Among them, they were driving me mad, all of them pressing me to undertake what I have passed on to you. They would not believe, even my own father who taught me this very thing, that since I have done homage to Stephen I would not break that oath and carry arms against him. Also—" Storm shut his mouth and set his jaw.

"So you feel it too," Hereford said softly. "What is it? In the name of the Merciful Mother of Christ, tell me, what is it?"

Storm shook his head and looked down at his hands. "It is different for every man. Even if I could tell you what specters I fear, it is not needful that yours be the same. You must seek out your own black places and cast light into them."

Distracted momentarily from his own problems, Hereford looked with undisguised surprise at his friend. "Are you afraid of things too, Cain? I never believed you to fear anything on earth or in heaven. I have known you so many years; I have never heard you speak of fear before or seen you look afraid."

"It is not something one speaks of ordinarily." He smiled

sadly. "There are few men to whom one can speak of such things at all. They think you soft or a coward or a fool."

"Is it not so?"

"Is it? Am I a coward or a fool? A little soft I am, perhaps, but I cannot think that so great a fault. And you—do not eat me, Roger, but you are one of the most fearful men I ever knew."

Hereford paled and put out a hand as if to stop the older man, then let it drop. "How have I given myself away? Nay, do not answer, I do not wish to hear. You are not any of those things and I do not believe you. You speak only to comfort me. You were ever one to see what is in men's hearts and ever kind to me." He paused and added bitterly, "Of what are you afraid? You cannot even think of a thing to fear, so you name nothing. These are but words."

"I am afraid of everything," Storm replied, his mouth suddenly gone hard and ugly as Hereford remembered it in the past. "My father is old, soon he will die and I will be left to decide what is best for my people. I am afraid of that burden. I am afraid to die myself, leaving him so old, my son so young, and my wife so rich. Ay, look away. A man's insides are not a pretty sight, but you asked to hear and hear you will. I am even afraid of the pain of wounds. I can bear it with patience from long schooling, but if you think I am not afraid—and that every man is not afraid, just as you are—you are the fool, not I. I will tell you something more, Hereford, that will make you look aghast. I am even afraid to lie with my wife. Oh, I cannot help it, a fire of desire for her rages in my blood—." The dark eyes showed red and angry. "But even the pleasure is spoiled by fear. I am so afraid that she will begin to breed again that I am sick with it. Have you ever seen a woman in childbirth, Hereford? A woman—that is a jest, she was but a child herself. They made me hold her. It is more than a year past and I still—" He rose so suddenly that he overturned the chair and made for the doorway that led out on the battlements.

"Let me go," he cried as Hereford started to follow. "I have ripped myself open for love of you. I can bear no more."

The Earl of Hereford rolled his wine goblet between his hands and looked sidelong at Lord Storm, who was sunk into the chair beside him. The sullen expression on the dark face did not invite conversation, and for the moment Hereford too was satisfied to be silent. He understood well the flash of affection and generosity that could make a man open his heart for another and also the resentment against the object for whom the gesture had been made that followed. They were seated at the table, a regular meal having been served instead of the usual light supper of cold meat or cheese, bread, and wine because Hereford had missed dinner while traveling. Just then he was free of the depression which had plagued him recently because his mind was so filled with the host of new ideas he had received.

The earlier conversation circled round and round in Hereford's mind as he tried to determine whether he was afraid or whether the premonition of disaster was a warning which came from outside himself. Nothing new had been added to his knowledge of the situation because Gaunt had come in tired, eaten, and gone straight off to bed. Storm, cajoled into eating by his wife after something of the situation had been explained to her by Hereford, had uttered hardly a word beyond monosyllabic replies to his father's questions and now that Lady Leah had left the table seemed to be almost in a stupor. Finally Hereford let the goblet rest.

"Storm."

"What?"

"I swear it is not that."

"Not what?" the big man asked irritably.

"I am afraid, it is true, but no more than I have been all my life and of no new things. Death, pain—these things, as you say, I, like all men, fear. But so I have always felt and yet I have always been happy—or nearly happy. Why am I so far from happy now?"

"Why ask me? Surely you know best what frets you."

"But I do not know. Storm, you are always looking at your own guts. Why should a man who has whatever he has desired be so uneasy."

Lord Storm made a gesture of pushing something away

and truly focused his eyes on his companion. He shrugged his heavy shoulders. "Because you are afraid to have that which you have snatched away. That is one reason, but not yours, I think. You do know what frets you, Roger, but you do not wish to acknowledge it."

A spark of anger shaded the color of the blue eyes that fixed the brown ones. "I tell you I have done my best to be honest."

Storm shrugged again. "You wish me to put it into words? I wished to spare you that. So be it. You are an honorable man. Miles of Gloucester bred you and raised you up, and now your honor is torn two ways. You are pledged to Henry and your heart is with his cause, but you know and I know that Stephen of Blois is King of England, God's anointed king, and it is wrong to wrest the throne from him by force."

"No."

"Yes. If it were God's will, Hereford, that Henry be king now, he would be. Stephen would have yielded the throne for reasons of his own, or the plague would have had him, or—any of a thousand things could happen."

"Then you are advising me to give up and not even try. You are mad. You are as deeply caught in this affair as I, even if you will not sully your honor by bearing arms against your king. You guard the word honor and deny its meaning." Hereford's voice was bitter with chagrin and sarcasm, but Lord Storm did not react to the tone and regarded the excited young man with no change in his thoughtful expression.

"Certainly I am involved in this, and more certainly I do not advise you to give it up. You are ever hasty, Roger. Would I have urged my father and the others to offer you what I felt to be wrong and hopeless? You have known me so long, is that my way with those I love? I am only telling you what I believe to be the cause of your distress."

"You are talking around me in circles again, Storm. You say you are my friend, do not do it. Speak simple words with plain meanings."

"Look you, Hereford, man is only mortal and does not understand the workings of the Infinite Wisdom. All we can do is what our hearts and minds tells us is right and just. That is what I meant when I said earlier that you should not do this thing if you have no stomach for it. On the other hand, if you think what you attempt is for the best—how do you know you are not God's instrument to bring about Henry's succession?"

The seriousness of the discussion could not prevent Hereford's easily tickled risibility from awakening. "God's instrument, eh? Satan's infernal weapon is more like. Do you know the count of my sins?"

"No, surely from your looks you must be the angel and I—seducing you to evil—the devil. Look at my face and my hoof." Storm touched Hereford with his clubfoot and laughed. "But this is no matter for jest. From what I can see and what you say also, you have doubts of the right of this action. I think that is only the result of your training and breeding. We are taught from the cradle that our duty is to our overlord. Stephen, as King of England, is your overlord even if you did not give him your personal fealty. It seems to me that it is the contest between what you truly feel to be right and your lifelong training that burdens you. More I cannot say. If I am wrong," Storm turned a palm up in a gesture of resignation, "then I am wrong because I have misread you or put into your heart what is in mine."

Hereford made no reply at all. Vaguely he heard, as if in echo, his own conversation that first day with Elizabeth, heard himself saying that Stephen was King of England and that he should be fighting for the king instead of rebelling against him. He watched Storm playing with the scars on his face with mild irritation and then smiled, thinking of how often Elizabeth had told him that the gesture gave him away, and stopped pulling his ear. Well, he should be fighting for the king and would be if Henry were the king. Around and around. He yawned and stretched.

"Ay," Storm commented, "we should stop talking and get to our beds. You are blue beneath the eyes with too much thinking. Sleep on it, Hereford, remembering that there is yet time to move either way without shame. But for God's sake, if you decide to go ahead, do so with a firm heart and a sure mind. For you to be unsure in this matter will be a worse disaster than abandoning the entire affair or trying to accomplish our purpose without the strength of Gloucester's army behind us."

Yawning again, Hereford shook his head. "I wonder if I will ever sleep again. These nights I feel as if I would drop, and when I lie down I am full awake again." He laughed as Storm looked questioningly at him with the same glance upward to the women's quarters that Beaufort had used. "No, thank you. I took a wench at the keep we stopped at last night and that did not help either—much. When my mind lies quiet, my body will lie quiet also."

"Yes, that and—you were never one for planning and scheming. When you come to the fighting you will rest easier—if you have time to rest at all." Storm clapped Hereford hearteningly on the shoulder. "It is dirty work, Roger, treason—ay, that is what it is, call it by its name— and you do not like to be splattered." He laughed. "When you are as drowned in the mud as I am, you will find it easier."

CHAPTER 4

"I CANNOT SEE," Roger of Hereford was saying in the dark just before dawn, "that we can make it more certain than that until we have Norfolk and Arundel with us to hear whether they are willing or not."

He was fully armed and ready to travel as soon as it was light enough to leave. A week of intensive and detailed planning at Painscastle had not improved his appearance or temper although his depression had lifted somewhat because his mind was so filled with the incidentals of war that he had no time to worry about whether he was happy or not.

"Norfolk may be depended upon. He agreed to help in whatever way was most fitting so long as he might remain near his own lands and I believe he will do it. Arundel is less to be trusted, I fear, in the fighting, but what we ask of him is little enough and I hope he will not fail. Indeed," Lord Storm added smiling grimly, "I know he will not because I plan to be with him at the time he goes to meet Henry. All he needs to be trusted with is getting Henry to Devizes, because I think it possible that it will be needful for me to go to London to see what Maud is doing at that time."

"Yes, yes. We have been over this and over it. Of more significance to me is the garnishing of the strongholds on Gloucester's land. If you will use that money you promised me for that and see to it that it is done properly, that will take a great weight from my shoulders and allow me to concentrate on the moving troops which I fear are in sad condition."

"You may trust me for that. It is perfectly proper in me, after all, to help my foster brother in such matters. Maud will know something is afoot, but it could not be long hidden from her anyway, and it will draw her attention in the right direction. Roger, give some more thought to the barons who are sworn to Gloucester. Can you bind them to you in some firm manner?"

"In two months? If Gloucester continues to insist that he will not appear as an active partisan, what can I do? Idiot that I am, I did not foresee that part of the problem when I agreed that he should allow me the men and money pretending that he had dismissed the mercenary troops and I had gathered them in. No, it was not idiocy," Hereford said, smiling like a naughty child in spite of his worn looks, in reply to Storm's raised brows, "it was pride. I did not wish that he should have the glory for the blood I spilled." His expression sobered. "But this is more important than my pride. We can make do without them, if Gloucester bids them offer us no resistance—which he has already promised—but they would be a welcome help. I have already decided that I will speak to him at the wedding and see if I cannot induce him to leave the court and join us at the nominal head of the forces."

"Ay, if you do all the work and allow him to sit safe in some keep he may agree, but not at first. He will want to see some hope of success before he commits himself."

"You are right, no doubt, but that will be soon enough. Until Henry and I return from Scotland and the heavy action begins, I have more than sufficient forces for my needs. Look, there is the first light. It seems scarcely worthwhile to say farewell, for you will be after me in a week's time. You will bring Lady Leah with you, I hope—and the boy too if she will not be parted from him—Elizabeth asked specially that she come if possible."

"You need not fear that," Storm laughed, "I would not be parted from her. My father makes a jest of me for it, but all in all I am so little at home—. She likes Elizabeth too. You would not think it, they are so different in every way, but it is true."

"We are not so much the same either, Storm."

"No. I suppose not. It will be nice for her to have someone to visit when I am from home and Elizabeth could come here too. Of course, your wife will not be so lonely with your mother and sisters in the house—but it is light enough to travel now and this talk is nothing of sufficient value to hold you for. God speed you, Roger. Travel well."

"God keep you, Storm." Hereford kissed his friend, smiling at the innocence and ignorance that imagined that his mother and such a daughter-in-law as Elizabeth would be "company" for each other. It just went to prove that a man who could see into the hearts of other men so easily was as a babe with women. I can hope, Hereford thought as they mounted and rode out, that I will have sufficient address to keep them from killing each other until time has brought them patience to bear one another. Otherwise, I will be forced to set my mother in her dower castle, which would be a shame. She would not like it and Elizabeth should not be troubled with washing underclothing and planning every day's meals. My mother could take those chores from her. Well, he was still smiling, I can do no more than try to keep the peace between them, but I hope Elizabeth has not yet arrived; I could do with a day's respite.

There was another reason he hoped Elizabeth and Chester would not have arrived. He expected the Earl of Lincoln to be already at Hereford and he wished to use the relationship to be formed between them to induce that notably unscrupulous magnate to attack Nottingham for him. Hereford had not mentioned his plan to destroy the Constable of Nottingham to Lord Storm because it was a private matter not really connected with Henry's affairs and because he was unwilling to discuss Elizabeth's involvement, but he had not forgotten. For a good-humored man who showed the true generosity of forgetting an injury he had forgiven, he was nonetheless an implacable enemy. What he had not forgiven, he never forgot. He had been forced, regretfully, to put aside the idea of attacking Nottingham at once himself as the pressure of work he would have in the next few months became more apparent through the discussions at Painscastle. He was too honorable to allow any personal problems to interfere with what he had taken on as a duty, but he could begin matters by inciting Lincoln to attack Peverel. Later, if things went well, he might be able to find time to finish the matter himself, but in any case he did not wish Chester to involve himself in that. He had other uses for Chester, for one thing, and did not want him distracted. For another, Chester was in enough trouble with Stephen without becoming more odious by attacking a favorite. One could never tell what small incident would set Stephen off on a path of revenge, and Hereford had no desire to have his wife's property attacked when he was too busy to protect it.

As they rode it became apparent that the weather was warming slightly. Hereford expressed himself freely, although in an undertone, on what he thought of the English climate, and gave instructions to Alan of Evesham that the men should keep a sharp eye on their beasts because he intended to push on directly to Hereford even if they had to ride at night. Lady Hereford, according to her letter, was frantic with the necessity of such great preparations in so short a time and Roger felt that his presence would lend stability to her efforts and calm his sisters, who were no doubt hysterical with excitement. Besides, he would be needed to hunt. His guests would expect better fare than pork, mutton, and beef, and the slaughter of game went better under the master's eye than when left to the huntsmen alone. He would have to hunt every day; Hereford looked disgustedly at the sky and the ground and cursed the weather anew. He could think of greater pleasures than hunting in this muck.

In the event, his prognostications were correct. Hereford's squires were just unbuckling his sword and lifting off his mail shirt when his mother and two younger sisters rushed in. Anne threw her arms around his neck at first without a word and kissed him all over his dirty face, but wordlessness was not Lady Hereford's problem once she had caught her breath.

"Roger, you are mad. Mad! Where are we to put all these people in the dead of winter—and such a winter? Where are we to get fattened animals—you cannot fatten winter stock in two weeks. Who ever heard of having a wedding—this kind of wedding—at this time of year!"

"Oh, thank you, brother, dear, sweet brother, thank you—"

"Roger, Roger, have you make up your mind about me? Mother told me you were to think of my marriage. Will I see him at the wedding? Will I?"

The three female voices in varying degrees of shrillness all impinged together on Hereford's ears. Nothing could be more likely to put a tired, cold, hungry man, already ill-humored, into a blazing rage, yet nothing was further from the fact. Hereford's women always exerted a most soothing effect upon him, even when they plagued at him. He shook his head as if slightly stunned, detached Anne from her stranglehold around his neck, although he retained an affectionate grip on her waist, and with his free hand drew his youngest sister close to kiss. Embracing both girls he faced his mother with his usual grin.

"Now, Mamma, I know you are quite capable of arranging these matters—Anne, do not kiss me on the ear like that, you will make me deaf—and I am sure you only wish to scold me."

"Scold you! I wish you were still three years old and I could smack you. Could you not at least have told me before you left for Chester that you were planning this insanity? That would have given me almost two weeks more. I said Anne must be married quickly, but I meant in the spring, in the normal manner. Do you know what everyone, Rannulf included, must think is the cause for this unmannerly haste? What a name you will give your own sister and worse, your own wife."

Hereford let out a long low whistle at that. "Good God, that had not occurred to me." An instant later, however, he laughed again and released his sister's waist to slap her rump. "Rannulf, at least, will know better soon enough, eh, Anne?"

Anne blushed and dropped her head. Her hair was darker than Roger's and her eyes gray rather than blue, but even if she had not the striking beauty of her brother she was a very pretty girl. The modest fit did not last long, because the more she blushed the more her brother laughed. Lifting her head, she too smiled, with a softer imitation of Roger's impish grin.

"Yes, he will, so there, you can stop laughing—and I still thank you. Oh, Roger, I will be a married woman, a lady with my own castle. And Rannulf himself seems very nice, I saw him yesterday and he—"

"Never mind her—"

"Oh, Roger!" Anne kissed him again with a sound enough smack to make him wince in assumed anguish as he turned toward Catherine.

"Never mind her. She knows who is to be her husband. Roger, do tell me what you have decided. Do! You will not make me wait and wait and tell me at the last minute, will you?"

"Catherine, you will tear my shirt. And if you do not stop hopping about from one foot to another, I will decide only that you are too young to be married at all because you cannot behave properly. Good Lord, you will bear me down between the two of you. Let me breathe. I have decided nothing, sweet Cate," he punned on her name and the word used for small sweet cakes sometimes served at breakfast, "but when I do, you will know."

Lady Hereford had been steadily losing patience with her sons' absorption in his sisters. Their affairs were important to her and she was pleased by the affection which she had been at great pains to instill into her eldest son for the younger children, but she felt that there were more pressing matters to be discussed.

"That is enough, girls. Let your brother be. Either help him to undress quietly or go back to your quarters. And you are worse than they are, Roger, encouraging them to hang on you the way you do. You should have more sense."

Shaking free of his two limpets, who finally set about the business of getting his bath ready and bringing him fresh clothing, Hereford stepped forward to embrace his mother. "It is no light task, I know, Mamma," he said quietly and seriously, "but you must believe me that I could not wait till spring. I will be otherwise occupied then, and it is part of my purpose to cement the relationships with Chester and Lincoln before the spring. Indeed, you have a perfect right to scold; I have put you to a heavy labor and there is very little time. Still, we must manage as best we may."

"But the betrothals are as firm a bond as the marriage,

why could you not wait until early harvest if you will be busy in the spring? Could Lady Elizabeth have agreed willingly to such a scramble?"

Hereford's eyes were momentarily shadowed by the specter that haunted him. "The autumn may be too late, at least for me. Elizabeth agreed willingly enough, for she understands what is before me."

Lady Hereford had paled at her son's first statement, but the pang of jealousy that pierced her with the second made her turn literally white and reach for a chair back for support. Hereford noticed but made no comment because he did not recognize the second, stronger emotion. For her fears he could offer little comfort; women had to accept the death of their menfolk if war took them no matter how dearly loved. So ran the pattern of life, but the girls were back, and Hereford shook off his troubles to joke and laugh with them as they undressed him and washed him. From the tub he called his mother to come closer.

"I can do nothing but plan tonight. Tomorrow we shall set out in earnest to make ready and you will see that nothing will be wanting. You have cleared the three floors of the keep already, I hope, and the bottom of the manor house is also prepared. That will give us sleeping room for fifty or sixty noble guests—on the two top floors of the keep—another fifteen or, if we press them close together, twenty may be put in the hall of the manor house. There are sixteen tower rooms which will take two to four guests each. At the best that will give us room for almost one hundred and fifty. I do not believe we will have more than that. From the east and the far north few will come. The way is too long, the travel too hard."

"I am not exactly a new-made wife and I have entertained a few guests in the past. You need not tell me how to keep house. I would be grateful though if you would tell me how we are to house the retainers and what we are to feed everyone."

That was that. All he needed to do was be there and everyone knew everything. If he was away, it was all impossible to accomplish. Hereford climbed out of the bath and permitted his sisters to dry him. For a time his conversation with Lady Hereford was suspended again as he answered excited questions about where he got this scar and that one. Like all gentle ladies, Catherine and Anne were fascinated by tales of war and enjoyed the bloodiest descriptions in a way that one would not believe from their gentle manners. Eventually, however, he was dressed; then he smacked both girls fondly, kissed them, and firmly dismissed them to their own duties in their own quarters.

"The retainers can be packed like salted fish into the ground floor of the keep and this building and into the passages. For the remainder, we will only need to drive the serfs out of their huts in the village, give those sties a rough cleaning, and let the men-at-arms sleep there. They will be warm and sheltered, and if the quarters are not elegant, they will have to put up with it. The village cattle will have to be sacrificed to the table too. I have sufficient money at present so we can forgive them their *aide* for my marriage and take the animals instead."

"Those scrawny beasts. What is there to eat on them?"

"Whatever there is, we will have. Tomorrow I will go to hunt. Lincoln and Rannulf—I gather have arrived and that Anne is pleased with the young man from her manner—can help, and when Chester arrives he will be out from morning till night. Nothing could give him greater pleasure. If worst comes to worst and we are still short of provender, we can raid the town. I do not like to infuriate the merchants, but what is needful is needful."

"If it is settled, you must have your way, of course. What do you plan to do to entertain the men? They will murder each other if they are kept pent in this keep so close together all that while."

"That is the worst of all, Mamma. We can have no tourney in this weather to lighten their hearts. The animals in the forest will be fewer because of the heavy hunting for the feast and the sport will be poor. Nonetheless, I will have the boarhounds out and I think I will send men to beat game from the furthest bounds of the woods. Also, you had better send a man to each of my vassals and tell them to bring with them any minstrels and jongleurs who are staying at their keeps or whom they meet on the way. At least we can dance."

"If there be room," Lady Hereford said wryly. "You will not have a mil left when this is over, Roger. Why does not Chester bear the cost of his daughter's wedding?"

"I have not come to ruin yet, and am not like to. You make ready, let me take heed for the cost. Come, Mamma, smile at me. I swear I did not do it to plague you but because it was the best path. Can you not trust me to do the best I may for all of us?"

Lady Hereford did make shift to smile then and stroked her son's hair. "For everyone else, yes, you do your best. Only for yourself, sometimes, you do not take proper heed."

"That is my mother talking. Who but she so blindly fond as to think I do not seek my own advantage."

"Your father was just such a one. Ever he spoke of his own advantage, yet he went first where duty led him without one thought for his safety or benefit."

"Yes, and was it not to his advantage to do his proper duty? Did it not bring him this earldom with wealth and honor too? Now, Mamma, you know I do not like this kind of talk—also, I am hungry, and I do not think I should avoid my guests longer lest they take offense. Let us go."

Hereford woke in the dawn with an urgent need for a woman. He reached out automatically, but the bed was empty except for himself, and he opened startled eyes to look around the room. Then he smiled rather wryly and lay still, fighting the urge. His mother had been very efficient indeed in dismissing his erstwhile favorites from the castle—he had not even remembered to ask what she had done with them—and it had seemed impolitic to take another maid to his bed when Elizabeth was due to arrive any day. Soon enough, he told himself and got up to urinate, which he knew would help. He shivered in the cold, and, knowing quite well that he would have to dress to hunt in a few minutes, plunged back into the warmth of the heaped featherbeds. He lay looking at the canopy above his head and thinking with some satisfaction of the accomplishments of the previous evening.

Anne and Rannulf seemed to have taken to each other very well. That was not surprising; she was pretty, affectionate, gentle, and Hereford was dowering her richly so that Rannulf had good cause to be well pleased. The young man was not ill-looking and was well-bred. He was brave enough and a strong enough fighter to make his wife proud of him, and his father was rich enough to give him a keep of his own to hold as a vassal upon his marriage even though he was a younger son. That was a piece of work well done.

The matter of Peverel was well in hand too. Hereford had spent a good part of the evening telling Lincoln how rich the Constable of Nottingham had become through being the king's favorite. He had also gently reminded him of the insult to the family in the attempted poisoning of Chester that had gone unavenged. Chester, he said, as if it were a matter of no real interest to him and he was merely relating interesting gossip, was bound by some oath exchanged before Peverel had proved an enemy not to molest him and had given surety of that. Since the king was Peverel's friend and Chester's enemy, it was scarcely safe to void that promise lest the king require that the surety be yielded in spite of the fact that Chester was in the right. Hereford had sighed gently and commented that it was too bad he could not take the excuse offered by that insult and his marriage to attack Nottingham Castle. He had heard that Peverel was close as a miser and had chests full of gold and jewels, but he had been away too long. His men were in no condition to fight just now; no new recruits had been trained, and, what was more, he leered, he had other plans. That he had repeated more than once, always with the leer which directed Lincoln's thoughts to his marriage, but the statement was insurance against Lincoln's saying that Hereford had lied to him when he began his spring campaign for Henry.

The light of avarice had wakened in Lincoln's eyes, and he assured Hereford that the insult would not go long unavenged. He had not known of Chester's oath, he explained, and thought his half brother had some private reason for sparing Peverel. After all, Chester had not died from poison although three of his vassals had. It could have been, Lincoln said, that Chester wished to be rid of them and Peverel had obliged him. He was not on such terms with his brother that they confided their secrets to each other.

Hereford suppressed his disgust with himself and Lincoln and concentrated his mind on the fact that even evil was attended with some good. If his brother Walter had not often behaved just as Lincoln did, he would not have known how to bend the man to his will. Then too, Lincoln's avarice, which was certainly an evil in itself, would probably lead to the just punishment of the Constable of Nottingham. What a father for his brother-in-law. Hereford yawned and threw off the covers, wondering whether it was worse to have such a man for an enemy or for a relative. It was done, he thought, and there was no use worrying; Rannulf seemed a good enough sort in spite of his background so that Anne would be happy, and if Lincoln finally ended on the gibbet where he belonged Hereford was sure he could protect Anne and Rannulf from any evil consequences.

"Roger."

Hereford groaned inwardly. "Yes? I am awake. Come in."

"Awake, but still like a bear in winter. Are you coming to the chapel this morning?"

"Yes, I am coming. Do not wait for me, Mamma. Send William in to help me dress and you go ahead and tell the chaplain to wait. Save a seat beside yourself for me and set the girls elsewhere. I want to talk to you about Catherine."

"During Mass?" Lady Hereford asked, her eyes opening wide with surprise.

That was a mistake that might get him a long lecture. Hereford took his lower lip between his teeth. He had forgotten that his mother was truly pious. He had been too long with Henry of Anjou who always used his time in church to write letters or plan strategy or just gossip.

"No, Mamma, but for a few moments before and after. With Lincoln here and the press of your duties and mine, I will have little other time."

"As you like, Roger, but do hurry. I do not like to ask the chaplain to delay."

The chapel was even colder than the manor house since it was not fitted with a fireplace. Hereford's mail struck cold through tunic and shirt, and his scabbard banged against his calves painfully and clanked on the stone floor as he genuflected to the Living Presence in the tabernacle. The mass of servants who stood at the back and sides, shifting uneasily from foot to foot and surreptitiously rubbing their arms and hands in the cold, hastily made a broad path for their master. He was usually kind, but in winter even Hereford's temper was strained by the continual minor discomforts he suffered and he had been known to knock someone in his way clear across the room when he was crosser than usual. He genuflected again just before he assumed his seat, but absently, and began to speak almost before he had risen from the bow.

"It would be very nice if I could settle the preliminary contract for Catherine's betrothal at the wedding since it would save time and trouble. There are not too many young men available, but—well, I cannot decide whether it would be better to contract her now, thereby gaining another firm ally or wait until—until later when I may well be able to look as high as I desire for a husband for her."

"How much higher can you look anyway? Roger, what are you about? What is this thing that is hanging over us?"

"Not an affair for a woman to trouble about, but if I succeed I will be one of the first men in the kingdom."

"You are not far from that anyhow, and what if you fail?"

The chaplain had entered and begun Mass, but Lady Hereford did not even notice.

"Then if I do not contract her now, you will have to settle Catherine as well as you can yourself, or, better, leave her to Walter." Hereford smiled grimly. "It is too bad Storm's son is so young. That would be perfect, but he is not yet two. If she were the man it would not matter—oh, well—"

"There is Shrewbury's eldest boy—"

Hereford's complexion changed color and his eyes darkened. "Mayhap I have sinned in uniting one sister to the son of a greedy boar, but I will not unite the other to the offspring of a serpent. Let me not hear that name again."

Lady Hereford looked somewhat startled, since the events that preceded her son's hasty departure for France had never been fully explained to her. Shrewsbury's treachery had contributed largely to Hereford's troubles at that time and he was not likely to forget or make alliance with that house.

"Chester's son is out too," Hereford continued more calmly, "the Church would never permit that, and it would be ridiculous anyway since Chester is more tied to Elizabeth than to the boy. I favor Bigod's second boy—I would like to make alliance with the east, but I have never seen him and they are a hard family."

"That is so far away, Roger. Norfolk is across the whole breadth of England. What of Gloucester's son? He has a boy of Catherine's age, has he not?"

"Yes—" it was a long-drawn-out sound, "a sickly creature like his mother with his father's vices, I fear. Of course I wish to marry Catherine well, but I also wish that she should be content. You have put me in mind, however, of someone quite suitable—two young men, in fact. Best of all, I like John Fitz Gilbert's eldest—"

"Fitz Gilbert is a bastard!"

"So? The son is not. He will inherit Fitz Gilbert's lands without let or hindrance. Robert of Gloucester was also a bastard. Patric's mother, moreover, is Salisbury's sister—"

"And his grandmother was a tanner's daughter!"

"So was our late king's. William the Bastard's mother was a tanner's daughter and he honored her all his life." Hereford laughed. "Speak well of tanner's daughters, Mother, they breed good men."

"There is no sense in my arguing with you, Roger, you will do as you like anyway."

"Yes, I will, but not so much as I like as what I think is best. You know I will listen to anything you have to say that is reasonable. That is why I am speaking to you about this matter at all. It is not reasonable, though, to object to a marriage because a man's father is a bastard."

"It is a sin to breed children out of wedlock! A punishment will fall on those—"

At that Hereford laughed so loud that the chaplain turned protesting and admonitory eyes upon him. "Most certainly, but look where you step, Mother, you are pinching my toes now."

"It is as great a sin for you as for another, even if you are my son."

"No doubt," the son replied, still chuckling, "so you had better pray for me. The other boy is not blackened with that pitch, but he is of more doubtful quality and less weight. That is Salisbury's third. He has fought on his father's right hand for some years now; he is some ten years Catherine's elder, and that is about right. William is younger, not much more than Catherine's age, and for two people so young to mate, Catherine being somewhat headstrong, I doubt—"

"You are full of wise saws and good advice that you do not follow. Elizabeth is scarcely your junior in years, and as for being headstrong—"

Already, Hereford thought. Winter or no winter, it would be hot as hell in Hereford Castle when Elizabeth arrived. "I am not fourteen, mother," he said pacifically, "and although it is true that Elizabeth is double the twelve years which would make her ten years younger than I, and, as you say, headstrong, you need not fear that she will rule me." A wry smile flitted across his face and was suppressed. "I can give as good as I get. What I desire from you, is that you watch Catherine and see if she looks kindly on either of those two lads—or on any other who seems suitable to you—and let me hear where her fancy lies if you can. If God is willing, I will be able to be generous, and a strong fighting arm, even if not backed by a great alliance, is not to be scorned."

"Roger, you put me out of all patience. I raised you to love your sisters, it is true, but you carry a good thing too far. It can make no possible difference where Catherine's fancy lies. She must love the man you choose for her. You did not ask Anne's opinion."

"And I am not asking Catherine's. I will allow her to do nothing unsuitable, I assure you, but Catherine is different from Anne. You are their mother, have you not seen it?"

"I see only that if you go on as you are there will be two Elizabeth Chesters in one family."

His patience was rapidly slipping, but he drew a deep breath and held it. There was no advantage in losing his temper and this was not the place for it. "You must not speak of Elizabeth like that," he said quietly, but it was plainly the end of the conversation, "and you must not fret her. I will have peace in my household even if there is war everywhere else."

When Hereford arrived home just before the light failed in the late afternoon, frozen, soaked, and panting almost as hard as his hunting dogs, the peace of his household had not yet been broken in spite of the fact that Elizabeth was there. The atmosphere, however, had all the aspects of a brewing thunderstorm rather than a quiet and settled calm. He kissed his betrothed's hand, which had been extended rather coldly, and then her lips, although she had not offered those, and escaped to the welcome and soothing ministrations of his squires and his sisters.

At the late supper, a full meal including potage, roasts, and pasties, as Hereford had eaten nothing since his breakfast at dawn, the clouds hung even lower and he could almost hear the thunder rumble. He was tired right into his bones by the chase—they had killed five does and three stags and the stags had fought hard—but he exerted himself to soothe Elizabeth, and failed. She was perfectly polite and proper, her manners left nothing to be desired in company at any time as a matter of fact, but she was cold as the weather outside.

"What is wrong, Elzabeth?" Hereford asked, drawing her out of the circle that was listening to a tale read aloud by the chaplin after the meal.

"Wrong? Nothing. You have a beautiful home and I see that every preparation for a magnificent wedding is being made."

"Come into my chamber where we can talk. There is a fire there and comfortable chairs."

"And display further my immodesty and impropriety? I am shocked that so gently nutured a man as yourself should put forward such a suggestion."

The sarcasm in the voice made Hereford raise his brows but told him what he wanted to know. Apparently his mother had wasted no time in expressing, in the most deferential manner, her surprise at Elizabeth's acquiescence to this hurried marriage and her hints of why the bride was so agreeable. Hereford would not have put it beyond his mother to indicate, in the politest way, that Elizabeth had seduced him—after all, her son could do no wrong.

"Do not be so silly. I have something important to say to you—something I would prefer the others not to hear." He allowed his irritation to show on his face. "Go in, Elizabeth dear, and make yourself comfortable." The softness of his tone, however, made it plain to Elizabeth that it was not she he was annoyed with. "I will follow in a moment. I have a few words to say to my mother."

Elizabeth's rigid expression softened. It was plain that she thought Roger was going to remonstrate with Lady Hereford for being rude to her, and Roger knew what she thought and held his peace although nothing was further from the truth. It was odd, he thought, how little women understood each other. Nothing could be more disastrous to him or to Elizabeth's and Lady Hereford's future relationship than for him to intervene in Elizabeth's favor. When he reached his mother and bent over to whisper in her ear, nothing but the physical weariness he could not hide showed on his face.

"Mamma, will you do me a favor?"

"Anything, darling."

Roger sighed. "Be kind to Lady Chester. Keep her occupied; talk to her. She frets Chester unbearably and then he comes to me with his troubles. I am too tired to deal with him, and it is important to me that he be in a good humor."

"Of course I will, love. You go to bed."

"I will, but I must have a few words with Elizabeth first."

This time there was no softness in Hereford's voice and his mother was also allowed to think that his interview with his betrothed was to be rather unpleasant. Again the woman was wrong. Hereford knew Lady Mary Chester only very slightly, but he knew that her personality and ideas would be exactly what his mother liked least. If such a woman complained about Elizabeth, as Lady Chester was bound to do since she hated her stepdaughter heartily and with a certain amount of justice, Lady Hereford would rise in Elizabeth's defense and Hereford's work would be done for him without his lifting a finger. He went into his chamber and sat down opposite Elizabeth, allowing his body to sag into the chair. The posture was unusual for him and drew Elizabeth's attention. She looked at him closely, really seeing him. Even in the candlelight the mauve shadows under his eyes and the grayish hollows under his cheekbones were apparent.

"Perhaps we had better leave this talk until tomorrow, Roger," Elizabeth was moved in spite of herself. "You look tired to death."

"That is kind of you, for I am sure you are curious about what Gaunt had to say." He smiled. "I will not lie to you, my very bones cry out for my bed, but it is pointless to delay. Tomorrow I shall be only a day more weary. As soon as I lie down, Elizabeth, my mind whirls with plans and dreams and I cannot sleep. You will do me a great kindness by letting me talk. Mayhap if I talk the matter out with you I will be able to rest."

Elizabeth glowed with pleasure. This was what she wanted. With an impulse wholly unplanned she went to sit on the footstool at his feet and took his hands in hers.

"I will listen to anything you wish to tell me. Take your own time."

Hereford closed his eyes. She was leaning toward him, her breasts lightly pressing against his knee and he had to fight the desire to take her in his arms. He permitted himself no more than to turn his hands so that he now held hers and could press them lightly. She was warm now and alive, but was it only for the news? He began to relate the decisions arrived at during his stay at Painscastle, giving her without hesitation details that could ruin his plans and destroy him if they came to the wrong ears. He had no doubts about Elizabeth's loyalty or her ability to hold her tongue, and she knew some of the people involved better than he did and could advise him as to whether his estimates of them were correct—only Hereford did not care about that just now. The question of paramount importance to him just then was a purely personal one. He wanted Elizabeth's estimate of her own affection for him, not of other men, and the question tugged at him until his voice faltered.

"What is the matter, Roger? Can I get you something?"

It was her first interruption. Until now she had listened to him silently, her eyes almost unnaturally bright, unconsciously pressing closer as her admiration for him increased. As he talked it had become less important that he was sharing his ideas with her, more important that the ideas were his. There was more to Roger of Hereford than she had guessed. He shook his head.

"You are a woman, Elizabeth, and you know Maud. She is the weakest link in my knowledge for if I cannot fool her, she can keep Stephen and Eustace both from acting as I know they would if left to themselves. Is my reasoning right? Will she think the way I expect?"

Elizabeth's hands stiffened under his and she dropped her lids as she drew her mind from the man before her to concentrate on her knowledge of the queen. "Not completely. The very fact of all the military activity will warn her that something more is going to happen, but you can do nothing else, and if you begin long enough before Henry comes she will be forced to let Stephen protect his vassals. Certainly Storm and Arundel should be warned to take great heed lest her spies be in their entourage."

Hereford nodded. "Storm is no problem. He can hold his tongue and so can that babe who is his wife, surprisingly. For a girl so seemingly innocent she has a mind that amazes me sometimes."

Suddenly Elizabeth's eyes were dancing with merriment. "Yes, Lady Leah is wily as the serpent. Did you ever find out, Roger, how you fell into that quarrel with—with Lady Gertrude just before you left London to go to France?"

"Lady Gertrude?" For a moment Hereford's eyes were blank and then he did remember. He had gone to stop the Earl of Pembroke from coming to court and had been drugged and fooled. On Pembroke's evidence he could have been imprisoned as a traitor, and, in a desperate attempt to make the evidence one man's word against another, he had been about to spread a tale that he had spent the time with a woman. Matters had been taken out of his hands, however, by Lady Gertrude, who had been his mistress briefly. In front of Elizabeth and a whole crowd of loose-tongued court hangers-on, she had accused him of infidelity, raging and weeping and reviling. The tale had spread like wildfire and Hereford, embarrassed, chagrined, and unable to defend himself, had been believed to have been illicitly disporting himself in a manner that no efforts of his own could have brought about.

"Yes. That was Lady Leah's doing. She came to me and told me of your trouble. Even I could not think of how to help, but she bid me set Lady Gertrude on to you. How we laughed; I nearly choked to death trying to look outraged while that—that whore let you have the edge of her tongue. Not that you did not deserve it in general, even though that once you were innocent. Leah told me that Storm nearly had a fit when she described the scene to him."

Hereford had to join her laughter although he was stung. "No, I never knew. I have a score to even with her then—and you too. Could you not warn me of what was to happen?"

Shaking with remembered merriment, Elizabeth leaned her head against Roger's knee. "Oh, no. We counted on your shock and surprise to give veracity to your dumbness, and it did. Oh, Roger, Roger, never will I forget the look on your face." She sighed and sat up again, the laughter fading. "But this other affair is no laughing matter. If any definite hint of Henry's place or time of arrival comes to her or if she finds out that Arundel is involved in it, I would not put it beyond Maud to lead an army herself or risk military disaster in Norfolk or Gloucestershire to recall Eustace or Stephen. You know what taking Henry would mean to her."

"I do know. I wish I could meet him myself, but—"

"That would be worse. Once the fighting starts, not all your vigilance will be able to exclude her spies from the mass of men surrounding you and you will be watched closer than any other. If you move any force other than your own household guard, she will know. Another thing, be careful how much you drink at the coming celebrations so that your own tongue does not wag too freely."

"Do you think I need that warning, Elizabeth?" Hereford frowned and bit his lip to prevent himself from pointing out that if she slipped a word to her father or uncle they would be far more likely to be indiscreet sober than he would be drunk.

"Every man needs that warning. When the wine flows at table, men are all children together," she retorted dryly. "I think," she added, as if reading his mind, "that perhaps it would be as well to tell my father nothing more of Henry's coming. So long as you plan to take him to Scotland with you, his interests will be well served by that exhibition of his loyalty. You must tell him something, however, or he will look for trouble. It could do no harm to confide the plans for the fighting in Gloucestershire and Norfolk to him. He will be content to stay clear of it, I believe, if he knows he is to go to Scotland, and if he does talk it will not matter too much, because you want Stephen to know you are launching that attack."

The words barely made sense to Hereford because his desire was drowning his reason with the irresistible pressure of the incoming tide. With his last bit of resistance he asked steadily, "Will you tell him, or shall I?" But then, without waiting for her reply, he rose roughly and walked away. "I cannot bear to be so near you, Elizabeth. I am no more than a man, after all. You want of me what I cannot give. I cannot love you without desiring you. If that must lower me in your eyes to the level of a beast, then a beast I am."

Elizabeth stood up too, frightened by the change of mood. He had hidden his feelings so well that she had no hint of what was coming. An impulse to run away touched her briefly, but she was not the kind who ran away, and even if she had been, he was back beside her too quickly to have allowed her to act on it.

"Let me kiss you, Elizabeth. Let me have you. It is only six days more until our wedding. We are already betrothed—"

"If you have such a need," she gasped, "there are other women."

His eyes were almost black and glistened with the tears of his aching desire. "I do not want another woman. I am only a man, and I love you. Let me but touch you. If you are not willing I will force you no further."

Elizabeth went livid with her fear. She was only a little afraid of the act itself, having heard much both good and bad about it and seen every variety of domestic animal mate. What terrified her into near paralysis was the fact that she was willing—at least her body was willing. Her mind cried out that once she showed the willingness she would be only one more body. She would be Elizabeth no longer, no longer the companion whom a man could ask about the thoughts and temper of the queen, only another breeder of young who warmed a man's bed. Worst of all, though, was the little whisper that ran under all the thoughts telling her that the struggle was useless for once she gave in she would like it better so.

While she was frozen immovable between her strong will and her stronger craving, she lost the time in which she could have acted. Hereford pulled her hard against him, her back to his chest so that he could hold her, caress her, and press himself against her all at once. It was, perhaps, not the usual way to hold a woman, but to Roger of Hereford love was a fine art and he was not content with the usual. As long as he held Elizabeth thus, every sensitive part of her body was open to his hands while against her buttocks rose the insistent demand of his manhood. Her lips alone he could not reach, but her lips were given often to her father, her brothers, and even for courtesy to favored male guests. He had accessible areas that were most unlikely to have been touched by other mouths, her throat, her shoulders if he could open her tunic, her ears, and the little spot just under and behind the ear lobe that had brought shudders and sighs from more women than Hereford cared to remember.

He had won many reluctant females to his will, from terrified serfs to previously faithful wives, and he was familiar with the rigid resistance that melted into uncontrollable trembling or helpless weakness. He knew too just the stage at which the trembling or weakness would change to voluptuous moans of acquiescence, only it had all been a game to Hereford previously and now he was in earnest. If by some chance he brought a woman so far in the past and she still rejected him, he might have been a little piqued but he had always known that any other woman would do just as well. Now the contrary was true; there was no substitute in the world, for him, who could take Elizabeth's place, and his recognition of that fact made him clumsy. His hands were not quite as sure as usual—he himself was trembling—and when he had brought her almost to the point of yielding his urgency robbed him of his controlled gentleness and he hurt her.

For some time Elizabeth had been leaning back against him without resistance, and he was no longer making any attempt to restrain her. He was unprepared, therefore, for the sudden desperate effort which tore her loose from his arms when that tiny, unexpected pain woke her from her sensual trance. The thrust carried her some three feet away and she faced him; both were panting, both trembling. Roger raged inwardly at his own stupidity. It was too soon for pain; that would come later when every aspect of gentler pleasure had been often savored. He moved slowly, cautiously, to his left to block the path to the door.

"Roger, do not—" Elizabeth faltered, with a pathetic attempt to keep her voice from openly pleading, "you said you would not force me."

"If you were unwilling—you cannot lie to me. I care not what your mouth says, your eyes, your hands, everything, tells me different. Elizabeth—" He came toward her, his gait a little stiff because he dared not move quickly for fear he would stampede her into flight. He could have rushed her; she would not run, now or ever, from him or anyone else.

"Perhaps you are right, Roger," she whispered, "but do not make me do this. Do not take my maidenhead from me before my wedding. Do not break my pride."

Pride, it was what he loved in her, what made her different from other women; he would not touch her pride. "Then tell me you are willing. Let me hear you say you love me and you want me and I will let you be. It is not easy for me to let you go—give me something."

What he asked of her was far more difficult, however, a greater blow to her pride than physical yielding. Unwittingly he had twisted a knife in a bleeding wound. Elizabeth's eyes were suddenly as alight as the golden flames leaping in the hearth.

"Yes, I am willing. Because I am sinful, because my will is not as strong as my lust, therefore I am willing. You will rule my body, I see it. No matter how I struggle, you always win because my lust answers yours; I cannot help it. Only remember that my soul is not willing, and when you have your desire of me the more eager I seem the more I will hate you, and myself, and the tie that binds us."

Hereford looked at her helplessly. "Elizabeth," he protested, "Elizabeth." But he was drained of strength and even of will, and he let her go, hurt more deeply than he realized himself.

CHAPTER 5

THE SIX DAYS THAT FOLLOWED were a nightmare to all concerned in what Lady Hereford silently referred to as "this unhappy match." The nightmare quality was intensified to the Earl of Hereford who was living a life split in two parts and who was tempermentally totally unsuited to it. With the majority of his guests he had to remain madcap Roger while all the time his mind was busy with treason and his soul was sick with the knowledge that it was treason he was engaged in. From Elizabeth, who could have eased his burden greatly by carrying on many of the negotiations with the men of the court who knew her and trusted her of old, he was completely estranged. It seemed, on top of everything else, horribly appropriate that with his companions he should hunt and hunt, kill and kill, until even that passionate sportsman, Chester, when wakened to ride out in the dawn of the day before the wedding, groaned that he never wished to hunt again.

"This is not sport," Chester grumbled at table that morning, "we are no better than butchers cutting the throats of sheep."

And Hereford, sitting beside him with hanging head, too tired to eat, felt that Chester was predicting his future. That was what he was to come to, a butcher. First a butcher of animals for the table and then a butcher of men. Of the two, the first was more laudable for that at least had some clear purpose. Was he to spend his life thus, drenched in blood? Crazed, he told himself when the thought first passed through his mind, you are crazed; what is a little blood? Always there was blood, hunting as a boy, fighting as a man; why does it matter now? But he drove his uncomprehending sisters distracted with his demands to be washed and to have his clothes cleaned, ignoring their pleading that he release them to serve the multitude of guests who by now had arrived, and his squires cursed him with elaborate oaths as they labored every night far into the dark hours to clean his armor and hunting equipment. Still the odor and feel of blood hung about him, and he felt like the little stuffed figures that the jongleurs sometimes amused them with, laughing and jesting with his guests as the dolls did, without reality. Stuffed with odds and ends of fleece and rags as they were too, without bones, he went moment by moment in dread that the soft stuffing would collapse leaving him in a shapeless heap.

That evening was the worst of all, and Elizabeth, hearing her lord's high-pitched, nervous laughter, had ample cause to regret her hasty words. She had been regretting them all week, blaming herself with clear insight for more than Hereford realized she was responsible. She had tried more than once to have a few private words with him, but although he was unceasingly kind, courteous, and painfully gay, he had avoided any personal conversation, and his eyes were like blue ice, clear and cold and fathomless. Elizabeth swallowed the tears which rose in her throat and looked down at her hands to hide her emotion from the women with whom she was sitting.

"Elizabeth," said the sharp voice of her stepmother, "Lady Hereford is speaking to you."

"I am sorry, madam, I did not hear."

A smile passed around the circle of women; Lady Hereford repeated her question, some unimportant query about Elizabeth's clothes for the morrow which she answered without really being conscious of what she said. All she could hear was Hereford's laughter. She started as a small, warm hand touched her cold one and looked up to meet Lady Storm's large, greenish eyes. For days she had dared meet no woman's eyes, for her behavior had been unnatural and the glances she met were so often filled with contempt, compassion, or jealousy that she had been hard put to control her tongue. Leah's eyes held nothing but warning, however, and Elizabeth focused on the conversation around her with a sense of urgency.

"She is nervous, poor thing," Lady Hereford was saying, and speaking with sincerity. She did not like Elizabeth and told herself, untruthfully, that she never would, but Roger's treatment was working. So many women did not like Elizabeth that Lady Hereford was forced to protect her to vindicate her son's choice, and that sense of protectiveness was unconsciously making a place for the girl in her heart. "Roger keeps talking about great doings in such a mysterious way that he has even made me quite nervous. It is no wonder if the girl is upset. What with pushing her into this sudden marriage and threatening to run away almost the moment it is consummated to—"

"Surely not, madam," Elizabeth intervened. "He has said nothing to me of leaving Hereford, except, of course, to make a tour of my dower lands. It is true"—she laughed self-consciously—"that his lordship was so kind as to offer to allow me to stay behind because of the dreadful weather, but I could not allow that and I will attend him."

Another series of glances and smiles passed around the circle. Apparently Hereford had no intention of giving up his loose way of living and was already seeking to make his shackles as light as possible, while Lady Elizabeth seemed equally determined to watch her prize closely. Elizabeth recognized what they thought, but she did not object to blackening her husband's character or making herself ridiculous in a good cause. Lady Leah's hand closed imperceptibly on hers. Elizabeth cast her brilliant eyes around the watching group, daring any comment, but Leah leaned a little closer and spoke, her soft voice lowered but clear enough to carry well.

"I think Lady Hereford is right though. My lord has also been restless since Lord Hereford has come home, and I know messages have traveled to and fro from our keep to Hereford."

"I do not think," Elizabeth replied stiffly, "that these are matters we should discuss."

Leah opened wide the innocent eyes of seventeen. "Surely we are among friends here. Lord Storm is not one who allows me to know too much of his business." Elizabeth resisted a sudden impulse to laugh in spite of the seriousness of Lady Hereford's slip and the desperate effort she was making to cover it, for a woman more closely in her husband's counsel and looking less like she might be was impossible. Leah was party to every thought and plan in Lord Storm's head and was not unlikely to have put some of the ideas there. "But," the childish voice continued, while an expression of happy vacuity played over the innocently pretty face, "I listen, and it seems to me—"

"Lady Storm, I think you should not discuss what you hear talked of among your menfolk," Elizabeth interjected sharply, playing the game.

"Let the child speak," Lady Warwick said. "What she says will go no further."

Elizabeth looked acutely uncomfortable, as was necessary if anyone was to believe what Leah said. She herself could not make idiotic statements, she was well known to be in her father's counsel if not in her husband's, but she could give weight to Leah's wild remarks by pretending reluctance to allow her to make them. She blessed Lady Warwick, who was her senior by many years and at least her equal in social position, for providing the necessary opening which she could not with courtesy oppose.

"Well, I think that Hereford and my lord intend to settle a few old scores." . .

"Old scores?" Lady Warwick was, by virtue of her husband's association, at peace with King Stephen, but she always had an eye to the main chance and kept both ears open.

"Yes. The Earl of Shrewsbury caused both of them a great deal of trouble some years ago, and I believe they intend to make him pay for it. They know the king is powerless to stop them; they are too big for him. Also Shrewsbury has fallen out of favor, and—"

"Leah," Elizabeth interrupted again, "I never showed you my wedding dress. Perhaps you had better come and see it now since you will have to help me dress tomorrow."

"I would love to," Leah cried, getting up at once.

"But, Lady Storm," the Countess of Warwick tried to hold the young woman, "do you not think—"

"You must pardon me, madam," Leah replied light-mindedly, "I have been teasing Elizabeth to show me her things all day and she has been too occupied. I cannot forego this pleasure. I will return straightaway." They escaped. Leah's voice and expression changed at once. "Elizabeth, you had better go and tell Hereford to stop his mother's tongue. Good Lord, how can a woman of that age say such things! I will tell Cain what is going forward and what we have done so that he can drop similar hints among the men, and then I will go back and see what other bad fish I can cast along the trail." Elizabeth nodded and began to turn away. "Elizabeth," Leah said, detaining her, but with averted eyes, "Roger looks horrid and you look unhappy. If I can help you in some way, I beg you will allow me that favor."

Elizabeth shook her head and murmured her thanks. The bed she had made, she would sleep in without complaint. She found Hereford without trouble in a group of gambling men.

"Roger, I must speak with you." She could see the muscles bunch in his jaw as the teeth set together.

"Just now?"

"Please."

"Very well. You must pardon me," he said to his companions, "if this lady speaks, I must obey." He followed her docilely into his own room but stopped a few feet past the door and spoke in a rigidly polite voice. "How may I serve you, madam?"

"You are not going to like what I have to say, but it is more important that you act upon it than like it."

"Elizabeth, if you have any sense, do not now tell me that we are making a mistake and you do not choose to have me. I will not argue with you, and I will marry you even, as I have said before, if I must drag you to the altar by the hair."

She bit her lip. "I am not that much a fool. This is something far different. Roger, your mother is telling a whole group of women that you have been talking mysteriously of great plans. Leah and I turned it so that it would seem that you plan to attack Shrewsbury, but if she begins to speak of your having met Gloucester—"

"Women!" Hereford groaned. "She loves me more than her life, she says, yet she will get me hanged. I wish she loved me less and thought a little more. Who was there?"

Pressing a hand to her lips, Elizabeth looked away. In a quieter way than Hereford, she was equally unstrung, and little things loomed as large as mountains. "I am sorry, Roger," she faltered, almost sobbing, "I have failed you in this. I know I should have paid attention, but I did not. I do not know. My stepmother was there, and Lady Warwick, and Lady Lancaster." She covered her face with her hands. "There were others, five or six, but I do not know. I was not thinking or listening. Your mother must have said other things too, because Lady Leah drew my attention. I am sorry, I was thinking of other things."

"So you might. Do not be so troubled about so little. I can do nothing now in any case. To call her would but make her words of more note. Tomorrow I—I will see what I can do."

His voice slipped off into indefiniteness and Elizabeth spoke impulsively. "Go to bed, Roger. You are pale and cold as death." To that he made no reply, almost seeming not to have heard; she went and grasped his wrist as he started to return to the main hall. "Roger, you are asleep on your feet. Have some sense—go and lie down."

"It does no good," he answered dully after a slight pause. "I am so tormented—" He stopped. There was no need to load his problems onto Elizabeth's shoulders; she had troubles enough of her own. Without meaning to, once again he hurt her for she took the remark as a deserved reproach to herself instead of a general comment. She flushed painfully; Elizabeth did not like to apologize but she knew she had been wrong to speak as she had and this was her first opportunity to try to redeem herself.

"If those words said in haste and shame hurt you, Roger, I am sorry. You know I often say things I should not. Nonetheless, it is your own fault," she added, quickly reverting to a more natural imperative tone, "I have tried all week to tell you this, and you would not listen. I swear," she cried, her voice rising, "if you have suffered you have deserved it for your stubbornness."

Hereford's face started to come alive then; he covered

her hand, which still held his wrist, with his own. He would not for anything disabuse her of the notion that she was the single cause of his unhappiness although it was not completely true. One of the surest roads to a woman's love was that she should believe that the man loved her beyond anything else. Hereford had been greatly distressed by Elizabeth's reaction to his love-making, but he knew enough about women, when he was calm enough to consider the situation objectively, not to be hopeless of winning her or alarmed by the violence of her words. He told himself that a greater immediate problem was his sexual frustration. He had not practiced so much continence since his first experience—at twelve—with a girl in the fields, and it did not agree with him. Elizabeth had virtually given her permission for him to take another woman, but he was not fool enough for that; he would not make her ridiculous in the eyes of her peers by taking a mistress to his bed while the guests were assembled for the wedding. Other men did so, perhaps, but even if Hereford had not loved Elizabeth he would not have done so because he was naturally kind. Nonetheless, his sense of righteousness made it no easier for him to sleep, and the sleeplessness gave him too much opportunity to think. The sense of futility which had been suppressed by active planning returned, and the physical fatigue of hunting instead of bringing him sleep only intensified his depression.

Women, however, were a central point in Hereford's orientation, and he could close the door on matters he knew to be more important temporarily while he attended to them. "As you say, I have well deserved it, but not for my stubbornness, Elizabeth, for my stupidity. Nay, I will not make myself worse than I am. I am so tired that it is no wonder I did not realize you had something special to say to me. Have I been coldly polite to you? Then we are even, for if you hurt me, I have surely done the same without meaning to."

Elizabeth made no direct reply, but she was pleased with Hereford's graceful acknowledgement of her apology. "I can see you are tired, the whole world can see it. You look dreadful. Even if you cannot sleep you could lie down and rest." She took his arm persuasively. "Come, let me see you lie down."

Hereford's smile illuminated his tired face. "Elizabeth, you delight me. For all your sharp words, you are going to spoil me worse even than my other womenfolk."

"Now you are flattering me so that I will forgive you for denying what I ask. Is it not so?"

"Yes." Hereford was still smiling. "I cannot—I was winning. The gentlemen will never forgive me for retiring suddenly with their gold in my purse."

"It is no matter for jest, Roger. In spite of what you say, I am not given to coddling my men, but you will make yourself ill."

"I am never ill."

"As you will." Elizabeth might have urged him further, he was plainly willing to listen and to be cajoled, but she was ashamed of seeming tender and a little afraid because any prolonged private contact with Roger woke both his sensuality and hers. His eyes were already brighter.

"Kiss me, Elizabeth." It was as if he read her mind, however, for he spoke gently and added, "For courtesy's sake, to seal our mutual pardon. I will not touch you."

"I will sell you a kiss."

"Sell it! Holy martyrs, listen to her. Chester has brought me a changeling, a tradesman's daughter, worse, a usurer's." He was holding her hand tighter now, smiling with a more relaxed expression. "What is your price?"

Elizabeth colored; it was not easy for her to display the softer emotions which came so naturally to most women. She had buried them too deeply in her struggle for recognition as an individual and she was now awkward and ashamed.

"One kiss for one hour's rest, two for two, and if you will allow me to undress you so that you can go to bed I—I will give you whatever you ask for."

She was afraid; it was plain on her face, but she was more afraid for him, that near hysterical laughter still echoed in her ears. Hereford slowly closed his eyes and reopened them as slowly.

"Do you care so much?" His voice was unsteady. He was continually surprised at the violence of his reactions to anything Elizabeth said or did. He no sooner convinced himself that her influence was only slightly greater than that of any other woman when she would show another side of her character that threw him off balance again.

"That is a fine question," Elizabeth replied tartly. "Of course I care. A fine sight it would be if my bridegroom fell flat on his face on his wedding day. There is enough scandal about me without adding the fact that marriage to me is enough to fell a man." The tone and words could not hide the sentiment; Hereford's answering smile was as uncertain as his voice.

"I wish—what excuse can I offer?"

Swallowing nervously, Elizabeth moved closer. She had proposed a bargain and now it seemed must yield her surety. "Your face is your excuse. Everyone has been telling you to go to bed for hours. What excuse do you need? Come, let me remove your gown."

"No, dearest." Relief and chagrin mingled almost comically in her face. Hereford would have laughed had he not been so moved. He drew her close and held her gently against him, rubbing his face on her hair. "I will go to bed, since you desire it, but you shall not undress me. Therefore you need pay no forfeit. That was what you said—if I allowed you to undress me. You shall have your will of me and yet go scot free, but you must remember not to mock me for keeping the word of a promise and violating its spirit."

William Beauchamp shrugged his shoulders at Hereford's two junior squires. "Do you remember when we were envied because our master was the best-humored and most considerate of men? Do you know what has come to him this last week to make him walk about half the night?"

Patric glanced up briefly from running a thread of coarse wool through the links of Hereford's mail which looked now as if it were made of silver rather than steel. "I can guess. What need to lie abed if there is nothing to keep you warm in it?"

"Ay, so what is he doing there now when he should be up and preparing to fill that empty space? All week he kicks us out of bed before dawn when we need only throw any old rag over him and ourselves. This morning when it will take us hours to get everything just so—his chausses perfectly smooth, the tunic to show just so much at the neck, the gown to have only certain folds and no others—when he will feel his face ten times over for one hair missed in shaving and keep us an hour combing those silken locks—this morning he sleeps."

The youngest of the three, Harry, straightened Hereford's scarlet velvet robe—just a shade off the so-called royal purple—where it lay ready on a chest. "Mayhap it is better he sleep," the boy interjected shyly, "he surely looked to need it last night."

William laughed. "He will get little enough tonight, if I know him—or she either. But at least he will not be walking the floor and waking us for one thing or another. I can only pray that this new wakefulness will mend his temper."

"If there were special prayers for it, I would pay the priests well to say them, and join them myself. We will have to wake him soon anyway. How long do you judge the sun has been up, William?"

"What sun?" William pushed back a shutter cautiously and pulled it to again with a disgusted grunt. "It is raining soft ice. By Christ's holy blood, even heaven is cold and weeping at this match."

"It must be almost six. I heard the chapel bell some time since."

"Good boy, Harry. Go, you wake him. He is usually soft of speech to you."

Hereford would have been soft of speech to anyone that morning. He woke easily and gently from a deep, dreamless sleep, greatly refreshed and, after lying for a while, drowsy and relaxed, allowed himself to be helped out of bed and bathed. He had been shaved and half dressed in the same lazy, acquiescent mood when some comment of William's about Rannulf's clothing made Hereford start upright and say, "Anne! I must speak to Anne."

"Oh, God, what new crotchet is this?" William groaned. "Not now, my lord, there is no time."

"Time or not, I must see her at once. Look you, dress yourselves now to save that time at least. I will not be long away. Give me that box of jewels."

"At least let me finish with your cross garters, my lord."

Hereford was looking hastily through the contents of the chest which he had unlocked with a key chained around his neck. "Make haste then." He extracted a ring engraved with the arms his father had borne before he became Earl of Hereford.

"Haste," William grumbled, "if you wish them to lie properly I cannot make haste. Will you go with baggy chausses to your wedding?"

Fond of clothing as he was, Hereford had to laugh. "As long as something else is straight and tight I hope to be satisfied."

William choked, pleased at his master's apparent return to normal. "Thanks be to God I do not have the arranging of that. Now, whatever you do, do not sit down. Those are molded like marble to your legs. If you crease them, I will die of a broken heart."

There was a mad flurry of excitement in the women's quarters when Hereford demanded admittance, for he rarely invaded his mother's private apartments personally. Lady Hereford came into the outer chamber to him.

"What does this mean? Are you crazy, Roger? We must be at the church in two hours and look at you."

"I want to see Anne, Mamma."

"Anne! With two women to dress in bridal clothes, do you think we have time for your nonsense? This is no time to tease your sister. Go away."

"I am perfectly serious. I do not intend to tease her. Let me go in."

"You cannot. Elizabeth is in there as well as Anne."

"Oh, Lord. Send Anne out then."

"She is not dressed."

"God damn it," Roger said impatiently, "send her out naked then. What harm do you think I will do my sister? I tell you I have something important to say to her."

A moment later Anne came out in her thin linen shift, looking frightened. "What is it? Is something wrong? Rannulf—?"

"Nothing wrong, love. I did not mean to frighten you." He took her by the shoulders and looked her over frankly. "Well, he is a fortunate young man. You are very well, very well indeed." He took her face between his hands and kissed her gravely, first on the forehead, then both eyes, and then her lips. "Listen to me, Anne, my love. I have done the best I know how for you and I have every expectation that with your sweet face and your gentle nature you will be very happy. Mischances, however, can befall even the best of plans."

"Oh, Roger, what is it? Is this a time to speak of mischance?"

"Dear heart, in a few hours you will be mine no longer to care for. I think I have chosen well, but—. Anne, love, I will always be your brother, and, as long as I live, you will never lack for a protector. This is your father's old ring. I do not believe anyone except myself and your mother will remember the crest. If—now I do not want you to be afraid, but if Rannulf should prove to be different from what I expected and prove unkind or if, God forbid, he should be hurt or killed—nay, child, such things happen—then you must write to me. Listen closely and try to understand. Do not write of your troubles. Write a letter as if all were well. Write that you are in good health and desire to know of our well-doing, or any such matter, and seal the letter with this ring instead of your husband's seal. When I receive a letter sealed with this seal, I will come to you at once. Do you understand?"

"I—I think so."

"Now, love, be very careful. Do not lose the trinket and do not seal any other letter with it. It would be a terrible thing if you made a mistake and I came to ravage your husband's lands with fire and sword. I could destroy him, and you, and myself also if you were careless."

Anne began to tremble. "At such a cost, I would not wish to be saved. Do not give it me, Roger."

"Now, now, you will not be so foolish as to make such a mistake." He kissed her again. "And be a reasonable girl too. If your husband gets drunk and knocks you about, you are not to send for me to settle your quarrels. Run away or hit him back. Only for really serious trouble—and

I do not mean another woman in his bed either—are you to use that seal."

"You are always so kind to us, sweet brother."

"Who else will be if I am not?" He held her close and patted her shoulders. "Now, for lesser matters you may write and complain, and if I can help, or your mother can, with advice or admonition, we both will. Do not ever feel that we have deserted you. God keep you, love. God make you happy."

Anne began to cry. "You sound as if we would be parted forever. I do not go so far. You will come to visit me, will you not? And Rannulf will let me come home sometimes, is it not so?"

"You must not cry, Anne. You will spoil your face and make your poor husband think you are unwilling. You would not wish to grieve him so. Your home is in Rannulf's keep now, and do not forget it," Hereford said firmly, and then, softening, "but you and your husband will be welcome guests at Hereford whenever you wish to come. I will also very gladly come to visit you—if *Rannulf* should be willing to invite me. You must go and dress now, dear heart, you are cold." She clung to him, sobbing. "Enough, Anne, I must dress too. Hide that ring well and tell no one—no one at all—that you have it or what its purpose is. It might be used to set a trap for me that would cost my life. Have a care to your tongue. Now go."

Lady Hereford received her sobbing daughter with thoroughly exasperated affection. As she comforted her, she felt a surge of gratitude for her daughter-in-law's perfect calm in that roomful of bustling excited women. Elizabeth was a little pale, but not enough to spoil her complexion, and was completely collected. She was fully dressed already except for her bliaut, which she chose not to put on until the last moment because it was so stiff with gold-thread embroidery that sitting in it might damage it. She was watching Anne with a rather reflective softness in her lovely eyes while she braided gold thread into her thick, black plaits. The tunic she had chosen was a soft wool of coral color, its tight wrists and high neck also embroidered so thickly in gold that they were stiff. The bliaut had called forth gasps of astonishment from the attendant ladies; it was a dull gold velvet covered all over with a branching pattern of oak leaves and acorns in glittering drawn gold. The magnificence was not what startled the women, however, that they had expected, it was the color—yellow was the color of mourning and Elizabeth's dress was barely a shade removed from that sad tint.

No one could deny its perfect suitability for her. The tunic, close to her face, gave her skin warmth, and the gold matched her brilliant eyes and set off the black braids that hung beside each breast well below her hips. Elizabeth had just been helped into the garment by Leah, who was holding the bride's icy hands in her own warm ones when a page asked for admittance. He carried a soft leather pouch and a small piece of folded parchment which he said must be delivered to Lady Elizabeth alone. She went forward slowly and took the note first and then the pouch. Opened, it poured a necklace of gold and rubies into her hands. The women had cause to gasp once more.

Elizabeth swallowed once, then again, and reread the note accompanying the necklace. "Elizabeth: I send you this, not as a dower gift, but for yourself. The stones are my own to give as I choose, having been paid for in France with my own blood and agony. I beg of you to wear them for love of me, but if you love me not, do else with them as you will. Hereford."

Clever Roger, he never gave her time to think, and he made it so easy for her. She needed to say nothing, only don the necklace. What woman could resist that rich beauty? Moreover, if she did not wear it, she would need to explain to all the women there why she chose to ignore a gift of such value.

"Who is that from, Elizabeth?" Lady Mary was upon her, the sharp, peevish voice even shriller than usual with the hope that she would catch Chester parting with some of the dower property, or even better, that she might catch Elizabeth receiving something from a lover. "Let me see that note. Who could send you such a costly gift?"

She reached for the note, and Elizabeth tore it away from her, dropping the necklace in her anxiety to hold the parchment. Whatever was between herself and Hereford, now or in the future, it was their business alone, not that of a roomful of gossiping women. She folded the scrap of parchment and pushed it up the tight sleeve of her tunic, her face crimson with anger and excitement.

"The gift is from Lord Hereford," she cried. "Who else would send it to me?"

"That is no part of the dower jewels of Hereford, Elizabeth," Lady Hereford put in slowly and reluctantly. She did not wish to seem to support Lady Mary Chester, but she felt obliged in Roger's interests to inquire.

Elizabeth's body grew rigid, drawn up to her full height, which was not inconsiderable for a woman, and she fixed her mother-in-law with eyes that made the older woman recoil a step.

"They must be something his lordship brought from France," Lady Storm said softly, picking up the necklace and putting it back into Elizabeth's unreceptive hands. "He would wish to give her something private for a wedding gift, something for herself alone. The dower jewels she may only use, but they cannot be hers, belonging as they do to the sons who will come after her. Here, Elizabeth, let me put this on. It will be more beautiful than the topazes you had chosen to wear."

Now, of course, Elizabeth was trapped. If she did not wear the necklace, every woman there would think that Hereford was not the giver and that she was trying to hide the jewels from him. She started to tell herself that she was angry at being forced into the situation, and knew that she was lying. She was glad that she could wear it without having to confess that she did it only to please Roger of Hereford. Leah was still speaking in the gentle, aimless way she adopted in company, rambling on about Lord Storm's gifts to her and displaying an armband with necklace to match of square-cut emeralds bound in silver, which, she said, he had given her upon the birth of their son. That was no part of the Gaunt collection either, she pointed out, but hers alone, and the women came to examine the work and exclaim so that the cold silence was covered and Elizabeth had time to regain control of herself.

Finally it was time to go. Leah did not sigh with relief,

for she was too well trained to give expression to such an emotion, but she sent up little thankful prayers as she wrapped Elizabeth in her furlined cloak and pulled the hood up to protect her head, and, since neither of the elder women who had that right did it, she kissed her friend.

"You will be happy in the end, Elizabeth," she murmured very low, "even if you do not think so just now. You need to be a person. I know, I need to be a person too. Go gently, it will come to you."

Perhaps, Elizabeth thought, as the sleet stung her face while they rode to the church in the town of Hereford, if she could go gently it would come to her. For Leah it was easy. She was the type who could kneel and cling to her husband's knees and weep until he had no strength to deny anything she asked. That gentle soul was not cursed with the sin of pride that locked her own knees and back so that she could not kneel to save her life. She had not even knelt to the queen for her father's life. She glanced at the Earl of Chester riding beside her, and her heart contracted at the thought of leaving him. They had been so happy.

Because of the weather, the bridal couples would not exchange their vows at the church door, which was customary, but went in to perform the entire ceremony before the altar. They stood there in two pairs, Anne weeping softly with Rannulf holding her hand, Roger and Elizabeth both still, not touching, apparently intent upon the two bishops who had chosen to share the honor and the guilt of this marriage. Hereford looked a little worn in spite of the rest he had, but his eyes were bright and the corners of his lips alternately turned up and were pulled down into a more becoming gravity as he considered the mischief he had created by his gift to Elizabeth. His mother had given him that information by protesting that he should have told her of his plan, and, although he knew he could not count on warmth of heart being Elizabeth's reason for wearing the necklace, he was glad she had done so. If he pretended ignorance of the disturbance among the women, as he would in any case, he could pretend he believed her to have acted out of love alone, and that would serve his purpose almost as well.

There was a little confusion because Hereford had to act both as bridegroom and as guardian of his sister, but all was finally smooth and both men kissed their brides on the priest's instructions. On their way out of the church, a gust of wind slammed the heavy door to with a loud crash. Hereford laughed as he released Elizabeth whom he had instinctively pushed behind him to protect as he whirled to face the sound.

"There, I told you the church would come down upon us," he chuckled. "No, it is not that, the Lord has closed the door so that we might be alone. Elizabeth, let us run away. You do not wish to eat, drink, and dance to make a show for our guests, and I do not wish to go boar hunting tomorrow. Let us go and hide so that we can quarrel in peace."

"How can you be so ridiculous?" Elizabeth replied, laughing too. Roger sounded so ordinary. In spite of being her husband now he did not appear to have changed. His expression was frankly teasing and he squeezed her finger-tips just as he used to when he was trying to convince her to do something outrageous at court.

"A nice way to speak to your lord and master. Come, pick up your skirts and race me to your horse. If we get to the house first, we can eat all the dessert and say dinner is over and get to bed."

"Roger, if you pull me into that mud and splatter my dress, I will use this necklace you gave me to strangle you. You are drunk already." She shook her head and pushed him away as he attempted to bite her ear, laughing harder instead of being frightened because it was obvious that he was mischievously attempting to discompose her just as he used to before he went to France. "Stop that! Behave yourself. They will have that door open in a moment. Ouch! Roger!"

He pinched her and she slapped him, just as the door opened. Hereford's eyes danced with merriment and Elizabeth, torn between amusement and embarrassment, could have murdered him very cheerfully just then.

"Wait," she said between set teeth, "wait, I will pay you

back for that. I will make you black and blue where it counts."

Hereford choked. "Elizabeth! How vulgar! Is that a nice thing to say? You may well, but do not tell the whole world of it."

Elizabeth blushed hotly. She had not, of course, meant what Roger pretended she did, but to protest would only make him more outrageous. He might well appeal to the crowd now surrounding them for support; nothing was beyond him when in this mood. He remained completely ungovernable right through dinner, which was eaten in the great hall of the old keep where there was more room. Two soups were served, one of vegetables and beef, the other containing various types of sea food, but largely oysters. Of the last he soberly filled a bowl and presented it to Lord Storm because, as he loudly explained to everyone in hearing, a man who never looked at any woman but his wife must need oysters for their medicinal effect. As oysters were commonly reported to be an aphrodisiac, the ladies and gentlemen roared.

Lord Storm, well accustomed to Hereford's sense of humor, merely replied that he hoped Roger would need them for the same reason soon, for there was no other way, since he had returned, of insuring a wife's virtue but to stay in her bed yourself. That turned the laughter of the guests upon their host for his problems with irate husbands had been almost proverbial. It was then obviously necessary to ask Elizabeth what methods she proposed to use to keep him faithful. He never allowed her to answer, but her wits were kept on the jump countering the insane proposals which Hereford was making for his own restraint.

His next happy notion took the form of plucking a peacock which the cooks had roasted and painfully refeathered to distribute the beautiful tail plumes as consolation prizes to the ladies he had loved and lost by this marriage. By this time, as his eyes were definitely not focusing too well and the wine in the great tuns was being rapidly depleted, Elizabeth really exerted herself to divert him from his purpose. She was not successful, but at least made him promise to keep to women whose husbands were sufficiently sober to recognize his actions as a joke. Even so there would have been some angry looks had not Hereford first convulsed Elizabeth herself and the entire group by presenting a feather to William of Gloucester's wife. That poor lady, unlovely and constantly pregnant, was so unlikely a choice for amorous adventure and her husband so notorious for his faithlessness with both men and women that the most jealous of husbands only laughed when their wives were chosen.

The *pièce de résistance*, however, came with the introduction of the pasties. Hereford left the hall, ostensibly to relieve his bladder, but actually to collect every small hawk from the mews—his own and his guests' indiscriminately. These were surreptitiously carried by the falconers to regular stations around the hall and, when five unusually large pasties were cut open, ten live doves were released from each. The hawks were loosed and pandemonium reigned. Every noble and most of the ladies leapt to their feet to halloo the hawks on; the hawks shrieked, the doves screamed as they were struck, and blood and feathers rained down on the guests from the roof of the hall.

"How could you, Roger?" Elizabeth gasped as she swung a lure seized from a nearby falconer and called to her own merlin which had missed its strike and was shrieking angrily and circling near the roof. "You idiot! It will take us days to straighten them out and calm them down."

Hereford laughed like a madman as he watched his guests caper after the hawks, oversetting the tables and benches. He tore the lure from Elizabeth's hand and pulled her back just in time to save her from being trampled by her own father and the Earl of Salisbury, and then stood over her in a corner, warding off a number of other men and women who, half drunk and mad with excitement, careened into him blindly.

"Nay, Elizabeth," he said over his shoulder, "I am not such an idiot. Drunk as they are with no fighting to look forward to to ease their hearts, they would be at each others' throats if they had nothing to tire them. By the time the hawks are taken, most of them will be worn out and fairly sober again."

"You are a fine one to talk. You are drunk yourself."

"That I am," he giggled. "I could not help it, for everyone presses drink upon me, but I am not so drunk that I wish to see swords out in my hall." He burst then into raucous whoops. "Look, Elizabeth, there is Gloucester in the middle of a pasty. I know not who tripped him into it, but they have the right idea. He would look better baked than he does half roasted as he is now."

"Hold your tongue," Elizabeth gasped, trying not to laugh with him. "He will hear you. How will we ever clear up this mess?"

"Better birds' blood than men's—Ouf! Storm, for God's sake take your elbow out of my ribs."

"Everyone always told me your head was screwed on wrong, Hereford, and I defended you. Bless me, if I ever do so again. Here, do not let Leah be trampled on, or better, let me stay with the women and you go and keep Chester and Lincoln from murdering each other. They are laying claim to the same hawk."

Hereford plunged off into the crowd, singing something about the glory of losing one's life for one's honor, and Storm watched him, his dark eyes warm with affection. Elizabeth and Leah peered out behind his bulk, laughing when people slid about on the floor, which in spite of the strewn rushes, was now slippery with spilled food. Leah had to cling to her husband for support when one of the dogs bounded into the air to seize a weakly fluttering dove using a portly and highly born abbot's stomach as a springboard.

"I am glad to see Hereford back in his normal spirits, Lady Elizabeth," Storm said, wiping his eyes when he returned to his charges after helping the abbot to his feet, "but was there no less disastrous way for him to express them?" Elizabeth explained, and Storm nodded. "I give him credit for it." He hunched a shoulder off which William Beauchamp bounded as if it had been a stone wall, "but I wonder, if this is the way he has begun, whether it is safe to stay. Tomorrow he will probably let boars loose in the hall so that we may hunt in comfort."

"Lord Storm," Elizabeth gasped, half laughing, half horrified, "I pray you, do not say such things in his hearing. You jest, but Roger would very likely think it an excellent idea in all seriousness."

When the servants came in to renew the torches in the wall holders a second time after dancing had replaced bird catching as the sport of the evening, Lady Hereford caught up with her son who was leaning breathlessly against the fireplace.

"Roger, I am taking Anne up. Collect Rannulf—if he is in the same disgusting state as you are you had better look under the benches for him—and the rest of the men. If we do not start now, we will not get you and Elizabeth bedded until tomorrow night. Roger, do you hear me? Can you understand me?"

"Yes, Mamma." He hiccuped and laughed. "I am not that drunk—though in all good faith, I have been soberer. Where do you propose I start to look for him?"

Lady Hereford took a deep breath and held it. If she spoke again, she would scream, so she took her unresisting but giggling son firmly by the arm and led him away. She steered for a dark head well above the rest in the crowd; Lord Storm was usually given to sobriety and could usually manage Roger. When she addressed that gentleman, however, he bowed gravely from the waist so far forward that his wife had to catch him and push him upright—no light task for a small girl—and then, with a vague, but pleased smile of surprised recognition, he embraced Hereford and began to sing.

"Cain," Leah protested, trying vainly to pull him loose, "where is Rannulf of Lincoln?"

Storm stopped singing. "What do you want him for?" he asked aggressively.

Plainly, as if speaking to a retarded child, Leah explained. "He must go to bed with his new wife. Remember, my lord, you are celebrating his wedding."

A puzzled frown crossed Lord Storm's face. "I thought it was Roger that was married. Roger, were you not married?" Hereford giggled. Storm regarded his companion for a moment and then looked around the room. "How did we come to Lincoln? I could swear we are in Hereford Castle. It looks like Hereford Castle."

"Is there one sober man in this place?" Lady Hereford cried.

Leah wished to laugh too, but she was sorry for Lady Hereford, who was faced with coping with the bedding ceremonies. "Cain!" She shook his arm. "You are drunk. Go soak your head, and soak Roger's too. You must sober him up enough to get his sister and her husband bedded and himself also." The men began to wander off vaguely in the direction of the doorway. Leah shook her head. "Madam, he cannot be trusted, he will forget before he is halfway across the room. I must go after them. Where is Lady Elizabeth?"

"With Anne."

"Good. If they go out in the cold for a bit they will be all right. Anne will not notice that I am missing. I will come as soon as either of them knows what he is doing."

It was not easy, but finally Rannulf and Anne were safely ensconced in Lady Hereford's old solar in the keep. Then the entire party trooped out of the keep and across the court to the manor house. The cold sobered everyone a little, but they were still drunk enough to take a very long time to get Hereford undressed, and Elizabeth, sitting naked in the great bed and listening to the obscene jokes, became more and more terrified as the minutes passed.

She had been happy all day after the ceremony. Roger was just Roger—mad, wild, amusing—teasing her and accepting her teasing in return. Now he was suddenly a stranger. The candlelight gleamed on the soft golden hair of his arms and legs; his body, nearly hairless, like alabaster, was unreal, unrelated to her. In the course of her duties as mistress of Chester Castle, she had bathed Roger of Hereford more than once and knew his body well, but it did not look the same to her now.

Leah left the head of the bed where she had been standing near Elizabeth. She had been so amused at what was going forward that the restrained but increasing tension of the bride had escaped her notice. Now, as she went to her husband, she hoped she had not delayed so long that Elizabeth's reserve would break into hysteria before she could get the guests out of the room. Fastening on little things, anything, to make herself deaf to the talk and keep her mind from what was coming, Elizabeth watched the way Leah walked, watched how quickly Storm, drunk, aroused, and laughing, responded to her touch, watched her say something to him that made him stare as if surprised and then smile slowly and sensuously. After that, however, he went quickly up to Hereford, kissed him, and ruffled his hair. Elizabeth drew a breath that was nearly a sob. It was the beginning of the end; they would go now.

Hereford watched the last woman pass through the doorway and close the door with a sense of relief. He had been enjoying himself, but he was glad it was over now. He scratched his buttock and then stretched, reaching as far back as he could first and then pulling his shoulders forward to ease their tension. Rubbing the back of his neck, he turned toward Elizabeth and smiled, about to make easy talk on the success of his first night's entertainment. His wife, however, was sitting tensely erect clutching the bedclothes to her breast, her eyes so wide that the whites showed all around the iris. His smile faded; dizzy with drink, he was faintly annoyed by her rigid attitude.

"Elizabeth—"

"Do not touch me. Do not come near me."

"Do not be a fool!" He strode over to the bed, adding sharply, "Do you think I am going to stand here naked all night?" Then the realization of how very frightened she was came to him through the haze in his mind. "For one thing, I am cold," he said lightly, trying to calm her. "Move over and give me the warm part of the bed—be a good wife—pander to your selfish husband."

She did not look at him or move; her eyes did not blink or flicker. It was as if she were turned to stone by terror. Her hair was loose around her and he lifted a handful of the silken strands. Looking down he could see the division of her breasts, greenish in the shadow created by the sheets she clutched. He was not accustomed to continence, and, all in all, she was the most desirable woman he had ever seen. He was swept by the desire to seize her and force her to his will because the drink weakened his control over himself, but for Roger there was no pleasure in the rape of an unwilling woman. His full satisfaction could only be gained by winning willingness, not by breaking resistance. He would try, but one way or another he could not wait much longer. He turned her face toward him.

"Elizabeth, you have known me all your life. Look at me. I am Roger, the same Roger you have teased and tormented for years, and I love you. How can you fear me?" Her chin trembled. "Love, do not weep. Will you be less afraid in the dark?"

She did not reply, but all intimacies were easier in the dark so he doused the candles and made his way back to the bed in the fitful glare of the fire. He got in beside her but did not pull the bed curtains; the cheerful flames were a reassuring sight, and they provided little light. Gently but inexorably he forced her down onto the pillows. Her skin was so warm to his touch that he knew his hands were cold and his heart was pounding thickly; he too was afraid, although of different things. It was so important to him that she be content. He had never really cared much before. Of course, he had wished the various women who had been his bed companions to find the association pleasant, but he had not much cared whether they found heaven or a pleasant garden—they were only women. This was Elizabeth; for her it had to be heaven.

"Roger—"

"Yes, it is Roger," he replied to the trembling question almost in a whisper, slowly, making his voice relaxed and soothing.

"Help me," she cried.

Hereford's stomach turned. For a split second he really thought of going away and leaving her alone, but he knew that was insane. Sooner or later she must truly become his wife and the sooner the better for them both. The longer he delayed the more frightened she would be and the less able he would be to command himself.

"I will, my dearest," he said finally in the same low tone. "Can you tell me of what you are afraid?" Then she made her first voluntary movement. With a violent shudder she turned into his arms. "I wish, Elizabeth, that I could tell you I would not hurt you, but that would be a lie. I must hurt you—are you afraid of that?"

"No—yes—only a little."

He found her lips then but did not kiss her full upon them. Often it was better to touch only the corners of a woman's mouth. Her face was wet with tears although she was not sobbing and the salt taste made Hereford's breath catch. He stroked her arm very gently a few times and then, still stroking the arm with the palm of his hand, extended the fingers so that they just brushed her breast.

"Oh!"

It was a little startled cry, half gasp, half groan. Hereford had to stop kissing her, had to stop thinking about her physical being; she was not ready and she was not helping him, but neither that knowledge nor the long experience he had of restraining himself while bringing a woman to the proper pitch made any difference. He knew well he should wait, continuing his caresses until a new tension gripped her, but he could wait no longer.

She cried out and twisted her shoulders as if to get away. "Lie still, Elizabeth," he murmured softly.

Relaxed after the last shudders of his satisfaction had passed, Hereford continued to caress his wife, murmuring endearments. His eyes were closing, but he did not wish to leave her hurt and angry while he slept. She was not crying now, it was true, but for all he could tell she had turned to stone again.

"Elizabeth?"

"Yes."

"Are you all right?"

"Yes."

"Are you angry?"

"You have only had your right. Why should I be angry?"

"Elizabeth, do not use that cold tone to me. I did my best to be gentle with you. You are my wife, and I love you. Are you still afraid?"

"No. Oh, Roger, let me be. Do not ask so many questions. Go to sleep."

"I cannot sleep," he replied huskily, "when I think that you are dissatisfied with me or, even worse, when I feel that I have made you unhappy." He sat up. "What have I done wrong? Where have I failed you?"

"Nay, Roger, if there is a failure it is mine." She reached up to put a hand on his shoulder. "I warned you not to take me to wife. I cannot be other than I am. Lie down now and sleep; I am not angry or even much hurt. I only want a little peace to think."

"Think?" About what, at such a time?"

"What do you care?" she blazed furiously, touched on the raw. "Do you believe that because you have used me like a sow that I have become one? We have mated, but I can still think."

"Is that how I have used you?" Hereford asked, missing the point completely. He lay down then, flat on his back and stared up at the draped curtains. "I have sinned much, Elizabeth, and often have I been told of my evil ways, but never before this have I felt so foul."

"No, Roger, no. I did not mean that—it was not—. You were very kind, and you used me most gently, I am sure." She turned and put her arms around him, for she knew she had hurt him without purpose. It was not his fault if he could not understand. It was not right to torture Roger because she had made a mistake. She kissed him gently, contritely; it was the first kiss she had ever voluntarily bestowed upon a man not her blood relation.

"Elizabeth," he said softly, after a long pause during which she had almost drawn back, thinking her wordless apology had not been accepted, "I pray you to have a care what you say to me."

"I will so often make you unhappy, Roger. I am cursed with a wicked tongue."

"If it is but your tongue, dear heart, I can bear it." He turned now and looked earnestly into her face. "It is when your heart pours out of your mouth that I—I am distressed."

What he saw in her face must have satisfied him, although Elizabeth felt no different and had no idea what it was, for he sighed and pulled her so that her head rested on his shoulder. Throwing a leg across her, he gave a satisfied grunt and rubbed his cheek on the top of her head. Not two minutes later the change in the rhythm of his breathing told Elizabeth that he was asleep. Across the smooth curve of his pectoral muscles she watched the flames in the hearth. Roger was one of the best, she thought, unconsciously caressing his shoulder and bearing the unaccustomed weight on her thighs with a certain pleasure, but it had been a bad mistake to marry at all. Pride and vanity had originally driven her to it, together with the physical desire for him which she denied, for Roger was the best catch in the kingdom and she wished to show that the hopeless spinster of twenty-four could win him. Now that she had him, she knew that the satisfaction of pride and vanity were not enough. "Love" gave her no happiness, only a craving which she would not permit Roger to satisfy and, worst of all, she knew her position to be untenable. She could not give a little of herself as she could to her father and retain the rest separate, for herself alone. Either she must give Roger nothing of herself, or give him all.

It was warm and comfortable in the bed, and Roger's even breathing was comforting too. He tightened his arm around her in his sleep; perhaps it would not be so bad. It was very pleasant to have that breath pass her ear and feel his firm flesh pressed against her. She did not need to decide now, Elizabeth told herself, not realizing that she had decided. Certainly it would be wrong to disturb Roger with personal matters when such great political stakes hung in the balance. Until Henry of Anjou was on the throne of England, she would do her best not to distress her husband. I will just stay as I am, she told herself, and realizing that the sheets were cold snuggled closer to Roger's warmth, putting the seal on the change she had already made.

CHAPTER 6

ELIZABETH, LADY HEREFORD, looked with distaste at the sheets her mother-in-law was displaying to the assembled guests. She had bled very little, the combination of her very active life and Roger's experienced gentleness and consideration mitigating to a great degree the usual results of defloration, and she had to leave the bed before the few spots which bore witness to her virginity could be found. Elizabeth had not seen Anne although she understood by the chaff that flew back and forth that she had given a better display of her maidenhood or, as Roger protested, laughing, of Rannulf's clumsiness. He certainly seemed in excellent spirits, capping every remark made with one still more suggestive, but when the witnesses to the successful marriage night left to allow the married pair to dress, he sobered suddenly and sat down thoughtfully silent.

The men were going out to hunt, for sport not food this time, and Elizabeth had merely drawn on a robe since there was no hurry for her to dress. She was assembling her husband's clothing somewhat awkwardly, not knowing exactly where his things were kept.

"Roger, I cannot find any cross garters except these fine silk ones. Where—"

"Never mind that now, come here."

"What is it?" He pulled her into his lap. "Oh, Roger, enough. You will be late."

"There can never be enough," he replied slowly with curving lips although he had not been thinking about that. "You were better pleased with me this morning than last night, were you not?" Elizabeth colored slightly but lifted her chin with an arrogant gesture to which Roger reacted with more laughter. "Nay, no smart answers now.

126

Will you admit that the right man is needful to a head-strong woman?" He put a hand against her mouth to dam the quick, angry retort. "The truth—I have a reason for asking."

"The truth then—yes. But that does not mean—"

"That you will admit that I am right for you." He finished the sentence for her with dancing eyes. "You little viper. You will sting me when I have sweated so to please you. Of all the ungrateful—no, no, you must not strike your husband." Now he had her hands and laughed harder than ever at her frustrated fury. "Gently, my love, I was only teasing you because you are so beautiful when you are angry. But I do have a real reason for speaking. My mother—"

"Hates me, and I am to be good and proper this day to please you—you have begun well to put me in such a humor. I am fit to please no one, and your mother—"

"Least of all. Stop, Elizabeth. I care nothing what lies between you and my mother. You are both old enough to fight your own battles. So long as you do not draw me into them, you may both do as you please. Let me finish what I am saying and do not put words into my mouth."

"Only you have that privilege, being my lord and master. Well, I—"

He kissed her, damming her lips. "And so will I do each time until you hold your tongue and listen."

"You will have enough of kissing then, for—"

Her words were smothered again, and this time when he let her go she was silent and turned her face away. A toy, so swiftly had she become just that—a toy. Only a little while past her body had answered to his, just a little, because she could not completely control it, and what she had feared had come to pass. Desperately she strove to stiffen her resistance, but too much had happened too quickly.

"Elizabeth?" Roger was saying, gently, questioningly. "I was only jesting with you because your lips are sweet. Dear heart, what is wrong?"

"Nothing. Say what you would say. I will listen."

"Love, it is funny to make you angry, but you are not angry now. Somehow I have hurt you. That I did not mean."

Of course he did not mean it, she thought. To him it was only natural that all woman should be playthings. "Roger, I can bear no more explanations. Whatever you will have of me—take."

He was much disturbed by her depressed passivity and totally without a clue to its cause, but it seemed safest to question her no further. "I have only a small favor to ask of you—you need not trouble yourself with it if you do not wish."

"A favor?" To go to bed again or to cook a special potage, Elizabeth thought bitterly. "What is it?"

"You have seen my youngest sister, Catherine, I know, but have you ever spoken with her?"

"Not much." There was more life in Elizabeth's voice. Certainly this was not what she had expected.

"Do. She is an interesting girl—spoiled—my fault, I suppose, and Walter's too because he dotes upon her—bold, headstrong—and—"

"You mean, just like me?"

"Yes, my dearest love, just like you. Quiet—I will kiss you again. If you continue to interrupt me, I will be late for that hunt. I am looking for a husband for Catherine." He explained the choice available and mentioned the question of whether he should seek alliance just now or chance obtaining a greater match by waiting on the outcome of the spring campaign. "My mother will not look to see the girl's preference—if she has any—because she says it does not matter and that Catherine must be pleased with whom I choose. Since she will not, will you do that for me, love?"

"Do you think that is right, Roger? That a girl should make such a choice?" Elizabeth's voice was carefully noncommittal, but she fixed her eyes on her husband's face with a painful intensity. A great part of the future pattern of her own life might hang on his words.

Cheerfully unconscious of the importance of his answer, Hereford wrinkled his brow slightly over her question. He was often troubled to find the proper words even though the ideas were perfectly clear in his head. "Right? What is right? This is not a matter on which the Church or the Law may speak with authority; this is a matter of a person. Every person is different. Look you, Elizabeth, I did

not seek to find Anne's preference. I chose Rannulf
for her; she never even saw him before he came here for
the wedding. That was right for Anne. If I had given her
a choice, or she knew that I wished to know her preference, she would have been terrified. Unless he turn into a
monster, Anne will be happy with Rannulf—or any other
man for that matter—she is like unto my mother as two
peas in a pod. Catherine is different."

"How different?"

"I do not know, I cannot tell you, but this I know. If
Catherine were not pleased she would not weep and pray.
No, love, nor like you rage and storm, for though in jest I
said she was like you, she is not. You have a light that
shines within and shows you the true path. Mayhap there
are times," he said, smiling, "that you first cast thorns and
boulders in the way and then climb over them, but you do
not wander from the road. Catherine—though I love her
dearly—like Walter is the sort who would easily bring dishonor on her name."

"Roger! She is not yet fourteen years old. How can you
say such a thing of your own sister?"

"Have I not already laced her bloody for fooling with
the servant boys?"

"That is a child's trick; it does not point the way of a
whole life."

"Did you ever do so?"

Elizabeth thought. "No—but—"

"You see!"

"But Roger, it was because I did not like the way they
smelled, not because I thought of right and wrong."

"Ay, but there was something that held you back. With
her there is nothing. The teachings of the chaplain she
laughs at; my mother's admonition she is deaf to; my
whippings she scorns. Only with love can she be led at all,
and of late she obeys me because she loves me. What
would become of her then if she loved her husband not?
Bless us, there is the belling of the hounds and I am still
stark naked. Think on it, Elizabeth, and lend an ear to
Catherine. My mother is a good woman, but sometimes—"

He did not need to finish that, and Elizabeth was already off his knees gathering clothing. Boar hunting was
rough work and called for no use of the bow, nonetheless

it was not safe to wear homespun in the woods—thus had his father died, shot by a friend who thought the grayish-brown woolen surcoat was the coat of a deer. Roger wore homespun under his mail, woolen shirt, tunic, and chausses for warmth, but his surcoat was of the most brilliant green dye available. Buckling on his sword as he went, Hereford started for the door, Elizabeth following. He had it half open when she laid a hand on his arm.

"Roger—"

"Yes?"

"Do not do anything mad."

That stopped him and he turned to look at her. Boars were dangerous animals, it was true, but for Elizabeth to caution him was a strange thing. He kissed her long and gently, then drew back with his eyes already laughing rather than tender.

"I never do anything mad. Did you not know my new role in life is that of the staid and sober counselor? Besides, I am married now and that, I am told, takes the heart out of a man. Elizabeth, do not be so alarmingly wifely or I will tell you to mind your needle instead of—. Good Lord, I forgot all about my mother's talking too much. I have cautioned her, but—I must go. Liza, keep your ears open."

He was off, running lightly across the hall in spite of the weight of his armor; Elizabeth closed the door and sighed. Perhaps it would not be too bad. There were compensations. She stood still, leaning back on the door seeing Roger laughing like a boy with head thrown back, Roger's golden hair haloed by candlelight, Roger with blue eyes fixed in the distance, intent, saying that certain things were matters of persons. The noise in the courtyard came up through shuttered windows, and Elizabeth shook herself, stuck her head out to call her maids, and picked up the thread of daily living.

Hereford, greeting and greeted, made his way through the press of talking, gesticulating men to where his chief huntsman was conferring with his underlings, giving orders to the dog boys, and endeavoring to calm some of the hounds that leapt about him. Some of the beasts remembered Hereford well and turned their passionate attention to him as soon as he appeared. For a few moments he was busy patting familiar heads, calling familiar names, lifting lips to look at gums and teeth, and feeling paws to remark on swollen pads and split nails. Even the vicious alaunts and lymers strained at their leashes at his well-remembered scent, associating him with many a half-gnawed bone kindly thrown, and Hereford slapped at the slavering muzzles affectionately.

He wiped a wet leather glove on his surcoat and clapped his huntsman familiarly on the shoulder. "Well, Herbert, what have you for us?"

"Good sport, my lord, if we do not founder in the mud and soft snow. We have tracked three full-grown boars for a week and driven them slowly closer together. This morning I had word they were gone to earth only a half mile or so from each other. God send they have not come to fight among themselves, but it is not the rutting season yet and my men report no sows nearby."

"Are we ready then?"

"You have but to sound your horn, my lord."

It was not as simple as that, actually, for the organization of such a large hunting party was a complicated affair and many of the participants were presently more interested in talking over past experiences than in starting a new one. At last they were on their way, however, and Hereford found himself riding beside his brother-in-law.

"I trust, Rannulf, that you found everything quite satisfactory," he said gravely, concealing behind his open curiosity a real interest in his sister's welfare and a mild amusement at the self-conscious glance Rannulf cast at him when he first pulled up beside him.

The young man cleared his throat in embarrassment. He was actually Hereford's senior by a few years, but totally lacking in the poise and assurance which his brother-in-law had gained through the necessity of being master of his own fate and head of his family. The Earl of Lincoln was not a man who encouraged independent action in his sons, especially not in a younger son. He was suspicious and believed that safety lay in suppression. Too many lenient fathers found their sons their executioners, and Lincoln did not allow his genuine fondness for his male children to blind him to their potential dangerousness; therefore Rannulf, though properly educated, had never been to court and had traveled off his own estates very little. Even when he had visited with his father, the elder man had kept him largely under his own eye, allowing him little opportunity to converse with strangers on his own for fear that he would get ideas. It had taken all Hereford's ingenuity and the yielding of a good part of a fair bride price to induce Lincoln to give the young man a castle of his own to hold.

"You are providing magnificent entertainment, my lord."

Hereford roared and slapped his thighs, startling his mount and Rannulf's and causing the greyhounds running alongside to burst into short, excited barks. "Now that is a perfect reply. What tact! But you must thank my mother for your entertainment. After all, I had little enough to do with Anne's creation." Rannulf flushed. That was not what he meant and he suspected that Hereford knew it. "You should call me Hereford, or even Roger if you prefer, Rannulf, you are my brother now. I hope we will come to be truly brothers," he added more soberly.

"I too."

"When do you plan to take up residence in Corby?"

"I hardly know. My father has not mentioned the matter and I—I scarcely like to press him."

Hereford maintained his indifferent expression with an effort. If Lincoln thought he was going to void that part of the contract so easily, he was mistaken. "It will be a great disappointment to my sister if you do not take her to her own home directly. She has been greatly looking forward to being a lady in her own keep."

"I—I know. She has spoken much to me of it, but my father says as she is so young it might be better to stay a while at Lincoln until she is more able to manage her own household."

"Anne is well trained and perfectly capable of running a home." Hereford replied stiffly. "Her youth is nothing to do with the matter. There is no better housewife in the kingdom than Lady Storm, and she was a year younger than Anne when she took Gaunt Castle under her hand."

Rannulf turned away looking really distressed. "She—I might have pressed the point if she continued to urge it, but—she—. When I spoke of it in the night she was most cold to the proposal, and—and this morning she would not speak to me at all."

Clumsy ox, thought Hereford, irritated. "You should have handled her more gently—are you as much of a virgin as she that you knew not what to do?"

"Plainly I know not as much about the matter as you do, my lord." Rannulf's voice was cold, his eyes angry, and Hereford cursed himself for a worse clumsy fool than the young man beside him. What a stupid thing to say.

"Wait, brother," Hereford said as Rannulf raised his legs to put spurs to his horse. "That was an uncivil and unkind remark. You must pardon a brother's blind fondness for a gentle sister." It was true, too, that it was blind fondness. Anne should have known better herself than to behave in such a fashion to her husband. He would have to talk to her, and firmly too. If she followed this path she would lose her chance of a hold on her man and her chance of happiness also. "Moreover," he continued, putting a hand on his brother-in-law's wrist, "it is not even true. All maids are so." He was stretching the truth a little, of course, but in a good cause. "And the more gently nurtured the worse they are. Mayhap it is my mother's fault and my own for watching her so close. She is very ignorant of such things."

"I do not suppose my cousin Elizabeth acted the same. But then, Lord Hereford no doubt, knew just how to make all easy."

Hereford laughed. "You should know better than to ask if Elizabeth would not speak to me. That could never be my trouble. Indeed, she had much to say, but none of the words were so sweet as you might expect from a new bride. If your ears were offended with silence, at least you may consider yourself fortunate that they were not scorched as mine were."

Resentment dissolved in laughter as Rannulf looked at Hereford's rueful expression. "Each man must carry his own pack. I suppose if we measure burdens I prefer that of silence." The frown returned almost at once, however. "Yet it is no pleasure when a wife will do nothing but weep and cringe away when a man seeks her lips. What difference then between that and taking a woman in the fields?"

That rather pleased Hereford as indicating that Rannulf was interested in a good relationship with his wife rather than seeing her only as a brood mare. "Custom will make her more yielding, and if you have a little patience and use her gently in the beginning, pardoning her youth and inexperience, she will become willing—even eager—in the fullness of time. You know, Rannulf, she will be more docile if you have her to yourself. When she comes to realize that you alone are to make her life, she will seek by all means to please you—thus has she been bred. But if there are other women to hide behind and perhaps to give her comfort, like your mother who will be sorry for her, she may be slower to come to terms with your ways."

Hereford had not lost sight of the main point which was to get Rannulf into Corby Castle. Plainly the young man was not given to brutality for brutality's sake or he would have enjoyed Anne's resistance. It was best for them both, under those circumstances, to be alone together, and best also for Hereford's interests.

"I did not think of that. Certainly there is sense in what you say, but—"

"If you like, I will talk to your father. In a sense it is really my business because the contract was made with me, and it is a matter of my sister's consequence. Our arrangement was that she was to be a lady in her own manor."

Relief was clear in Rannulf's expression. The fear and respect engendered by many years of domination were difficult to shake off quickly, even though the desire to be a man on his own stirred his very bowels. "If you really take it to be your affair, of course, it would ease matters for me. I am no coward, I hope, but it seems disrespectful to me to quarrel with my father."

"Good. Leave the matter in my hands then."

"One more thing," Rannulf said, blushing hotly and looking with great interest at his horse's ears. "Anne says she will not stay with me, that she will run away and you will protect her."

"Me?" Hereford exclaimed, really angry with his sister. "I am more like to school her with the buckle end of my belt for such a trick. When my mother hears of this she will flay Anne alive. She is no believer in women with minds of their own. If she ever speaks to you so again, let her feel your hand. That will amend her manners shortly."

"There is no need to be harsh with her." Rannulf was moved to rise to his wife's defense by his brother-in-law's ferocious look. "She is, as you say, young. Belike she was frightened and sought protection where she was wont to find it. My father uses my mother in that way too often for me to find pleasure in it. Mayhap if your mother were to speak to her—"

A light dawned in Hereford's mind. Here was a way to rid himself of two problems at once. "Do you like my mother, Rannulf? You do not find her company a burden?"

"Nay, she is a most gentle lady, I like her well."

"You could do me a service then, help Anne, and still your father's objections all in one breath. Do not feel that I wish to push this upon you, however. If you have the smallest doubt, speak your mind and be assured I will be in nowise offended. Let my mother go with you and Anne to Corby." Hereford smiled mischievously. "I said she was no friend to headstrong women, and she and Elizabeth— well, it has been a little warm in Hereford Castle this last week, as you may have noticed."

"I would have said it was a little chilly, but have it your own way, Hereford." Rannulf was flattered by being asked for help and spoken to as an equal by the important Earl of Hereford. "I will take her gladly."

"Warm, chilly, whatever you will, but it was not comfortable. It will only be a few weeks at most. Elizabeth and I will move on to her dower lands very soon so that her people may come to know me. Then my mother must return to guard Hereford in my absence. By then Anne should be well settled."

"I hope—hark!"

The alaunts somewhat to the fore had begun to bay on a new note. They had picked up a scent. Hereford and Rannulf both spurred forward, leaving the track to follow the direction of the sound. The greyhounds leapt forward, too, leaving the horses in the rear with their burst of speed. They had not scented the quarry but responded to the baying of their hunting companions. Hereford drove his golden spurs deep into his mount's side in an effort to keep up with those silent coursers. He grunted as a low-hanging branch slashed his face and bent over his saddle-bow to avoid a repetition of the experience and to ease his horse's stride. Behind him Rannulf pounded hard, and the corner of his eye caught a flash of a surcoat banded in black and gold that could only be Lord Storm as could the husky "Ha" with which the big man urged his black stallion.

The baying changed, the deep notes of the lymers and alaunts now mixed with the sweeter belling of the braches. The boar was on the run. Hereford's blood pounded with excitement and the cold air stung his nostrils. The hunt turned; Hereford's left knee pressed hard against his horse to change its course. They crashed through a section of bracken, the thorns catching and tearing backs and chausses and further maddening the horses with the pain of deep scratches.

"On him, on him, so my loves, soooo."

That was Chester urging the dogs forward, and Lincoln's voice followed his.

"Earth him. Bring him to ground. Hold hard my sons. Courage! Courage!"

The belling was now an excited chorus of yelps and Hereford knew that the boar was standing at bay. A moment more and he could see the dogs leaping back and forth in sharp charges and retreats. He dismounted, nearly tumbling off his horse in his hurry. The serfs and huntsmen following on foot would catch the mounts if they did not stand where they were left. The short, sturdy boar spear was out, and in swift and automatic motions Hereford pulled at the crossbar to be sure it was firm and pulled at the long knife in his belt to be sure that was loose. The crossbar, set eighteen inches from the tip of the spear, was to prevent a speared boar from running right up the shaft and killing the hunter. So vicious and stubborn were those beasts that the agony of the piercing spear meant nothing to them if they could get at the man behind it.

An agonized scream indicated that the boar had killed or injured one of the dogs. Hereford broke into a run, Rannulf panting beside him. Another scream and a series of yelps; the boar would charge in another moment. Hereford and Rannulf moved apart by about five feet and knelt in the snow. They were in a fairly open space blocked at one end by the trunk of a huge fallen tree. That was where the boar had turned on his tormentors as was evident from the crowd of leaping dogs and the bloody, trampled snow. Hereford set the haft of his spear firmly into the ground, holding it point forward about two feet off the ground at the tip. No man could hold back the rush of a matured boar; the earth would take that shock. Rannulf was to his right, Lincoln and Chester equally spaced to his left, and Storm coming up more slowly, because of his lameness, to Rannulf's right. There was little chance that the boar would run between them and escape because once those animals were enraged they desired to attack their enemies, not to escape from them.

The dogs flew off in all directions, yelping in anguish as the great beast charged. Hereford had a few seconds clear sight of him, black and ugly, the tiny eyes blazing red, the bristling lips pulled back to show tushes four inches long emerging from a froth of blood-flecked saliva. Then there was nothing but the thunder of his hoofs as he made for Rannulf, straight as an arrow, seeming irresistible. There was a bellow that made the wood ring as the creature ran onto the spear, but it was too low. Rannulf had caught him in the abdomen rather than through the chest. Insane with pain, the animal writhed in an arc, tearing the spear from the ground and from Rannulf's hand. Hereford, leaping up to help, saw Rannulf go down, saw the flash of his hunting knife as he stabbed, heard his cry as the boar went over him head lowered to slash. Then he was on the animal himself, his left hand reaching for the snout to pull up the head and stab in the throat. He heard his own voice cry out as a searing pain tore his left calf just as his knife went home.

A sharp flash passed his right arm as Lord Storm thrust under it with his boar spear behind the animal's foreleg, the power of the thrust smashing the ribs as the spear went home into the heart. The *coup de grace* was not necessary, however. Hereford's thrust had cut the jugular, and the boar slipped in the blood that poured from his torn throat and went down jerking in the convulsions of death.

"Are you all right?" It was a chorus from Lincoln and Chester, Lincoln addressing his own son, Chester bending over Hereford.

"Here, Roger, tie up that leg of yours, you idiot. What

were you trying to do, wrestle with the creature?" Storm handed Hereford a strip of cloth cut from his tunic with his hunting knife.

Hereford laughed a little shakily. "I could not chance that he would turn and charge Rannulf again. I did not know that you could cover ground so fast."

"Here, that wants to be tighter, you are bleeding through." Chester knelt beside his son-in-law and Lord Storm turned his attention to the dogs, whipping them off the boar.

"Never mind me, I have come to no hurt." Hereford remarked impatiently, getting to his feet with a grimace. "How badly is Rannulf hurt?"

"No harm done here either," Lincoln replied, "except that he is a little short of breath."

"I think the son of a sow stepped on my stomach," Rannulf gasped holding his upper arm from which blood streamed, dyeing his blue surcoat purplish.

"Take your hand away," Lincoln growled, "and let me stanch that bleeding. Did he tear your shoulder?" Rannulf shook his head, still breathless, wincing as his father tightened a band around his arm and drove the torn ends of the leather jerkin into the flesh. "Do you want to go back or will you continue with us? What about you, Hereford?"

"I will ride on, I am barely scratched. Rannulf?"

"I too, if I can ever catch my breath, only I am not sure my hand will be steady enough to hold a spear. When my father gets through trying to kill me, I will see. I would not miss seeing the sport anyway. Ouch!"

"Ah," Lincoln remarked, putting the finishing touches to the bandage and then hitting his son affectionately in the head, "if your hide was as thick as your skull you would be better off."

Storm was blowing the mort, and the other hunters were streaming in to look at the kill. "Whose kill is he?" he asked Hereford in an undertone.

"Rannulf's. Had I not thought the beast would charge him again even in his death throes I would not have interfered. He hit him firm, the spear is still imbedded."

The huntsmen cut the animal open according to im-memorial custom, threw the entrails to the leaping, yelping hounds, and then tied and slung the beast to be carried back to the castle. Ordinarily the entrails would have been mixed with blood and bread and cooked as a reward for the dogs, but there were two more boars to hunt and no time to bother with that particular refinement. Hereford, with his master-of-hounds, limped over to the dogs who were too hurt to come for their prize. A quick look sufficed to show that none could be saved, and the two or three that were still living were quickly dispatched with kind words, tender hands, and a quick, sure blade.

Elizabeth, having been dressed in a favorite combination of beige tunic and brilliant red bliaut, dismissed her maids and turned her attention to the room around her. There was very little to be done, it was nearly perfect as it was. She decided quickly where to put her prize possession, a very large flat plate of silver, polished so smooth that one could see every mark and hair on one's face reflected back from it if the light were good. A table inlaid with various precious scented woods was beside it and the chests with her clothing near by against the wall. All that was needed else was a cushioned, low-backed chair to set before her mirror so that she could comb her hair and dress herself in comfort and the room would be as she wished.

She made a mental note to tell the steward to bring her a suitable chair and turned her attention to Roger's things. Basically there was no need for this. Under Lady Hereford's excellent management there was a large and well-trained group of women who wove, sewed, and even embroidered with great skill, and Lord Hereford was always beautifully dressed. He even had a body servant who folded and cleaned his clothing and helped him dress if he did not wish to have his mother or sisters about for some private reason or simply did not wish to trouble them. Elizabeth had decided that the personal attentions of that servant must now come to an end. She herself would dress Roger, bathe him, and perform other similar tasks. She had no sentimental idea of making herself necessary and beloved by taking over these duties, merely she did not want any servant about who had the right to walk in and out of her chamber. Elizabeth was clear-sighted enough to know that she and Roger would have many tussles, and, whoever won, she was determined that no servant should carry the tale of their strivings. It was this thought which made Elizabeth's voice rather sharp as she called out in answer to a sound at the door.

"Who is it?"

"Lady Elizabeth, may I come in?"

Elizabeth looked up from the contents of the chest she had turned out. That was a gentlewoman's voice. "Certainly," she said more civilly as she rose and then, "Why, it is Anne. Do come in."

"May I speak with you a moment, Lady Elizabeth?"

"Of course." Elizabeth smiled and came forward. The smile faded as she got a good look at Anne's face. "Why, my dear, whatever is wrong?"

"Lady Elizabeth, you must help me, I am so very unhappy."

Receiving the shuddering and sobbing girl in her arms with surprise but very little sympathy, Elizabeth wondered whether Roger, discussing Anne so glibly that morning could have been wrong. "If I can help you, Anne, I will, but—"

"I am sure you can. Roger loves you so much he will do anything you ask, I am sure of it. He will not listen to me or to my mother, but he will listen to you. I do not wish to be married," the girl burst out. "Please, I wish to stay here. Make Roger let me stay. Make him send Rannulf away."

"Anne, no matter how much Roger loves me, I do not believe I could convince him to do such a thing, especially without a reason. What in the world has happened? I know you were looking forward to being married and you seemed to like Rannulf very much."

"It is not Rannulf's fault. I am not fit to be married. I cannot bear it. He—he hurts me. I am afraid."

"But Anne," Elizabeth exclaimed, finally comprehending that her problem was sexual, "you cannot be sixteen years old and not know what was to be. Have you never seen the beasts mate? Did your mother tell you nothing?"

"Yes, she told me, but I—" Anne burst into tears again and sobbed, "I thought it was going to be wonderful. I must be ill-made. There is something wrong with me. I am not fit to be a wife." She cried despairingly in Elizabeth's arms, adding pathetically, "And I wanted to be so much, so much—"

Elizabeth was temporarily stunned but slowly began to understand. Roger was right, after all, about his sister. She was apparently a very simple child and either had not understood what Lady Hereford and the other women told her and suggested to her or had been guarded too carefully, told nothing, and had drawn no conclusions from what she had actually seen with her own eyes. Too timid and obedient to question and experiment on her own, Anne was sexually ignorant, and Elizabeth was ready to wager Rannulf was almost equally ignorant, since his experience was confined to whores and serfs. Elizabeth smothered a smile as she saw herself cast in the role of preaching obedience and patience and counseling a girl to be yielding and receptive to the sexual desires of her husband. A fine situation for her to be in. Nonetheless through the confusion of ideas in her own mind welled an intense sense of gratitude to Roger who had made everything so comparatively easy.

"Do not weep, Anne. Come here and sit down with me." Seated on the bed, Elizabeth put her arm around the girl and drew her close. "There is nothing wrong with you. It is the same for all maids—ay, do not look so surprised, for me too. It is very long since your mother was married. Mayhap she has forgotten or mayhap she did not wish to frighten you. Also it is possible that Rannulf was a little sudden and eager, but you should be glad of that for it shows that he loves you." Elizabeth's voice faltered a little over that because she was not at all sure it was true and she did not like to lie.

"Lady Elizabeth, is that really true? You do not say it only to comfort me?"

"Yes," Elizabeth replied firmly, "it is true." Roger *was* right, all people were different. Anne was sufficiently blind and trusting so that if she believed her husband loved her she would probably be happy even if it were not so. And, since Rannulf was not overly complicated himself, his wife's love and faith would no doubt bring him to care for her even if he was originally indifferent.

"Oh dear," Anne cried, beginning to sob again, "oh dear, whatever have I done?"

Oh dear, Elizabeth thought too, raising her brows, I hope it is less serious than she thinks. "What is it now, Anne?"

"I—I did not understand and I pushed him away and I would not let him kiss me—and I would not speak to him. He was so angry, but I thought—"

Not so bad after all. Doubtless Roger could calm Rannulf down with tactful explanations of Anne's ignorance. She would have to catch him as soon as he came in. Poor Roger, as if he did not have problems enough without this.

"That is too bad, Anne, you should not have done so, but what is done amiss may often be amended. Dress yourself in your prettiest robes and when Rannulf comes home greet him kindly. If he will go aside with you, tell him you are sorry and try to explain, if he will listen, how you came to be so foolish."

"But what if he will not go with me or allow me to speak—he was so very angry. Roger is never so cross."

Elizabeth was again forced to restrain a smile. Roger did not have the same cause to be cross with Anne; he could be furious enough, Elizabeth knew, when he was properly pricked. "Then you must be patient. You will certainly be alone in the night." Anne shuddered. "Do not make the same mistake again, Anne. Receive him willingly. It is—it is very bitter to live with an angry man. Now do not spend the whole day weeping." Elizabeth said sharply, "and do not go and gab your troubles to everyone. I am your sister and I will hold my tongue, but others will not, and you will make yourself ridiculous. Furthermore, crying will spoil your face and your husband will find you less pretty, and also men do not like to find their women always bathed in tears. Come, tell me where Roger's things are kept and how he likes his garments matched."

That was an appeal well suited to Anne's taste, and she regained much of her natural cheerfulness in Elizabeth's bracing company. Eventually they were joined by Catherine and Lady Hereford and finally spent the rest of the day with the ladies, gossiping, roasting nuts in the huge fires, and talking about affairs in the world around them. For many of the women a social occasion of this kind was the only chance they had to leave their own keeps and exchange news, views, and gossip with other women of their own class. Many husbands did not care to have their wives mix in their affairs and did not bring them along when they went to court or to other political functions. This did not reduce the women's interest in these matters, however, and they talked with equal eagerness and ignorance, doing their best to get information from those whose menfolk were more liberal in their ways.

Elizabeth bore the brunt of much of the questioning since she was well known to be deep in her father's counsel. As she fenced off question after question with harmless tidbits of information or laughing rejoinders, she could not help seeing that it was her own pride and vanity which put her in this fix. She had always been eager to have the world know how high she stood in her father's estimation and now she was bound by the pattern which she had established. She could not help envying Lady Storm who had all of the advantages of her position with none of its disadvantages. Leah had adopted, since her first appearance in public, the manners of a sweet, innocent simpleton. Thus she had gained much information, since no one was afraid to speak their mind before her, believing she would not understand, and could spread much misinformation with which to help her husband's cause. She had even tried to establish the fact that her husband was indifferent to her, caring nothing for the sneers of the other women if she could serve Lord Storm's purposes better that way, but in this she had failed because Storm would not cooperate. He was passionately in love with his wife and made not the slightest effort to hide it, hanging over her even in public, jealous and protective. That, thought Elizabeth, watching Lady Storm laugh like a child with her big, soft eyes open as wide as they could get, she did not envy Leah; such attention would smother her. Roger might wander, but he would never dote.

She stiffened slightly as her mother-in-law made a remark about Roger not being able to take a much needed rest, prepared to cast her reputation, his, or both to the wind, and then sighed with relief as a page ran up to tell them that the hunt was on its way home. This caused a natural flurry and changed the thread of the conversation. Elizabeth was amused by watching the reactions of the different women. Lady Salisbury and Lady Warwick were clearly indifferent and did not even hesitate in their talk; Lady Lancaster was mildly pleased and interested, while Lady Gloucester was mildly annoyed; the longer her husband stayed away the better she liked it. Lady Storm rose at once to run to the door or even down into the courtyard to greet her darling. Someone would expect a man so anxiously awaited by his wife to be handsome and delicate, possibly in ill health, instead of a redoubtable giant, ugly, arrogant, and deformed.

Having made these observations, Elizabeth laughed at herself wondering what she would see in her own face if she could watch it. Her first move, however, was to Anne's side where she urged the girl, nervous and frightened again, to go forward and greet Rannulf. So much initiative unsupported was impossible to Anne, however, and Elizabeth took her hand and went with her.

Fortunately their bloodstained husbands arrived together, exhausted but happy. The women's reactions were typical. Anne ran forward crying, "Rannulf, you are hurt, oh, let me see. Is it bad?"

Elizabeth stood still, placing her hands on her hips, and remarked in an exasperated tone, "Roger, how could you? Could you not be more careful? I hope, considering where you keep them, that your brains have not run out."

The men's reactions would have been equally predictable to anyone who knew them. Rannulf looked embarrassed, although Anne's concern had done a great deal toward making him forget and forgive her behavior the previous night, and said in a low voice, "It is nothing. Do not make a fuss here."

Roger seized his wife by her ears, effectively paralyzing her, and kissed her soundly, laughing. "I have been accused of having my head screwed on wrong, and of keeping my brains in my ass, but never before of keeping them in my ankles. Anyhow, what kind of a greeting is that to a wounded hero? You should swoon all over me, weep floods of tears, and marshal every leech in the castle to attend to my hurts."

"Let go of my ears, you pest. Do you want them to grow pointed like a witch's? That is all I need to add to my good name. Roger, you stink. Come and change those foul clothes."

"All right, but I still think I deserve a little more sympathy. Look at Anne—that is proper behavior. For pity's sake, Rannulf, go with my sister and let her see to you before she faints from anxiety. She will never believe that you are not dying if she cannot see with her own eyes."

Rannulf hesitated for a moment, then smiled faintly at his wife and went with her to the room they were using. At first neither spoke, both were embarrassed, but when Anne removed the bandage from Rannulf's arm and he winced, she murmured that she was sorry.

"It is nothing," he said indifferently, reminded by the place and being alone with her of her rejection.

"N—not for th—that alone," Anne faltered, her eyes filling with tears. "I—Rannulf please, forgive me. I—did not understand."

He made no reply, a little awkward about how to accept her apology and wondering also whether it would not serve his purpose best to frighten her a little. He had almost forgotten his hurt arm in spite of the dull ache, for like most men he was accustomed to the pain of minor wounds, so that when Anne pulled off his leather jerkin, tearing the clots loose, he cried out more in surprise than pain. Anne began to weep in earnest, thinking he would be more angry because she had hurt him, and the jagged tear began to bleed again.

"You had better stop the bleeding, Anne," Rannulf said quietly. "What do you mean, you did not understand? What do you understand now that you did not before? To whom have you been speaking of us?"

"Lady Elizabeth told me—told me—oh, Rannulf, I am ashamed to have been so stupid." Her voice trembled but her hands were steady as she washed the wound and rebandaged it.

Rannulf's lips twitched. At least they were keeping matters in the family. He complained to Anne's brother, she to his cousin. He looked at his wife's tear-wet face.

"Have you changed your mind then about leaving me?

Do you still wish to ask your brother if he will offer you his protection?"

Anne slid down to the floor and embraced her husband's knees. "Please do not tell Roger," she whispered, "he will tell my mother and everyone will laugh at me. Please—"

Rannulf pulled his wife up rather roughly. He did not then mean to hurt her or frighten her but the position disgusted him; he had seen his mother and sisters kneel that way too often. "Do not kneel to me like that, Anne. I do not like it." There was a pause while he studied her expression. "I am glad that you have mended your manners with no need of schooling from me," he said more gently, "and perhaps it was also my fault. I should have been more gentle with you." He bent his head then to kiss his wife's lips. They were yielded willingly now, although the quivering tension of her body still proclaimed her fear. Rannulf forgot about dinner, forgot he would be honored by the presentation of his kill, forgot his steadily throbbing arm. There was something intensely exciting about that fearful eagerness, something different at last from the harlot and the serf.

The conversation taking place in Roger's bedroom was far different. For one thing Elizabeth was certainly not either silent or embarrassed. At first she asked eager questions about the hunt, plainly regretful that she could not have been present, which Roger answered with willingness. Then as it was borne in upon him that Elizabeth was pouring water for him to wash with and laying out his clothes he stopped in the middle of a spirited description of the second kill.

"Really, Elizabeth, you could not yet have spent all my money nor alienated all of my servants. Will you tell me why, considering our circumstances, you feel obliged to act like a maidservant?"

Elizabeth merely cast an exasperated glance at him. "Because I have something to say to you that I do not wish all the servants in the keep to know about. My women do not come to me unless I bid them, and I have taken the liberty of telling that pasty-faced manservant of yours to adopt the same custom. I hope you do not mind," she added as an afterthought on a note of sarcasm.

"A lot of good it would do if I did. Well, what is the bad news? Good can always be shared."

"Not bad, just private. Anne has behaved like a little fool with Rannulf—"

"I know, but how did you hear of it?"

"From Anne. I suppose Rannulf blabbed the whole to you. Men!"

"Why men? Did not Anne come running to you with her troubles? Why you, by the way? Why not my mother?"

"She thought I would have more influence with you and would urge you to keep her here and send Rannulf home."

"She did, by God's eyes, did she?" Hereford said, flushing slightly with anger. "That is what comes of being kind to a woman. I hope he takes a stick to her."

"Well, it was not her fault, poor thing," Elizabeth retorted hotly, flushing in turn. "She was told nothing to the point and he must have acted like a stud in heat."

Hereford bit his lip; he had forgotten that this was still a rather sore point with Elizabeth. "Was all else quiet?" he asked, changing the subject.

"Untie those chausses and let me look at your leg, Roger. I hope so. It took me most of the morning to calm Anne, but the talk was innocent enough when I joined it. If I get a chance to talk to Leah I will ask." She had been removing his clothing as she spoke and then pushed him toward a chair.

"Take it easy, Elizabeth, that hurts," Roger said sharply as she loosened the bandage and pulled at the chausses.

"I cannot help it," Elizabeth replied without a trace of sympathy. "If you had come directly home when this happened the cloth would not have stuck to the flesh." She looked more closely at the wound. "That is an ugly tear," she said more gently, "perhaps it would be better to have it sewed. Do you want me to take the time to soak the cloth loose?"

"No, only be quick."

The cloth off, Elizabeth could see better and decided that it was unnecessary to stitch it. The wound was long and ragged but not deep and would heal well, she thought, with just a dressing. Hereford made no pretense of hiding his sigh of relief; he was stoic enough when necessary but did not believe that pretending to be a hero about such things was necessary.

"You might tell me," Elizabeth said, wrapping linen smoothly around his calf, "what catastrophic form of game you are planning to amuse us with tonight. I want to know whether it is safe to wear a light-colored bliaut."

"I can tell you nothing," Hereford replied in a whisper, "I am too faint."

His voice was, indeed, so unsteady that Elizabeth jumped up and was just about to lean over him anxiously when she saw one eye open slyly to see the effect of his statement. Pretending not to have noticed, Elizabeth came closer and then with sudden violence boxed his ear.

"Faintness," she cried, leaping out of reach, "is due to a failure of blood in the head. That is the best treatment I know for it."

"Fiend! If I ever saw such a woman. You have not a drop of compassion in your soul. I could bleed to death and—"

"Not in this room," Elizabeth interrupted severely. "If you plan to bleed to death, do it outside or in the hall. In here you would get blood all over the rugs and I do not approve of such filthy habits."

Hereford gave up and laughed heartily. With a movement swifter than her own in spite of the hurt leg he seized her, running his hands over her with the passionate insolence of ownership.

"Let me go, Roger. We have wasted enough time talking. Roger, let go! Do you wish to offend your guests so that they all depart in anger?"

"Yes." He spoke with surprising intensity, all trace of laughter gone from his voice. "I wish there was not a living soul in this keep save our two selves. I could eat you from the shoes up, Elizabeth." She made a convulsive movement, and pain shadowed Hereford's eyes as he released her. "Perhaps if I had you to myself—all to myself with nothing else and no one else to think about—I could some day come to understand you."

CHAPTER 7

ELIZABETH WOKE WITH A STARTLED CRY OF PAIN. She had just been struck with great violence. Gasping, she struggled upright, prepared to defend herself before she was awake enough to realize that she was in bed and the man who had hit her was her own husband. She dodged as Roger struck at her again, staring at him with wide, frightened eyes and thinking he must have gone mad when she realized that he was still asleep and was again struggling with phantoms.

"Roger!" She shook his shoulder. "Roger, wake up, Roger!" she shrieked, a real note of terror in her voice as he reached smoothly for the naked sword lying beside the bed.

"What is it, Elizabeth?" The sword gleamed as Hereford sat up and put it in his lap. "Hush, do not cry out. Of what are you afraid?"

"Are you awake, Roger?"

"Of course I am awake. How could I sleep with you shouting in my ear? Were you dreaming?"

"No, you were. Roger, do put that sword down. You have already blacked my eye, I fear. A fine time I shall have explaining what happened. You were fighting something in your sleep."

"I am sorry, Liza. Did I hurt you?"

"No," she replied sarcastically, "there is nothing I like better than a black eye and a swollen jaw."

"I would not hurt your for the world, Liza, you know I would not," Hereford murmured, lying down and pulling Elizabeth on to his breast.

"What were you dreaming about that disturbed you so much?" she asked hastily. Roger knew of a number of

149

methods of soothing women, but only one would occur to him in bed.

"I cannot remember," he said vaguely, tightening his grip on her.

Elizabeth had learned in the two months of her marriage that it was fruitless to tell Roger to let her alone. Whenever she did so he compromised by caressing her until she was willing and, however pleasant the experience was, it was humiliating to her to appear so weak-willed. He could be distracted sometimes by jesting or by questions.

"Having done trying to beat me to death, I see you are now about to strangle me." Her voice was still sharp, but she wriggled an arm free to touch his face and hair in the dark. "Was it demons or something real?"

"Real enough. Let us talk of something else," he replied shortly, and Elizabeth could have wept with frustration.

By and large her fears about marriage had not been completely realized. Roger seemed willing enough, even eager sometimes, to discuss his plans with her, but it was plain enough too that he was hiding something, and something very important. This nightmare, recurring every two or three nights was part of it, and more than once Elizabeth had found her husband with his head sunk in his hands and his face drawn with worry. He always laughed when she questioned him, making some light reply about general matters or that he was only assuming the burdens of a married man, but he was obviously avoiding her interest in this particular aspect of his problems.

"Will Walter do as you desire, Roger?"

Hereford's younger brother had appeared suddenly out of nowhere and had stayed at Wallingford with them for two days almost a week ago. He had not come to their wedding and had not come as he had promised his mother he would after Epiphany. When he did arrive at Wallingford, unexpected and unwanted, he brought with him a rowdy band of ill-regulated landless knights and men-at-arms. The troop was so undisciplined that they had respect for nothing and had quickly lost one member who had inadvisedly attempted to be a little too friendly with Elizabeth. Her startled cry and his shriek of pain as her poniard pierced his arm brought Hereford, who had dispatched him summarily without a word of question or an instant's hesitation. Elizabeth was not thinking of that, but of the scene following when Walter had hurried up to defend his man. Roger had been standing over the corpse calmly wiping his hands and his knife, having already been reassured by Elizabeth that she was unhurt. He had, at first, made no reply whatsoever to Walter nor given any sign that he heard his brother's violent questions. Even when Walter had put a hand on his shoulder to spin him around, his other fist raised to strike, Hereford did not deign to answer. Knife in hand, Roger made no move at all to defend himself, and Elizabeth, a silent witness, externally unmoved, had held her breath. Only Hereford's eyes met and held Walter's and Walter had turned purple and dropped his hands, crying that he would stay no longer in a place where he and his men were insulted and murdered over a woman.

Elizabeth thought Roger would burst; she was accustomed to her father's violence, used to cover his weakness, and to Roger's quick rages about little things, as quickly dispersed, but this was something quite different. Eventually her husband had said quietly, almost gently, "This is Elizabeth Hereford, my wife, as well you know, not—a woman. Moreover, you may not leave now, Walter. I have something to discuss with you and I will say what is in my mind." There had been a short pause in which Walter, shifting his gaze under his brother's, had made a remark about Roger's oath that this was no trap. Hereford had swallowed, looked carefully at his hands as if to be sure they were clean, and had spoken in the same gentle voice. "Do not do it, Walter, do not bait me. You are flesh of my flesh, my brother, blood of my blood. Do not force me to hurt where I love so dearly."

Roger had touched her arm then and taken her away, and Elizabeth, no coward, had been afraid even to mention Walter's name until this moment. Even now she could feel the tensing of the muscles in his shoulder which supported her head, and she regretted opening the subject. It would have been simpler to let him have what he wanted, but Elizabeth was ashamed of being afraid of Roger. It was unreasonable; she knew he would not hurt her. Nonetheless she was afraid, and, characteristically, she pushed herself into a position where she did not really want to be.

"Will he, Roger?" Elizabeth insisted.

"I do not know. Yes, at first, while he remembers he is afraid of me and while the booty runs in freely. But he is like, at any time, to turn and strike his nearest and richest ally. For God's sake, Elizabeth, can you ask nothing of me that does not touch me on the raw?"

"You are too proud. If a tree in the orchard bears one rotten fruit, is that a reason to distrust the whole tree?"

Hereford moved restlessly. "Mayhap, but it is not only pride. I cannot lift from my heart the feeling that I have done amiss with Walter. Yet, I cannot think where I have failed him either. Heaven knows, I have given him more than is due a younger son. I have ever treated him as my heir."

"How can you talk in that way? Even if you did or said what was not perfect—you were so young yourself at first. How can you blame yourself?"

"I do not—at least, I tell myself I could have done no other way. Even now that I know better, when I look back, I cannot see that I did so ill. Still—"

"But if you cannot trust him, Roger—to talk of what you did or did not is fruitless now—how can you employ him safely in such work as you have in hand? If he should turn upon you—or worse, upon your allies—he might bring you to disaster."

"Do you think I know it not? Let be, Liza. I need no more trouble than I have already."

There was such a long silence that Elizabeth thought Roger was asleep. She had just started to doze herself when a gleam of firelight penetrated the dark as Roger drew back the bed curtains and woke her completely by slipping silently out of bed. He dropped the curtain, but Elizabeth could hear the rushes rustle as he moved restlessly around the room, stirred the fire, and poured wine into a drinking goblet. This too was nothing new to her; usually he returned to bed in a short time, chilled and passionate, but sometimes she would find him in the morning slumped in a chair before the fire or still pacing the room. His mood changed with lightning swiftness when he knew her to be awake and he showed her only his usual laughing tenderness or teasing, but Elizabeth now recognized that the merry-mad façade was just that, a façade behind which the Earl of Hereford concealed himself.

Tears rose to her eyes and she fought them back; tears availed nothing. It was wormwood and gall to know that she, so wise and clever as she thought herself, did not know her own husband, had never guessed that there was more to Roger of Hereford than his obvious gaiety, intelligence, and strength of character. Even bitterer was the knowledge that Roger did not trust her sufficiently to share his troubles with her.

It never occurred to Elizabeth that what Hereford was hiding was only his weakness and his fear, and that she herself had unconsciously made that concealment a condition of their marriage. She had made it very plain that in spite of her great love for her father she despised his weakness and that Roger was attractive because he united Chester's charm with great determination and fixity of purpose. Furthermore, she had given him no reason to believe that her love for him was sufficient to overcome the disappointment she would suffer in knowing him to be as riddled with fears as any other man. Aside from his subconscious perception of Elizabeth's demand that he be strong, the concealment of indecision and fear was now second nature to Hereford. A sixteen-year-old faced with the overwhelming task of maintaining his birthright in a country almost completely devoid of law and order where rights can only be established by force, either leads his men so that they believe he is forceful and fearless and takes out the change in bad dreams, or yields his rights and honors and sinks into poverty and insignificance. Hereford had chosen the bad dreams and battled his terrors alone in the dark.

Elizabeth listened intently for what seemed hours and hours and actually was about fifteen minutes. She could hear nothing more, however, and finally could bear the suspense no longer. Drawing back the curtain, she peered out. At first she did not see Hereford at all, and her heart sank, but almost immediately she heard a faint creak and realized that he was standing in the shadows looking out through an arrow slit.

"Roger, you will freeze. What in the world are you do-ing?"

He stiffened as if she had hit him, lifting his head and squaring his shoulders. "I am sorry if I disturbed you. Go back to sleep, Elizabeth. I am only restless."

"About what?" That was unwise and she knew it. Roger was in no mood to be questioned.

He had not turned and now replied in a rather muffled tone. "That is my affair. I assure you that it is no matter that could possibly be of any concern to you." He meant by those words exactly what he had said and no more, and his voice was kind, if a little weary. He never thought of excluding Elizabeth from any practical situation, political or personal, but his struggle with his own depression seemed outside of her sphere of interest to him.

Elizabeth, thinking in entirely different terms, put the worst possible construction on his simple sentence. Before she could stop herself, she had burst into a spate of bitter words, the sum and substance of which was that no concern of Hereford's was any affair of hers because she did not care a piece of broken silver for him, and if he chose to refuse to answer her civil questions it was a matter of complete indifference to her. "I desire merely to put a good face upon this unhappy relationship between us so that the whole world need not know of the mistake we have made. If you do not care that people laugh at you for refusing to answer civil questions asked only to make conversation, why should I!"

Hereford had finally turned to face his wife during her tirade, which he made no attempt to interrupt. At her assertion that she did not care for him, a spasm of pain crossed his face, but her last statement, so obviously the result of bad temper and so silly in view of the hour and the room empty except for themselves, distracted him from the nameless terrors that pursued him and restored his good humor.

"You are always just what I need, my darling wife. Not, I admit," he added laughing, "always what I want, but what is good for me. Do not, I beg you, say that we have made a mistake. I doubt there is another woman in the world that could do for me what you do."

He returned, still laughing, to the bed, and Elizabeth hastily moved to the other side and turned her back on him. That too was most unwise for it left her defenseless. If she had faced him, she could have pushed him away and continued her scolding, but one cannot scold a bed curtain with dignity or push a man who kisses the small of one's back. Gasping and indignant at first, Elizabeth soon yielded, ashamed and angry, but docile to her husband's demands. She had learned also to simulate an exhaustion and a desire for sleep which she did not feel on the completion of Roger's lovemaking because, if she did not, he would either continue to caress her, which disturbed her further, or whisper questions and endearments to which she could not reply. What Elizabeth did not know was that she had not deceived her husband as completely as she thought. He had been too successful a lover in the past to mistake Elizabeth's mild pleasure for a genuine and ultimate response. He was, however, patient with her inability to respond, putting it down correctly to the factor which was causing her general dissatisfaction. Only in misunderstanding the basis of his wife's unhappiness did Hereford err; he believed her not to be in love with him, thus far having completely misunderstood her fears of subjection and her relation of those fears to sexual satisfaction.

Having conceded defeat once more in his attempt to win his wife sexually, Hereford slept at once, leaving her to struggle with her fury until she too slipped into the unconsciousness she had feigned earlier. He was not left long in peace, however, and neither was Elizabeth. A rider, splattered with the mud of the first thaw, was led to his room barely an hour later. When Hereford heard what he had to say and had read a brief missive which he carried, unheaded, unsigned, unsealed, but in the well-known scrawl of Gloucester, he woke Elizabeth. His face might have been carved in marble for all the emotion it held as he told her that she must pack her things and leave at the first light.

"Where must I go? Why must I go?"

"Where you like." Roger meant to be kind, but he was stupid with fatigue, abstracted with concern over the news, and he had no idea of the cold indifference of his voice. "The king is on the march. Too soon—always too soon. We had meant to take—no matter. I have no time to indulge you with talk, Elizabeth; I must go at once to join my men."

"But, Roger—". .

"No words, Elizabeth, no argument." His eyes had a wholly deceptive depth. Elizabeth realized that for her there was nothing in them; he hardly saw her. "I said to go—now go. Alan of Evesham and my household guard can escort you wherever you like. When you are safe they can return to me. I will await them or leave word for them at Devizes."

He did not look at her again as his squires armed him, and he left without a word of farewell. Elizabeth wept with rage, telling herself that she would not go, she would not be ordered about like the meanest serf. She knew, however, that such thoughts were vain. Roger was Alan's god on earth, and he would obey his master even if it came to tying her to her mount. To resist would only mean more indignity. She dried her tears and packed with burning eyes and a heart throbbing so that at first she could scarcely think. Later, as the need to consider what to take and the physical activity calmed her a little the notion of teaching her husband a good lesson came to her.

Elizabeth knew that Roger expected her to go either to Hereford or to Chester, or, as a remote possibility, to Painscastle to stay with Lady Leah. She would teach him. She would go to Corby to Anne and Rannulf. It was not as far as Chester so that his men could return quickly; for all her rage she had no desire to endanger Roger by keeping his most faithful men from his side. She would be just as safe at Corby, but he would not be able to get at her easily and he would be worried sick when no word came from Hereford of her passing through.

Alan of Evesham's surprise when she announced her destination she stared down coldly, and he had no choice but to obey her since his lord was already on his way and had left no contrary instruction. He did not like it though, and made no bones about saying so. To pass so near Oxford, a firm stronghold of the king, and then through Northampton, which did not love the arms of Hereford because Walter had been busy there, seemed foolhardy in the extreme to him. Elizabeth remained adamant. Had she been given time to think, she would have yielded, for she was not foolhardy; but now, in the first flush of her rage, any opposition merely hardened her purpose.

Walter of Hereford lay in the open staring up at the slowly lightening sky and chewing a bitter cud. He was wet and cold, but he made no attempt to go to his tent where there was a fire and dry clothing. The physical discomfort added to his misery, and he was savoring his bitterness to the full. Twice now they had raided small keeps of the king's according to Hereford's plan, striking just before dusk when the guards were at their evening meal and coming off nearly scatheless with much booty. At full light they would be away northward to strike again and gain another rich prize. There could be no doubt of it, Roger had accurate information and advised him for his own good. Walter turned his head and spat. Roger always advised him for his own good; Roger did everything right, he was perfect. But it was Roger's good too—always Roger's good. Roger sat with a fat army and gained praise and honor for doing nothing while he fought in the dark and ran in the dark like a rat and was called thief. With what I know and what I guess, Walter thought, I could hang him. Hang him like a common thief on a gibbet for being a traitor. Walter laughed without mirth or pleasure. How my mother would weep, he thought, seven others of us she has and none of us worth a hair on dear Roger's head to her. I need only to go to the king, the bitter thoughts continued, to gain booty far richer than what I could gain by ten years' fighting. Even the earldom of Hereford would be mine. His lips drew back in another mirthless smile. Mine, but with what dishonor! Mine, to be known as the man who sold his brother. Mine, but not long to keep with Chester on the north and Gaunt to the west. They love Roger too well to let his murderer go scot free. Roger, Roger, the whole world loves Roger.

He rose and kicked his master-at-arms awake and gave the orders for carrying out the next step of his brother's plan. The sky was blue and the clouds golden in the early light. Walter did not notice them, but if he had even they would have reminded him of Roger, for his coloring was dark and he envied his brother even that accident of birth. They did not ride far but beyond their objective to the east so that it might seem that they had come from that direction. This assault too prospered, as all of Roger's plans seemed to do with Walter; the treasure chests of the main dwelling house quickly found, quickly taken, and they horsed again and away before the stunned guardians of this previously peaceful town knew what had befallen them. This time they did not stay to divide the booty but rode hard, still northward, until long after dark. In a keep at Oundle they would hide for a day or two to lick their wounds, refurbish their armor, and count their gain.

Roger of Hereford did notice the clear blue sky and golden clouds, but only as another factor in his tactical plans. All his energy was bent upon reaching Devizes, and his mind was busy with men and horses and supplies. Too soon. He had hoped to begin the assault himself. In a week or two more with the forces at his disposal he could have fortified several small towns along the line of march to harass Stephen so that he would need to break up the mass of his army or at least slow his advance. Now he was not sure whether it would be better to disperse his army into the various strongholds and make sporadic attacks with no danger of any serious loss, retreat westward to draw Stephen beyond hope of any aid, and then attack, or stand the ground he had now, which was well known to himself and his men, and take the chance of gain or loss that came with a major engagement of two nearly equal enemies. The balance was in his favor anyway. His men were near friendly strongholds that would receive them in case of defeat; they were rested and well fed; and for a good many of them their homes lay behind them in the direction the king would pass if they did not beat him back. They would fight hard to keep Stephen out of Gloucestershire, even the mercenaries, many of whom now had wives and children in the towns where they had been stationed for so many years. Hereford calculated from the date the messenger had set out that he would have sufficient time to order his battle and make all ready. Retreat was repugnant to him personally too. They would stay, he decided, and face the king unless his reconnaissance parties brought back reports of an overwhelming force.

Hereford released a long breath of relief; for good or ill his decision was made. He looked up at the sky again. If the weather held they would have dry ground to fight on, but it would not hold unless it grew colder. Tomorrow, Hereford thought, let it rain tomorrow, and rain and rain. Mayhap we will be wet and slip in the mud, but Stephen's men will need to ride through the mud and drown in the swollen fords. That will teach him to trust an English spring and chance attack before the first thaw dries.

In the late afternoon of the second day out, Alan of Evesham was looking at the sky. He, however, was not pleased in the least to see it graying over, not knowing that rain suited Hereford's purposes. Thus far they had made a really remarkable distance for a troop traveling with women. Her ladyship, he thought, rode as well as any seasoned trouper, cared nothing for the comfort of her attendant ladies, and was plainly anxious to reach her destination. She had ridden, that first day, from dawn until after dark without a murmur of complaint and was up and ready to ride again at dawn the next day. Nonetheless, if it rained they could go no further than Geddington that night. It would make a long ride to Corby the next day and a miserable one if the rain continued.

When Elizabeth felt the first drops she bit her lips with nervous chagrin. She had long since recognized her folly and bitterly regretted it, but it was more dangerous now to go back than to move forward. She desired only to reach the safe haven of Corby so that when Sir Alan asked if they should return a half mile to Kettering she said that the wet was nothing.

"Let us press on, Sir Alan, I beg you. I am not made of salt."

The knight looked up at the sky. Dusk was gathering quickly now over the gray clouds, but Geddington was only a few miles ahead. "Very well, my lady," he replied.

A mile further down the road, however, he would have given much to have made a different decision. Behind them he could plainly hear the sound of a large body of mounted men coming. They were gaining steadily on Alan's troop and, having no way of determining whether they were friend or foe, he had no desire to meet anyone at that hour and in such an indefensible place.

"My lady—"

"Who is that coming?"

"I do not know, my lady. Mayhap it would be well for us to move off the road."

"You know best, Sir Alan, but look, there are only open fields. Where can we hide?"

"There is a small copse ahead. See that shadow? Let us spur forward. It may be that we may reach that shelter in time."

Walter of Hereford wiped the wet out of his face and expended a good part of his not inconsiderable store of obscenity. He was miles and miles from Oundle and separated from his companions. He cursed the stag he had been coursing; the dogs that had lost the scent and, finding a new scent when his horse was too tired to follow, had left him; the weather, and himself for being so absorbed in the chase as not to realize how far it had taken him. He was not even sure just where he was, but plainly there was a road ahead. At least he had a purse heavy with gold and was, as his habit was, well armed. There was nothing for it but to take to the road and seek the first shelter he might find. He walked his tired horse slowly toward the opening in the trees and then pulled it up suddenly. Just below him were the unmistakable sounds of battle—the clash of arms and the hoarse cries of men. Walter edged closer cautiously. It was most unlikely that anyone would notice him even though it was not yet completely dark, and he was curious.

A small troop was engaged with a much larger one— that much was clear—and the larger group were plainly well-drilled soldiers fighting under a banner. Walter shrugged and began to back his horse. He could not make out whose banner it was, and the outcome was clear although the small group fought well and desperately, clustered about a central point as if protecting something precious. It was dangerous to stay longer, Walter thought, and of no real interest to him until a girl's voice rose over the sound of the fighting in a shrill scream of pure terror.

"Help! Lady Hereford, help me."

"Hew them down to a man if you must," was Ralph de Caldoet's harsh reply, "but do not harm the women. One among them is Hereford's bride. Our lord will make us all rich if we bring him this prize."

Walter pulled up so sharply that his horse nearly slipped. Lady Elizabeth! What was she doing here? He began to laugh, but carefully and silently. So the omniscient Roger had at last made a mistake. Good for him, let him win his own way free of it. He moved back into the shadow of the trees, and the sounds began to fade, but his mount moved ever more slowly as an unconscious guilt made his hand heavier and heavier on the rein. Finally the horse stopped. Who was the lord of whom they spoke? What did he want with Hereford's wife? Hereford's wife. Hereford was his name also and his father's. Roger said always that he brought shame upon his name. What shame? He touched his horse with his spurred heel. All men gained what they could for themselves in these black times. So he was worthless and shameful. Then let Roger mend the shame of sending his wife ill-protected through a country hostile to him. Fool. It was more shame to be a fool than a thief.

With a soft-muttered oath, Walter of Hereford turned his horse again and moved to the edge of the wood. It was his name and he would do as he liked with it, but no other man would smirch it under his very eyes and go scatheless. Now he could do nothing—one man on a tired horse—nothing but follow and see where his enemies went.

William Beauchamp yawned and rubbed his eyes. He wondered why, just because his master had given up sleep, he too must do so. They had ridden a day and a night, stopping only for an hour or two to rest the horses, from Wallingford to Devizes. After that it was true they had slept—for three hours. William could not even remember clearly the passing of the following days. They were full of scribes writing messages and riders going forth and returning. Men accoutered for war poured in from all sides and camped on the downs around Devizes, small parties riding forth day by day to spy out the countryside and to discover what they might about the king's advance.

Something had apparently delayed Stephen, possibly the rain which Hereford had wished for and which had certainly come in abundance. William wished that the elements had not been so thoroughly at the service of his master; he was tired of being wet and cold. He lifted his head, which had dropped to his breast, as Hereford's voice rose in argument against some proposal of Lord Storm's. Great leaders of a great army—William shook his head. No one looking at them now could tell the difference between the leaders and the meanest landless knight. Both were unkempt and unshaven with surcoats and chausses so splattered with mud as to make the original color unrecognizable. No, William thought, smiling grimly to himself, there was one way to recognize them. The lesser knights did not have eyes sunken an inch into their heads; they got to sleep once in a while.

He looked at his master consideringly. Sunken or not those eyes were bright and clear now as they had not been since the return to England. For all the hard labor, discomfort, and anxiety, it was plain that his master had recovered his spirits. He was ready to be merry whenever he had time, and nothing but outright disobedience to his orders seemed to have the power to discompose him. Perhaps it was the prospect of the fighting. William was looking forward to that himself because fighting behind Hereford's banner was thrilling and inspiring. He did hope, though, that he would be able to get some sleep before the battle took place; his head dropped forward onto his breast again.

Moments or hours later, he never knew which, he woke with a shock as a man-at-arms stumbled over his feet and fell headlong into the tent, crying out as he fell. William was on his feet at once, sword drawn to protect his master. For that there was no need, the man made no effort to rise; it was clear that he was at the end of his endurance.

"My lord," he gasped, "your lady is taken."

CHAPTER 8

THE FROZEN SILENCE following those painfully articulated words endured only for a moment. Hereford was on his knees beside his man, turning him face up roughly to recognize with horror that it was Alfred of the Southfield, truly one of the men sent to escort Elizabeth.

"By whom?" Where?"

"Easy, Hereford, you will throttle the man and he is sore wounded already. Beauchamp, wine. Lift his head and pour it down his throat."

"Where was she taken? By whom?" Hereford insisted, blind and deaf to all else, shaking the fainting soldier.

"I know not by whom. It was nearly dark and they set upon us so suddenly—. It was near Kettering, a mile or two north."

"Kettering! You lie!"

That gave the wounded man more strength than the wine. "My lord, I am your faithful servant and have ever been. I do not lie. Lady Elizabeth commanded us to go to Corby to your sister, and thither were we riding."

Hereford had turned a ghastly color, even his lips white.

"How long since?" That was Lord Storm, almost as pale but less disabled by shock.

"I do not know. They left me for dead, else I had not been here. I know not how long I lay beside the road nor how long I have been in coming hither. There was no other man alive there and no horse within sight or call. I crawled along that road till I came to the nearest cot. There I waited for night, stole a horse, and I have ridden since, when I could for weakness, stealing other mounts when that I had fell or wandered away."

"My God, my God," Hereford moaned, "what possessed her?" Before Storm could protest that this was no time for useless lamentation, however, he was in full control of himself. "Go call Elizabeth's and my own vassals to arms, Beauchamp. Let them take riding food only. We do not stop day or night until we come to Kettering."

"Wait, Hereford," Storm said, laying a comforting hand on his friend's shoulder. "Is it not possible that this is some trick to drive you and your men from a position of strength to where you may be easily destroyed?"

Cold and white, Roger of Hereford looked at his liege man's bloody face. "I do not think it. Go, Beauchamp. Alfred has ever been a true man to me, as he said, and to my father before me. What does it matter anyway," he added savagely. "Could I take such a chance? Would you?"

Grimly Storm shook his head. "No, I would not. But where shall we go, Roger? What use to go to Kettering? They would not keep her there. It is no small robber band that has taken your lady. Doubtless there is some purpose behind this and you will hear what—"

"Are you friend to me or enemy? Ay, I could wait here, wait until she was in the White Tower or a stronghold equally safe. What would be the price of her ransom then, think you? My lands? My faith? My head? What use to go to Kettering? Someone must have seen that troop and known who it was. Someone must have seen them passing later, bearing prisoners. I will have that information even if I must burn every house and cot and keep and rip the bowels from every man, woman, and child for a hundred miles around Kettering."

"So be it, Roger. I go bid my men also arm to ride."

"For what? If the king has her, which I greatly fear, you will lift no hand to help me for your oath. You had better stay here—"

"For the rape of my friend's wife I will lift my hand, oath or no oath, against any man. What can I do here? The keeps are safe against Stephen. There are yet no crops to burn. We can take no serious loss except the loss of the chance to defeat the king. I have three hundred good fighting men in my train, and we are like to need every man who will fight with a will."

They rode out hours before dawn, more than two thousand men, armed and angry, for Hereford had made plain the cause for which they rode. "Is that honor?" he had cried aloud. "Is the coward so much afraid of us that he needs to make war upon women traveling in peace?" And those who could hear passed the message through the ranks. Some of the men knew the hot-tempered and beautiful Lady Elizabeth because they belonged to her dower property and were her own men; some because they were Hereford's own troops and they had seen and heard her during the stays she and their lord had made in various strongholds. Many thought of their own wives and sisters who might be similarly treated, and all desired to right the wrong done their master.

Even in his haste, Hereford had chosen only those troops who would have a personal interest in this fight because a few men hot with rage were better for this kind of work than a huge army half-hearted and unwilling. Any man would fight when threatened, but it took a different kind of man to assault a well-defended keep, and that was exactly what Hereford planned to do when he found who had his wife prisoner.

Day dawned and the morning passed. Those who were hungry ate dried meat and hard bread on horseback and drank water from the leathers at their saddlebows. The sun reached its zenith and began to decline; still they rode, until the beasts went with hanging heads, stumbling at every unevenness on the track, while the men on their backs dozed in the saddle, too worn to be watchful. In all those hours the Earl of Hereford had spoken not one word, nor had he looked elsewhere than at the track before him. Lord Storm looked at him often, but forebore to break the silence. He could offer no comfort, and mere words at such a time were better left unsaid. In the dusk, however, he at last touched his companion.

"Hereford, call a halt. The beasts can go no further even though the men are willing to ride until they drop. Look, my own Fury and your Shadow can barely stand, what must be the state of the weaker beasts?"

Hereford looked at him sullenly. "We have miles yet to go."

"Not far. I do not know this country well, but I think not more than ten. The men must rest, Roger, if they are to fight."

"Very well. For an hour. We cannot arrive before nightfall anyway."

When they had dismounted and were about to eat, Hereford and Storm raised their heads simultaneously, looking into the gathering dusk across the fields toward their right.

"Ware arms! Horsemen to the right."

The tired men mounted again and drew their ranks closer, but only one horseman approached. Stopping at a respectable distance, he called out to know whom he faced.

"The Earl of Hereford. You have leave to approach but not to depart."

A clear laugh rang out. "You would be ill able to catch me, Roger, if I desired to go. My men and mounts are fresh, and we know this country well."

"Walter!" Hereford exclaimed. "What do you here? You should be across the breadth of England by now."

"To speak the truth, dear brother, I was waiting for you. I have had spies set on every northeast track for two days now. What delayed you? Did not my messenger reach you in good time?" The tone was light, a mocking triumph filling eyes and voice as Walter of Hereford approached and sat looking down at his brother.

"Messenger?" Hereford's face which had been white flamed suddenly. "What messenger?"

"Ah, now you are less anxious to have me across England. Nonetheless, dear brother, I am so eager to please you that, although I have something of note to say to you, I will gladly leave right now."

"Do not play with me, Walter. I am far past the mood for sport. If you have aught to do with my purpose in being here, I—"

"Roger!" Storm caught at his friend as he started forward.

"Sweet Roger, clever Roger—oh, stupider than any ass

to send your wife nearly unguarded into the hands of your enemies. Did you think the terror of your name alone—"

Storm's grip slipped as Hereford wrenched loose and tore his brother from the saddle. Too angry to reach for a weapon, he used his hands like a beast, seeking to tear the jugular from Walter's throat. His fingers were foiled of their purpose by the close-fitting mail hood, so that Storm had a chance to drag them apart and interpose his bulk between them. William Beauchamp and two others hurried up, permitting Storm to consign Walter to their care while he wrestled with Hereford himself.

"Hold him and let me speak," Walter gasped, "my precious, loving brother who tries to choke the life out of me before he will hear one word. God knows, I am close to holding my tongue and letting him sweat blood, but my revenge is too sweet."

"Say what you must and quickly," Storm growled, fighting to hold Hereford, "or I will stick you like a pig myself."

"Pig am I and foul? Evil am I and black? Always it is Walter that is black and Roger white. Why then did I go two days and a night without sleep or food to discover where the lady that bears the name Hereford was taken? You think I took her? You think I am so common that there is no deed too filthy for me to touch?"

The young man was trembling, his eyes filled with tears of pain and pride. Still clasped in Storm's arms, Hereford had stopped struggling. As far as Lord Storm could tell, he had stopped breathing too, so quiet had he become.

"What will you give me, Roger? What price will you pay for the news I bring?" Walter tried desperately and without success to keep the sobs from his voice.

One of the men holding him growled and spat. He took the sobs for fear and the words for open greed. Lord Storm, wiser by bitter experience, bit his lips. He could hear his own voice saying just such venomous words in the not distant past. He could have told much, had there been time, about what happens to a man whom others believe to be evil. But there was no time, and it was not his place to meddle between the brothers. He released Hereford and limped away; he would be witness to no more of this scene by his own will.

"Let him go," Hereford ordered his men. "William, pass the word for the men to dismount and take their rest."

"Do you not fear that I will bid my troop fall upon you in the dark for the booty you carry?"

Hereford ignored that. "Walk down the road a way with me, Walter. I am tired and cramped from riding. I would stretch my legs."

They moved off into the gathering dark silently.

"Well," Walter prodded with an ugly laugh, "what will you offer me? You are out of hearing now. Your men will know nothing of your chafering with your commoner of a brother."

"Nothing. I offer nothing, neither price nor threat. I have an hour's time—until the stars are clear, if we can see them. I would make my peace with you. Walter, for love, will you tell me—not where Elizabeth is, that you must do as you like about—tell me what man you sent as messenger to me."

Walter stopped and turned to face his brother squarely, striving to see his expression in the dark. "What difference can that make to you?"

"If it makes no difference, answer my question—if you please."

"How polite you are grown."

"Am I by custom so rude?" Hereford asked in a smothered voice.

"I do not believe you have ever used those words to me before. For them, then, not for love—you do not know the man, though he knew you, but his name was Red Olaf the Scot. Now are you the wiser?"

"Ay, I am the wiser and the sorrier too."

The anguish of guilt was so clear in Hereford's voice that Walter was startled, the more so as neither answer nor emotion made any sense to him. He had always been unaware, and always would be, of Roger's unease in dealing with him, because uncertainty was the one emotion that his brother had learned to mask completely. Walter noticed only the positive aggressiveness or condescending kindness with which Roger covered his sense of failure, and now he put down his brother's pain to hurt pride.

"Sorry? So you should be. The all-wise Hereford has made a mistake, and who must pull him out but the brother who can do nothing right. Nay, if you offered me the crown for the information I have I would not take it. I desire only that you know yourself for a fool and the satisfaction of hearing you beg me for the whereabouts of your lady."

"Your price is too low. I would beg on my knees the whereabouts of Elizabeth from the merest stranger—to you, Walter, I owe more, for I have wronged you and you are my brother. Will it ease your heart to see me on my knees, Walter?" Hereford took his brother's hand preparatory to kissing it as he kneeled, but Walter jerked away nearly oversetting them both with his violence.

"You make me sick," he stuttered, and although it was the literal truth he realized that there was something wrong. He should have been enjoying his triumph or have been filled with contempt; instead he felt frightened, as if he were about to lose something of importance, something without which he could not continue to live. "Nay," he added hurriedly, "if the woman means so much to you as that—. She is at Nottingham. Peverel has her."

Instead of thanking him, or for that matter cursing him and turning away, to Walter's amazement, Hereford made a sick sound and staggered. The younger brother caught the elder in an unkind but steadying grip. "What ails you, Roger? At least she is not yet in Stephen's hands. It could be worse."

"No," Hereford groaned, "no, it could not." And then, without thinking, racked for the first time by a real fear for Elizabeth's personal safety instead of the political danger to himself, he poured out the tale of her relationship with the Constable of Nottingham.

Walter listened without a sound, keeping his grip on his brother's arm. At last out of a stunned silence that had endured for several minutes after Hereford had stopped speaking, he said uncertainly, "He would not dare touch her. Not Hereford's wife." And there was no mockery in his use of the name then. "Have sense, Roger, he means only to give her to the king, for what could hurt you more?"

Hereford shuddered and made a defeated gesture. "I fear that it is not me that he wishes to hurt. Mary shield her—oh, my Elizabeth, my Elizabeth," he cried remorsefully. He had been so angry through all the long hours of the ride, dwelling with increasing rage upon the disaster that her thoughtlessness might bring upon him that he had not spared a thought for her fear or danger.

Tightening his already excruciating grip, Walter growled impatiently. "Brace up, man. Call your men and let us go. If this tale of yours is true—nay, he could mean no such insult I am sure, for he must know that to lay a hand upon her would be to write his death warrant—still, the sooner we wrest her from his grip the less the chance of trouble."

Hereford shook his head. "My men can go no further, Walter. Certainly not to assault Nottingham. We came from Devizes last night and we have ridden without rest since three hours before dawn."

"Fool! Fool again. Did you not trust my word—but no, I know you did not. I sent Red Olaf to you four days since, but you are so wise, you needed to believe me a liar and send to Hereford—"

"No, Walter. Your messenger never came. Do you not see that that is how I came to think—God forgive me—that you—"

"Never came! Then how did you know to come here? Where were you going?"

"One man of mine escaped and made his way to me. He knew no more than that they were set upon past Kettering, and I was going there to harrow the countryside until I found a man who could tell me who had taken my wife."

"What could have come of Olaf? He was as hard and trusty—never mind. It is true, however, that if your men have come from Devizes they will never win to Nottingham this night. So be it. I will go. I have five hundred armed men, fresh and ready. We will wake the Constable of Nottingham early. I will knock on the gate in such a way that he is not like to forget that Hereford will not be trifled with."

"Walter!"

"What now?" Hereford's face was invisible, but Walter stiffened at the familiar imperiousness of the tone. "Do not fear, the price for my service will not be too high," he sneered.

"If you do not have a care what you are about it may well be too high for me to pay. I will not pretend that I do not hold the woman very dear, but not so dear that for a day's more time I would sell my brother's life. You also are dear to me, and five hundred men will not take Nottingham Castle."

"I am no child to be thus chidden."

"Walter, if my tone was sharp, you must pardon me. I am so weary I can barely think. I do not mean to chide. You have done me a great kindness and are offering more—"

"You mistake me. I had no mind to do you a kindness. You are ever telling me I smirch the name of Hereford—well, if I do it is my own name and my own affair, but no man else will hold it lightly while I live or insult those under its protection. Take not unto yourself what I do for my own pride's sake."

"Whatever your reason, your actions have been kind, and I will take it for kindness. I have great need of kindness from you, Walter."

"You," the younger brother vented an ugly, jeering laugh, "you have need of nothing—you are perfect; beautiful of face, faithful of word, rich—let me go or I will lose my temper and not go at all."

He left Hereford standing in the road, and a few minutes later his troop thundered by, headed north. Roger returned slowly and gave orders that the men move off the road and make camp. They could rest until dawn, after which they would ride to the assault of Nottingham. He told Lord Storm briefly that Elizabeth was held by Lord Peverel, knowing that the fact that Peverel was a king's man would be sufficient explanation, and wrapped himself in his furred cloak to pretend sleep and escape discussion.

Lady Elizabeth was not asleep either. She had, indeed, slept very little since she had been taken six days previously, but it was not because she was frightened. She was only tormented by guilt. There was little doubt in her mind that she could hold Peverel at bay, and no doubt at all that Roger would come to her aid as soon as he knew where to go, but she was sick with the thought of what her freedom would cost him either in money or in men and time. Hour after hour, day after day, like a squirrel in a cage her mind circled seeking the smallest possibility of escape.

The first two days of her imprisonment had been horrible, for Peverel was not at Nottingham and the men had cast her into a foul den. She had been well fed but cold and uncomfortable, and she could hear nearby the groans of the wounded and dying men-at-arms that Hereford had sent to protect her without being able to give them aid or comfort. When Peverel had returned, she had been moved to much more comfortable quarters, though just as closely guarded. Personally, thus far, she had been treated with every courtesy, but when she had unbent from the attitude of scornful anger she had maintained so far as to ask politely that the men be eased, Peverel had laughed in her face.

Her women, also, had not fared overly well. They were with her now, but they had been brutally misused, first by de Caldoet, the captain of the group that had taken them, for he had the distorted nature which took pleasure only in unwilling women. When he was finished, he had cast them to his men. Peverel had finally returned them to her, but they were helpless and terrified still and Elizabeth knew that they would be of no assistance if she found a way to win free. She still hoped, but more and more faintly. She had no jewelry with which to bribe the guards, all had been taken from her. Nor did Peverel allow the same man to bring her food or mount guard for more than one day at a time. He in no way underestimated Elizabeth's cleverness or beauty. She did not even know where her men were being held with relation to her own prison, for she had been blindfolded and carried to her new quarters. All that she knew was that she was in a tower room and that it was an inner tower of the keep since each of the three arrow-slits showed only inner courts and gray stone walls.

A key grated in the lock, but Elizabeth did not look up. Peverel again, no doubt. Hands folded in her lap, her eyes upon them, she remained outwardly unaware of his presence.

"Good even, Lady Hereford."

No reply.

"Are you comfortable, my lady? Is there aught I can do for you?"

No reply.

"You do not ease your situation by this sullenness. Much might be gained by a little courtesy, Elizabeth."

She raised her eyes. "I will give you thanks if you will not foul my name with your tongue."

"You are not at all wise, madam," Lord Perevel snarled. "Do you not realize you are totally at my mercy? If I were you, I would mind my manners."

Elizabeth laughed and looked insolently up and down her captor. "If you were me, I would be groveling on the floor craving mercy, but I am not a miserable wretch who preys on women. Nonetheless, you have some merit for you have begun a good work. Men who have no quarrel with the king will rally to my husband to punish one who has unjustly and without provocation taken his wife prisoner. You, no doubt, will call on the king for help. Then will the battle be truly joined. And, if you do not call for help, how long will you endure against the might of Hereford, Chester, Lincoln, Gaunt—. Will you have me go on and list the names of those welded to Hereford and myself by blood and love?"

"You have said all this before, madam."

Ay, Elizabeth thought, and I shall say it again, for each time I do your face grows more uneasy.

"But you do not say how the Earl of Hereford will know where to find you. You know that every man who was not slain outright was taken prisoner."

Elizabeth wondered too, because although Roger would soon know, if he did not already, that she was missing, how he was to tell that she had gone east instead of west she could not guess. She did not allow the doubt to show in her face, however. The smallest sign of weakness would be the key that unlocked all of Peverel's malice, now held in check by the fears engendered by her calm and scornful manner.

"Doubtless when he does not hear that I have arrived safe at my destination he will follow my road to make inquiries."

"And what was your destination?"

For a brief flash Elizabeth felt as if she were merely having a bad dream, so often had they been over this conversation. "That is my affair," she answered, as if by rote.

"See here, Elizabeth, let us have done with this dicing. I have come here one last time. If you will be reasonable, I myself will send to your husband and he can have you—for a price. I know you think I am an enemy to you, but it is not so. I am very fond of you, very fond indeed. You can make all easy—"

He came closer, and Elizabeth drew back into her chair although her eyes held his.

"You have no choice anyway. If you are willing, I will sell you to Hereford; if you are not—" he laughed, but it was an ugly sound, "I will have my will of you anyway and then I will sell you to the king."

He was leaning over her then, and Elizabeth spat full in his face. Startled for the moment, Peverel stepped back and she had a split second's time to leap to the wall and seize a flaming torch.

"Back, cur, before I singe you. Have your will of me?" Elizabeth laughed too, on the border of hysteria, "You will need help for that. Go call your men and bid them take and bind me. Show yourself in your true light—so weak, so foul, such a craven coward that one feeble woman, alone and helpless, a prisoner in your keep can hold you at bay. Back, I say, I will set your clothes alight and give you a foretaste of what you will come to in the hereafter."

For a while Peverel merely gasped with fury. He would have killed her then, could he have got at her, but he soon recovered. Self-interest ruled even his lust and he knew without being told that Elizabeth was the kind who would gladly destroy herself to gain revenge. He had thought that a week's isolation without hope would frighten her enough to make her yield to win her freedom. Had her spirit broken, she would have held her tongue to protect herself. As it was, if he forced her she would not be still. She would cry aloud to the world what he had done and sooner or later, whether he recovered her or not, Hereford would hear. Peverel was brave enough for the ordinary chances of war and life but not brave enough to face the thought of the relentless quest which would be sparked by that insult. He had known Miles of Hereford, and it was plain that his fierce pride burned in the spirits of his sons. Even if Roger of Hereford did not care for his wife, the infamous act he had planned could not go unavenged. Peverel felt himself go cold. Even now he had gone further than was safe, perhaps. If Hereford took him, it would not be for ransom or to kill. Death would be a thing to pray for and plead for. There was no other way to be safe in this but to be rid of the woman. For a moment Peverel coldly considered killing her, but that would not help, for it was known in Kettering that his troops had been there shortly after Hereford's men passed through. He could not muzzle the whole town. His greatest safety and profit would lie in sending her to the king at once with no dickering over price. Then if Hereford came he could deny that she was there, even open the keep to him and allow him to search. He would have to admit that his men had taken her, but he could truly say he was not at home at the time and that they had carried her direct to the king.

Elizabeth was doubly fortunate that Peverel did not know that she had told her husband of his earlier attempts on her or that Hereford really had no idea of her destination. His knowledge of either of those two facts would have been her death warrant for the first would have pushed his fear past the point of reason and the second would have given him a great although erroneous security.

"Very well, madam, have it your own way. Plainly my desire had blinded me temporarily to your need for chastening, but your torch has shown me the light. At dawn tomorrow you will be taken to the king and queen. No doubt your husband will rejoice greatly to hear of your safety. No doubt his joy will be such that he will be happy to have you as hostage for his loyal behavior to King Stephen."

Elizabeth gasped and went white. Not for an instant had she thought that Peverel would yield his prize to another, at least not without force or long bargaining. The torch trembled for the first time in her grip and her eyes stung with tears. For a moment she was so shocked and terrified that she considered casting away her weapon and yielding. Anything seemed better than knowing that she—out of pure spite—had brought disaster upon all of her husband's plans and dreams.

She was never given the opportunity, and even if she had acted Peverel would not have accepted her offer now. Her terror had salved his pride, and he suddenly saw that sending her to Stephen without asking a price for her would be a triple act of genius. Not only Hereford but Chester too could be controlled if Elizabeth were in Stephen's grip, and he, who had put this power into the king's hand, would be raised higher than ever in the royal estimation. High enough, very likely, for an earldom of his own. Peverel laughed all the way back to his quarters, thinking of Hereford and Chester dancing on a chain which he could twitch as he liked.

He lay in the dark somewhat later that night, remembering Elizabeth's blanched face and terror-filled eyes. It was not any man he told himself, who could make Elizabeth Hereford tremble, and his ego was such that he never realized that it was not Peverel Elizabeth feared but Hereford.

Another man was seeing Elizabeth Hereford's face that night, not as it was then but as it had been a week since. Alan of Evesham, temporarily free of the fever which had been consuming him, cast his mind back to the orders given by her ladyship that dawn. He tried to remember every word she had used, every expression on her face, seeking for a clue that would indicate whether Lord Hereford knew of their destination. It was useless. It had been too long ago and he was not, at the time, paying close enough attention. One of them had to get out. One man must win free to his lordship even if it cost the lives of all the rest, for he had news thrown at him by a guard when he asked about her ladyship's welfare that sometime very soon she would be transported elsewhere. That was the moment to strike. No matter how large the force traveling with her, it would be easier to overwhelm them in the open than to take Nottingham keep, and once gone from Nottingham, God alone knew where they would hide her.

If Lord Hereford did not know where his lady was and was searching to the north, a man might bring him in time to strike down the party moving her, if he did know, then someone must warn him not to strike and not to make his presence known for a day or two. Alan of Evesham closed his eyes, and tears of weakness, pain, and despair ran down his face. It was such a tiny, tiny hope, so far away. How was a man to get free? All were wounded and even those who had been lightly hurt were now much weakened by near starvation and the effects of the filth and vermin of their prison. If one was to go, which one? He could not; he tried again to move and groaned aloud. He did not even know who of his men were left to him, or where to tell a man to seek his lordship except at Devizes; and, if Lord Hereford were at Devizes still, he could not come in time or, if he were in the district prepared for battle, it was too late to hide his presence and Peverel would not dare send her ladyship forth.

He lay and wept, hopeless and ashamed, crying out softly to his Maker that he wished for death. He had failed his master and only God knew what that failure would bring. That state of mind did not last long. Alan of Evesham was of too tough a fiber to yield to despair without struggling until his last breath was drawn. He steadied his voice and spoke quietly to the man close beside him, instructing him to begin a tally of their numbers and their state. Each man was to give his name and the nature of his hurts. Nearest neighbors passed the word along and passed messages back. Those who could walk felt their way along in the unrelieved darkness to squat down around Sir Alan. In spite of all they were so oriented that their spirits rose because their leader was, to some degree, functioning again. At least he could talk and think. The men were so trained to obedience that the loss of a leader who would give them orders and tell them what to do was more terrifying to their spirits and weakening to their bodies than the dark, cold, and hunger.

Forty-seven, there were forty-seven men in that room. There had been halts in the flow of information from time to time when a man found that the thing next to him did not answer, but by then those who could move easily were helping with the count and in half an hour Sir Alan had his information straight. Of the forty-seven, twenty-three were conscious and able to move, eleven more, including himself, were conscious but too badly hurt to be of help, three were unconscious and as good as dead, and ten were dead. Twenty-three men out of a hundred who had started. Alan of Evesham winced; never while he was Hereford's master-at-arms had he lost such a tally of men.

The voices murmured low; after Sir Alan had stated what they were to do—get one man or two free to ride for help—they felt that their lives had direction again and they were willing to offer suggestions on how best to accomplish their ends. Who was to go was quickly enough decided. Adam, the tanner's son, dark of hair, of medium build, and without any scarring that could make him noticeable had been knocked unconscious by a blow on the head but had received no other hurt. He was still fairly strong, not too stupid, and very trusty. If chance offered for more than one, Herbert, the huntsman's nephew would accompany him. Here the talk faltered a bit. To decide who was to attempt to escape was easier than suggesting how that attempt should be made. None of them knew Nottingham keep, so that there were problems beyond merely passing the locked door.

"Water," Alan said faintly. "Is there any water? I am perishing for a drink."

A leather was held to his mouth. "If you can drink it, you must be near perishing."

Foul it was, and something moved in it as Alan drank so that he gagged. Nonetheless it was liquid.

"We can plan no further than the door," the master-at-arms said finally. "There is no sense in wasting thought and time on what we cannot even guess about. This much I know from what you have told me. We have lain so still that they are grown somewhat careless. Two men or even one alone bring this—" his term was so foul that the men laughed softly because Alan was usually fair-spoken, "that they call food. How long do they stay? Fifteen seconds? Thirty? In that time, not longer, they must be overpowered without a sound. You understand? Without any sound—no ring of mail on stone, no grunt, no whisper. They must be divested of garments and Adam and Herbert clothed in their stead. Pray God they wear helmets with nosepieces."

A little time longer was spent in polishing the plan, Alan trying to suggest a pattern of behavior to his men which would make them inconspicuous. They were to relock the door, the others could not go anyway without arms or weapons. They were to go without haste, always outward. There must be many new men in Peverel's forces and they should claim to be such if they were questioned. They should ask their way boldly to an obvious place like the kitchens. He stopped speaking at last, exhausted by his hopelessness and his pain, grateful for the darkness which hid his quivering lips and streaming eyes from the men so that they at least could continue to hope. It was better that they should not know how impossible it was for the plan to work, for they were not bred, as Alan was, to set duty above all else. Everything rested on a thread of chance, and the thread was so very, very slender.

"God help us," he sighed.

"God help us," the men murmured devoutly. It was no time to doubt God.

CHAPTER 9

———◦◦——◦◦◦◦——◦◦———

"My Lord!" Peverel's squire was crying aloud and shaking him. Peverel came reluctantly awake from a very pleasant dream. "My lord, the village is in flames. Some enemy is upon us."

"What?" Peverel shrieked, starting up. "Who is it?"

"I do not know, my lord. Thus far not a soul has come up from the village and the guards have lifted the drawbridge and closed the gates."

From the battlement Peverel saw that his squire had spoken no more than the truth. The village was certainly in flames and what remained of the ricks were burning, too, as was the stubble in the fields. Then Elizabeth had spoken the truth and Hereford had found her. No one but a man mad with rage would cause such wanton destruction as to burn the ricks, after all he had to feed his own men and mounts. But how had he come questioning through Kettering without the spies Peverel had set in that town hearing of him or seeing the host? A treacherous man suspects all others of being the same, and Peverel muttered to himself of what he would do to those faithless hounds when he laid his hands upon them. He could tell nothing of the raiders, not even their numbers, although now and again a man spurred past one of the fires and the light glittered on helmet and drawn sword. It would soon be dawn, however, and they would then know enough. Now Peverel was frightened. He had been so sure he would have more time and adequate warning. He could send for the king and he knew that Nottingham Castle was strong and well stocked. It could withstand a long siege, but men who burned ricks of fodder were not planning a siege. Nor, apparently, were they planning to wait

180

before Nottingham until help could come to him; they were planning to attack, and at once as far as he could tell. Well, let them try to assail the walls. As long as he was not drawn out into the open, he would suffer little loss and they would suffer greatly. Peverel looked out at the fires and tried to steel his nerves. He assured himself of the strength of his fortress and swore to God that no trick of his enemy would lure him or his men out of the castle until they showed themselves openly and he knew what force he had to contend with.

Orders rang throughout the keep; the archers mounted the outer walls first, bows ready, staring through the darkness for a mark. Under their protection others made ready the remaining defenses of the outer walls. The round stones for the trenchbuts were moved to more commodious positions and the leather ropes that operated them were tested for brittleness, replacements laid ready in case they should tear. Heavy-shafted, iron-shod arrows for the catapults were also carried up from the storehouses in the bailey where they were kept, and the operators of these machines oiled the great wooden screws that drew back the thongs so that they would turn smoothly, whispering endearments to their instruments of death. Those shafts could pierce a horse right through the body and made no work at all of tearing through a ringed-mail hauberk.

In the inner keep fires were set under huge cauldrons of fat and pitch. These would be kept boiling hot, to be poured down trap doors and over the walls should the attackers penetrate the outer defenses, and large stones were set on the battlements to be pushed over for the same purpose. On the north side of the castle a rather sharp drop in the land eliminated both the need for and the possibility of a moat. Here the largest numbers of defenders were concentrated, armed with hooked staves to push over scaling ladders as well as the ordinary weapons.

It depended, Peverel thought, pacing the walls and seeing that all was progressing according to order, on how large a force Hereford had brought and how many men he was prepared to lose. If he had brought enough men and was so furious as to count no cost, even Nottingham keep could be taken. The Constable of Nottingham was shaken with a dreadful indecision. There might still be a chance if he sent out half a dozen riders now under cover of darkness that one would win through to the king. The trouble was that such a plea for help would commit him to holding his keep without attempting to come to terms with Hereford. Peverel shook his head and muttered that such behavior was foolish. Hereford might have only a small force and might be beaten back without help. Also he had a very powerful bargaining point in Lady Elizabeth and might come to terms very profitable to himself. On the other hand, Stephen was very undependable in such matters. He might not come at all or might dally until too late. Peverel growled that an ill master was worth only ill service and decided to do both. He would send to Stephen who knew nothing of his captive and parley with Hereford also. If he came to terms with the latter, he need only lie to Stephen and say that the besiegers had grown weary seeing that Nottingham was well defended and had departed, or even that he had joined battle and defeated them. He even had prisoners—Hereford's men—to give credence to the tale. His own men's mouths could readily be stopped with gold, they were used to it. At the worst he could say that he was overmatched and had to make treaty lest the keep be taken and the lands destroyed.

If he could delay Hereford with parley until Stephen came, his position would be even better. Hereford would be trapped between two fires, his pride well humbled, and he himself could keep his captive, sell her for ransom, or sell her to the king as a hostage. Peverel's spirits had risen while he considered these alternatives, but they soon fell again. It was entirely likely that Hereford would wait for no parley but would attempt the keep with the coming of dawn. Peverel shuddered and wrenched his thoughts away from his fate if the castle should fall, but he had a plan even for that eventuality. When the attack came, he would stay near the tower where Elizabeth was kept prisoner. If things went ill with them, he could retreat to her chamber, bar the door, and bargain for his life and freedom against hers. He was sure that if he threatened

Hereford with killing her and himself the young bridegroom would yield him anything reasonable.

"De Caldoet," he said, turning to the large, brutal man beside him. Peverel had taken Ralph de Caldoet into his service after that knight's own greed and ferocity had ruined him. He was a dangerous man, even when well paid, for he was totally untrustworthy, but no one, it was said, even Hugh Bigod, Earl of Norfolk, or Cain, Lord Storm, was a better jouster, and few men could match him on foot with a sword either. These qualifications were adequate recommendation to Peverel whatever type of beast a man resembled, and thus far he had no cause to regret his choice. He was becoming conscious, however, that it was easier to gain de Caldoet as a retainer than to rid oneself of him if he became unnecessary. Peverel had been about to order de Caldoet to command the defense of the outer walls when suddenly a notion that gave him much pleasure lit up his eyes.

"De Caldoet," he repeated, "how would you like to have a keep of your own again—perhaps even several?"

The big man beside him at first made no reply, only turned upon him the small, mad, greedy eyes of an old boar. The voice, when it came although gratingly harsh, was cautious. "Such things do not fall from heaven without aid. What I like and just how much I will do to gain what I like do not always lie together."

"Nay, de Caldoet, you will enjoy the doing as much as the prize for it. What do you say to the chance to kill Roger, Earl of Hereford or to make him crawl and crave mercy?"

"All I need do," de Caldoet answered, looking out across the moat to the raging fires, "is to pluck him out of that little crowd he brought, eh?" He laughed and shook his head. "Find another cat to pull your hot chestnuts from the fire."

"No, no," Peverel said impatiently. "I do not think you a fool, and you need not think that I am. What I desire to know is whether, if I can arrange a duel, you will fight him. Besides, the chestnuts are yours also. Hereford will scarcely love you when he discovers that it was you who took his wife and slaughtered his men."

At that de Caldoet's eyes seemed to become even smaller, a red glow of greed and hatred flickering in their
depths. Still he was cautious. "Him alone I fear not. He is
a good man, but no match for me. What warrant will I
have, though, that when I have him down his men will
not fall upon me."

"If you are sure you can beat him, all else will be arranged to your satisfaction—you can make the arrangements yourself. If things do not suit you, you need not
fight."

De Caldoet's glance strayed again to the occasional figure of a knight passing like an evil phantom before the
flames. The only thing on earth that he had ever loved
was the earth itself. To burn the earth was the only
outrage he had ever considered a sin and now he snarled
with fury as a ball of fire flew high in the air over the
moat and fell into the bailey. Greek fire. Another rose and
this time hit its mark. A storehouse with a thatched roof
began to burn. Cries of fear from the serfs mingled with
quick shouted orders from the men-at-arms. De Caldoet
shrugged, but he was angry.

"If he does not fall upon us tonight and end it all, I will
kill him for you."

When Lord Peverel had left her, Elizabeth had stood
quietly for a long time. She was alike unconscious of fatigue or of the maids weeping hysterically on their pallets.
She was not even really conscious of thought or fear for
she was in a state of shock. At last her muscles relaxed of
their own accord and the torch fell to the ground. Starting
as if awakened from sleep, Elizabeth, finally moving, did
not seem to be able to stop. Back and forth she paced the
rather narrow confines of her prison, back and forth while
her mind moved from one phase of self-condemnation only
to a still bitterer one. She knew only too well the pressure
that could be exerted on Roger through her captivity, for,
free of her wrath, she knew he loved her. Her father too
would press him to conform with the king's wishes for her
sake, and beyond that, the king might try to claim her
dower revenues for her support while he held her which
would hurt Roger when he needed money most. Stephen

might easily succeed too, for those barons did not yet really recognize Hereford as their overlord and would likely be very happy to free themselves from his closer dominion by paying their dues to the king. Stephen was much further away, a far weaker man, and by virtue of both of those facts far less likely to interfere in what they considered their private concerns.

Elizabeth did not weep; her grief and self-loathing were too deep for lamentation. It was well that everything that could be remotely thought of as a weapon had been taken from her, for just then, with less than ever to fear on her own account, she was desperate enough to take her own life in removing herself as a threat to her husband. With her own hands, as she sometimes spun wool into yarn, she had spun the rope that would bind her husband's hands. Never had Roger himself seemed so dear, his integrity so precious.

"Why cannot the punishment fall upon the sinner?" she cried. "What will he do, blameless as he is of evil in this matter, what will he do, torn between his oath to protect me and his oath to support Henry? Is this a choice a just and merciful God gives a man, a choice of doing only evil to those who trust him no matter which way he turns?"

How long she had been walking she did not know, but the sound of her own voice roused her somewhat from the inner recesses of her own mind and, as if in answer to her question, flung defiantly at the feet of God, she heard the tumult in the castle. For another long period she clung to one arrow-slit or another, fearing that her desire was deceiving her eyes and ears, but at last it became sure that the men of Nottingham Castle were preparing to defend it. Roger! Elizabeth's heart leaped. Roger had come. Now tears came, too, and she went down on her knees to give thanks to God for what seemed to her like a miracle. She was not thanking God for her deliverance, she never gave that a thought, and if she had she would have realized that freedom was no closer and personal peril was. All Elizabeth cared for in that moment was that Peverel would never be able to carry out his threat and use her as a chain to bind her husband.

The men imprisoned in the lowest chamber of the north

tower were even slower than Elizabeth to realize that the keep was arming for defense. This was in no way due to lack of vigilance on their part but to the excellent construction of the towers of Nottingham. There were no windows, not even arrow-slits, in the area in which they were confined, and the walls at the tower base were close to twelve feet thick. No sound could come through that depth of stone and earth, and at first no one came near enough the small grilled opening in the heavy oak door to be seen or heard.

Alan of Evesham emerged easily from a light, feverish doze. He took his responsibilities to his men and his master very seriously and was receptive for that reason to very slight changes in the atmosphere around him. Just now, however, he did not trust himself. The fever would make his ears abnormally sensitive, it was true, but it also might deceive them completely by confounding imagination with reality. He lay and listened, trying to localize the sounds in the dark, then sighed and closed his eyes again. He had heard the clang of arms it seemed, but he knew that to be impossible. He had been dreaming, he supposed, of the past or hoping for the future; they could fight against the very walls of the tower without sound coming through. Then he was staring into the darkness again. He could not be dreaming, for there was the sound still and it was coming from above him. Sir Alan almost laughed. He might easily dream in his fever, but not of battles in heaven. His smile was short lived as he strained to hear better; there could be no doubt that in the chamber above men were moving arms. But why?

"Herbert," Alan whispered.

"Yes, sir?"

"Who has been watching at the door grill? Bid him come here."

A hand fumbled at his feet, slid gently up his leg. "Sir?"

"Have you seen aught?"

"Ay. Men have come running up the stairs and down carrying arms."

"You blackhearted idiot! Why did you not tell me?"

"None came here. You said to warn the men when they came to bring us food."

Sir Alan ground his teeth as well as he could for pain; he had been much cut about on the face. "Ass! If we ever get out of this alive, I will have you flayed. How long?"

"As long as it might take to go a mile at a foot pace."

"Herbert."

"Sir?"

"Spread the word among the men—but quietly—that they should seek along the walls and floors for anything, metal, sharp stones, the buckles of their belts, anything that may be used to pick the lock or work around the wood and loosen it."

"Sir Alan," Herbert protested, "that door is oak as hard as iron itself, and the lock is no child's plaything. Our first plan is better."

"Oh God, why am I cursed with a troop of moonlings? Did you not hear? The keep is under attack. Why do you think men came to carry arms? Do you think they will stop to bring us food? I know not who Lord Peverel's enemies may be, but if enemy to him then friend to us, and my heart cries out that it is our own lord seeking his lady and his men. Mayhap we will not win free, but will you sit here in the dark while your lord fights and not try to give him aid?"

He stopped, gasping with weakness, but he had said enough. The spirits of the men near enough to hear rose almost to gladness. The insults and threats of their captain were old familiar friends, indicating to his men only that he was feeling better, and they had all been with Hereford in desperate situations before. His name was, to them, almost a magic password of success.

"The earl is come."

"Lord Hereford has come for us."

The words were whispered from man to man together with the orders of Alan of Evesham. Hastily but carefully, one man still watching at the door to guard against surprise, the search was begun. Patient hands, hard as the pitiful implements they found to use with much handling of weapons, began to work at the wooden frame near the lock and around the lock seated in the door. That the task was very nearly hopeless did not discourage them; at least there was work to be done.

With rage and disbelief Lord Peverel had watched the first cask of Greek fire, a flaming mixture of tar, pitch, and oil, fly over the outer wall. The second, which set a storehouse in the bailey alight, sent him into violent action. He shouted at de Caldoet to send out messengers to the king and to assume the defense of the outer walls. He himself would hold the inner keep, he added in a voice which he managed to keep firm only by a great effort. He need not have bothered, for de Caldoet was not likely to be deceived by a firm tone in a man who abandoned his outer defenses to another before they were even threatened. The mercenary was a trifle surprised. Peverel was not ordinarily a coward, although he plainly was no man to cling to his courage in a forlorn hope. De Caldoet could only assume that Peverel knew more about the strength of the attackers than he admitted. Well, well, de Caldoet thought, that was no problem. If they were too strong, he would open the gates to them upon promise of freedom for himself and his men. He would even help them take the inner keep for a price, and there was no doubt he would get his price for he knew the castle well and could be invaluable to his master's enemies. At present there was no particular danger and he could afford to stand his ground.

Peverel was thinking very similar thoughts as he made for the great inner donjon with rather unseemly haste. He recognized the irrationality of his behavior but could do nothing about it because a cold fear had a grip on him that he could not shake. His mind was sure that Nottingham could not be taken if well defended and that he had done the one thing that could endanger it. Nonetheless he was terrified, too shaken to give orders to urge his men to fight. In fact it had taken all his strength not to seize a horse, order a company to follow him, and ride away. All he could do now was to hide until he could command himself again. To try to command his men in the state in which he was, was to make cowards of them all by convincing them their situation was hopeless.

In the gray light of a dawn that promised more rain, Walter of Hereford drew rein on a rise to consider how best to trouble Peverel. He had no expectation of being able to storm the keep with five hundred men, for he had none of the machines or weapons necessary for such an effort. Nor, in spite of his elder brother's fears, was he mad enough to try to take Nottingham Castle by surprise. He could, however—the thought stopped dead in his mind as his eyes took in the landscape before him. Burnt out! It was burnt out, and lately. Smoke was still curling lazily from the ruins of ricks and huts. Walter raised his eyes from the fields to the walls of Nottingham. There was fire within the keep also!

The first notion that came to him with a flash of rage was that his brother had made a fool of him again and had beaten him to the attack. He very nearly cried out and ordered his men to charge. He was, however, an experienced soldier in spite of his youth and was restrained by his own good sense. It was impossible. Even if Hereford had lied and his men were fresh he could have come no quicker, and what he gazed upon was the work of several hours. Walter frowned. The Constable of Nottingham had many enemies, but unfortunately not all of them would, for that reason, be friends to Hereford. It was plain enough from what he saw, however, that Nottingham keep was in no immediate danger of falling into the hands of its foes. Walter lifted the mail band under his helmet to scratch his forehead. What now? He could see no sign of the raiders, had no idea of their strength or even where they were. One thing alone was certain; he could not sit there forever. They would have to move one way or another soon because the darkness was rapidly yielding to morning and in that scorched area there was no place to hide.

Walter turned his head to speak over his shoulder. "Let four men ride back along our trail seeking my brother Hereford. Say unto him that Nottingham is already afire but not by me, and that he should make all haste to join me here. Send another twelve round about to see who has set these flames, but let them have a care not to fall into the hands of the raiders. I have no desire yet that they should know we are here. Let the men ride a little below the ridge also, that they do not show themselves when the sun rises." Without more ado he dismounted, his squire running up to take his horse, and lay down on the ground.

It was cold and damp, but he was used to that. It might take his men ten minutes or two hours to return with the information he wanted and he would use the time for rest because there might well be heavy fighting ahead.

The messengers found Hereford without difficulty, and the army made what speed it could. The horses were still tired, however, and the terrain difficult so that it was midmorning before Hereford finally flung himself off his mount and shook his brother awake.

"I have half killed us getting here, Walter. It is good to find you so much at ease. What the hell is going forth?"

"You need not knock the teeth out of my head. Why should I not take my ease? Our work is being done for us—look."

They walked to the rise and looked over the fields which were no longer smoking but lay black and sodden under the light drizzle. Nothing moved in those fields nor, as far as either of the men of Hereford could tell, in the keep itself. The drawbridge was up, the gates tight shut; if a man moved on the battlements, it was impossible for him to be seen from where they stood. At that hour of the morning there should have been work parties going and coming in time of peace or war parties going out to make forages against the enemy in time of war. Strangest of all was the fact that there was not a sight or sound of the attackers.

Walter looked into his brother's puzzled blue eyes. "So it has been since I came. Then the fields were still burning and there was fire in the keep too, but not a man have we seen except the slain in the village."

"For what do they wait? Why do they not come out, more especially since there is no army camped before them."

"Why ask me? I have been waiting here since dawn for that very thing, thinking to fall upon them and take to myself credit for what I have not done. He who has thus laid his shoulder to our wheel is gone like smoke in the air."

Hereford shrugged and turned to consult Lord Storm, who had not dismounted. Roger was not as blankly surprised at finding Nottingham under attack as his brother was, since he had had a hand in arousing feeling against

Peverel in more than one quarter. He could not, however, understand the tactics being used. It was mad to fire the fields and the keep and then ride away. Still he could not doubt the word or efficiency of Walter's men who had sought for miles around and found nothing. The quiet prevailing over the castle itself was also a puzzle, unless—unless the keep was already taken, the battle over when Walter arrived.

"No." Storm replied definitely to that. "It could not be. At the least there would be wains carrying forth the plunder. I do not know what this bodes, Hereford, but I say we are big enough. What profit to sit here wondering? Let us go down and camp on the fields before the keep, let us cry our defiance, and take him if we can."

"Walter?" Hereford questioned, turning to his brother with deliberate courtesy.

The younger man looked up in surprise. His brother was much more in the habit of telling him what to do than asking his opinion. Such deference made him suspicious, but he could see nothing in Hereford's face or manner that was not reasonable in the circumstances.

"We can do naught else unless you think to tempt them out by showing only a small portion of our men. Somehow, I do not think they will fight unless we attack, no matter how we move. I am willing to do as Lord Storm suggests."

They had, in fact, little other choice. There was no longer any chance of storming the keep by surprise, although Hereford had never counted much upon that opportunity anyway. Most castles were always on guard and quickly defended and Peverel's surely would be because he was cordially hated by most of his neighbors. They could have done little more than what was already accomplished for them, except, perhaps, to have kept the livestock and grain to feed themselves and their horses. The men moved down over the rise in a long column behind their leaders and around the keep well out of arrow range. Somewhat beyond the embers of the village a camp was begun while Storm, Hereford, and Walter continued around to see what they could learn of the construction of the keep and the lay of the land.

It took them about half an hour, for they went slowly and then more slowly, looking at the gray stone walls and looking even oftener at each other. Not a sound came from within the walls, not an arrow was loosed at them, not a sign of movement did they see. The silence weighed on the spirit. It gave the feeling that eyes, not human and angry but cold and dead, watched from behind dead walls. On the north side of the castle they stopped. Without the elaborate equipment for the assault of a keep which might take weeks to build, this was the place to attack. By common consent, yet without speaking a word, they moved closer to the walls, closer still, tempting the bowmen to make them a mark—nothing.

"Can they be all dead?" Hereford murmured, somehow unwilling to break in upon the stillness with a normal speaking voice. He had the feeling that if he spoke aloud he would wake something horrible behind the quiet walls.

The others too suffered from the same sensation, and for a long minute they were still. Suddenly the tension was too much for Walter. His sword sang with the swiftness with which he drew it, and he clashed it against the metal bosses of his shield, waking echoes and crying out, "Come out. Come out and fight, you rotting lepers. You toads who eat filth—fight—or open your gates and make way for men to enter."

Storm and Hereford half raised their shields now expecting the hail of shafts so long delayed, but nothing came except one coarse laugh. A postern door, so cleverly concealed that they never would have seen it, opened surprisingly near them. A man, as large as Lord Storm, even heavier, and a good deal uglier appeared in it.

"Come in, my little cockerel, if you will. Mayhap on our dung heap you will not crow so loud. It might be also that you will crow to get out even more vainly than you crow to come in."

Hereford's horse was in front of Walter's, blocking his, even before he could set spurs to it, but the spell was broken. The earl's clear laugh rang out shattering the stillness again. "Upon your kind invitation, O avowed dweller in a dung heap, we will come. But we are the masters here. We will come in our own time and in our own way. Tell

your master for me that Roger, Earl of Hereford, comes to
reclaim his jewel from the dross." His face grew suddenly
so grim that even de Caldoet was a trifle shaken. "He may
save his life and his keep by sending her out to me with
my men, but if there is one stain of his filth upon her, I
shall not leave one stone standing upon another to mark
this place, nor will gold or blood buy either his freedom or
his death."

All three turned and galloped away, the arrows they
had vainly expected before singing around them now. Fortunately they took no hurt, and when they drew up out of
bowshot, Hereford laughed again. He clapped his brother
heartily on the shoulder. "Good for you, Walter. You
pricked the fool and he showed us the gateway to our
desire. Let us mark the place well. My heart, too, is
lighter, for I had almost thought they were under some
evil enchantment."

In a way Hereford was correct and the keep enchanted.
The spell of Peverel's fear was spreading, paralyzing the
defenders and filling them with despair and the expectation of defeat. That was the price paid when men fought
largely for reasons of personal loyalty. Since they had no
goals of their own to strive for, they responed to the slightest sign of discouragement or weakness in their leaders. De
Caldoet could have given them confidence, for he certainly
was not yet afraid, but he did not care to stiffen their morale before he was sure whether fighting or yielding would
pay him better. He climbed rapidly back up to the battlements to watch the three companions ride off around the
keep to return to their camp. Then with a half smile he
went to bring Hereford's message to Peverel. Partially he
wished to judge whether Peverel really did know anything
more of Hereford's strength than was apparent, and partially he simply wished to enjoy watching Peverel squirm.
He had that pleasure, but not to the degree he had expected, and the information he gained was of an entirely different sort. Peverel had spent the night hatching a plan
for saving his skin in any event and one which he hoped
would gain his ends without endangering his keep. To this
plan de Caldoet listened and agreed, although he would
be the one to take what risk there was. He would also

stand to gain a good deal, and from his point of view the risk was small.

Peverel's chief squire was armed and sent as a herald to Roger of Hereford's camp. His message was brief. If Hereford would agree to his safe coming and going, de Caldoet would meet him in the field before the drawbridge to discuss terms of peace before useless damage be done to Hereford's men and Peverel's. The herald was instructed to cry his message aloud in the camp, not to give it to Hereford privately. Peverel knew that this would force Hereford to come to the meeting even if he was unwilling to do so, because he could not chance that his men would think he was afraid or that he would sacrifice them needlessly.

"It is a trap," Lord Storm said.

"The coward will yield us all," Walter laughed.

Hereford pulled the lobe of his ear, a worried frown wrinkling his brow. He did not believe either of his companions to be wholly right or wholly wrong. It did seem likely that Peverel was afraid, from his behavior, but that a man so completely devoted to his own self-interest could mean to yield so easily seemed impossible. Nor was it likely that even a treacherous brute like de Caldoet would take the chance of attacking him in the full sight of his army with his friend and his brother free to direct a fearful retaliation. De Caldoet's death in such an event would be certain, and he was too self-interested a creature to take such a risk.

"What surety of safety does de Caldoet ask?"

The herald was primed for that one and he called the answer loud enough for many of the armed men pressing close to hear. "None but your vaunted good word. Lord Peverel holds your household guard. If you betray his man he will send you a piece of each prisoner he has. So tender a master as you are reputed to be would not sacrifice your men and your honor for one stroke which could gain you nothing."

"Tell your master that I will come and be as tender of his emissary as if he were my own flesh and blood. But he can gain nothing by talk. He would do better to send out my wife and my men at once. I will make no peace for lesser terms."

Hereford turned away, rubbing his unshaven chin. Everything that had happened in the past three days had the quality of his constantly recurring nightmare, even though the events which had taken place and which he dreamed were not related. There was the same sense of pursuing an unknown goal in the midst of events that were totally inexplicable and beyond his control. Once again he felt like a stuffed puppet performing antics directed by someone else's will.

"If you go, Roger, I go too." That was Lord Storm, for once breaking impatiently into Hereford's thoughts.

"I also."

"No," Hereford replied slowly. "One of you at least must remain behind to lead the men in the small chance that Peverel does intend treachery. I ask you, Walter, to take that duty. You are my heir. Miles is too young to avenge us. Peverel could look for no greater temptation than that you and I should come under his hand together."

Walter burst out laughing. "You are a fool, Roger. How do you know this is not set between Peverel and myself? The temptation you offer me is greater than that you offer him. You are giving the Earldom of Hereford into my hand."

"If you want it on those terms, Walter, you are welcome to it. Much joy may you have of gain so gotten." Hereford dismissed that comment without a thought. "Storm, you should have more sense. Why stretch your neck for the ax blow when there is no need?"

"Have you never taken your head in your hands for my sake? Besides, I am curious to see this de Caldoet who even William of Gloucester could not stand. His brother was hung two or three years since and this one is reputed to be a worse man yet."

Hereford smiled slightly acknowledging Storm's mild jest. "You are old enough to know your own mind and too big to manage. Well, then, let us go. We have nothing to wait for." Storm moved aside toward the horses and Hereford turned to his brother. "I charge you, Walter, as you would have me rest in peace, to have my wife out of that keep whatever happens. And have a little sense; do not loose arrow or sword upon them unless it be really needful."

A few moments after they arrived at the meeting place, the drawbridge groaned its way down and the gates opened briefly to let ten full-armed men ride out. Storm glanced briefly at them and leaned toward Hereford.

"I could have saved myself the trip. The foul-mouthed oaf at the postern was de Caldoet."

For once Hereford did not respond to his friend's effort to lighten the tension. He was too caught up in the sensation of being whirled along against his will to an unknown destination. Seldom had he striven against a more unpleasant feeling, for although he had had as many fears and more worries than most men of his age, previously he had always felt that he controlled his own life within the limits of God's will.

"You are de Caldoet?"

"And you the Earl of Hereford?"

"Is your master sending out my wife and my men?"

"You have no right to ask that. You are a rebel against your king, and your wife was taken as a prisoner of war. You have further outraged law and justice by willfully burning Lord Peverel's lands without even due notice of hostility. My lord is generous, however; he does not wish to bring needless suffering to anyone."

Lord Storm made a low sound of contempt between a snort and a snicker but Hereford, expressionless, did not even shift his eyes. De Caldoet, speaking formal words that everyone knew were empty of meaning, cast one glance of envy and hatred at the pair and hurried on.

"Therefore, if you will withdraw your forces and pay for the damage you have done and, of course, a reasonable ransom, Lord Peverel will be happy to restore your wife and men to you."

Hereford lifted his rein preparatory to turning his horse. "I will pay nothing. I have come to take what is mine and avenge the insult done me. If this is what your lord sent you to say, you have wasted my time and your own. If anyone has suffered damage, it is myself, for whatever I am, no man has the right to make war upon a woman and you have attacked and injured the men of my household who offered you no provocation."

"High words and mighty, Lord Hereford, but hard to put to the proof. Nottingham is not so easily taken, and you dare not wait, for my lord's messengers have gone to the king and he will be upon you long before you can hurt us. Furthermore, Lord Peverel bid me say that if you attack us, he will kill your wife."

Hereford's bowels tied themselves into knots. Fortunately he was already so pale that his color could not change, and he had full control over his expression which remained totally impassive. The faintest indication that he could be moved by fear for Elizabeth's safety, that his attachment to her was emotional rather than financially and politically expedient, would have changed the entire course of the interview.

"If one hair of Lady Hereford's head has been discomposed when I come into your keep, I will spare no living thing in this county—except mayhap yourself and Lord Peverel. He, at least, I will keep alive—parts of him—for many, many years."

The tone was so pleasant, so even and measured that the men behind de Caldoet instinctively drew closer together for comfort. De Caldoet himself felt cold, and, experienced as he was in brutality, he had to repress a shudder. There were things far worse than death that could happen to a man, and Hereford was known for keeping his promise. There was a tale of how he had gained information some years before, using methods that had caused that old-time persuader, Chester, to plead for mercy for the victims. De Caldoet's emotion was fleeting. He knew, of course, that Peverel had not the slightest intention of harming Elizabeth in the first place, and in the second he was secure in the knowledge that he could change sides if things did not work as he expected and save his skin that way.

"You are stupid and stubborn as an ass," he snarled at Hereford. "You would do well to accept an offer so generous. Lord Peverel, however, expected no less, so he has empowered me to make one more offer out of mercy to your men and his, who are innocent of wrongdoing but who would be the sufferers. You say you are injured; he says he is. Let God decide between you. The Constable of Nottingham offers you trial by single combat to decide who is in the right."

Of all the offers Hereford had expected, this was to his mind the least likely. His mouth dropped with surprise. "Peverel offers to meet *me* in single combat?"

De Caldoet laughed. "No doubt that would just suit your courage—to meet a man thirty years your senior and long out of practice in feats of arms." His tone was deliberately, insultingly comtemptuous. "At that, even at his age and in his condition he would probably beat you for your successes are well known to be between sheets of linen not of steel."

Hereford's pale face flamed with rage. He knew he was being baited deliberately, but his response was instinctive, not intellectual, and was beyond his rational control.

"No, my little lordling," de Caldoet continued, sneering, "I have offered myself as his champion. Ah, that you like less. Nay, I told him you would have no lust to meet a *man* in the field and that, unprotected by an army, you would shrink to your proper size. Come now, pay his price and you may go scatheless."

Storm had hold of Hereford's forearm. "Do not do it, Roger. You cannot—"

"Done!" Hereford gasped, restraining himself with difficulty from falling upon his tormentor then and there. His hand clenched upon his sword hilt. "Where and when you will. Name your time and place."

"Wait," Lord Storm protested, "will you trust that snake? Say you fight and win, what surety do you have that he will open his gates?"

"And what surety do I have that when I win the little lordling's men will not fall upon me? We take even risks."

The scars on Lord Storm's face turned from white to red with fury. There were few men who dared openly question his honor. He pushed back his helmet and mail hood violently so that de Caldoet could see him clearly. "Do you know who I am?"

"Certainly. You are the devil's spawn who has taken the name of Gaunt. So what? I do not fear you, be you man, beast, or demon."

"You may have cause therefor some day." Storm mastered his temper with an effort, realizing that the angrier he and Hereford became the less chance they would have of making an arrangement which would protect Hereford's interests. Plainly de Caldoet was trying to enrage them to the point that they desired nothing but to kill him. A better revenge for his insults was to bring him to their terms. "Let that craven beast who shames a once honorable name send out the Lady Elizabeth and Lord Hereford's men under guard—up to three hundred men—to the east side of the keep wall on this field. I will bring an equal number—my men, not Hereford's, so they will not fight unless I order it—to the west side. The army will withdraw beyond that ridge so that they are no danger to you. You can fight between us."

The bargain was not readily made, for Peverel had indeed hoped that Hereford would, in his rage, fall into the trap of agreeing to fight without such precautions. He had every intention under those circumstances of doing exactly what Lord Storm suspected. He was reasonably sure his henchman would win, but he could see no reason to take any chance at all. Furthermore, even if Hereford won it was likely that he might be too badly hurt to pursue his attack on the castle, so that if he kept Elizabeth within he would have lost nothing. Storm could not be moved by any argument however, and Hereford by this time had cooled sufficiently to agree with him.

De Caldoet then began to play for time, attempting to put the day of combat off for a week. It was possible that for once Stephen would be spurred to rapid action and would arrive before that date, in which case Hereford would probably be defeated or forced to retreat. In this too de Caldoet failed, largely because he really did not care to be adamant on the subject. He was very certain that he could beat Hereford without great difficulty, and his personal interests would be more fully served by that than by having the king intervene. He was already looking forward with pleasure to seeing the Earl of Hereford crawl and weep and beg for mercy and could see no reason to wait a week for that pleasure. Therefore he did not really become insistent upon his own terms until the actual method of fighting came under discussion. In this he was successful in arranging three passes with the lance to precede the battle with sword or mace. Storm argued long and bitterly, for Hereford was no great jouster and de Caldoet was one of the best. He was defeated finally by de Caldoet's rigid insistence and by his own principal's impatience, Hereford saying irritably that one or three made no difference, for God would protect him. Lord Storm slammed one mailed fist into the other and gave up, muttering that even the Lord needed some help from a little good sense once in a while. De Caldoet smiled, silently agreeing, but satisfied. Capable of judging men only by himself and his personal experience, and to a certain extent misled by Hereford's apparent physical delicacy, he was rather contemptuous of his opponent. He was not overly clever and had the stupid person's habit of forgetting what was unpleasant to him, so that at the moment he did not remember that twice the same day Roger of Hereford had almost frightened him by his expression alone. His basic reason for wishing to fight and beat Hereford, however, was far more rational and practical than a mere sop to his ego. De Caldoet believed that when he had Hereford at his mercy the defeated man could be forced to cede a handsome share of his property to save his life. This would restore de Caldoet to independent status as a war lord, the thing he wanted most in life.

The terms of the agreement finally made were essentially what Lord Storm had proposed, and the following morning was set for the time of combat. Hereford had held out for some time for that very afternoon, but both Storm and de Caldoet had opposed him, Storm because he wanted Hereford to have some rest after their grueling ride and de Caldoet because he wanted a good night's sleep so as to be at his best. That was not, of course, the reason he had offered. Aloud he had insisted that he would need time to have Peverel ratify the agreement and did not propose to have the battle terminated by darkness.

"I do not desire to offer you that method of escape," he had sneered at Hereford, "and I wish all men to see clearly how you kneel before me."

CHAPTER 10

WHEN DE CALDOET AND HIS MEN had returned to the keep and the drawbridge had screamed its way up again, Hereford turned his horse toward the camp. If he had heard de Caldoet's final remark, he gave no sign. It was true that he had accepted the offered challenge in a fit of temper, but he would have accepted it even had he been perfectly cool. He could do nothing else. The captains of his army had attended the parley, and to refuse would have been tantamount to admitting either that he was personally afraid or that he knew his cause to be unjust. Hereford's hand tightened on his rein as if holding it firmly would improve his control on a situation that seemed to be slipping out of his grip. Lord Storm had been equally silent, although he kept his horse standing beside Hereford's while the others had ridden ahead to spread the word among the men. His dark face worked momentarily as he came to a difficult decision.

"Roger."

Hereford started. Lord Storm called him Roger only when he had something intensely personal to say or when he was emotionally much moved. "Yes?"

"You had better let me fight as your champion."

With eyes widened with shock and insult, Hereford studied the expression of the man who had made that flat, unemotional statement. "What?" he said, doubting his ears.

"Curse you, Roger, I like to say this no better than you like to hear it, but let us speak plain words without flattery. That man is a jouster that even I think twice about meeting. You cannot hope to withstand three passes with a lance against him. He will kill you."

The delicate mouth, fine and sweet despite a week's

growth of beard, took on an ugly, stubborn line. "I am not so easy to kill."

"Have some sense," Storm cried, his husky voice sharp with fear and exasperation. "This is no time to be proud. Your wife's safety and, more, the success of our venture hangs upon your life."

The earl shook his head. "No. No to all. If I am killed, Elizabeth will be safe because she will be valueless. Chester will pay her ransom—or Walter even—and Peverel will let her go. Stephen will not want her if he cannot use her to control me. About the other matter—I do not know. You know my feeling about that. Mayhap it was not meant to be, or I was not meant to be part of it. Such great things are in God's hands."

"Ay," Storm answered furiously, repeating his previous sentiments, "but sometimes God needs a little help on earth. Man has free will, and yours seems to be directed to destroying yourself."

"Do not fret me, Cain," Hereford said miserably. "You mean to be kind, I know, but even if I desired to accept what you have offered, I could not. I agreed to fight. My men expect it of me. How will they believe in me if you guard me as if I were a helpless child? How will I face my wife, proud as she is, if you ride for me in that field?" He smiled wryly. "Nay, what is more to me—how would I face myself?"

There was a little silence. Storm muttered to himself, but no matter how strong his impulse to interpose his own great strength and skill to save his friend he recognized the truth of what Hereford had said.

"Besides," Hereford continued, his tone becoming more brisk and animated by interest, "I am not so doubtful of my prowess as you are. That de Caldoet thinks I am nothing is all to the good. I have a lust to meet that great braggart."

In the long sleepless hours of darkness, however, Hereford wished more than once that he had accepted his friend's offer. He was afraid and desperately ashamed of being afraid. Finally, some time after midnight he went to find his brother. Walter responded so quickly to his low question that it was plain that he too was lying awake.

"Walter, I have a few things to say in private to you. Tomorrow—. Do you go with the men or stay with Storm?"

"I would not miss that sight for the throne itself, nay, not for the assurance of salvation."

The voice was hard and cold. Hereford had to pause a moment to be certain that his own would be steady before he spoke again. Whatever his aching need for comfort, he would not find it here. He suppressed the angry impulse of self-pity that urged him to leave, reminding himself that he had misjudged Walter in the past and that his brother's bitter tongue did not always accurately describe his emotions.

"Mostly I have come to ask that you have a care for our mother and our sister Catherine."

"Oh, ay, I need that warning. Doubtless you think I will wrest their dower rights from them and sell them as slaves. You alone can be fond."

Hereford sighed faintly and moistened his dry lips. He knew Walter would care for their womenfolk, he had only wished for a gentler tone even if not addressed to himself. "About matters of the estate, you will find written instructions if you wish for them, but I do not feel that I have the right to leave orders. As for the political matters in which I am involved, heaven only can tell whether I have done well or ill. With you as a man, I have certainly done ill, yet I know not wherein I have failed. I only pray you, Walter, if you know where I have trod amiss that you guide Miles more kindly."

Hereford waited, but there was no reply. He could hear Walter's steady breathing, nothing more. He continued to sit for some time after all expectation of an answer had passed, simply because he did not wish to be alone, but finally his pride asserted itself. There was one thing more only that he had to do, for he had already arranged with Storm about Elizabeth's ransom. He touched Walter's face, briefly and gently, and went out to seek quietly through the sleeping camp for a priest to whom he could make a confession.

Freed by his brother's departure from the self-imposed necessity of denying emotional reaction, Walter of Hereford clenched his jaws and cursed silently. Roger was a devil, he thought, a devil. No one else could devise more subtle tortures; no one else could so wrench the soul in his body. He had been contemplating with self-satisfying amusement the vision of Roger overthrown and humbled, it was true, but such a vision had no reality for him. Walter had for his elder brother, in spite of his struggles against it, an admiration that amounted almost to worship. He could not really believe that Roger could be defeated by anyone, and to dream of his humbling up to that moment had been only a childish act of rebellion against his brother's authority and a sort of emotional revenge for the many times Roger had curbed his actions and desires. Hereford's words, presupposing his death, had brought sudden reality to Walter's conception, and the violence of his reaction made him turn on his face and bite the mailclad arm his head rested on. When Roger was dead, he, Walter, would be the Earl of Hereford. He would have everything that was now Roger's, the wealth, the respect, the position, the power. Roger would be gone—gone forever, never again to say him nay, never again to chide or shame him. Walter clung to those thoughts desperately, but tears came anyway. Roger would be gone, never to laugh again, never to hunt with him, fight with him, play chess with him, never again to praise him for a clever thrust when they fenced, or, with eyes clear and shining with amusement, to give him advice on how to manage a recalcitrant mistress. Walter was torn apart. From the depths of his being he desired Roger's position, but in those moments of agony he admitted for the first time since childhood that he loved his brother. He did not know whether he wanted him dead.

Morning brought him no closer to a resolution as to which desire was uppermost, and Walter's face was more haggard than Roger's when they ate a meager breakfast and prepared to mount up. Hereford himself had slept well for the remainder of the night. Confession had calmed him and absolution brought him comfort. His affairs were in good order, and, best of all, the bright sun, the first they had seen in days, brought him confidence, shining on him like an omen of good will. He was able to smile easily and naturally at Storm's absorption in testing the girthing of his destrier and the sharpness and soundness of three jousting lances. The only shadows he had to contend with were his natural fear of death and his regret that he might not be able to keep his promise to support Henry's try for the throne. Storm moved away to give last minute instructions to his men. Hereford glanced at the sun to judge the time. Walter stared stiffly at Nottingham Castle across the burnt-out fields.

Within the keep, morning brought good spirits too. De Caldoet, sure of his victory, armed and checked his harness with grim exuberance. In a few hours he would be free of his servitude. The knowledge that he might be hurt did not depress him at all. A little blood was a small price to pay for the wealth and security he expected to win. Peverel, too, was well content. He was relatively sure that his man would conquer and had given instructions to the men who were to guard Elizabeth and Hereford's retainers that he felt sure would relieve him of the necessity of keeping his part of the bargain even if de Caldoet was defeated. He had everything to gain and nothing to lose.

In a decided mood of triumph he went personally to fetch Elizabeth. Peverel told himself on the way to her prison that he was very glad now to have resisted the temptation to take her to his bed. He had convinced himself that his attempt on her was a mere feint to frighten her and that, had he been earnest, he would have had her, but his complacent mood was shaken when he saw her. Elizabeth was smiling, her eyes glowing like live coals, and she replied to his order that she put on her cloak and accompany him only with a look of contempt and assurance. There was not the faintest remnant in her bearing of the shaken and trembling woman he had parted from two nights previously. Peverel could not bear it; goaded beyond endurance he described what she was going to see and even his plans for violating his agreement with Hereford in case of an "accident" to de Caldoet. She did not even deign to look at him. She went, apparently willingly, lightfooted, even gay, but only her great courage upheld her. She was not yet afraid that Roger could be defeated or that Peverel could succeed in holding her; fortunately she did not know much about de Caldoet and was spared a little pain. What she feared then was her reunion with her husband. In the two nights and a day that had passed since her thanksgiving, she had time to realize what Roger's rescue must have cost in terms of disruption of his plans, and what it might yet cost. He had been forced out of a position of great security where he had every hope of engaging and damaging Stephen's army seriously, possibly even bringing it to complete defeat and disorder. He was now in unfriendly territory, country not well known to him, where his enemies might fall upon him with great advantage. If the king moved swiftly, Hereford would be caught in a ring of fires, Peverel to the north, Stephen to the south, and Stephen's loyal adherents to the west between himself and his friends. He might even be hurt in this mad trial by combat, for Peverel would not have suggested it if he had not a worthy champion. If he was badly hurt, he might not have recovered before Henry was due to arrive and total disaster might be the outcome of her willfulness.

Oh God, Elizabeth thought, lifting her proud head even higher and stiffening her back, I must be the most evil creature alive for what pains me is not the fearful destruction I may have wrought, not the pain and failure of my husband, but the fact that he will trust me no longer. That was the truth; that was where the iron bit the soul. It was the realization that she, who had spent her life rising above the normal state of women, had done something so irrational and petty—so womanlike—and for such a womanish reason that she could be held up as the perfect example of the idiocy, untrustworthiness, and inferiority of womankind.

To the men, hopelessly gnawing like rats at the door of their trap, night and day were the same. They had no measure of the passage of time and it seemed that they had been years and years chipping splinter after splinter away from the lock and frame. Since the movement of arms which had taken place, no one had come near their tower. They had no food and, far worse, no water, but they worked on desperately, the knowledge that they would die of thirst and starvation spurring on the effort begun out of loyalty.

"Hsst, stop," Herbert whispered. "Tell Sir Alan that someone is coming. If they bring us food and water, ask him, should we try our first plan?"

The question was passed back while the men waited, silent, in the dark. They could hear the outer door of the tower as the bar shot back and it groaned on its unoiled hinges. Herbert bit his lips. If Sir Alan did not reply quickly, every chance was gone, but it never occurred to him that he could act without Sir Alan's permission even in such desperate straits. Meanwhile Alan of Evesham struggled back from the thin edge of oblivion. He had not even sufficient strength to be angry that he had been re-awakened to pain and fear. He fought hard to understand what the man bending above him was asking so urgently, but he could make out only a few words. Those few his mind turned over, mixing them with matters from the past dizzily until one particular word caught his attention.

"Out," he managed to murmur through swollen, unwilling lips, "yes, out."

The men sighed with relief and drew back against the walls. They were even weaker now, but six of them should be able to manage two men encumbered with a bowl of slop and a leather of water. They knew what would happen. The door would open and close and the man or men would take a step or two into the room, cast down the burdens, usually spilling most of the food into the filth on the floor, and leave. The men tried to swallow and lick their lips, tried to banish from their minds the desire for one taste of that water. There was no time to drink; they must kill and go at once, all of them now. There would be plenty of water outside, they told themselves, plenty of water, and with nothing crawling about in it.

There were steps entering the outer chamber, bodies tensed, waiting. "No!" Herbert whispered tensely. "lie down, it is a whole armed troop."

"Let us go," Walter of Hereford said harshly to his brother. "They are lowering the drawbridge. It is time."

"Ay," Roger replied, smiling rather rigidly as the lust to

fight and kill rose, temporarily blocking his fears. "Ay, let us go."

The contending parties reached the field at approximately the same time, Storm's men holding their mounts well back toward the west end of the wall as the men filed out of the keep. Hereford alone moved forward close enough to make sure that one of the women who rode with them was Elizabeth. He should have still been furious with her; his life was at stake because of her behavior, but at the moment he felt nothing but an overwhelming gladness to see her again safe and sound and a desire to hold her again in his arms. His men were there too, some on foot, some slung across the backs of pack animals like sacks of grain. Hereford's expression hardened. That was no way to treat honorable enemies. He wheeled his horse and set spurs to its side to gallop back to his end of the field.

The preliminaries were very brief, for this was no formal contest to be judged upon nice points. There were no rules, no bright colors and graceful pennants. Hereford's arms and surcoat were rust-stained and mud-splattered, and both men's shields were so battered with hard wear that the devices were all but obliterated. The combatants' own strength and skill were judge and jury; they would fight until one of them yielded, was incapable of fighting any longer, or was dead. The field was dead silent except for the soft sound of the horses' hoofs on the scorched turf as Hereford and de Caldoet drew apart and an occasional creak of harness as one of the watchers' horses shifted position. The men faced each other and slowly fewtered their spears, each watching the other. Hereford settled his lance firmly between his arm and his body. It lay straight and steady at the proper angle in his light grip, the well-sharpened iron tip gleaming slightly, but his heart was pounding so that he could hear it and his mouth was dry and tasted foul. For him, this was the moment of greatest danger. If he could last through these three passes unhurt, he would have a better than even chance of beating de Caldoet. If—. He was far lighter and needed a longer run to gain greater thrust.

Hereford raised his legs and drove his spurs viciously into his gray stallion's sides. The horse leapt forward into full gallop. A split second later de Caldoet was also moving. Above the roar of the pounding hoofs there was a sharp crack of splintering wood, which covered the grunts of the men as the air was forced out of their lungs by the impact. Hereford's spear had caught de Caldoet fairly in the near center of his shield, but de Caldoet was immovable and the shaft gave way. De Caldoet, a little too sure or simply amusing himself, had been careless. His point, landing off-center above the metal bosses of Hereford's shield, had slipped harmlessly over Hereford's shoulder.

There was a faint whisper of released breath from both groups of watching soldiers. Walter of Hereford licked his lips nervously. Lord Storm muttered instructions and advice helplessly and uselessly under his breath. Elizabeth, almost as knowledgeable as a man in arms, seeing for the first time the kind of man Hereford fought, became frightened and began to pray. Alan of Evesham, sensing the cold air of spring on his face, dreamed gently of past days in the field, dreamed of the many times he had heard the crack of lances and the thunder of hoofs while riding behind a laughing, brilliant lord, dreamed that he had won free and brought his men away scatheless to his own and his lord's honor. Dreaming, with the wind cooling his fevered body, he slipped gently, gently, into oblivion, and gently, almost happily, he died.

Both men took fresh spears from their squires and returned to their starting points. Hereford tightened and relaxed his grip on the hand hold of his shield, trying to restore the circulation in his arm. De Caldoet's blow, even misdirected as it was, had been powerful enough to numb his hand. One pass was over, but he took no comfort from that because it was plain to him that de Caldoet had been playing with him. As if to prove him right, this time de Caldoet did not wait for him to start the course. The master jouster had been surprised by the slight man's strength, and his jaw was bruised where his shield had sprung back and hit it. Nonetheless he had no qualms about his ability; he was merely annoyed at having been careless. The horses thundered across the turf again. De Caldoet drew a steady aim, in spite of the rocking gait of his mount, on the right shoulder Hereford was forced to expose in order to hold his lance. He still had no desire to kill his opponent for Peverel, but it would be useful to disable Hereford's sword arm and reduce him to helplessness early. That would be simpler than fighting him to a standstill later. In the instant before they met, Roger of Hereford took a desperate chance. Hazarding his life on the estimate he had made of de Caldoet's character, he threw his shield across his body, exposing his left side. He had guessed right; de Caldoet was stubborn and single-minded, incapable of swiftly reversing a decision he had made. His lance never wavered toward Hereford's naked heart; it hit his shield's edge and slid off once more without damage.

Hereford gave a low cry of triumph though he was shaken again by the blow. Two passes were over and he was still alive. Moreover this time it was no carelessness on de Caldoet's part, but his own ability that had saved him. It was true that he had not even touched de Caldoet this time, but his hopes rested on his swordplay and his blood was well up. Once more and the game would be his own, for he knew that de Caldoet's strength was no match for his quickness with the blade. He was given no breathing space at all now. De Caldoet, thoroughly angry, whirled his horse at the end of the field and started back without taking a fresh lance or considering whether the one he bore was sound. Now there was nothing at all Roger could do to protect himself from the enormous shock de Caldoet chose to release on this last course. The lance caught the inner edge of Hereford's shield with the full power of two galloping beasts and de Caldoet's own huge strength thrusting behind it. Irresistibly the shield turned inward and the point slipped between the bosses to slide against Hereford's breast. De Caldoet threw himself forward into the thrust; Hereford felt the point pierce his mail, felt the pain of his tearing flesh. With the clarity of vision that such an instant gives, he even saw the shaft bend under the pressure applied. With a crack that sounded loud as thunder to Hereford, the strained shaft gave. The point fell away, but nothing could stop that thrust and the broken truncheon struck him such a blow that he was unseated and fell heavily.

Fortunately Hereford fell to the left, away from de Caldoet who would have gladly ridden over him if he had a chance, but it was not all good fortune. His left arm was virtually paralyzed by the heavy shield which dragged against the stirrup, and he could do nothing to ease his fall or to protect himself. He cried out with pain as he hit the ground, for something had broken in his left shoulder. There was no time to think of pain, however. There was no time for anything but to roll to his feet and draw his sword. Behind him he could hear de Caldoet's horse thundering down upon him again and he turned to face his enemy, shaking his head slightly as if to clear it from the mists that fogged his brain.

Tears poured down Elizabeth's cheeks unfelt as she watched her husband stand to be ridden down. She prayed no longer; she was capable of no feeling at all except the desire to close her eyes and her mind and blot out the sight and knowledge of what was happening. That power was not granted her, and she knew she deserved her punishment. For the rest of her life she would see it, over and over. Over and over she would see her husband die.

Lord Storm gripped his saddlebow with such strength that the ivory creaked protestingly and a carved figure broke off cutting his hand. He felt nothing. Through gritted teeth he groaned, "Jump, Roger. Wake up man. Jump."

Walter of Hereford neither moved nor spoke, for his personal agony was too great for outward signs. His hands had not tightened on the reins he held and his body had not tensed for he was not mentally interposing his body between the combatants as Lord Storm was. At the one moment when love and fear had submerged his hatred and envy of his brother, he was incapable of helping him. Walter of Hereford was frozen solid, the only moving thing about him was the blood that dripped down his chin staining his surcoat from the gashes he had bitten in his lower lip.

De Caldoet raised his sword to strike with a grin of pleasure. His lance had not held and he had not killed Hereford with that stroke as he intended, but he was better off, for he had apparently stunned his opponent. One good stroke should disable him completely; then he could dismount and bring Hereford to his knees to plead for mercy and promise anything to buy his life.

Hereford's breath rasped noisily. He was at a tremendous disadvantage on foot against a mounted man, but he did not hope even for an instant that de Caldoet would do the proper knightly thing and dismount also. With an almost unbearable effort he lifted his shield arm so that he could wind the fingers into the edge of his surcoat. If he could hold on, his body would be protected even though the arm was useless for any further movement. Once more Hereford was going to hazard his life on a guess. Under normal circumstances, he would have counted on his quickness to dart in and attack the rider, being able to defend his head and shoulders with his raised shield. Now that course was impossible. It was not honorable to hurt a horse willingly in combat, but he had no choice. Every motion now caused him pain, and that clogged his swiftness; worse, he could not use his left arm at all. He stood perfectly still, allowing de Caldoet to bear directly down on him, his sword lifted a little, pointing upward. Trembling, Roger of Hereford ground his teeth, repressing the impulse to jump aside. His mouth was full of the bitter slime of fear and his stomach was heaving with it. Agonizingly he swallowed, gasped for breath, took one long swift step, thrust—and finally leapt sideways. The scream of de Caldoet's horse was music to his ears, and the crash as the beast fell was a door opening to life. Now, unconscious of the grinding pain in his left shoulder, he could run, hoping to catch de Caldoet still on the ground.

He was not swift enough for that, but the big man was not fully erect nor completely on guard. Hereford launched a blow that could have cut de Caldoet in half, but the older man was too experienced to be caught by that. Even half dazed he thrust the sword away and continued the upward swing so that the edge of his shield caught Hereford on the temple. Roger could feel the side of his face grow warm as blood ran down it, but he had no other sensation of discomfort. He leapt aside to avoid de Caldoet's counterstroke; he could not chance taking the blow upon his shield, for his fingers were growing steadily number and might lose their hold. That would expose his left side to de Caldoet's sword, but worse, it would expose his weakness to de Caldoet's mind.

Hereford was sick with pain and bleeding now from two minor wounds, but he was no longer afraid. His heartbeat was hard and fast, but it was steady, and if his mouth was dry, it was only from gasping air through it because of his exertions. His eyes were alight with blood lust, and his mouth was curved in the hard, merciless, fixed smile of the victor. He knew that all was not well with him; he knew that he could not continue to fight indefinitely, hurt as he was; he knew also that he would not need to. From de Caldoet's stance and behavior, Hereford could see that his opponent was the one who was now afraid, and he knew that that fear was better than two armed men at his back. Roger of Hereford knew men of de Caldoet's type; he knew that, unlike himself, de Caldoet was not used to doing his duty in the face of his fear. Terror could not break Roger of Hereford, but it had already destroyed Ralph de Caldoet.

De Caldoet swung his sword at Hereford and missed. His breathing was uneven and his timing was off. Hereford's blade slipped under his shield and nicked his hip; his fear grew. Never had de Caldoet jousted against an opponent he so plainly overmatched in strength and skill and failed to make his point exactly as he had intended. He knew that he had seriously underestimated Hereford, and now he exaggerated his ability, confusing luck with supernatural aid. He raised his sword over his head and brought it down hard, hoping hopelessly to cleave head or arm of the slight man with glittering eyes who smiled so tauntingly and surely into his face—but Hereford was no longer there. As he bowed with the power of his own blow, Hereford's blade came down on his back, missing the nape of the neck at which it was aimed. The edge was not perfectly aligned and de Caldoet's mail held, but he was slightly cut and badly bruised. He twisted aside, gasping and crying out, and Hereford's leg was behind his. With a shriek of terror, de Caldoet went down. Hereford would have liked to kill de Caldoet. He felt that he would be ridding the world of something strong and evil, but he knew he could not do it. It was no spirit of mercy nor any psychological repugnance for the act of murdering an enemy who was already beaten; it was simply that he recognized his physical inability to strike hard enough and quickly enough. The best he could do was to set his sword point at de Caldoet's throat and lean against it.

"Drop your sword. Ay, I know there is mail at your throat and I have not opened it, but I need only lean my body against the point. You will choke, de Caldoet, even if your mail holds."

Lord Storm turned his head and issued a low, sharp order. Five men set spurs to their mounts and galloped off toward the rise behind which Hereford's army waited word of the outcome of the battle. Another word and the whole group moved down the field, not toward the combatants but to block the entrance to the drawbridge. The men drew their horses close against the wall uneasily, expecting a hail of arrows or worse, heavy stones and hot oil, but there was no other method, to Storm's way of thinking, of preventing Peverel's men from making a dash for the castle, carrying Elizabeth with them and bringing the battle Hereford had fought to naught. They only had to hold their ground for a little while; soon the entire army would be pouring over the ridge to reinforce them. On the wall of the keep, Peverel screamed curses and danced with rage. De Caldoet was down, and that spawn of Satan, Lord Storm, had read his mind. He had one chance to bring off his planned treachery successfully and that was to order his men to shoot the five messengers—clever Storm to send five rather than one—and bring the full defensive measures of his keep to bear on the few hundred men beneath the walls. His own terrors once more defeated him, for he was frozen with indecision, unable to give orders until too late. Far better now to pretend innocence, give up his prisoners, seal his castle, and hope that Hereford would keep his part of the pact and, having his wife and his men, retreat. In any case, with Storm blocking the entrance he might lose the prisoners and sacrifice men badly needed for the defense of his castle.

De Caldoet's sword dropped from his hand without

even a token protest. He was finished fighting and had been finished from the moment Hereford killed his horse. Had he known Hereford was so soft as to accept his yielding, he would have thrown down the sword while he was still on his feet. Like most men who were as nearly irreligious as a man could be in the year 1149, de Caldoet was deeply superstitious. To him it was obvious that Hereford, inferior physically and in experience to himself, had been aided by forces beyond man's power to defeat. Had he not seen with his own eyes and heard with his own ears the murmured incantations of Lord Storm? Indeed, it was easier and pleasanter for de Caldoet to believe that than to acknowledge that his own powers were waning or that Hereford was cleverer than himself. He did not blame the supernatural or Storm, however. Hereford was the man who had brought him down, the first man who had defeated him personally, and it was against Hereford that the full hatred of his brutal and limited mind was directed. As he cried aloud the formal words of yielding and the acknowledgment that Hereford's quarrel was just, de Caldoet vowed revenge and sought an escape route, for although Hereford had spared him, Peverel's assassins would not. He shook his shield loose so that he was totally without armor or weapon other than his mail and caught at Hereford's ankle as he was about to step back.

"My lord," he said softly and intensely as Hereford raised his sword again, "listen quickly. Lord Peverel has instructed his men to carry your lady back into the keep if I should fall. He thought I did not know—" His voice died as Hereford's expression did not change. De Caldoet did not know that Hereford, standing, had seen Storm's men move in to guard the gate.

"My lord," he cried more desperately, "I am Perverel's man. I needs must do his bidding. I fought against my will. I did not fight my best—you must know that." Something came into Hereford's face finally, an expression of revulsion which did not endear him to de Caldoet any further. He added it to the score he owed the earl and hurried on. "You have spared my life, you are accountable for seeing that I receive mercy. Peverel will kill me. Take me out of his hands as your prisoner."

Hereford wrenched his leg free and stepped back just as Walter came up leading his horse. He did not glance at the man still lying on the ground.

"Are you all right, Roger?"

"Yes, but you will have to give me a leg up into the saddle. Something went in my left shoulder. Will we have to fight, think you?" Hereford sheathed his sword without wiping it and put his left foot into Walter's hands to be thrown up into the saddle.

"I think not. You, at least, certainly not. You have had fighting enough for one day." Walter's voice was angry, but it was still the anger of relieved tenderness for he had not had time to readjust his emotions.

"My lord!" de Caldoet cried aloud.

A spasm of acute distaste crossed Hereford's face. He would not turn and look at De Caldoet, but he acknowledged his responsibility. "Walter, if there are two men to spare, let them take that—that thing prisoner."

A little surprised, for one did not usually make a prisoner of one's opponent in a trial by combat and Hereford was ordinarily a stickler for the rules, Walter did not answer directly. He urged his brother instead to go back to camp and assured him that he would oversee the arrangements for transferring Elizabeth and the remainder of the household guard to Hereford's protection. The next half hour passed in a daze of horror for the earl. The black reaction of his fear overwhelmed him as it always did while his wounds were treated by the rough and ready methods available in the camp. He remembered later that he had screamed when his squires dragged off his mail shirt and again when the bone was set. He remembered also that both Walter and Lord Storm had troubled him with excited remarks and questions, but what they had told him and what answers he had made were lost in a fog of nausea and dizziness. Finally he gave up the struggle to control his body and vomited wrenchingly, clinging to William Beauchamp for support, groaning with pain and then, as if he had cleared the fog from his head as well as his undigested breakfast from his stomach, his mind was clear again. Only when he looked up after wiping his mouth he thought for an instant that he was seeing things. The Earl of Lincoln was looking down at him and laughing.

"Well, Hereford, I know many people do not love me, but I did not expect you to react quite so violently."

"Lincoln!" Hereford gasped, amazed. For the moment his own arrangements had completely slipped his mind.

"Who did you expect? Did you think fairies or elves had set Peverel's fields alight? After all, it was you who urged me to it."

Hereford wiped his mouth again and looked at Beauchamp. "Find me some wine if you can." When the squire left he turned to Lincoln. "Sit down. I have had little enough time to think of anything. But why did you—where did you go?"

Lincoln laughed again. "Peverel keeps strongboxes in places other than Nottingham, places easier of access than this keep. I merely wished to cause a diversion and keep his attention fixed here. Therefore did I burn the ricks, for that could mean only an assault without a siege. Had I known you were on your way I would have saved my men a hard night's riding, but I do not grudge you the help I lent. I would have been back last night—the men I left as spies to watch what he would do gave me news of your coming—but it took me a little longer than I expected to reduce Carlton." Lincoln raised his brows at the expletive Hereford shot at him.

"Nay," the young man added hastily, "that was not meant for you. But had I known, our forces together could have—well, last night would not have been soon enough." His face was bitter. "I have passed my word that I will do him no hurt and that I will withdraw my forces. May he rot piecemeal, he has tricked me out of roasting him over a slow fire and you out of my help in taking him. You know what brought me here?" Lincoln nodded. "And how it was settled?" Another nod. Hereford shook his head angrily, and then winced. "Mayhap I have done you an evil turn unwitting. His henchman told me that he had sent for the king. I know Stephen would not be like to come merely to lift a siege for Lord Peverel, but to catch me— that would be worth his while. If you plan to stay, watch the south."

"I do not know. There is a good beginning here, and Stephen is ever slow. Still, a long siege—"

Hereford shifted his eyes to the floor. He wanted to think and did not wish to expose himself. Possibly he was making a mistake, he decided, but mistake or not, he would not keep de Caldoet near him if he could help it. "One good thing has come out of this," he said slowly, "I have taken his most skillful captain, one who knows the keep well, inside and out. He has adherents within also, I think."

Lincoln's eyes gleamed. Whatever might be said of him, he was no fool. Briefly he considered what Hereford's purpose might be in offering such information, but he replied automatically and characteristically. "How much do you want for him?"

"Nothing. I will give de Caldoet to you for love, because I hate Peverel. No doubt he will ask his own price to betray his master, and what that will be I do not know." Hereford hesitated, then stung by his conscience and the knowledge that Lincoln was his wife's uncle and his sister's father-in-law, doubly related to him in blood, he put his hand on the older man's wrist. "For love also I will give you this warning—whatever you pay him, however you seek to bind him, do not trust him."

Lincoln did not bother to reply, merely laughed again. He trusted no one—at this moment certainly not even Hereford—and scarcely needed his warning. A shadow fell across them and both looked up at Lord Storm.

"Greetings, Lincoln. Roger, how are you?"

"Well enough."

"Then finish your business, for if we do not stay to attack, since you have passed your word, the sooner we are away the better."

"We are finished." Lincoln rose. "I will get back to my men. We will stay out this day, at least, whatever I decide, Hereford, so you may be sure of a good start. Where may I find de Caldoet?"

"Walter has him—my brother Walter. Fare you well. If you send word to Rannulf, send also my love and blessing to my sister Anne. Storm, where are my men—what is left of them. I have need of Alan." He spoke a litle irritably and then, more irritated by Storm's silence, looked up. His friend's expression was not lost upon him, but he kept looking at him for a moment longer almost pleadingly. Lord Storm shifted his eyes, knowing what was coming. "I should have known," Hereford said quietly. He rubbed his good hand across his face, strove for control, and then burst out bitterly, "Is he missing altogether? May I not even have the comfort of knowing him to lie in peace in hallowed ground?"

"Gently, Roger," Storm said softly. He too had retainers who were really dearly beloved friends, closer in tie than blood. "He is here. I have found a priest to give him extreme unction—"

Hereford rose hastily. "I will go to him. If he is not yet dead—"

"He is dead. He was still warm so the priest was willing. I thought you would wish it. Do not go, Roger. Why tear your heart further? He fought well for you, that was plain. I will care for him with all honor."

"Nay, dead or alive, I must bid him farewell. My heart, I think, can come to no further hurt through Alan. What worse could befall?"

Lord Storm could not find the words to tell him, but as he watched Hereford's face when he looked at the mutilated thing that had been his master-at-arms, Storm almost wished he had restrained him by force. Hereford turned away from the body and spoke quietly to the remnant of his household guard. When they had been dismissed he returned to look again at Alan of Evesham.

"That is enough, Roger, come away."

"Why?" Hereford whispered to no one in particular. "He was a good man, none better. Why should he die in such a way?"

"Because men die as God wills. You know not how he died for there was neither fear nor pain in his face. You were like to be finished yourself today in no better manner. Come away and rest while you can. If your weakness holds us back, more men than one may die. You will have time for grief when we are safe."

"I am well enough. I am glad I came. I will grieve less for his death now. I could wish no man to live in such case. Certainly not Alan. You will—"

"Yes. Trouble yourself no further. In any case we must part soon. If it agrees with what you desire, Hereford, I will take Alan and those of your men who are wounded too badly to go south with you back to Hereford. It is on my way home." Storm hesitated and stopped his companion just before they reached the tent. "I would be happy to escort Lady Elizabeth home also. You have not seen her yet, but do not—"

"You manage your wife in your way and leave my own to me," Hereford snapped, his white face flushing slightly. Storm dropped his eyes to hide his satisfaction for the stunned, dead quality had disappeared from his friend's voice. He knew that his remonstrance would make Hereford furious, not with him but with his wife, and he was perfectly willing to sacrifice Elizabeth so that Roger, venting his anger on her, would suffer less. Like most of Storm's little plans this one worked well. The rage that should have come earlier and passed was rekindled. Hereford walked purposefully into his tent and sat down. He did not glance toward the figure standing in the shadows which he knew was Elizabeth. William had returned with a flagon of bad wine, culled from Lincoln's men, and Roger seized it and drank, choking a little in his haste. Elizabeth, whose eyes had become accustomed to the dim light, saw more than shadows, but she neither moved nor spoke. She looked at her husband, whose face was gray with fatigue, pain, and grief, his bright curls matted with blood. More than anything, she wanted to throw herself at his feet and beg his pardon, but her stubborn knees were locked and her eyes were dry. She could only wait.

"Did Peverel do you any hurt, Elizabeth?"

"No."

"Where were you going, Elizabeth?" Hereford's voice was quiet and deadly cold.

"To Corby." She spoke too low to be heard.

"What?" He turned toward her then, his right hand clenched into a fist on his knee.

For a moment Elizabeth had the surging hope that he would beat her, but he did not move and the hope died. "To Corby Castle," she said a little louder, "to Anne and Rannulf."

"Why?"

Elizabeth's lips parted to answer, but she could not speak. She would not lie, and she could not bring herself to confess that she had acted in a fit of childish chagrin, not yet. She thought she had suffered for her mistake, but she could not even guess at the refinement of torment that was to come. She thought she knew what it was to bear guilt, but she was still too proud to confess her folly.

"I asked you why you were going to Corby. Do not tell me that you, of all women, have become mute."

"I am not mute. I—I do not wish to answer." Elizabeth's tone was as calm and proud as it had been in Peverel's keep because that was her automatic reaction to the threat in her husband's voice. They looked at each other, and, as Elizabeth saw the pain in Roger's eyes, both her pride and her calm were washed away in a wave of remorse. Her eyes dropped. "Oh, Roger, I am sorry—so desperately sorry for the harm I have done. I will cause you no more trouble, I swear it. I will never do such a thing again."

Her voice, now broken and unsteady, for once failed to move him. He could only believe that she had been about some private business of her own or her father's. Hereford did not think for a moment that Elizabeth would willingly become involved in anything detrimental to himself, but in the midst of his other troubles the feeling that she cared more for anyone's interests than his and that he could not rely upon her absolutely was simply too much to bear. He took one step toward her, not sure whether he was about to ask again what she had been about or whether he would kill her, when they were interrupted.

"Roger, I thought I had better—sorry, I can come back later."

"What is it, Walter? I am at liberty." That was said as a deliberate insult to his wife, his manner dismissing her presence as of no account.

Walter looked uneasily from one face to the other. "I only wanted to be sure that de Caldoet was to go with Lincoln. I—"

"Yes, I am glad to be rid of him. Wait, Walter, I have something to ask you."

"Later, Roger, I must—"

"There may not be time later, for we move soon and you must decide the path you will take. I have lost—" Hereford stopped to clear his throat. "I have lost my right hand in this disaster. Alan of Evesham is dead."

There was a small choked gasp from Elizabeth, which Hereford heard but ignored.

"Alan! I am sorry, Roger. He was a good man to you and a good friend also. I could ask for no one better to be back to back with in a desperate strait."

"Not now, Walter. I cannot bear it. One more word and I will begin to weep and be good for nothing. I spoke only because I wanted you to understand what I am about to ask you. I need you. Will you come with me and fight behind my banner?" Walter's face hardened with consideration. Hereford sat down again as if his knees had gone weak and, desperately trying to hold his brother, made a bad mistake. "I can promise you very little immediate gain," he continued in a low voice, "nothing to what you would have if you continued with the plans we made earlier. If we fail, also, I can promise you a rope's end for a necklace. But if we succeed, Walter, there is almost nothing you will not be able to ask—land, an earldom, any heiress in the country to wife—"

Walter's eyes narrowed, and his mouth tightened. Watching, Roger was aware that he had trod amiss again. He wanted to cry out to him to come back, not to recede into hatred or indifference.

"Your price is not high enough," Walter said finally. Roger always tried to buy him like a common mercenary and always that action aroused in him the same burning shame and bitter resistance. He failed to realize that he himself had blocked his brother from all other methods of approach by his venomous tongue and manner. Elizabeth cried out softly at the expression on her husband's face, but neither man looked at her. They were totally absorbed in the struggle between their wills. Walter now had his bloody lower lip between his teeth again, defeated already because he knew that Roger always won, but unable to give up the struggle. With a sharp intake of breath Hereford looked aside. He had realized that this was one thing in which it was more dangerous to force Walter to his will than to be without help. He must follow willingly or not at all.

"Forgive me, Walter. I have no right to push you where you do not wish to go. I thought I had learned that lesson. I can only plead my great need to excuse me. What will you do now?" He laughed shortly then but not pleasantly. "Nay, you need not tell me. You are a man, not a boy in my care. You may do what you will."

Walter did not answer, but he did not seem to be able to leave either. Hereford lay down, shaking, incapable of further effort of any kind.

"Can I do something for you, Roger?" Elizabeth asked quietly, coming closer.

"You have done enough for me already," he replied. It was a cruel thing to say, but Hereford was beside himself, on the thin edge of complete loss of control. Elizabeth winced; she felt, however, very strongly that she was receiving her just deserts and made no effort at extenuation.

"Curse you, Roger," Walter burst out. Elizabeth started, thinking amazedly that Walter was about to defend her, but he had not even heard the exchange. "If you want me, I will come with you. You are a fool to ask me though. I am no man of yours, and I care nothing for your cause. One day you will say or do the wrong thing, and I will turn on you." He came up and looked down at his brother. "You cannot buy my loyalty, Roger, for you have by birthright the only thing I desire, and I hate you for it." Hereford did not look up. His face shone a little in the dim tent, possibly with sweat, but Elizabeth wondered if he could be crying. If he was, Walter gave no sign of noticing as he bent over his brother and put a hand on his sound shoulder. "You are right in one way though. You once said you were flesh of my flesh and blood of my blood. I can refuse you nothing you ask of me for love."

He straightened up and walked away, turning again almost immediately to say more briskly, "Let us settle it thus. I will come and do my duty as long as I may. Do you meanwhile look about you for another man who will suit you. When you have him, give me leave to return to my own affairs—or, if I can bear you no longer, I will give you warning and go when I must."

CHAPTER 11

THE SUN SHONE ALL THAT DAY, but for three members of the party that rode from midafternoon to late evening its brightness was overcast by the shadows on their spirits. Walter, leading the force, wondered, panic-stricken, whether he would come out of the commitment he had made with a whole soul. Hereford with Elizabeth beside him, unarmed and with his left arm bound lightly to his body to protect his shoulder against the jolting of his horse, traveled well in the center of the group where he was best protected. He had accepted the suggestion from Walter without comment, indifferent. He understood that he would be of no value either front or rear if they were attacked and actually an additional source of danger to his companions who would be obliged to protect him, but he would have accepted the suggestion anyway because he simply did not care. He was silent, absorbed in his thoughts, struggling with the pain of his partial comprehension of his brother's problem and the depression caused by his emotional turmoil over Elizabeth. His wife did not dare address him, not because she was afraid but because the sight of his dumb suffering was steadily swelling her remorse. She watched him, however, with her heart in her eyes. It was unfortunate that Hereford never looked at her, for he did understand women and could not have misinterpreted her expression. The knowledge that would have given him would have cut his burden in half.

They made camp that night, Walter and Lord Storm having decided that it would be better to take the chance of camping in hostile territory than of pushing Roger past his endurance. He did not argue even against that, suppressing his sense of urgency, partially because he was exhausted and in pain but largely because the next day would bring them to the parting of the ways. Storm would take Elizabeth due west to Hereford, and Walter and he would travel south to Devizes. Roger would not admit it to himself, but he really had offered no objection to camping in the hope that somehow in the privacy of that night he could mend matters between himself and his wife. When the raiding parties had returned with food and he was alone with her, however, he sat stupidly staring at the fire.

"Roger," Elizabeth ventured at last in a voice that trembled slightly, "eat something."

Automatically Hereford started to reach out to tear the chicken before them in half and stopped with a grunt of pain. Elizabeth paled a little and dropped her eyes. She was the cause of his discomfort and felt that he would be reminded of her guilt. Hereford's mind, of course, did not work that way. He associated wounds with battle, and his recollection of how he had broken his collarbone, if it could have any effect at all, could only lift his spirits. He would be very proud of that encounter when he had time to consider it in a less emotional moment.

"Let me, Roger."

Elizabeth broke the chicken into quarters and offered them to her husband, who looked at her without being blinded by wrath for the first time that day. He was shocked by her appearance, having been too taken up with his own emotions to consider that Elizabeth, knowing the havoc she might have caused, must have been living in hell herself for an interminable week. He took a quarter of the bird slowly, seeking for some ground of conversation.

"You had better eat something too. You will have a long ride tomorrow."

Elizabeth did not raise her eyes because they had filled with tears at the kindness of Roger's tone. "I am not hungry," she faltered.

"Neither am I, but that is no reason for starving oneself."

"Are you ill? Do you have fever?" Elizabeth was now too distressed by more important matters to be ashamed of displaying her tenderness. She reached over to touch Hereford's face, lifting the hair off his forehead to feel it, and then, still dissatisfied, she came closer and put her lips to it. "No," she sighed, torn between relief and regret. Perhaps if he had been feverish she could have brought him home to Hereford Castle for a while.

Her husband permitted the caress with pleasure, allowing his eyes to close sensuously. "I am only tired, Elizabeth. Tired and sad."

That was unfortunate; it reminded them both of their quarrel. Hereford stiffened slightly and Elizabeth withdrew. There was a silence in which he began to eat, finding it surprisingly difficult to swallow and watching his wife surreptitiously. Perhaps his rage should have reawakened, but Elizabeth was so close to him now, her beautiful head drooping disconsolately, that there was no anger in him, only a desolation of sorrow in which he wished to comfort and be comforted. Had he been sure she was willing, he would gladly have taken her into his arms to kiss and caress. He had not yet forgiven her for what she had done, he might never be able to do so, but he could not live in a wrangle with Elizabeth and he was growing increasingly certain every moment that, no matter how angry he was, he could not live without her.

"I wish I knew—" he began, only to be interrupted.

"Do not ask me, please, Roger. I am sorry, as God is my hope of salvation, I am sorry for the hurt I have done you. You may beat me, or lock me up. I will not complain nor defend myself for I have surely deserved it."

Elizabeth began to cry then in a horrible, wrenching, unaccustomed fashion. She really wept so seldom that she did not know how, and her sobs racked her apart. They tore Hereford's strained emotions to tatters too. He was always affected by women's tears, yielding readily even to the gentle weeping of his mother and sisters. To stop Elizabeth's violent grief he was ready to give or promise anything. He cast down his uneaten meal and pulled her against him.

"I will ask nothing. Do not weep, Elizabeth. When you are ready you will tell me whatever you like, or nothing at all if you like. I pray you, do not weep."

At that Elizabeth's sobs choked and a moan like a tortured animal was torn from her. She slipped out of his embrace down to the ground and embraced his knees. "Oh, do punish me, Roger. Do. Do not be kind to me, I cannot bear it." She did not realize that she was kneeling before him; the posture was no attempt to soften her husband's heart, it was an unconscious attempt to ease a sense of suffocation and the pain that gripped her across the breast. "I am sorry," she moaned, "I am sorry. Oh, the pain I have wrought you, the harm I have wrought you. Your men, your plans—. What have I not brought to naught. But I meant you no harm. Mary be my witness, I meant not to hurt you thus. Roger, I cannot live if you will not believe that."

He lifted her to sit beside him again. "I believe you. Nay, Elizabeth, calm yourself. Even when I could have killed you for rage I never thought you meant me harm." He kissed her, holding her against his good shoulder. "All in all, it was not so bad as it might have been," he began, trying to quiet her, but a sudden vision of Alan's dead body rose before him, and he choked on the words. He could kiss her and love her, but that he could not forget or forgive. Elizabeth who had become quieter sensed his withdrawal and began to sob again. The vision faded as Hereford directed all his attention to soothing her, first with wordless caresses and finally, as she lay against him limply, shuddering intermittently, with reflective speech.

"At least this has brought me to some understanding—or rather to some working arrangement with my brother. Understand him, I never will. There is good in him though, which it has lightened my heart to know. Then too, that business with de Caldoet was not all bad." Elizabeth shuddered and Hereford kissed her. "Come now, you were ever a woman who appreciated skill in arms. I flatter myself I did right well, for I was overmatched in weight," Hereford smiled a little ruefully, "and not a little in skill with the lance. Ay, I did right well." He began to laugh outright as a thought completely foreign to his present troubles occurred to him. "It will behoove me to improve my jousting now. Word of this will spread, as I guess, and there will be many who wish to try the man who endured three passes and conquered de Caldoet."

Elizabeth drew a shuddering breath, turned her face into his breast, and put her arms around his neck. For Hereford the memory of that encounter was becoming steadily more pleasant as his fears faded from his memory and his success stimulated his ego. Elizabeth would never see eye to eye with him on that subject. She had only to close her eyes to see him standing there, waiting, while de Caldoet's horse thundered down upon him.

"Go to," Hereford was saying, almost gaily, "you are acting like a cloistered maid. Have you never seen men fight before?"

"Not in such deadly earnest and when one of them was my husband." She tightened her grip and Hereford winced.

"Easy, you will unseat that bone again, and it was not lightly set." He smiled at her and pulled her back as she jumped away. "You need not leave me either. Only do not hang upon my neck. It is warmer together, the night has turned cold."

Elizabeth nestled again him very willingly, and not because of the cold, although Hereford did not know that. Nor was she comforted by his embrace, for the kinder Roger was, the more he attempted to soothe her, the more enormous her sin seemed. She was crushed beneath the weight of her guilt and she sought some way to lighten it. "What will you do with me, Roger?"

"Do with you?" He shook his head and smiled with rather twisted lips. He loved her, but she had cost him seventy good men, one as dear as a brother. "I suppose I should lay the buckle end of my belt to you till I could lift my arm no more, but I am scarce in a condition for that. Truly it would hurt me more than you. What would you have me do? I love you. I cannot even be angry with you any longer."

Desperately Elizabeth tried once more. "Roger, please! I have done ill. Let me suffer for it."

You are suffering for it, Hereford thought, gazing at her. Perhaps I am more cruel than kind to let you go scatheless. All he said aloud, however, was, "I cannot bring myself to hurt you, Elizabeth. Not now when we must be parted for so long and so perilously. You go to Hereford tomorrow and I—mayhap to meet the king."

"Tomorrow? Am I not to go south with you, Roger?"

"I cannot risk that." He spoke slowly, seeking briefly for a reason to take her, or to go home himself, but his sense of duty would not permit him to think seriously of such a thing, not even briefly. He was conscious now of Elizabeth's body, warm and soft against his own, for he wore no mail, conscious that the preparatory stages of his rebellion were over and that there would be fighting to come. His ever growing sense of foreboding was increased by his depression over Alan's loss and Walter's unpredictability, and Hereford felt suddenly that he might not live to see Elizabeth again. The knowledge that this might well be the last chance he would ever have to enjoy Elizabeth made her infinitely desirable to him. He began to tremble slightly, and color rose into his pale face, making his eyes intensely blue.

"Elizabeth," he murmured in an entirely different voice, bending his bright head over her dark one, "Elizabeth, you are a fire in my blood. Will you share my bed tonight?"

She was startled. It was the last request she expected of him, but immediately it seemed perfectly logical to her. He said he loved her, yet he could no longer trust or respect her after what she had done. What other use could Roger have for her now? She deserved it; she deserved it. That at least she could give him, however, willingly, with no reservations. Perhaps her complete yielding, free of the initial resistance she customarily displayed would make up in some small measure for the trouble she had caused. Love, Elizabeth knew, was very important to Roger. She lifted her mouth to his.

"Yes, with all my heart, but—"

He smiled faintly although his face was already rigid with passion and his trembling had increased. "Do not worry," he said through rather stiff lips, reading her mind, "I will show you a way that will not hurt me. I know many ways, Elizabeth."

They kissed good-by very tenderly in the morning, but the eyes of both were shadowed. Hereford's burdens weighed heavily upon him after the sweet oblivion of that night, increasing with the light, and Elizabeth, recalling every word and act of his tenderness, could scarcely breathe under the weight of guilt she carried. Her state was far worse than his. The pressure of Hereford's duties and military anxieties would soon blot out everything but a distant uneasiness. Elizabeth, on the other hand, would return to a peaceful household which ran itself smoothly needing no attention, to a mother-in-law who disliked her and from whom her pride and honesty would forbid her to conceal her misdeeds. She faced days, weeks, perhaps months of idleness in which she would have nothing to do but consider what her bad temper and lack of consideration had wrought.

Walter of Hereford shouted orders at his men and opened his mouth to give directions about the disposition of men, the pace to be held, and the path to take. With a sudden expression of distaste he closed it again and went to find his brother. He had pledged himself to service, he reminded himself, for such matters he needed Hereford's approval. He found Roger remarkably easy to please, though not in terms of the indifference he had exhibited the day before. The elder brother listened attentively to everything Walter said, but he displayed none of the inclination to make unnecessary changes in the plans that was typical of the petty tyrant. Walter breathed a sigh of relief and thought that things might not work out so badly after all.

"The only thing I cannot plan on is how far we may go. I do not know how much traveling you can bear, Roger. You do not carry yourself much easier that I can see."

Hereford laughed. "No, and I feel, if anything, worse. Still I doubt not to go as far as is necessary. We need make haste only into the borders of Gloucestershire, however. Once there, except for certain keeps, we are safe. It might be well worth while to plan only as far as Cheltenham this day. I admit that I have a mind to spend one night in a comfortable bed, and I can command one there. It will make an easy ride to Devizes tomorrow, and what has been lost by my delay will not be changed, I suppose, by one day more."

They accomplished their intentions without any hindrance at all but were met at Devizes by Patric, Earl of Salisbury, with the bad news that Downton had fallen. Hereford expressed himself fluently and at great length when he had this piece of news, repressing with difficulty an impulse to write to Elizabeth so that she might have another score to credit against her willfulness. In honesty, however, he could not do it. He had known that Downton was under siege for some time, but had not considered their plight to be serious. The failure to go to their relief was all his own, and he confessed as much to Salisbury, striding up and down the hall in a rage at his own stupidity and seeking a way to revenge his frustration on Stephen. The king was well out of his grasp, however. He had never arrived in spite of their expectations, and no further word had come from Gloucester. Hereford selected a whole new set of epithets and said what he thought of both Stephen and Gloucester so that Walter laughed heartily at his brother's masterful use of obscenity. He did not laugh long, however, for when Hereford recovered his temper he saw an entirely new aspect of the earl. Five clerks wrote at once as Hereford dictated, summoning his allies, his vassals, and the mercenary captains who had not yet arrived. He wrote also to those men whom he had ordered to disperse to the safety of various keeps a week earlier. Interspersed with this activity, he consulted a large piece of parchment he had unrolled, on which was marked the disposition of the various forces and keeps, those in the king's power in black, those avowedly favorable to his cause in red, and the neutrals in blue or green depending upon which side they leaned.

Walter watched in astonishment. By and large wars were conducted in a hit-or-miss fashion consisting of a series of individual encounters which were not specifically related to any over-all plan. Ordinarily this was logical enough, since the end in sight was merely to reduce the enemy to a state of exhaustion in which he would yield or be incapable of fighting any more. Hereford had not associated with the most astute soldiers in France to no purpose, however, and he had picked up from Henry a length of vision very unusual in that time. He knew that Stephen's forces and his own were very far from equal and that the advantage of time also lay on Stephen's side. Hereford's allies might easily become restless if he showed no signs of success, while Stephen's had nothing to lose as long as the king held his own. The salvation of Hereford's cause lay in planning his action in such a way that his successes even if minor would be apparent and his losses could be concealed, a thing Stephen either could not or would not do. The two major objectives Hereford had to accomplish were to appear successful and to draw Stephen and Eustace away from London, where they were virtually invulnerable, and from the southeast, where Henry would arrive. He interrupted his general activity to dictate a long letter to Hugh Bigod, Earl of Norfolk, and Walter seized the opportunity to study his brother's chart. A glow came into his eyes as he slowly made out its meaning and the purpose of the counters Hereford had placed upon it. For the first time in his life a spark of enthusiasm for a cause other than his own personal gain struck a light. It was not that Walter cared who was king. As a matter of fact, if he had a personal preference it would have been to retain Stephen, for what he heard of Henry indicated that such a king would put a major crimp in his favorite sport, raiding. It was merely that he could not resist being part of a game as fascinating and dangerous as that which Hereford had outlined.

"Roger—"

"Yes?" Hereford replied short but without discourtesy, "what is it?"

"I see the keeps you have marked, but why have you overlooked places like Faringdon and Henley? Both are thorns in your side and certainly important to the king."

Hereford had no time to give his brother a course in strategy just then, but he was pleased by Walter's interest and certainly did not wish to discourage him. He knew also that it was not wise to have admitted Walter so deep into his councils, but having been forced to do so by circumstance it would be madness to antagonize him. Walter would not sell him for gain; Hereford acknowledged that he had misjudged his brother when he assumed he would, but he was still not sure that Walter would not betray him in a fit of temper.

"I have not time just now to explain fully for so many things must be considered, but I can show you this. The keeps I have marked are those which I plan to attack—or have attacked by others—immediately. You see that each of them is thrust into territory friendly to our cause or surrounded by keeps held by our men. Yet, each is also on the borders of the lands of Stephen's adherents. Furthermore, all of them are not really strong points and are not strongly held because they are of little account."

"Then where is your gain in wasting time and men on them?"

Sighing because he hated to have to find words to explain what he instinctively felt was right, Hereford continued. "My gain is in the appearance of strength that so many quick successes will give me with those who do not know the complete tale. That will win me allies—admittedly of a questionable nature, but at least they will be afraid to fight against me—and satisfy those I have that I am busy. Also, Stephen's men, seeing us attack so near their lands, will cry to him for help. If he brings them help, we have drawn him out of London and perhaps have a chance to take him. If he does not bring them help, a doubt will be raised in their hearts of his good faith. We can raid their lands too for provender, thus saving our own people from the burden of supplying us and further injuring our enemies."

"So much I guessed myself. But Faringdon and Henley although strong also match this plan, and their value to our purpose should surely cancel the trouble their strength will give. Why—"

"Walter, think," Hereford said a little sharply for he was tired and in pain and felt the pressure of much that needed to be done in a very short time. "Faringdon and Henley are not only strong keeps but were originally ours. Therefore the garrisons are specially strong and alert. I wish to attack only where I can win with little loss of time and men and where I am sure of succeeding." He rubbed his face and forehead. "Let me put off this talk until we eat, I pray you. I am so pressed for time just now. The week Elizabeth cost me I could ill afford."

Hereford began to walk away, but Walter caught his arm. "You had better give me something to do, Roger. You know that the devil breeds work for idle hands."

The telltale hand stole up to pull the ear lobe. Hereford could have used his brother's help, because the task that Lord Storm had been engaged in was hanging half finished. Walter was well suited too for the checking of supplies and garrisons and would doubtless make a good impression on the men, but Hereford was still torn with doubt as to his brother's steadiness. He could not afford to hesitate, however. For one thing, he had no time for hesitation, and for another, his hesitation would offend Walter. He wiped his mouth with the back of his hand, sick with indecision.

"Are you all right, Roger?"

"No. If I had time I would be sick with a good will." Hereford seized eagerly on the excuse offered by his brother. It was true enough after all. "I cannot think. I—oh, yes, there is one way you may do me a great service. In the court and the lower hall there are men—some spies, some prisoners, some serfs we have picked up, some deserters—from the keeps in which I am interested. Will you go and see what information you can wring from them? Forgive me, I know it is dirty work and I had intended to discharge the task myself, but I have not time now myself and I know not whom else to trust. Besides, just at this time—"

Walter laughed. "Your stomach is uneasy enough. I know. I do not mind." He looked after his brother as Hereford went out, quickly sobered. He did not like to see Roger looking so strained and ill. For many years Walter had based his rejection of Roger on envy. Hereford was rich; he, except for his brother's generosity, was poor. Hereford was handsome; he was not. Most of all, Hereford always seemed carefree and happy, and he always knew himself to be miserable. To see Roger in this state shook the entire fabric he had carefully constructed to defend himself from helpless adoration. If his defense failed, he felt that Hereford would devour him alive as he had devoured his mother and sisters, who seemed unable to breathe but by his direction. Possibly it was not by intention that Roger reduced them to nothing, but his love was protective and enveloping—and smothering.

Somewhat earlier on the same day, Lord Storm pulled his horse to a halt. About a mile ahead the road forked. The right track would take them to Hereford Castle, the straight path went through the town and on west to Painscastle. He looked with pleasure at the peaceful land; the soft air of April touching his face made him spread his nostrils to scent the spring. His expression did not change, but his heart had been singing louder and louder since they had turned west and now the joyous noise in his soul was like the full choir at the cathedral. For a week, no, better, two weeks, he could be at home with nothing to do but attend to the affairs of his own property, play with his son, and make love to his wife. When he thought of Leah he felt, as always, a pleasant tightening in his genitals and a slight shortening of his breath. He sat on the quiet horse, apparently surveying the road before them and the general scene, but in reality his eyes were blind and he was savoring with delight the sensations of his own great body. Dizzy with the pleasure of the sight of a peaceful, unburnt countryside, the scent of spring, and the feel of his anticipation of love and comfort, Storm started when Elizabeth touched him. There was fear in her face.

"Why do we stand here so long?"

"I am sorry, madam, I did not realize you were in haste. I did but stop to pleasure myself with the sight and smell of a happy land."

Elizabeth sighed and steadied her lips. "I am in no haste. So long as you hear and see nothing to fear, we may stand here all day for all of me."

"You need fear nothing in my care, Elizabeth. I will keep you safe."

Lord Storm was a little surprised. He had known Elizabeth all her life, since her father was his godfather, and he never remembered her confessing to being afraid of anything before. It was one of the things that he had objected to about her; he felt that she had a courage unsuitable to a woman. As a matter of fact, although he often enjoyed Elizabeth's company while she was Elizabeth Chester, he had thought Roger mad to offer for her. He would not have taken a woman with such a temper and such a will for ten times the dower she had, he told himself, nor ten times the beauty. He was happily oblivious of the fact that his own wife, whom he thought gentle as a newborn lamb, had a stronger will and a temper just as fierce, if far better controlled. Leah ruled her husband differently, however, and the outward form of acquiescence and subservience which she accorded him satisfied him.

"Safe!" Elizabeth burst out, interrupting Storm's

thoughts. "What do I care for being safe? I wish I were dead." She looked away, mastering her emotion after a short struggle, and spoke more quietly. "It is only that I have caused Roger sufficient trouble and loss. I would not wish him to suffer further through me."

The dark eyes which Lord Storm normally kept half lidded to hide their expression opened wide with amazement. This attitude on Elizabeth's part was more of a shock than her confession of fear. He had never suspected that she cared for anyone at all other than herself and possibly her father. His face softened somewhat. Perhaps he had been unkind these last two days in his cold manner to his godsister. Perhaps she was bearing a heavy enough load in her recognition of the harm she had done without his adding his scorn to it.

"Elizabeth, would you like to come straight on to Painscastle with me? I fear you may not be comfortable at Hereford. Lady Hereford—I mean the dowager, of course, will surely hear of this—." He stopped, not knowing just how to phrase a description of the trouble Elizabeth had caused. "Leah will love to have you, you know I speak the truth in that. She is very fond of you, Elizabeth. Come to us for a month or two. Leah will amuse you, my son will divert you with his ways, and I will be gone in a week or two."

She did not turn to him because she could not control her expression. "You are very kind, Cain, but I think that the welcome I will receive in Hereford is perhaps what I deserve."

"Perhaps," Storm agreed dryly. His sympathy for Elizabeth was not sufficient to make him deny so plain a truth. "Nonetheless, I do not believe Hereford would wish you to be unhappy. You cannot blame him for being angry, but that will not last long." His voice grew even drier, as he remembered Hereford's stricken face when the news of her capture came. "Aside from other matters which make you valuable to him, he is mad for you, Elizabeth. I know not, and do not wish to know, why you played him such a trick, but it was not befitting conduct, for I know him well and know that he could not have merited it. If he was not kind, seeming to set your sufferings at naught, it was because his own were too great to forget so quickly."

"He was too kind," Elizabeth said in a stifled voice. "My heart would be lighter if he had been harsher. I thank you again for your offer, but I wish to go home."

That was firmly enough said to permit of no argument and they discussed the matter no further. Storm valued the little time he had to spend with his wife too much to really desire any visitors and Elizabeth was only too eager to seize the relief of less personal conversation. Storm stayed the night at Hereford keep, forestalling by his talk of his own affairs, for Lady Hereford was fond of him and deeply interested in his wife and child, any extended questions regarding the badly wounded men of Hereford's household he brought home. He could not avoid mentioning that there had been some heavy fighting in explanation of their condition, but he assured his friend's mother, somewhat mendaciously, that Roger was perfectly well, and cleverly turned the conversation elsewhere. It was Elizabeth's duty to explain, if she wished to do so, what had happened. That duty Elizabeth fulfilled the next day. She had gone to attend to the wounded very early, to be sure they were all cared for and denied nothing. Lady Hereford, coming for the same purpose, although with less reason for her anxiety, found her there.

"What happened, Elizabeth? Were you there when this battle took place? Now that I come to think of it, Lord Storm said very little to the point."

"He had his reasons, madam," Elizabeth replied. Her head came up and her shoulders braced. "If you will come where we can be private, I will tell you the whole. You have a right to know, and I have no right to conceal."

The facts were briefly related, Elizabeth indeed concealing nothing, not even her reasons for her actions. She was fiercely glad to display her guilt, for her need for punishment had reached such proportions that she felt she would go mad if it was not satisfied. If Lady Hereford told Roger, so much the better; she would be glad of that too because she had fretted herself into a state in which she believed she had no right to his love. Even as she poured this all out, she knew that the intensity of her grief would pass and that she might well regret her impetuosity more deeply than her misdeeds, but, as in all other things her immediate emotion swayed her, and unburdening her heart was all that mattered.

"I told him he would be sorry he took you to wife," Lady Hereford cried viciously. "He is a fool about women. A pretty face could always turn his head. I will write to him at once. You will not go scot free out of this, cajoling him against his sense and will with your beauty. He is free of your presence now and can think clearly. God willing, I shall free him of you completely. Roger will listen to me now that you have proved your falsity and untrustworthiness. You have no child of him. We are rich—and if we are not rich enough I will sell my dower rights for gold. We will buy an annulment of this horrible marriage from the pope. It is against the will of God for a man as good as my son to be mated with a woman so evil."

The second night they spent at Devizes, Hereford was wakened by his brother's hand on his shoulder and his voice calling his name. He came instantly out of his sleep, completely alert. "Trouble?"

"No, at least, I am not sure. There is a courier—"

"You are supposed to take the night watch," Hereford said with the irritability of a man freshly awakened from a pleasant dream, "and I assume you still know how to read."

"It is a great pleasure to me that you know so much about my abilities," Walter replied nastily, firing up. Service, however, he had pledged, and he swallowed his anger as well as he could. "The message is to be given into your hand alone. Shall I slay the messenger and take it by force? Or should I say that the Earl of Hereford is having his beauty sleep and does not care to be disturbed?"

Hereford scratched his head and yawned. "Very well, send him in." He levered himself up in bed with some effort, tried to move his left arm in a tentative way, winced as he desisted, and took the roll of parchment held out to him by a weary courier only to hand it to Walter again after a glance at the seal. "Break the wax, Walter, it is none so easy to do with one hand."

Walter also looked at the seal, but it meant nothing to him, the device being completely strange. Watching his brother's expression grow blacker and blacker as he read, however, Walter was moved to ask impatiently whether the news was bad.

"No. It is good news. It merely sits very ill with my own wishes. There is no help for it though, we must move at once or we will be too late." He turned to the courier. "You are Sir Ralph Pritchard?"

"Yes, Lord Hereford."

"How do you know I am the Earl of Hereford?"

"I have seen you at court. Once seen, Roger of Hereford's face is not forgotten."

That drew a laugh, although the compliment was accepted without a blink. "Do you return whence you came or stay and fight with us?"

"Whatever you will, my lord."

"Very well. Go and find yourself a place to sleep and something to eat if you desire it. In the next few weeks I will be glad of every sword."

Walter, holding the rolled parchment, listened, angry but admiring his brother's adroitness. Without being discourteous to the well-born messenger by forbidding him to speak or dismissing him without any conversation, he had effectively prevented him from giving any hint as to what was in the message or who sent him. Had Walter known Roger less well, he would have missed the significance of the exchange. As it was, in terms of Walter's feelings, Roger would have done better to be more direct. Walter dropped the chart on his brother's bed.

"Shall I withdraw and close my eyes and stuff my ears lest I hear something unsuitable? You asked me to come with you. If you trust me so little—"

A stricken look crossed Hereford's face for an instant, followed by an expression of resolution. He needed Walter, it was true, but it would be useless to have him if he continually went in fear of treading on his toes. The matter must be settled once and for all. "It is perfectly true that I do not wish you to know what was in that message or from whom it came. I am sorry if you are offended, but there are some things too dangerous for any man except myself to know. You must accept that if you are to serve under me. Now forget that nonsense and unroll that chart. You have heavy work before you, and I will be of little help. I had hoped to delay until my shoulder was healed, but," Hereford sighed, "as usual, there is no time."

"What work?"

"Tomorrow," Hereford had glanced at his markings although it was not necessary. He knew every mark on that parchment by heart. "You must move on Burford. You have not more than a week to reduce it. What will you need in men and arms?"

"You want to know now? Just like that? I have never seen the place."

"You have as much information as I have about it. For God's sake, Walter, bend your mind to the task. I have troubles enough guiding the others by the hand. Do not put me to that labor with you."

"Very well, very well," Walter snapped, flattered and on his mettle, although he knew quite well that it was that reaction Roger was trying to achieve. "Give me at least half an hour to think. You are unreasonable."

"Good enough. I must write to Salisbury. He is to take Stockbridge. That does not touch my men, however, since he takes it to hold for himself. John Fitz Gilbert, too, needs to be spurred a bit to attack Hungerford more seriously." Hereford groaned as he got up. "You would think there was a law against sleeping a night through in this country."

He took pen and parchment but did not begin to write immediately. His news really had been of the first importance. Arundel had passed on a message in Henry's own hand and bearing his seal naming his date of arrival as the first of May. Hereford knew, of course, that the date was subject to change, depending upon winds and weather, but even if Henry was delayed, he himself must be ready. It was necessary to choose carefully what to say, and though plans and needs were clear in Hereford's mind, words were less ready. The Earl of Salisbury and John the Marshal were probably completely trustworthy, they had been attached to Henry's cause for a number of years, but the fewer people who knew the time and place of the pretender's arrival the less chance there was of the news spreading where it should not. Hereford's brow furrowed with worry. He wished wryly that he himself did not need to know. It was hard to urge people to hurry and yet guard against a slip of the tongue which would explain the need for that hurry. It was hard, too, he thought, looking at a flask of wine, that he was not to be able to celebrate a victory or drown a defeat for fear of a wagging tongue. Hereford began to write slowly. His skill had improved greatly, but his hands were still clumsy with a pen, forming each letter painfully, and he ordinarily preferred to have a scribe write for him. In this case, however, the messages needed to be in his own hand and in a certain sense his lack of ability was an advantage, for he needed to think as he wrote. Finished with that task he leaned back for a moment to consider two questions nagging at his mind and then, with an exclamation of impatience, set the problems aside while he wrote to the master of Wallingford keep. They were, if possible, to engage the king's forces in that district closely. If they needed men or arms, he would help as he could. That he hoped would be another diversion to keep men's eyes from the sea coast.

Dawn was lighting the sky when Hereford looked up from his last letter. Walter had long since gone to begin preparations for the attack on Burford and should be returning in a short time to give him word of when he and the men would depart. It was time to take out one of those nagging questions and find an answer for it. Should he or should he not go with Walter? He would be of no particular value to his brother, who doubtless knew almost as much about taking a keep as he did, since he could not yet fight, but—. What was troubling him? Distrust of Walter? No. This was the kind of work Walter liked and would do for the love of the task alone. He pulled his ear and smiled a little, knowing that what drew him was a protective concern for his younger brother. If Walter knew, Roger thought, not so blind after all, he would have a fit. Even when they were children and Roger had sought to protect him, Walter had angrily rejected his care. Blessed with the saving grace of humor, even when he was the butt of the jest, Hereford laughed at himself. He could not resist; he would never learn and would probably go on infuriating Walter and hurting himself until they were both old men. The laughter was quickly quenched—if they lived to be old men.

He would go. He had known he would from the begin-

ning and could have saved his time, but as he squinted at
the growing light Hereford knew that he had been thinking about Walter to stave off a far more important and
more painful decision. Chester would have to be notified
to make ready to ride with Henry and himself to Scotland.
Certainly his father-in-law would need three weeks to a
month to summon his vassals and other forces, but how to
tell him and what to tell him troubled Hereford deeply.
Two weeks earlier he would simply have written the
whole to Elizabeth and left dealing with her father to her
discretion. Now his faith in her discretion was shaken, and
he sat rubbing his left arm and the fingers of his left hand
gently, frowning at the rosy glow coming into the room.
How pale she had been when he left her, how subdued.
How violent her protestations that she meant him no
harm. After all, he thought, it was more bad luck than
bad management that she was caught. An hour earlier or
later and she would have won safe to Corby. Hereford
shook his head. Chester was too difficult to deal with in
any other way, too vacillating and curious; he would have
to employ Elizabeth. She was chastened and would follow
his instructions, he hoped, without asking to know the
whole of his plans as she usually did. He drew pen and
parchment to him again with a certain feeling of satisfaction in having a reason to write to his wife without raising
the subject of what had last passed between them. Hereford asked Elizabeth briefly to induce her father to make
ready to ride and fight in Henry's cause by the second
week in May at the latest. He asked further that she arrange for Chester to wait in his own keep when he was
ready, offering no reason and giving no indication of
where the fighting would take place or who they were to
attack. That was quickly done, but Hereford sat a good
while longer with the pen in his hand. His impulse was to
add softening words of affection to make up for the obvious gaps in information, but Hereford found that to caress
his wife and whisper endearments to her was one thing, to
find words to put in a letter that would not sound foolish
was something else. Eventually he contented himself with
saying merely that he was in good health, his shoulder
and other wounds healing, and that she should not concern herself for his welfare.

CHAPTER 12

ONE DAY SHORT OF THE WEEK allowed him, Walter of
Hereford stood panting in the main hall of the small keep
at Burford. It was a neat piece of work, he congratulated
himself, particularly since the place was far better gar-
risoned and more strongly fortified than he had expected.
He had diddled them nicely though, having his men
dam off the stream that fed the moat and then burrow under the wall in the soft earth instead of attempting an assault over the walls. Walter smiled, his eyes resting on the
castellan and his family huddled together under the guard
of a half dozen men-at-arms, remembering the expressions
on the faces of the defenders when the ground under their
feet had collapsed and their enemies had poured out of
the hollow of the earth. That had been Roger's only con-
tribution to the fight. He had suggested the artifice of raising the tunnel bit by bit, supporting the earth above by
planks held up on wooden posts. When a large enough
area had been excavated, they had set fire to the posts
and the whole had collapsed. Meanwhile Walter had
diverted attention by making half-hearted attempts on the
walls and gates. The plan had worked as if charmed.

Walter's eyes had been resting on the eldest daughter of
the castellan, a pretty enough maid of fourteen summers,
as he smiled, and the conquered man was growing more
and more restive. As a matter of fact Walter hardly saw
her. He was not particularly interested in women, finding
an occasional serf or harlot sufficient to his needs when he
was not keeping a mistress, but the castellan could not
know that.

"What do you want of us? You have my keep, will you
not treat us with honor?"

Walter shifted his eyes to the man but did not reply. Instead he spoke to one of the men-at-arms who promptly opened a wall chest and brought him a cloth. It was a fine piece of wool, meant for a shirt or shift, but Walter used it to wipe his sword before he sheathed it. Then, still smiling, he directed the man to order the gates opened so that Hereford could ride in in comfort. Finally he redirected his glance to the nervous father.

"You should have yielded when we came as I bade you. Then you could have asked anything within reason. There is naught left for you now but to obey or die, and it matters not at all to me which you choose."

"I have yielded already. What more do you desire?"

Walter laughed but did not answer, issuing instructions instead that the kitchens be set into operation. There was no reason not to have a good meal when everything was available. For a time he watched the men collecting plunder, silently evaluating it, and realizing regretfully that it was not his to do with as he chose. That was the rub in serving someone else, even though it was convenient to have a full-scale army and plentiful supplies to fall back upon. Recognizing Hereford's step, Walter turned just in time to be seized in a tender if painful embrace. Instinctively he strained away at first and then yielded, allowing his brother to kiss him and hug him, and kiss him again.

"Enough, Roger. We have been parted only for a few hours, not ten years."

"Blessed Mary be praised, you are safe. Safe. My God, how I have prayed."

Walter pulled loose, frowning disgustedly, torn as ever between pleasure and irritation at his brother's open display of affection and concern. "Why should I not be safe? Roger, you have addled wits, I swear it. Do you call this fighting? You make me think ill of your experience."

Laughing with relief, Hereford tousled the brown hair exposed when Walter pushed back his mail hood. "Ay, you may growl all you like you ungrateful cub, but it is one thing to fight for yourself, or to fight with someone, another to stand helplessly by and watch. God grant I need not have that experience again."

"You have found that out, have you? Mayhap you will be less eager to thrust yourself always into the forefront to shield those who do not wish to be shielded then." Walter made an impatient gesture and changed the subject. "What are we to do with these—and the plunder?"

"Are the strongboxes here?" Walter pointed. "Take what you want first then, within reason, and set the clerks on to the rest. As to the men—are there any mercenaries here?"

"No."

"The serfs may go back scatheless to their fields. If they do not till, we do not eat. The men-at-arms—how many?" Walter shrugged. "Divide them and send them under guard to various of our own keeps." His eyes moved to the small group of nobles. "It is a pity he is alive. Frankly I would like to cut his throat and be rid of the problem." The wife and daughter began to weep, and the man himself turned an ugly shade of gray. "It is always these petty vassals who are the most bother. He is probably not worth much ransom to his overlord and is of no value as a hostage either. What is your name?"

"Sir Robert Trevor."

"Trevor, Trevor—" Hereford shook his head. "The name means nothing to me. Do you know it, Walter?"

"No."

"Well—"

"My lord, I yielded in expectation of mercy. If I needed to die, I could have done so fighting and cost you a score of good men."

Hereford looked bored. He was bored. The whole thing was a nuisance and not worth the time he had already spent on it. His inclination was to have the man executed and send the women away, but if mercy had been promised he was honor-bound to give it.

"Did you promise him mercy, Walter?"

"I did not strike when he knelt to me, but I promised nothing."

"He is yours then." Hereford shrugged. "Mayhap Oxford will pay a few crowns for him. Do as you will."

Some time after full light the next morning, Hereford wakened with a grunt of pain and a startled expression. Fully conscious a moment later, however, he burst into laughter at the outraged expression on his brother's face. There was only one good bed in the keep, that of the castellan and his wife, and the brothers had elected to sleep together as they had done often enough in their youth. Hereford's bed companions in the last years had usually been of a far different type, though, and apparently, from the way Walter was looking at him, the feel of another body in the bed had stimulated him to make advances.

"I do not usually sleep with men," Hereford offered in explanation, still laughing.

"I should hope not! If you have such disgusting inclinations, it is just as well to keep out of the way of temptation."

That convulsed Hereford anew. "No, no. I meant I thought you were a woman."

"Thought I was—so I feel to you like—" The words came out almost in a shriek, but as he spoke a look of realization came over Walter's face. At that point he too began to laugh. "All I can say to that is that you must have had some queer bedmates in your time. I am not particular myself, but a woman with chest, arms, and legs like a bear, even I would think twice about bedding."

"Ugh," Hereford grunted, revolted, "what a thought to start the morning on. Come on, we had better get up. Look at the light."

"You get up," Walter replied. "I have been up all night fighting you off. May I be damned if I ever share your bed again. Even when you do not make indecent advances, you want to climb all over your companion. Your poor wife."

By the time Walter joined his brother in the hall, Hereford's good temper was completely gone. His look was so black that Walter, still in a merry mood, backed away in pretended terror. "I do not wish to know," he said hastily as Roger opened his mouth, "with an expression like that as an introduction, I had rather you told me nothing. At least wait until I have eaten. I am braver on a full stomach."

Ignoring his brother's remarks, Hereford pushed two parchment rolls toward him. His mother's letter had irritated him because in his hurry he did not clearly understand what it was she was pressing him so earnestly to do, but the other, in Lord Storm's strong square script, had frightened him enough to make him furious. Walter began to read slowly, making out a word at a time, his lips moving with his concentration, but Hereford could not wait and broke impatiently into speech.

"You will be till next week at that. Gaunt is dead. Dead! I saw him not two months ago hale and hearty."

"So what is the to-do? He was old. I hope I may live so long and die in so much comfort."

"Can you not see what this means? I feel as if God has set His face against this venture. With Gaunt dead, Storm—I mean the present Gaunt—dare not leave his lands. Certainly not until all the vassals have done their homage, and that will take months."

"So what again? You never expected him to aid in the fighting. He will honor his father's word in the other help he will give you, no doubt. What ails you? Sit down and eat."

Hereford opened his mouth and shut it again almost with a snap. Two years ago he would have burst into tears and had a temper tantrum, but he had been in a hard school since then. Of course Walter could not understand what was troubling him. He knew nothing of the plans for Henry's arrival and nothing of the fact that Lord Storm was supposed to have met him. Arundel would still do his part, Hereford assumed, but he did not trust Arundel the way he trusted Storm, and, furthermore, Lady Alice was so zealous in Henry's cause that she was totally indiscreet. Without Storm to say him nay, Arundel might well bring her along or allow her—. What was the use of making things worse by imagining horrors, Hereford thought, biting his lips. He recognized the fact that he was doubly furious because of his carelessness; in his rage he had very nearly told Walter what it would not be safe for him to know. Swallowing tears of rage, he then began to wonder why he worried about Lady Alice when he was almost as bad himself.

Hereford called the emotion from which he was suffering rage, and the reactions he was displaying were very similar to those of anger, but the truth was that Roger of

Hereford was frightened. Again and again since he had begun this affair, his plans, so carefully made, so near fruition, had been twisted awry. And always it seemed that the damage was done without ill will to him by those he trusted most. Every time his spirits rose through some success which permitted him to throw off the cloud of depression he labored under, a new misfortune took the savor from the victory. Every time he took one step forward to his goal, he was dragged two steps back. It was as if he were being warned to go no further in this venture, as if a great voice was crying out that the harder he strove the greater would be his final defeat. The pattern seemed clear enough; he would be defeated by desertion. He did not believe it would be a desertion which a shift in policy might cause in Gloucester or Chester—that would be too easy to guard against. Perhaps it would be a desertion by death, Hereford thought, staring out at the tender green of new grass in the bright spring sunshine. Alan had already left him in that way, left him with Walter as his right hand, a right hand he could not have faith in. Alan's grave would still be raw in the earth of Hereford churchyard, but soon it would be green with new grass. Hereford's throat tightened and he pulled at the mail as if it were that which was choking him. Perhaps his own death—. He jerked his mind away. That was a sick fancy. If he must die, he must die, but to fear it beforehand when there was not even a real danger present was to destroy his own usefulness.

At that idea, a cold sweat broke out over his body. "O God," he prayed, "forgive me for not heeding Your warning. I hear, and I would obey, but I cannot. I have passed my oath on Your Name to help Henry to the throne. It is a just cause. Have mercy upon me and upon my bleeding land. God, O God, if I must fail, let it not be through weakness and dishonor. Let me fail through death, if that need be, but not through the desertion of my own courage."

Walter meanwhile had been frowning over his mother's letter, not because he was angry but because he was puzzled. He read it through once to make out the words and again for the sense, but was little better off after the second reading.

"Roger," he said imperatively, "do you know what Mamma is writing about? Roger, what the devil is the matter with you? I never thought you cared for the old man; I thought it was Storm you were attached to."

Hereford turned slowly. "I was just thinking of death in general. It is very hard to realize that I will never see Gaunt again—that Alan is lost to me in earthen bonds he can never break—. What did you say about Mamma?" he asked briskly, trying to shake off his mood. To Walter least of all could he confide his fears.

"I asked if you knew what this damn letter was about. Surely you cannot be considering breaking your marriage with Chester's daughter. You would do better, if you do not trust her, to keep her prisoner. To ask for an annulment and bring Chester down upon us at this time is madness."

Irritation was an excellent restorative in Hereford's case for depressed spirits. He came back and seized the letter, rereading it quickly. When he finally looked up, there was such a mixture of fury and humor in his face that Walter did not know which emotion to comment upon.

"Women!" Hereford exclaimed, "Women! As if I had not troubles enough. I swear God made men and Satan made women to be sure that all men would go to hell. It will be a miracle if I do not slay them both. Did you ever hear of such a thing? Did you? One insane creature is cross with me—God knows why, for I swear I had done nothing to enrage her—so she rushes across the breadth of England like a bitch with a sting in her tail, disrupts the plans I have painfully spent months bringing to the point of fruition, nearly costs me my head, destroys my household guard and my best and most loyal servant—and then she will not deign to tell me why. No, she must spill the tale to my mother—who loves her not. Heaven help me! I will beat her black and blue when I see her next. Then the other idiot—and how my own mother could be so addlepated I cannot tell—not content with the damage the first has done me, proposes that I should rid myself of my wife, and of course her revenues, to the tune of *my* entire fortune and hers, and, that loss not being sufficient to satisfy her love for me, bring political disaster upon myself also." Hereford gasped for breath, feeling much better already. "I will beat her black and blue too," he continued, when he had mastered a fit of coughing. "This not being enough, she informs that proud bitch of a wife of mine that she intends to write this to me and that I will surely obey her." He began to cough again. "I have not obeyed her since I was seven and left the women's quarters, but doubtless my wife, having less brains and more stubbornness than a sow, will believe her and write to her father craving redress."

Having worked himself up into a royal rage, Hereford became literally speechless. That rage was the best thing that could have happened to him at the moment for it permitted the transfer of all his frustration to a real object and his fury temporarily obliterated his fear. Moreover, it was not a rage that was likely to last long. Already his sense of the ridiculous was striving with his anger, and Walter, his head down on his arms on the table, was frankly helpless with laughter.

"It serves you right, Roger," he crowed, when he had breath to speak. "You will involve yourself with them. It does not matter though. You need only write to Chester and assure him it is only women's nonsense."

"I will write not only to Chester. Oh, could I but lay my hands upon them, I would mend their ways. I tell you I will blister both their ears for this." Hereford was still panting faintly, but a rueful smile was already curving his lips. In a few seconds more, he too was laughing. "The cream of the jest, Walter, is upon me, you know. I would not harm a hair on either of their heads, and I love them both, perhaps more dearly than ever, for being so—so like women."

Walter made a disgusted gesture. "I cannot see why you wonder about Mamma's brains being addled when you are so much like her after all. I have always said so and always will."

"I must suppose you are right, yet I have had much pleasure from this disorder. Strangest of all is that I would not part with Elizabeth even if she had acted in malice,

though I was sure she had not even before she told
Mamma—. Can you imagine that?" he asked, growing
heated again. "Can you imagine such idiocy? The course
of a whole kingdom's fate might have been altered by the
mad whim of one woman. Perhaps God is not against us
after all. Had He been opposed to our cause, that was the
moment to destroy us."

And Hereford, greatly refreshed and restored by the release of his emotions, stormed off to write his letters and
further relieve his heart. Having dispatched his couriers,
Hereford emerged from this epistolary episode like a giant
revitalized to plan his next move with his brother. The violent surge of energy provided by his fury had made decisions easy. Suddenly all seemed clear. With good fortune
he and Walter should be able to take another small keep in
the next week or two and begin an attack of a third. That
attack he would leave in Walter's capable hands while he
took a small troop of men as secretly as possible to meet
Arundel and Henry. Depending upon the success of Walter's lone venture, he might well be able to leave the raiding in the south to him—it was something he liked to do
and would not readily tire of—and to Salisbury and John
Fitz Gilbert, while he himself rode north with Henry to
Scotland, picking up Chester on the way. All that remained was to plan where to direct his attacks.

There was, of course, not the slightest need for Hereford to assure Elizabeth that he did not intend an annulment. She might be stubborn, but she was not stupid at
all and did not trouble herself for a moment over that part
of Lady Hereford's outburst. She knew her value politically and financially to her lord too well, and that would
outweigh in the long run any amount of ill will he had
toward her. Nor in any case would she have written to her
father in her present state of guilt and depression. When
Hereford's first letter directed to Elizabeth arrived, Lady
Hereford was so incensed that she actually considered
making Elizabeth's life in Hereford untenable. She too
had come to the realization that her son could not afford
to part with Elizabeth, but she had hoped that he would
be furious enough to drive his wife out to one of her dower

castles. Even that hope was destroyed when Elizabeth heard from him so soon after their quarrel, and Lady Hereford saw that the only way to be rid of her unwanted daughter-in-law was to drive her out herself and pretend Elizabeth had gone of her own free will.

One day, exceedingly uncomfortable for both ladies, although for far different reasons, passed before Hereford's second courier arrived. Lady Hereford had begun the ousting operation and was completely miserable about it, while Elizabeth, absorbed in her own problems, was so unhappy that she had not even noticed. Lady Hereford's uneasiness was caused to a very small degree by fear of what would happen if Roger discovered what she had done, but primarily her distress came from her own kindliness. Elizabeth did not look well, her skin having that greenish tinge pallor gave her; her eyes were sunken and ringed with dark circles; and she spent a good part of the day mutely staring into space. Had Hereford not interfered by writing either letter, his mother would very soon have been forced by her own compassion to try to comfort the girl. She told herself that Elizabeth was bad for Roger, trying to stiffen her purpose, but she was a pious, truthful woman, and the knowledge that she was acting out of jealousy was slowly forcing itself upon her.

For Elizabeth also, Roger's demand that she act as intermediary between himself and her father came at a bad time. Normally she would have greeted such a request with enthusiasm, feeling it to be a mark of her husband's recognition of her worth and being sure she could accomplish exactly what he asked. Now, although it was true that the worst of her agony had passed, she was in a numb state of convalescence in which her soul had begun to heal itself. What he wrote, however, flung her again into a bottomless pit of despair, because her faith in herself was broken. She was sure she would be incapable of handling her father properly, that he would ask questions to which Roger had given her no answers and which she was still too shattered to chance answering on her own. Chester was a difficult man to deal with sometimes—none knew that better than his daughter—and if something in her manner or his own situation set him off, he could easily refuse to have anything further to do with Hereford's cause. Elizabeth knew also that her father was quite capable of stubbornly adhering to a plan of action disastrous to himself to spite someone else, and she was terrified that in her present state she would do or say something wrong and start him on a path inimical to her husband and his own welfare.

The mirror before her reflected a face that Elizabeth stared at without seeing for some time as she automatically unbraided her hair to go to bed. When she finally focused upon it, she dropped her head on to the table before her and began to weep. If she showed her father that countenance, so drawn, so hollow-eyed, with a disconsolately drooping mouth, he would immediately conclude, no matter what she said, that Hereford was cruel to her, and again her very existence would bring about the failure of her husband's plans. She could not go to Chester, she could not. Besides, she did not wish to go. If Roger came home—perhaps, though, he would not wish to see her. After all, it was very likely that when she was not there to show him how very sorry she was and, she had to add, stir his passion, he might dwell more on the enormity of her actions. She reread those last lines in his note in which he said she was not to trouble herself over his welfare and which she took to be a cold rejection of her concern for him and then crept miserably into bed. How she longed for his warmth beside her; how she longed for the caresses she had so often repulsed. Elizabeth did not realize it, but it was a sign of restoration of her emotional balance that she now wanted Roger to comfort her whereas previously she had clutched her unhappiness fiercely to herself. His assurances of affection would no longer burden her with greater guilt. They could not erase her consciousness of evil-doing—Elizabeth would bear the scar of what she had done to her dying day, would treasure it in later years, in fact, when she came to realize that her sorrow had made her a whole woman—but now Roger's love could heal her heart.

The next day began evilly with the deaths of two more of the wounded men and blossomed into complete horror with the arrival of Hereford's second courier. Lady Hereford read her son's missive with wide, unbelieving eyes. Never before had Roger written in such a way to her. He was bewitched. That she-devil had enchanted him. Only, when she looked up at her daughter-in-law, who was also reading a letter of Roger's, she could see that Elizabeth had turned even greener. Apparently, enchanted or not, Roger was not writing love letters to his wife.

"I must leave Hereford keep, madam," Elizabeth finally said in a dull voice.

So Roger had ordered her out of the keep. Instead of being glad, Lady Hereford's heart was wrung. How could she have written that letter and betrayed Elizabeth's confession to him. "There is no need, Elizabeth. Roger is angry now, but it will not last. I know him well. If you go, you will only have to return for he will surely ask you to do so by his next letter. See," she said, holding out her own letter to Elizabeth, "he is furious with me also."

At first Elizabeth did not take what Lady Hereford offered, knowing full well that if Roger had intended either of them to see the other's mail he would have saved parchment and effort and written one letter to both. Her hesitation was brief, however, for she was moved by a sense of unity with Lady Hereford against Roger, another sign of her improving spirits, as well as by curiosity. The first glint of humor she had felt since her unfortunate decision to go to Corby Castle flickered in her eyes as she took one letter and handed Lady Hereford the other. Roger would have a fit if he could see them, she thought.

"But, Elizabeth, Roger says nothing about your leaving here. Indeed, he is very angry, and you should not fret him further by taking action on your own, even if you are insulted by what he says—and I must say, you have not much right to be taking it ill. At present, and, indeed, I mean this kindly to you, I would go nowhere without his order. You know what happened the last time you spited him." Lady Hereford could not resist that, and Elizabeth did drop her eyes, but the pain of the deliberate prick was much less than she had expected to feel when her trespass was mentioned. "If you think to go because of what he says about being a good daughter-in-law, do not trouble yourself over it. I do not expect it, and I will tell him nothing more since he does not desire my advice. Whatever is between us will be our affair."

That was fair enough, and Elizabeth was moved to volunteer a little more information. "I do go by his order. It was in the letter I received yesterday. I must go to Chester. I will return as soon as I may."

Elizabeth still did not wish to go and was still somewhat troubled about her ability to deal with her father, but now she was determined to try. Hereford's strictures had done something to improve her resolution by raising a tiny spark of resentment in her, resentment she had not known she could still feel. More important, however, was a brief, bald statement in his mother's letter that he still wanted and needed his wife. Elizabeth's lips curved into a faint, unconscious smile. He had not meant her to see that. How she would prick him for playing the heavy husband in her letter and not realizing that two women—even two who did not like each other—would combine against a man who sought to discipline them.

An excessively cold, wet March had run away into a lovely, soft, bright April. On the peaceful farm lands of Chester, the corn sprang from the earth in thin, pale-green blades, young, fresh, and tender. The oaks, beeches, larches, and aspens showed a mist of the same tender green on their branches, promising the rich shade and whispering grace of summer. Elizabeth, riding home to Hereford, broke into a soft humming of a song in praise of spring out of sheer lightness of heart. Perhaps in the core of her soul there was still a black spot of despair that could rise and overwhelm her, but today it was buried deep. She had a great many things to be glad of, even though her father had received her initially with anything but kindness.

Indeed, from Chester, Elizabeth had received the beating she had been longing for. He had heard of her folly through Lincoln, who had been only too glad to twit his half brother on the results of the way Elizabeth had been raised. Enraged almost as much by the shame she had exposed him to as by the things she had done, Chester had received his daughter with a blow which had knocked her flat. Elizabeth picked herself up only to be smacked again while her father raved at her. Apparently Chester believed that she had come to him for protection against her husband's wrath. At first she tried to explain, while warding off his blows, but Chester was beyond reason. He continued to strike her and shout curses at her until Elizabeth was forced to defend herself as she knew full well how to do. She was badly bruised, however, and in a full-scale fury herself before her father was tired, her indignation at being misjudged and misunderstood going a long way to lift her depression. In the end she cursed Chester with the fluency and originality of a man-at-arms and drew her small knife on him. From sad experience, Chester knew that her poniard could inflict nasty cuts and he gave over, father and daughter facing each other flushed with rage and panting for breath.

"Out," Chester shouted, "out! I will not have you here. If Hereford kills you, it is his right. Go hide from him elsewhere." Suddenly the anger on his face died out and changed to an expression of sorrow and bitter disappointment. "Elizabeth, why? How could you do such a thing? Why?"

"I would not answer you now if my life depended upon it. Nor need you be troubled with me. I will go. I would not spend an hour more than I must here for a king's ransom. Hide! I am more able to defend myself, from Hereford or anyone else, than you are. I would die on the rack sooner than crave your succor." She drew a trembling breath and steadied her voice. "I come upon my husband's business, and it is for him alone that I have borne so long with you."

"Hereford's business? That boy is mad to trust you now. I do not believe you. He is not so addlepated as that."

Elizabeth's angry flush subsided as she saw a way out of her dilemma. It was well that her pride had been humbled by her folly for she could never before have brought herself to say what she now must. "He had no choice. He could not send a courier past Shrewsbury. Nor does he trust me overmuch, accursed that I am, for he told me nothing save that I should bid you summon your vassals and gather your mercenaries in readiness for the second week in May."

She had shown him Hereford's letter after that, and Chester asked her no questions, believing her explanation of why no further information was offered. That hurdle past, all was easy. Chester readily agreed to do what was asked, so Elizabeth had succeeded where she had feared to fail for the very reasons she had expected to fail. In spite of Chester's angry words and her own, she had stayed several weeks, long enough to see the muster begin and to make her peace with her father. Therefore Elizabeth was happy. There was only one small dark cloud on her horizon; she had not heard from Roger again, but she buried that fear and enjoyed the spring and her success while she could.

The spring showed a far less pleasant face in the war-torn south through which Roger of Hereford was riding. The fields lay untilled, often showing still the burnt stubble of past raids, and what few miserable serfs remained on the land crept into gullies to hide or, so weak with starvation that they could not do so much, stretched out their hands to the passing men with whispered pleas for alms. Sometimes Hereford threw a few copper coins or ordered a bag of wheat to be left behind, but largely he did not notice, for the sight was so common as to render the senses numb, and, besides, he was taken up with his own thoughts. By and large these were satisfactory. Salisbury and John Fitz Gilbert had been successful and had moved on to other targets; Walter and he had reduced Bampton, and Harwell had yielded without resistance. Walter was engaged at Shrivenham at present. If he took it, Faringdon would be virtually surrounded. A faint qualm rose in Hereford's breast at the thought of Faringdon, for he had once come very close to losing all there—not his life, but his honor and his power. He repressed the sensation fiercely; they were not yet trying for Faringdon. Perhaps after Henry and he returned from Scotland, but not yet.

He was looking forward to seeing Henry. For one thing, a good part of the burden of his responsibilities would be lifted when Henry of Anjou arrived; for another, that young man's forceful personality and invincible if cautious optimism were difficult to resist. Shaky alliances would become firmer with the presence of the young claimant to the throne, and many would join them who did not previously believe that Henry would keep his promise and come. Independent holders of keeps would yield much more readily too, for Henry could confirm their holdings with surety, while Hereford could only promise.

There were only two shadows on Hereford's present satisfaction. One, the deep, abiding sensation of futility that he strove in vain to conquer, recurred periodically, largely in the dark hours of the night after one of his nightmares or at times of enforced inactivity. The other was a very active distaste for the necessity of bargaining with Henry. That he had to undertake at once, even before relating what had been won and what could be expected. Hereford felt that his demands were very reasonable, since they were mainly confirmations of what he already held by hereditary right or had won by his own prowess in war. He also wanted a title for Walter, another small matter, for the lands to support the title were Walter's already, although perhaps the method of winning them would not be completely to Henry's taste. Nonetheless, Hereford knew that Henry would not grant even reasonable demands with great readiness. He was closefisted with both lands and titles, feeling very justly that the less he gave the more he would have to give or to hold out as prizes in the future. Hereford had everything all written out for Henry to sign, and he knew Henry would sign in the long run, but he dreaded the thought of the wrangling.

"William." Beauchamp came forward. "Send a man ahead to Arundel—no, better, go yourself. Say whatever is proper. I believe Lord Storm—I mean the Duke of Gaunt, I will never get used to calling him that—has already written to Arundel, but in case he has not, explain why I am come in his stead."

"Yes, my lord."

"William—"

"Yes?"

"Explain tactfully. Do not set up Arundel's hackles."

Beauchamp laughed. "You mean I should not say out

and out that you do not trust him and that you think his wife is a lovely idiot? Nay, I will restrain myself. Shall I ride back to you?"

"Not unless he will not receive us."

Arundel did, of course, receive them, but he made no pretense of being happy about it. He had opposed the choice of Hereford as the leader throughout the councils, feeling that he himself had a better claim to that position. In a certain sense he had, being a more mature man and having been a partisan in Henry's cause far longer, but old Lord Gaunt had trusted his foresight less even than Hereford's, and, more important, Gloucester had set his face solidly against that arrangement. In Gloucester's opinion Arundel was already too powerful; he would not cede his authority into those hands. Also, Arundel's main fortresses were not in such easy striking distance of Gloucester's property as Hereford's. William of Gloucester knew well how to fight, even if he would not, and believed firmly in having deterrents to use against his allies.

Fortunately Hereford and Arundel did not have to bear each other's company for long without diversion. Henry was as good as his word, for the weather was fair and the breeze blew sweet and pungent with the fragrance of spring and salt spray from France.

May the first, May Day. Wherever there was peace it was holiday. Ladies and gentlemen dressed in their best and went to Mass, then to ride out, not to hunt or fight on this day, but to pick flowers, eat in the fields, and dance. It was holiday even for the serfs. Their lords had provided food and drink in plenty, Maypoles were up to dance around, the priests either watching with sympathy or turning aside from these forbidden totems. A few preached against the heathen practice, but it was May Day, and there was spring in all men's hearts. Lords smiled indulgently, as serfs, normally forbidden to enter the woods without specific permission and payment, brought back load after load of wood for the huge bonfires which would burn that night. They too would come with their ladies to watch the antics of the serfs, half drunk and half wild, as they danced in their uncouth manner in the red glare.

Hereford had no time for celebrating May Day, but its

spirit caught him so that his eyes were bright with laughter as he ran up the plank to greet his lord. He beat Arundel by minutes because of his greater agility and lack of dignity, and he had been raised from his bent knee and caught in an affectionate embrace by the time that more pompous gentleman had arrived.

"My Lord Arundel," Henry said, extending a hand to be kissed.

The older man started to kneel stiffly, not because he had any reservations about kneeling to Henry but because he disliked doing so while Hereford was still being held fondly by the shoulders. Henry was too keen to let that pass. He prevented Arundel from bending his knee with a gesture, since he cared nothing for the dignity of kingship, desiring only its power.

"There will be time enough for that, Arundel, when I wear the crown. You are looking well. How is your lovely wife?"

"In excellent health and perfect looks, sire, and waiting most anxiously to greet you."

"And yours, Roger?"

Hereford laughed. "I shall put Elizabeth in a box, my lord. She is too lovely for you to let alone and has too good an eye for a strong man to resist you. Truly though, I have not seen her for some time. I have been a little occupied on your affairs."

"Ah, what a reputation you will give me. For shame. Do you wish my vassals to withdraw their allegiance for fear I should tamper with their women? Not yours, anyway, Roger. After a face like yours, all other men must look like moles."

"If I ever see a mole with freckles and red hair, I will take the cloth—or eschew wine."

Henry struck Hereford a friendly blow that staggered him. He was somewhat shorter than his liege man, being a little less than middle height, but considerably broader. At eighteen his body already promised its full strength, square and stocky with tremendous shoulders and a neck short and strong as a bull's. The hair was not really red but sandy, and the face was liberally sprinkled with freckles. A mobile mouth, smiling now to expose good teeth, softened somewhat the square, determined line of the jaw that could easily look brutal. Beyond all else, however, the eyes above an indeterminate nose drew the attention. They were not large, and the lashes were short and sandy, but their gray was so bright and their look so keen that few except the dullest men were totally misled by the generally bland and good-humored expression of the face. Not that Henry was not good-humored, for he certainly was, although he had a fierce temper. Therefore, he looked, and was truly concerned when Hereford gasped and whitened at the blow.

"Good Lord, Roger, did I hurt you?"

"Ay, you are strong as an ox. I broke my collarbone a few weeks since and it is still tender. No matter, no harm done."

"Broke your collarbone? What a boy's trick! Were you climbing trees or did you fall off your horse dead drunk?"

"My lord," Arundel broke in, shocked and disapproving of this light badinage between king and liege man, "we should go ashore."

Arundel disapproved too of Henry's garb, both his own and Hereford's being far more magnificent. The young man was properly enough clad in excellent mail, but his chausses were of russet homespun as were his cloak and surcoat. Shoes and belt, instead of being decorated with gilding, gold wire, and jewels, were perfectly plain leather and, although of the best quality, were stained and marred by long use. Henry leapt ashore, too, laughing when he was splashed, without accepting the hands proffered to help him and mounted his horse with an agile spring, again ignoring the cupped hands ready to lift him into the saddle. He laughed and talked incessantly, as much to the men-at-arms as to the important men beside him, and stopped to jest also through an interpreter with the serfs around a Maypole. He has not changed a hair in two years, Arundel thought, frowning, and what was excusable in a boy of sixteen was less acceptable in a man who had come to make war to seize a throne.

If he had been present several hours later, when Hereford put his demands before Henry, Arundel would have felt quite differently, for Henry had sufficient dignity when he felt it necessary. He also had very winning ways and great charm so that it took all of Hereford's great power of determination to stick to his point. Henry yielded at last, signing and applying his seal to the charters, because he had no choice. He needed Hereford just then far more than Hereford needed him. His manner, having granted the demands, did him great credit, for he did not hold what Hereford had wrested from him against his liege man. Henry was not a grudge holder. He could do and say truly fearsome things in a rage, but cool, he was even too forgiving of an injury, especially to those of whom he was fond.

Late that night when even the bonfires which celebrated the coming of summer had died, Hereford and Henry were still hard at work. Arundel, more and more convinced that they were mad, nodded in his chair as the two fair heads bent together over charts and parchments on which plans of action, supply routes, escape routes, men and arms available, and even descriptions of terrain were detailed. Arundel had never seen anything like that in all his years of fighting and could not understand, although both obligingly explained, separately and in chorus, what they were about.

"Waste of time," he growled. "Let us attack where they are weakest and it is most convenient to us and take his keeps. When we have reduced him to nothing, he will yield."

"No doubt," Henry replied rather sharply, "and you will also have reduced the country to nothing. I do not come here for sport. I came first because it is my right to be king and second because there is power and profit in this land. Of what use is it to be king of a ruined realm? I wish to win, but I wish to spare the country as much as I may, that I may have something of value over which to rule."

CHAPTER 13

FROM ARUNDEL'S KEEP they rode west to Salisbury, Henry with those men he had brought with him and Hereford with his troop. They rode as quickly and silently as possible, starting in the evening and riding through the night. At present neither had any desire to be noticed, for they were not strong enough a group to hold off a determined attack, and some men of this part of the country were strongly in favor of Stephen and would have been happy to take such a prize. At Salisbury they picked up more troops and started on their way north. Hereford himself might have chosen to rest a day at Salisbury, but Henry seemed only invigorated by labor. No effort seemed to tire that squat frame, no problem to cloud his good humor. At Devizes they did stop—Henry suggested they stay long enough to eat and change horses.

"My lord," Hereford protested, "I urged haste, but indeed you need not have taken me so seriously."

"I am in no special haste, Roger, but where there is nothing to do, I can see no reason to dally."

Hereford began to laugh helplessly. "A few months away from you and I had forgot. My lord, the men must sleep, even though you apparently need it not—and I must sleep too. Furthermore, if we ride at this pace we will outstrip our own couriers to Scotland. Stay, I will find a wench to amuse you while the rest of us, weaklings that we are, snatch a few hours of rest."

"You would need to be quickly refreshed if you were to sleep only while I tumbled a wench. By the by, Roger, I do not believe I wrote to you that I have fathered a son—Geoffrey—a very likely boy he looks, though I had not time to stay long to observe him."

263

"You named him for your father?" Hereford was laughing again. Somehow that seemed a little outrageous.

"Well, he did not think it a bad idea—no, I gave the child the name common to the eldest-born of our family. When I am king I will bring him here. I would have been Geoffrey too but for the need to remind England that I am the heir of Henry Beauclerc through my mother. Go. You are asleep where you stand."

Hereford did not, however, go to sleep. He snatched the short period of freedom to dictate a letter to his mother, for he thought Elizabeth would stay at Chester. He bid her to make provision for entertaining "he whom I bring" and a large number of retainers, urging the man he dispatched to make all haste and providing him liberally with gold to buy new horses so that he would not need to rest his mounts on the way. His note was a bare two lines, terse and cold, although he did not mean it to be. He had certainly gotten over his rage and had almost forgotten in the press of other duties that he had been angry. An equally brief note went to Walter, merely to say that he would not return to the siege and that Walter should continue to follow the plans outlined as best as he could until he had further word. He fell asleep at the table eventually, his head pillowed on his arms, while he thought he was considering whether to write then to Elizabeth at Chester or to Chester himself, or wait until he had a little more freedom in Hereford.

They rode again that night but fortunately not far. Gloucester was at Bristol and wished to offer Henry his support personally. Henry was not fond of William of Gloucester, being repelled by the same characteristics that offended Hereford, although for different reasons.

"Is it worth it, Roger?" he had asked when the message came. "His father I would have ridden through hell to speak with—even Phillip—but William—. Of what value is he to us? Might it be a trap?"

"A trap—no. He is firm enough in your cause. I cannot believe that there could be any chance of that. And certainly he can be of great value, for I lead only his mercenary troops. He gave me his promise some months since that when we returned from Scotland he would summon his vassals to fight with us against Stephen. You know, my lord, I cannot command those forces without his will and presence. It would be most unwise to offend William of Gloucester."

"So be it. I too would not desire bad blood between us. He is, after all, my cousin, but I wished to be sure. Faugh, he makes my skin crawl though. What kind of a man is it that would allow another to do his fighting for him? I hear he looks with lust not only upon women—?"

Hereford made a moue of distaste. "That is true enough, and well I know it. There are times when I would be glad to have a face like Gaunt's. Nay, what troubles me most is that he *likes* to play the spy."

"I know, and I cannot help but wonder if that is not a disease too deep in the flesh now to cure. Will he, when I am on Stephen's seat, continue to play the spy, only now against me, for the love of the dirty game?" Henry's eyes were hard and narrow with suspicion. "Upon such a man it is never safe to repose too much trust."

Nonetheless, Henry of Anjou's opinion of Duke William did not prevent him from exerting the full power of his Angevin charm when they met. So successful was he that William's eyes hardly strayed even once to Hereford, who sat in grateful silence for a time and then excused himself. That charm, although it enchanted him when turned upon himself, made Roger uneasy when it was displayed for someone Henry plainly disliked and distrusted. It was true that Henry would usually keep a verbal promise, but that was largely because he almost never made one. Young as he was, he was a past master at the suggestive hint, the understanding smile, the glance that offered much without words. It was only when he was cornered and forced that he would speak or write a definite commitment. Hereford shrugged and acknowledged that a king without the art to keep his subjects faithful by hope of gain would need to be a bloody tyrant and keep them subdued by fear. In the end, it was the subjects, not the king, who were to blame. If they would keep their oaths to support him with honesty, he would not need to resort to procedures that certainly bordered on the dishonorable to control them.

How had he ever become involved in this affair, Hereford wondered. Where was the difference between Stephen, who promised with his mouth, and Henry, who promised with his eyes? Why had he not sat quietly on his own lands? That question answered all the others. Things had grown so bad in Stephen's reign that a man could not sit quietly on his own lands. The different between Henry and Stephen was not in their honesty, in that Hereford admitted there was little to choose between them, but in their basic characters and conceptions of kingship. Stephen was weak and desired the trappings of royalty. So long as men called him king, he cared little what they did, whether they fought among themselves or the stronger oppressed the weaker. Henry was strong and desired the power of royalty. Under his hand, by guile or by force, the barons would live in obedience if not in quiet. So long as his own personal interest was not at stake, Henry had a strong sense of justice, and, moreover, for his own great pride's sake, no man would cry to him for redress in vain. What he was doing was right and good, Hereford reassured himself; it was only because he was tired that his heart was so heavy.

A good night's sleep and a bright morning made that seem almost true as they set off again. They ate and rested a while at Gloucester, leaving the duke there with a sense of relief, and rode on again through the gathering dusk and on through the dark toward Hereford. Roger knew every foot of this road, night or no night, he had ridden it so often. He regretted not having asked Elizabeth specifically to return. She would have been useful in entertaining Henry—Catherine, Hereford decided, he would have to keep isolated because his lord would surely forget the courtesy due a noblewoman if the noblewoman showed any signs of encouragement. Besides—his eyes grew reminiscent, and he smiled—he could use some entertainment himself. He laughed aloud, and Henry, who had been silent for all of five minutes, turned to him quizzically and eagerly.

"I was thinking," Hereford replied to the look, "that I have been startlingly faithful to my wife. In four months of marriage—at least two of which we have been separated—I have not even looked at, not to mention touched, another woman."

"Is that something to laugh at? In your case I would suggest an immediate consultation with a good physician. Do not tell me you are in love with her."

Hereford laughed again. "Yes, I do love her, as a matter of fact, but truly, I fear, it was not love but exertion that kept me pure. Nonetheless, my lord, I am moved to reprove you—by your leave, of course—for your misspent life."

That sent Henry off into giggles. "Four months of holy wedlock and he wishes to reprove me. Roger, we shared the same whores in France, and even I was brought to admire your work. You have bettered me by one in the matter of bastards—and in the years in which you fathered them too. If you turn sanctimonious on me, I will hang you for a traitor. Still, who could better reprove me from a wealth of experience? By all means, you have my leave."

Both men were fatigued, both very young, and both overburdened with responsibility. The sweet spring air, the silent, starry night were headier than wine, and, drunk with the momentary release of tension which they knew would return all too soon, both because very silly. Hereford proceeded to preach a sermon on the joys of chastity that would have edified a saint; Henry, listening in awe, nearly fell off his horse with laughter.

The same sweet air and peaceful night were not affecting Elizabeth in a similar manner. She had returned from Chester just in time to witness the arrival of Hereford's courier, and the fact that he brought not even so much as a verbal greeting to her broke the peace that she had been achieving so slowly and painfully. Her mother-in-law's frantic activity to ready the castle for Henry's reception only embittered her further, for there was nothing for her to do. More bitter than gall was the knowledge that she was not even the lady of the keep, not even worthy to help in the labor of preparing for an exalted guest, more surely exalted because he was unnamed.

Possibly she might have regained some equanimity and sufficient reason to realize that her husband had not

meant to slight her had she been able to vent her emotions. That solace was denied, however, by her pride, for
she would not weep before the other women of the keep.
She could not even creep into bed to cry herself to sleep,
because she did not know what bed to go to. If the guest
was Henry, which both women suspected, there could be
no doubt that Hereford's own bedroom would be yielded
to him. Where Roger would decide to sleep then was any-
body's guess. He might decide on the semiprivacy of his
mother's quarters just above the main hall; he might wish
for greater proximity for ease of communication and
choose to sleep in the hall itself; or, he might wish to be
free of the exhausting presence of his guest and choose to
go to the solar of the old keep. In any case, Elizabeth was
not even sure that he would wish her to share his bed.
She had worked herself into such a state that, when the
exhausted foreriders arrived to announce that Lord Hereford was a few minutes behind them, she fled from the
hall up to the women's quarters. Whatever happened she
would not be shamed by being snubbed before the man
she believed would be the next king of the realm. She
would come down only if Roger sent for her, and sent for
her civilly.

Lady Hereford did not see Elizabeth leave and quite
honestly forgot all about her in the joy of welcoming her
dearly beloved son and the excitement of welcoming
Henry of Anjou. Elizabeth stood in the stairwell, listening.
She heard the confused noise of arrival, a man's voice
which she judged rightly to be Henry's, and her husband's
light laugh. She heard servants come with food and wine,
but Hereford never even mentioned her name, and no servant came with a summons to her. Fury replaced guilt
and self-reproach; whatever she had done, she had meant
no harm and did not deserve this. Step by step she was
drawn down those stairs by her rage and her curiosity until at last she stood just inside the doorway.

Had she been an active part of it, nothing could have
been more pleasing than the scene which met her eyes.
The room was ablaze with light, both hearths filled with
roaring fires, every wall holder with a lighted torch, and
every table and chest high enough to hold them supported

candelabra of burning candles. Both men looked tired but satisfied, Henry as usual talking and gesticulating vivaciously as he stood near Lady Hereford's chair. He nudged Hereford with his goblet, and Roger turned to fill it.

"Elizabeth! Where the devil did you spring from?"

Fortunately he did not wait for a reply but ran across to her to embrace her most heartily. For once in her life, Elizabeth was struck dumb with surprise and pleasure. Roger led her forward and presented her to Henry, saving her another few moments in which to collect her senses for she sank to the floor with bent head in the curtsy reserved for royalty. Those moments, however, also permitted Hereford to recover from his simple surprise and wonder what she was doing there.

"For God's sake, have you not set out for Chester yet? You knew my haste. If this is a new scheme of yours to bedevil me, you have gone too far this time. I will beat you witless."

That did it. All the resentment which remorse had swallowed up, rose at once in Elizabeth's breast and she rose from her curtsy as if she had sat on a hot coal. Henry took one look at that magnificent, flaming countenance, gave a low whistle, and began to laugh soundlessly.

"Whoreson! Is that a way to bespeak me before a guest! Watch lest I return to you better measure than you deal out to me. When you ask a question like a man instead of braying like an ass, mayhap you will receive a reply."

Hereford turned crimson and stuttered. His hand went to his belt, Elizabeth's to her knife. Henry laid his hand on Lady Hereford's arm to restrain her from intervening.

"Nay," he murmured, shaking, "let them have at it. Such love-talk is a wonder and a pleasure to hear. Doubtless they missed each other. I will not let them come to harm."

"You will answer however I speak to you, you lousy bitch, before guests or before the whole world, or I will flay you alive in the public square to make sport for my serfs."

"You and what other ten men? Toad! You will have to lay hands on me first. My hero! Call up your armies. With their aid surely you can subdue one woman."

Hereford was so enraged that his hands shook and he could not open the buckle of his belt. Henry, turning his head from wife to husband as if he were watching a game of catch-ball, suddenly gave way to his amusement, spluttered, and then howled with laughter. The sound hit Elizabeth like a pail of cold water. She was proud and in private would gladly have fought Roger to a standstill or been beaten unconscious. To shame her husband before his overlord was far beyond any salve her pride needed.

"Oh, stop, wait, oh, my accursed temper," she stammered. "Indeed I went to Chester. I returned from there only this forenoon. My father will be ready. I stayed to see the muster begin."

She stood her ground then, although she wished the earth would open and swallow her, more flushed and as magnificent in her shame as she had been in her rage. Before Hereford could speak, Henry stepped forward.

"Let her be, Roger," he said, very low. "You have won this round. Be generous." What he thought, though, was that Hereford should not tempt his luck. From what he saw of Elizabeth, the next passage at arms might easily be hers.

To say that the situation was not strained would have been fatuous, but Henry, suppressing his amusement as well as he might, did nobly. For a time he carried the whole weight of the conversation, while Hereford glowered and Elibabeth struggled to command herself. Eventually he was able to draw Elizabeth into talk with perfectly unexceptional questions about her father. Long practiced in public poise which covered private turmoil, she was able to respond politely, if briefly, at first, and then, as she warmed to her subject and her listener, with such intelligence that Henry forgot all about his reason for beginning the conversation in his absorption. He was not in the least shocked, although many men might have been, by such wifely behavior because it was the norm in the household of which he was a son. The only essential differences were that Elizabeth was far more beautiful than his mother and seemed to have better taste. Quite apparently she preferred to quarrel privately, whereas Matilda seemed to enjoy public squabbling. Henry was charmed and exerted himself to be charming. Elizabeth responded, warming steadily under his open admiration until she was flashing her magnificent eyes as flirtatiously for him as she ever had for Roger himself.

Completely incapable of joining them because of his inability to address his wife civilly, Hereford seized the opportunity, once he had caught his breath, to give his mother instructions about supplying a comely girl for Henry—not a serf and preferably not a virgin, and above all one who was willing—Henry liked complaisant women. Briefly he had thought of making the same demand for his own amusement in order to insult Elizabeth, but the notion was gone as quickly as it came. He did not desire any other woman when Elizabeth was obtainable. Angry as he was, his wife stirred his senses; he would never be sufficiently angry with her to forego that pleasure.

"My lord," he said finally, interrupting without apology Elizabeth's description of a tactical maneuver which had been beaten off at Chester, "it is long past midnight. We would all do well to seek our beds."

"Yes, yes," Henry replied absently, and returned to his absorbing interest. "But, Lady Elizabeth, it was the stupidity of your enemies, not your own strength which defeated them. With such a force they needed only dam off the water supply of the moat and fill it. Then—"

"Our water supply is not damable, sire. It is supplied a little by springs, but mostly by an underground outlet of the river. Chester is a hopeless place to attack; it will stand forever."

Henry's eyes flickered. Chester was for him at this moment, but Chester was sure only in his changeability. "Where is the outlet?"

"I do not know, my lord, nor does my father. He told me once that he had tried to find it because the fish from our stew pond escape that way and he thought to place some kind of barrier there—but he did not succeed."

Perhaps she was telling the truth, Henry thought, but very likely not. That was the trouble with intelligent women—they were interesting to talk to but not of much use, for a woman lied by nature and, also by nature, trusted no one. Such a combination allied with brains made them useless as sources of information unless they were overmastered by love.

"But I should not keep you longer with my foolish talk, my lord," Elizabeth continued, curtsying again. "I know you have come far and over a rough road. I am sure you desire your rest."

"Your talk is far from foolish, Lady Elizabeth, nor am I tired. Nonetheless, if I do not rest now I may well be tired tomorrow. I will hold you to your promise to tell me what you know of Maud in the morning, however."

Hereford led his lord away, murmuring that he should take whichever of the maids pleased him best. On his return through the hall, he passed Elizabeth, who had backed away a little, without a glance. At the door, however, he stopped to see whether she was following, and when it was apparent that she was not, he returned. His grip on her arm was brutal, his beautiful features distorted.

"And whose bed, madam, were you waiting to try? I assure you I have provided for Henry—you need not stretch your generous hospitality that far."

Elizabeth made no reply and did not attempt to pull away. When Hereford tugged at her she followed docilely, wondering what he would do. He dragged her out of the manor house and across to the keep. As they mounted the outer stair of the donjon, Elizabeth shivered, fearing he was going to imprison her in the dank lower floor or in one of the cheerless and unfurnished tower rooms. He never hesitated at all, however, and continued to yank her unmercifully across the great hall toward the stairwell which ascended to the old women's quarters.

"If you will tell me where you want me to go, I will go willingly," Elizabeth ventured to protest. She won no reply and when they had mounted the stairs, he thrust her into the old solar so roughly that she staggered.

"What were you waiting down there for?"

"Because I did not know where to go. Oh, Roger, have some sense. Do stop quarreling with me—"

"Me?" Hereford nearly choked. "Quarreling with you? You foul-mouthed bitch. Every time your lips part you spew venom. It is a wonder that your own spit does not poison you."

"Your own tongue is gilded with honey, is it? You have your just deserts of me. I warned you not to take me to wife—now you have me, enjoy me."

"That is just what I propose to do."

That was not, of course, what Elizabeth meant, and she struggled against him in earnest, but for once Hereford made no attempt to win her by caresses. He knocked her down and overpowered her, his rage as it mounted being such that even Elizabeth did not dare to fight any longer. Considering his initial fatigue and the violent venting of his passion, Hereford should have slept like one stunned. Instead he found himself wide awake when he moved away from Elizabeth. Her body had been unresponding, so cold as to be almost inanimate. Ordinarily Hereford was not a jealous man. In the past he had been too sure of his powers and not deeply enough involved emotionally to care much. Now everything was upside down. He was not afraid that Elizabeth's passions would lead her astray but that her ambition would.

"Elizabeth," he said in the soft voice he often used when he was in deadly earnest, "on my oath, if you ever betray me with your body for any purpose whatsoever, I will kill you."

"Lecher," she replied, but without heat, almost indifferently, "because you crave every woman you speak with, do not think that I am made in the same filthy mold."

"I do not think so. You are not honest enough for that. I could understand, if I could not forgive, an honest passion. You have none. When you sell yourself, it will be for gain. You have the heart of a trull."

Elizabeth should have been hurt, but she was not. Since she had a very honest passion, and since it was for Roger himself, the shaft was so wide of the truth that it did not prick her at all. She shrugged disdainfully. "And you say I have a venomous tongue. If I am to die for betraying you, I have consolation, for I will doubtless live forever." She turned on her side to look at him instead of staring at the bed curtains as she had been doing. "I have this to say to you, Roger, and I may as well speak even though you are in no mood to hear me. I am sorry I missaid you before your overlord. Mind, I am not sorry for what I said—that you deserved—but for the time and place of my speaking."

Hereford gave no sign of hearing her, but he had. The whole of his impossible relationship with Elizabeth was running in bright flashes through his mind. Elizabeth wantonly tempting him before his journey to France; Elizabeth coldly rejecting him when he returned as her accepted husband. Elizabeth warmly encouraging him in his political ambitions; Elizabeth nearly destroying them and himself because of a fit of temper. Above all the image of that very night returned. Elizabeth's dumb and joyous surprise when he greeted her so warmly, he had not missed that; her towering rage that met and matched his, and her sudden, unexpected capitulation. Interwoven with every memory of her was one of himself, invariably and inevitably doing and saying the wrong thing. Suddenly, helplessly, he began to laugh. He was remembering Henry's blatant admiration for his raving wife.

Startled by this most peculiar reaction, Elizabeth sat up. "What is it, Roger?"

"Elizabeth, oh, Elizabeth, we shall never act like ordinary people. We shall always laugh when we should weep, apologize when we should be angry, argue when we should make love, make love when we should sleep, and make ourselves a scandal and a hissing in all men's eyes and ears. When you do not drive me mad with rage, you drive me mad with love."

"Do you love me still, Roger?"

That made him sit up too. "Why not? Why should you doubt me? What sort of a love is it that fails for a little quarrel? Can I not be angry with you and love you also?"

She did not answer that. She wanted to ask what he meant by love, but did not dare. Instead she asked a little bitterly why he had written to his mother instead of to her regarding Henry's coming.

"Because," Hereford replied, his voice going cold and bitter too, "I was sure you would be still at Chester. I was certain once you were 'at home' with your father whom you love so dearly and in the only place where you are happy, as you have told me so often, that it would not be so easy to tempt you back to Hereford."

"My home is here now, Roger, and—"

"And?"

She spoke so low he had to strain to hear. "I love you too."

Her head was hanging. Hereford lifted it with a hand under her chin. "Those words are the sweetest I have ever heard from you, Liza. Why do you hang your head as if ashamed?" But she would not answer nor meet his eyes, and when he drew her against him, her head drooped again so that he could see only the white parting in her glossy hair. "For all I said of you in a rage, you are a truthful woman. Answer me. Why do you tell me this now?"

"Must I have some purpose other than that you have ever used me kindly—even when I deserved little kindness from you? You must think ill of me indeed to think me insensible of that."

"I do not know what I think of you. To speak the truth, I cannot think of you at all, for one way or another you put me into such a passion that I can do nothing except feel." He lay down pulling her with him, partly because he was tired but partly also to spare her his scrutiny. "I will ask you something I know you do not wish to answer, Elizabeth. Nor must you answer, although I desire to know. Why is your body so cold to me? No, not cold, that is not what I mean for I know that you desire me. You are not cold, you are—. You will not let me bring you to joy. Why do you deny me, and yourself too, that final pleasure? Is that no part of your love?"

"Part of it?" Elizabeth pulled away so that she could see Roger's face. "Is that not all of it to you? What use have you for me except that and my breeding an heir for you? Your home does not need a woman, your mother is here. Your business does not need a woman for you are too strong to want help or support—"

"Even if what you say were true, is it love to deny me the one thing I desire from you?"

There was a long silence during which Elizabeth crept miserably back into her husband's arms. He accepted her, but he made no effort to hold her close or to caress her. The candles began to gutter and first one and then another went out. The fresh odor of spring in the room was mixed with the scent of burnt wax, and Elizabeth became conscious too of the acrid odor of Roger's healthy male body against which she was pressing herself.

"I cannot," she whispered brokenly. "If my will could have given you that, you would have had it. It is true that at first I was unwilling to grant you that final power over me, but that night—the night we came away from Nottingham—I tried. I did try, Roger. I could not."

Hereford released his breath in a long sigh, and Elizabeth realized that he had been holding it while she spoke, so intent had he been on every word. "That was—that was not the right time, Liza." His voice trembled slightly and he put up a hand to stroke her hair, an expression of deep satisfaction softening his face. "Undo your braids, love, and try if you can sleep. I will torment you no more."

CHAPTER 14

THE SUN MOVED SLOWLY across the rush-strewn, stone-flagged floor, making motes of dust from the dry rushes glitter like minute stars. Hereford, with heavy-lidded eyes, watched them dance in the slight current of air that came through the open window. Today he would begin the muster of vassals whom he had not called to arms earlier, keeping them in reserve, although they had been warned to be ready for this ride north. It was unfortunate that Henry was here, for Hereford had no particular desire for any close contact between his vassals and the future king. It was not that Hereford contemplated changing his loyalties and feared that his vassals would remain attached to Henry; it was merely that he knew some of them would prefer to hold directly from the king and that Henry would by no means be impervious to this suggestion. Hereford had no desire to be engaged in a series of squabbles with his vassals and Henry as to who was whose overlord.

He needed only two days or three, but in the long hours of a sleepless night he had been able to think of no adequate way to rid himself of Henry for that period of time without rousing his suspicions. In his concentration he had forgotten that he had left the bed curtains open, and now the sunlight fell across Elizabeth's face, waking her. Her first sensation was one of loss, for she had fallen asleep in Roger's arms and now the bed was empty. She started up, half asleep.

"Gone," she cried, "he is gone without a word of farewell."

She sounded like a lost child instead of a mature woman. Hereford was so moved that he stumbled in his haste to reach her. "No, Elizabeth, I am here."

She clutched at him too like a child, but almost immediately became fully awake and drew back with a shamed smile which faded as she took in Hereford's blue-ringed eyes. "Did you not sleep at all, Roger?"

"Not much."

"But I thought—"

"It is nothing to do with you, Elizabeth," he replied, pulling her back into his embrace.

She was silent. As things stood between them now, she felt she could ask nothing further. Hereford's hesitation was due to no doubts of Elizabeth, however. In this matter they would surely be one, for her ambition could brook no diminution of her husband's power. He was mistakenly trying to spare her any worry on that score, failing to realize, as usual, that political problems reacted differently on Elizabeth than on himself. To her their challenge offered stimulation not depression.

"I must go," he said finally. "I should have gone down hours ago. Henry must be wondering what has become of me."

"Wait, I will dress and go also. Then you may say I kept you."

"May I, Liza?" He smiled and stroked her hair. A woman's hair was a lovely thing, silken, soft, and soothing. Hereford leaned forward and buried his face in Elizabeth's, breathing the scent she used and her warm, sleepy, animal odor. "Have you no shame?" he murmured mischievously.

"Better he should think that than that you were hatching plots against him."

"Nonsense, Elizabeth," Hereford replied sharply, moving away. "I am a rebel and a wolf's-head for his sake. I would need to be mad to do such a thing."

For an instant Elizabeth considered holding her tongue. Her husband's present warmth was very precious to her and she did not wish to make him angry, but in the long run his welfare was more important than his mood.

"Nonsense yourself, Roger." She could have bitten her tongue the moment the words were out; that was not the way to begin. She rose and went to him, catching his hands and holding them against her breast. "I only desire your good. I have no quarrel with your overlord, but he has not lived among people worthy of trust—you told me that yourself. Can you not see that he is so trained that he distrusts even himself?"

"Oh, in that way, yes, he is suspicious. I suppose you are right," he added grudgingly, and then burst out, "I wish I could be rid of him for a day or two."

"For God's sake, Roger, say nothing to him." She almost added that he should let her manage Henry, but recollected herself in time. Roger was not her father. She would have to do her best without telling him what she planned.

Elizabeth's plans, quickly made from long practice in dealing with Maud, whose mind was, if anything, even more suspicious and devious than Henry's, worked well. She found Henry restless, bored, and impatient, and, remaining blind to her husband's black looks, set herself to cajole Henry into good humor. She did tell him, as she had promised, as much as she could about Maud, but she pointed out that she could tell him only of that part of the queen which she exposed to women.

"The one who really knows her, who has matched wits with her more than once and come away scatheless—and that cannot be said of many—is the Duke of Gaunt, he who was Lord Storm."

"That I know. I had looked forward also to having speech with him on other matters—but he did not come as he promised." Henry's face darkened.

"Not through lack of loyalty. You know his father died and he was bound to take homage of his vassals. My lord, he could not let it wait, even for a few weeks. You do not know the Welsh. I have lived on the borders of the Marches all my life. They are a mad, fearsome people. They cannot be once conquered and then lightly guarded. Gaunt will be no courtier to you; nor will he send you men, nor will he send you money. Yet his life will be spent in your loyal service for it is he and his like that keep the Welsh from flooding back into England."

"That is because no strong force with a steady purpose has been sent against them. That is the king's fault. It is his duty to subdue rebellious provinces so that the land may lie in peace and the lords do their proper service to the king."

"My lord, I may not say you nay, it is not my place—"

Henry guffawed. "You mean you wish to sweeten me for something." His eyes were kind but calculating. "I am afraid that you, like Moses, would say even the Lord nay if that was your desire."

The golden eyes sparkled with shared amusement. "I cannot deny that I certainly wish to keep you good-humored, but in the matter of the Welsh, truly, I care not enough one way or another to oppose your will. I do not think they can be conquered in the usual way—you should see the country, it is full of bolt holes, caves, gullies, hidden valleys, and all covered with thick woods. And the Welsh themselves are as clever as wild animals at concealment, and brave—they are the finest fighters in the world, I think."

"Then why not use them? Into the king's armies with them. If they wish to fight, let them fight for their master."

"How simple and beautiful, could it be done. Nay, my lord, their trouble is that they will brook no discipline—not even from their own chiefs. If it were not so, I make bold to say we Normans would have set no foot in their country. The Britons are not Saxon clods."

Elizabeth was putting forth one of her greatest efforts to seem interested without eagerness, and she was succeeding. Henry it was who now seemed eager. All trace of ill-humor vanished, he questioned and questioned. Elizabeth obligingly stripped her brain for him, knowing that her fund of knowledge could never satisfy that insatiable desire for definite information. Only when she was drained absolutely dry upon every topic did she refer to Gaunt again.

"He knows more than anyone alive, save perhaps Mortimer, who will not tell, about them and the country. Since fifteen he has fought them in the forests and on the plains, in the hills and through the valleys. A good part of his blood is Welsh also and some of his kinsmen are full-blooded Welsh."

"I would like to look on that land, and I have a great

lust to speak to Gaunt. Also I would like to know whether he means to hold by his father's will and do me homage now that he wields all the power."

"Of that last, I believe I can assure you. He is in no way changeable. Painscastle is but an easy day's ride. It is a pity you have not time to go."

Hereford, who had been listening sullenly to the entire conversation, toying with a goblet of wine, rose suddenly from his chair and walked away. "There is no time," he said in a hard voice. "The Welsh can wait. My lord, we have spent too much time already in this idle talk. If I am to muster my men, I must do so."

"How long will it take? They have been summoned to be ready; you need only bid them come."

"Not less than three days. Furthermore, I wish to go to each keep that is near enough myself to gather them. Thus I can see that they give me their best instead of sending raw, untrained men in cast-off arms as they might do if I merely summon them. It is well for a man to have a close eye to his vassals' doings. You should come with me."

There was a bare hint of authority in that last sentence and the tiniest flicker of impatience. Elizabeth felt like applauding; she did not know that Roger had so much deception in his soul. In truth, he did not. The tone was perfectly sincere. All the time he had been listening to Elizabeth and Henry, he had been fighting a desperate battle between his jealousy and his knowledge of Elizabeth's purpose. Jealousy had won over reason. Although his mind was sure that his wife merely wished to get Henry out of his way, his heart would give him no peace. One of them would have to go with Henry to Painscastle—and it could not be himself. In spite of Elizabeth's confession of love, or perhaps because of it, he could not tolerate the idea of her being exposed alone to the full impact of "that Angevin charm" for three or four days. He would rather take the chance of contesting Henry's influence with his vassals, but he had not been sufficiently cautious and the direction of his desire showed.

"You do not need me for that," Henry replied stiffly. "I assume your men will respond to your call without my presence to reinforce your authority." He turned to Elizabeth. "Will Gaunt receive us if we arrive without warning, Lady Elizabeth?"

"I am sure he will, my lord, but that is not the point. He may not be at Painscastle, and you would waste your time if he were not. Why not wait until you return south again and give him warning to be at home?"

"I will have less time then and I like unexpected visits better than those for which my host is prepared. Besides, it is never a waste of time to ride through the country. There is always something to be learned. Will you accompany me, Lady Elizabeth? You give her leave?" he asked rather coldly of Hereford.

"As you will, my lord," was Roger's equally icy reply.

"Then if we go right now, we will have three or four clear days in Wales. I can ride north directly from Painscastle to Chester with no loss of time and meet you there, Hereford."

Roger controlled himself with an effort, repeating, "As you will, my lord," but when Elizabeth flew to make ready, knowing of Henry's impatience to set about anything he had decided upon, he followed her. "Have a care for yourself, Elizabeth," he said bitterly.

She looked up from what she was doing in surprise. "Why, Roger, I can come to no hurt between here and Painscastle. The land is all our own or Gaunt's and well guarded."

"The danger I fear is from our friends, not our enemies."

That puzzled her for a moment, but then she dropped the garments she was holding to throw her arms impulsively about Hereford's neck. "Roger, you darling, you are jealous. You have good cause too," she laughed mischievously. "That man must be a disaster to women, even though he is not nearly as handsome as you are. His manners are marvelous."

"And his morals are atrocious. You will be no safer, being Hereford's wife, than any servant girl."

"You cannot make me believe he would force me—"

"I do not try; he likes only complaisant women. I told you to have a care to yourself, not to him." But Hereford's tone was lighter. He had scarcely expected the stately Elizabeth to hang around his neck, particularly in the presence of her maids, nor to rub her cheek against his as she was doing now. He recognized clearly that he had been making a fool of himself."

"Oh, Roger, shame. You of all people to make such remarks. How many men have you cuckolded?" Her voice shook with amusement.

"That is no affair of yours, and all the more reason my wife should give no cause for similar rumors to be spread about me."

Still he was comforted and bid them farewell with commendable if not perfect calm. Subsequently he was too busy to spare them more than a passing thought now and again, so that it was not until a few hours before he himself left for Chester that his uneasiness returned. It was sparked by a note from Henry saying briefly that he assumed Hereford's permission would be granted to take Lady Elizabeth on with him to Chester since there could be no doubt of her welcome in her father's house. Hereford boiled. He liked neither Henry's calm assumption of authority over his wife nor Elizabeth's apparent docility, for she could surely have sent him word of Henry's intention in time for him to frustrate it had she so desired. What was more, he was furious at Elizabeth's being brought to Chester again. The further she was separated from her father these days the better he liked it. Of course Chester would be leaving with them so that Elizabeth would not be alone with him, but—.

Hereford could have spared himself a great deal of mental anguish if he could have applied his intelligence and what he knew of Henry to the problem instead of allowing himself to be carried away by his emotions. It was quite true that his overlord had no moral scruples, but he had an extraordinarily keen sense of what was to his advantage. It would have been criminally insane of him to take the chance of alienating Hereford for an hour's sport with his wife. At present Hereford was Henry's ladder to the English throne. On the other hand, Henry was a born tease and crazy for a jest. He could not resist the chance of tormenting his liege man—for he had seen that he was jealous—and twitting him later on his susceptibility.

It was not Elizabeth's wish to infuriate her husband that had prevented her from writing; indeed she was almost morbidly anxious not to displease him. She had admitted her love in the wake of her tempestuous outburst, had admitted too that she was willing to let down the sexual barrier she had built against him. Her temper had twice brought her serious defeats in her handling of Roger, a thing that had never happened in her dealings with her father, so that she had no weapons to use against him, and, worse yet, she was no longer sure that he would trust her with his confidence. For all that, she was strangely happy, even though she felt uncertain of what she wanted or in which direction she wished to move. It was very difficult for her to concentrate on any long-range object at all. When Roger had made a definite demand of her, unconscious though it was, her mind leapt into action to obey with its usual agility, but it seemed as if she needed some external force to activate her. She was content, as she had never before been, to drift on the current of things without desire to steer or propel herself. It was partly because of this languor that she had not written and partly because she did not know what to say. She wanted to go on to Chester because she wanted to see Roger again and because she enjoyed Henry's company; she wanted to return to Hereford because she knew that Roger would prefer her to do so and because pleasing him was now an object to her.

The drawn curtains of her own bed at Chester allowed only a dim red light to bathe Elizabeth. She sighed and turned on her side. She had long since missed Mass and there was nothing to get up for. They were all gone. For the first time in many years, since her childhood, in fact, Elizabeth was filled with a burning resentment at being a woman. A woman who was left behind to wait—wait and embroider and wonder what would happen if her menfolk did not return. She had not had that fear either for many years, but it had haunted her ever since she had watched Hereford fight de Caldoet. Now and again she had nightmares in which she saw her husband, unhorsed and helpless, waiting for death as a whole army rode down upon him. She wrenched her mind away from that, but not far away. It slid only to the scene between herself and Roger before dawn that morning. He had been coldly polite and very angry, not asking any questions or even giving her a chance to explain her actions in the two days they had all spent at Chester. Even his love-making had been cursory, an act to satisfy his own need with no regard for hers, unprecedented behavior in Roger which had reduced her to mute terror. In the last few hours he had become somewhat gentler, and Elizabeth's oppression had lifted sufficiently to permit her to help him dress and arm. She lingered about her duties, in fact, knowing that it might be many months before she saw him again, until he snatched his belt from her hands in impatience. She watched him belt his surcoat—the same belt he had tried to remove to beat her with, and reach for his sword belt. It might be more than months before she saw Roger again; he might never return.

"Roger."

"Yes?"

"Roger, I have asked you nothing of your plans. I know too that you are angry, but—"

"Please, Elizabeth. I have not the time—nor, in truth, the desire—for excuses or recriminations. Let us part as pleasantly as we may."

"You must listen. I will be brief for I have no excuses to offer and no recriminations to make. I only wish to ask you—" she hesitated and bit her lip. Hereford turned away impatiently, anxious only to end an interlude which he had found uninterruptedly painful, and Elizabeth caught his sleeve desperately. Her need was greater than her pride. Indeed, it looked very much as if she would soon have no pride at all where Roger was concerned. "Roger, I beg you, do not let me live week after week in fear. Write to me—even if it be no more than five words to say you are well. You do not know," she faltered, "you do not know how dreadful it is to do nothing but wait helplessly."

Hereford had started to pull away without replying, for he was still smoldering over her docility to, as he put it, everyone but himself, when the sick sensation he had lived with while Walter fought at Burford recurred to him. He swallowed; it was no light thing to live thus for weeks or months on end. That was a far bitterer punishment than any he had in mind for his erring Elizabeth.

"I will write." His wife looked strangely soft in the candlelight with her hair loose and a robe carelessly corded around her narrow waist. "Do not fret, Elizabeth, I will write everything I safely may to you. Shall I send here to Chester or to Hereford?"

"I had planned to ask Gaunt to send a force to take me home. He often has troops traveling to Rhos. It would not be far out of their way."

That was for his sake, and Roger had recognized it. He pulled her to him and kissed her, gently and gratefully. "I have not been kind to you, Elizabeth. You are generous to seek to please me nonetheless. If I have been unjust, I am sorry. I will write to Hereford then—every chance I have, but do not be troubled if time goes by and I am silent. We may have heavy work in the north. Always remember that if there is bad news, you will hear that most quickly of all."

It was something, but time stretched before her in a vast empty track. Who cared who was king, Elizabeth thought suddenly. If Roger had been a little man of no account, this lovely spring and the coming summer would have been a time of joy. A time to hunt together, to hawk together, to stroll in the garden and pick flowers in the meadows. Their greatest troubles would be the minor evil-doings of their serfs and the vagaries of the weather. Even the autumn and winter would be pleasant in their own way. Elizabeth could read tales by the fire, or together she and Roger could listen to the minstrels sing through the long evenings, then to seek the warmth and comfort of their bed—together. Elizabeth pulled back the bed curtains and prepared to rise. There was no warmth and little comfort in an empty bed.

Hereford leaned back against the bole of the tree behind him and yawned. They were making good time and should be at King David's court easily on the promised day. Then the knighting, then the fighting—all to the good. The quicker they were at it, the quicker it would be over, one way or the other. Chester and Henry had been in repulsively good spirits all the morning, and he might well have been too—except. Except for the nagging sensation which he could not kill that the enterprise was doomed from the beginning. Nervously Hereford yawned again.

"Short on sleep, Roger?"

"A little, my lord."

Henry looked quickly over his shoulder to make sure that Chester was well out of hearing. "You have a charming wife—charming."

"When she wishes."

"Still turning on the coals, Roger?" Henry chortled. "I had not thought a man so hot with rage could be so cold with courtesy." To that Hereford made no reply and Henry waited with a rather birdlike air of expectancy that was odd in a man of his solid appearance. At last he gave up and spoke again. "You disappointed me. I had hoped for a little more warmth in your manner when you met us at Chester. It needs only a small spark to set her off, and I have never seen a woman to match your wife in rage. Even my mother is nothing to it." Henry did not yet know that he was to marry a woman whose temper would make Elizabeth's rages seem like hymns of praise. He could still afford to laugh. Obviously Hereford was thinking that remark over.

"I am glad she afforded you amusement," he replied flatly.

A furrow appeared between Henry's brows. This was going a little too far. It was true that Hereford had said once that he loved his wife, but there had been so many other women he had professed love for with almost the same type of laugh. Almost, Henry thought suddenly, not quite the same. Now Henry was worried. Apparently this went deeper and Hereford was not concerned merely with his own honor but with his wife's feelings. It was ridiculous for Henry to protest that he had not touched Elizabeth. Plainly from his manner Hereford knew that. It would be no jest at all if Hereford were to remain in this temper over a woman, and Henry knew that, unlike himself, Hereford was capable of bearing a grudge for a very long time. A man whose heart harbors a grudge is a bad friend to have on the battlefield, even if his mind is loyal.

"I say, Roger, a jest is a jest, but our affairs are no laughing matter. If you are angry, say what is in your heart and be done. To carry such a burden is heavy work and grows heavier with time. You and I will have burdens enough without adding this load to our packs."

A jest, Hereford thought, I will teach him to jape thus with me. "I am sure you would do me no dishonor, my lord," he replied icily, "what then could burden my heart?"

"You are not sure at all, you great ass, although you should be. Nay, Roger, I do not pretend that your wife would be safe from me either because I love you or because you are my man. Nor do I make any promise for the future, but just now I would not treat the Virgin Herself with more respect. You hold the keys of my kingdom. Without you there is no gateway to my desire. You should know I would not throw the chance of a throne away for any woman, least of all for another man's wife who can bring me nothing."

Hereford had meant to hold out and give Henry a good lesson which might prevent him from a similar form of amusement in the future, but he could not. Henry's candid appraisal of himself was totally disarming; Hereford had to laugh, and that heartily. "I am not that much a fool. If I thought you had smirched my honor, you and I could not be sitting here in talk. Although I made an oath to support your claim to the throne, I made none to refrain from personal quarrels with you. You know, my lord, I make no fuss over other women. As you yourself have said, we shared our whores in France, but this is a question of my wife. I have been so gay a dog in the past that many are waiting for her to set a step amiss so that they may crow. Elizabeth—Elizabeth is too proud to let me fear dishonor through her, but her manner—. I have no desire to set up as a laughingstock."

"Well, she is safe enough now, so bend your mind to

your advancement and mine and leave off this brooding over nothing."

"What is there to think about? We go to Scotland to your knighting and mine." Hereford laughed again. "It comes a little late in our fighting careers I fear, but better late than not at all, I suppose. We will have time enough to think when that step is taken."

"Are you going to be like all the others—fight today with never a thought for the morrow. Wake up, man! Do you think that David is a fool? What will he want for what he offers? How much may I yield him?"

That opening was too good to resist. "That is easy. From your view, 'too much' is what he will want and 'nothing with ease' is what you will yield." Hereford then sobered and shrugged. "I can be no help to you in this, my lord. I have never had acquaintance with your uncle nor am I wise in the problems of Scotland. Old Gaunt is a great loss in this matter. I know little of King David's character and less of the needs of his realm."

The problem needed to be faced, however, and even Hereford began to be concerned with it after a while. King David's greeting was so cordial, his welcome so magnificent, and his plans for the knighting so elaborate that Roger's relatively unsuspicious nature was aroused. He came to Henry's lodging late the night of their arrival, unceremoniously interrupting his overlord's amorous activities. Henry had been a little surprised, but not really annoyed. He did not dismiss the girl but suggested to Hereford that they walk out together.

"You know she is probably in David's pay and would listen. A large open space is best for talk such as ours."

"What does he want?"

"Nothing. He tells me it is for love and to honor the bond of our blood, his wife being my mother's sister."

"Do you believe that?"

Henry laughed silently. "He is a fool. Seeking to gain all, he will gain nothing. Because I am eighteen and he is past forty, he believes I am a child. Child! Was I ever a child?" he asked bitterly and then laughed again. "But he has done my work for me. He will fall into the pit of his

own digging. A child I shall be to him. 'Yes, uncle,' 'You
are wise, uncle,' 'So, if I can, I will do, uncle.' "

"And I?"

"My unwise councilor are you, my dear Roger. Have
you not a reputation for hot-headedness and amorous dal-
liance? Indulge it. If David suggests something wise, oppose it. If he suggests something foolish, approve it—unless
it be so silly as to be a trap. In a word, I wish him to believe that when I am set on the throne, he will rule England. Thus will I buy him at no cost."

"Henry—"

"Yes?"

Hereford swallowed his sickness. "He seeks his own advantage, it is true, but—"

"But?" There was a hardness and brittleness to the tone
that Hereford had heard before.

"But he may do us good service. Is it fair to pay him
back in false coin?"

"What will I do with you, Roger? There is a time and
place for honor. Are we dealt by honorably in intention?
You are four years older than I and yet younger. Will you
never learn the way of the world? Moreover, who says I
shall pay in false coin? As he aids me against my enemies,
so will I aid him against his when that power is mine. Is it
false to deny him the whole when he has paid only for a
small part?"

"No, but to allow him to believe—." Hereford stopped.
Practically speaking Henry was right and he was wrong.
There was no other way if they wanted David's wholehearted support. He would never make the effort they
needed for the questionable benefit of armed support in
some unspecified crisis in the future which might, after all,
never arise. Only if he thought he could direct the actions
and policies of the English king and perhaps siphon off a
substantial portion of English gold or gain dominion over
the northern provinces of England, gradually eating his
way down to the rich midlands, would it be worth his
while to set so much at stake.

"Roger, if you block me, or foul my game—"

"Not by my will." Agreeing, Hereford's heart sank further. "But I am no great play-actor and no safe ally for you in this."

"You think I do not know you? Do your best. Doubtless the eyes will be on me so long as you do not try to change their direction."

The mild military activity of the next two weeks—the attack of some small strongholds of Stephen's in the north, largely to call attention to Henry's presence—was sufficient to occupy the minds of David and his courtiers; they saw nothing unusual in Hereford's alternating silences and bursts of gaiety. Henry could not avoid showing his true colors in these encounters because he judged it to be more important that all should praise his military wisdom and his valor. It also seemed reasonable enough that a young man might be a most valorous knight and effective soldier without being astute or certain in matters of state. Only Chester, the wily old fox, smiled and called his son-in-law aside to thank him again for his warning about pinning Henry down with written promises. They were just preparing to begin the feasting before the knighting ceremony, and Roger's squires could cheerfully have murdered Chester for interrupting the lengthy process of dressing him. The Lord knew that his temper had grown steadily worse and worse and nothing exasperated him more than discussions while he was preparing for an important function these days.

"He nearly fooled me with that boyish good humor and the way he nods when you make a suggestion, but, praise God, I believed you, Roger, and made him sign. Now that I have seen him in action, however—. Roger, are we doing the right thing?" He had dropped his voice and, embracing his son-in-law, was speaking directly into his ear to frustrate eavesdroppers. "When this one mounts the throne—as you said—he will ride us all, and I fear greatly that he will not spare the whip. We are tormented with unrest under Stephen, but under Henry we are like to be too quiet—like men in prison. Mayhap the ills we have will be less hard to bear, being ills of too much freedom, than those we will bring upon ourselves by this enterprise."

"Father, in God's name do not falter now." Hereford shuddered under his father-in-law's hands as a chill passed through him. Was this to be the desertion that would ruin them? "There is no path to return to Stephen's favor for either of us. Even if he were willing, we have too many enemies too close to his ear. For good or ill, Henry is our only hope."

"Are you sure, Roger?"

"Father," Hereford whispered desperately, "do not tear me apart. I have given my oath to support Henry, and you are bound in blood to me through Elizabeth. Do not make me choose between breaking my word and raising my hand against my blood kin. Oh, God, if you care not for me, think of Elizabeth's suffering. You will kill her."

"Oh, you need not trouble yourself about that. If you do not think with me, I will not involve you. If it is needful for me to change my plans, I will keep well out of *your* way. Whatever happens, *we* will not come to blows."

Chester patted Hereford's shoulders fondly as he left, but the young man was anything but comforted. He returned to the ministrations of his squires with a set expression, replying so absently to their questions that William Beauchamp lost patience.

"My lord, whatever greater problems you consider, will you kindly pay some mind to those lesser but more immediate ones that trouble me. Will you wear the blue or the green gown now?"

To Hereford, made hypersensitive with tension, everything had special meanings just then. Symbolically, blue was the color of truth, green the color of loyalty. Hereford looked from one gown to the other. Must he warn Henry of Chester's vacillation? Henry was suspicious enough. It would be a dreadful blow to Chester and one that he would never have dreamt would fall, for he trusted Hereford to keep their talk, which he regarded as personal, in confidence. Not tonight, at least, Hereford thought. Tonight after dinner they would bathe ceremonially and stand their knightly vigil. Hereford drew a deep breath. He would have time enough to think then for they would have to stand before the altar in the church from sunset to sunrise.

"Green," he said finally. "Let me wear green."

Beauchamp looked at his master, for the phrase was

peculiar. He had no time, however, to worry about Hereford's peculiarities just now. When he was rid of the trouble of dressing him, the clothing for the vigil had to be prepared, and the mail recleaned and checked for the jousting the next day. Somewhere also William planned to find time to enjoy the festivities. Hereford could stand on his head for all he cared. He had no time for discussions.

The feast was like all others. There was too much to eat and far too much to drink. If Roger of Hereford's gaiety was febrile, it passed easily without comment in that roaring place. The bath, taken just as dusk fell, was warm and scented and soothing, except that Chester attended his son-in-law, for whose knighting he was the sponsor. The vigil, to Hereford, was endless. The first few hours he spent moving restlessly from one foot to another, wrestling with his problem, but the more fatigued his body grew, the less clearly could he see any honest solution. It was his duty to Henry to tell him Chester might defect; it was his duty to Chester to hold his tongue. His eyes rested on the steady flames of the votary candles on the altar, flames that were like two tiny, rosy hands cupped and lifted to pray. Hereford went down on his knees on the cold stone flags and sought prayers, but none of the ones he had been taught seemed suitable to his situation. He set his sword point down into a crack in the flags, holding it by the hilt, and leaned his forehead against the holy relics set in the pommel. Now his mind kept drifting away from Chester to his daughter. Elizabeth would have loved the panoply and excitement and the honor done him in knighting him with Henry. It was too bad he could not chance bringing her, for his pleasure as well as her own, because he missed her. Not that he lacked for female companionship. Of that there was, if anything, too much, too willing, too often. Hereford had to smile. He would not have been so tired if Elizabeth had been here to protect him—nor so frightened either. Elizabeth would have known what to do; Elizabeth would have handled Chester; Elizabeth would have told all the right lies at all the right times to the right people and left him with nothing to do but fight so that his heart could have been at peace.

Hereford closed his eyes. Elizabeth would break her heart if Chester were disgraced.

The shriek of steel on stone as his sword point slipped woke Hereford just before he fell forward. He judged that he had been asleep for some time because his knees were numb from kneeling and his hands from clutching the sword hilt. It took him four tries to get to his feet, and, at that, he probably would not have made it but for a strong hand which lifted and steadied him from the right. That would be Henry. Hereford did not dare look at him for, although he was not very pious, he was usually respectful of the Church and all religious ceremony, while Henry's behavior bordered on the blasphemous. If he turned his head, sure as he lived, Henry would begin to talk. Besides, he did not want to talk to Henry just now nor to look at him because he felt guilty. Sometime during his sleep he had made up his mind. As long as Chester made no active move against Henry, he would hold his tongue; he could not, and would not, hurt Elizabeth for a scruple of his conscience. What was the addition of one more feeling of guilt to the load of it he already carried compared with her pain? He was used to it, and she had been hurt enough by her father's ways.

Hereford glanced impatiently at the high window slits; as yet there was no sign of dawn. He should be using this time for prayer and contemplation, but the knowledge only made him smother a smile. How could a man lift his heart and mind to heaven when his feet hurt? Mayhap a saint, but saint he certainly was not. Besides, what need had he to pray to be a good knight? He *was* a good knight, and a better man than most. Damn Henry and Chester also. How could a man tread the path of honor when those around him—. No, he would not cast the blame elsewhere and he would think no more of the matter lest his tongue betray him by accident.

The coming of the morning light brought priests to say Mass and to release the young men from their vigil. The real ceremony was only just under way. First they would have a chance to eat, then out on to the jousting field, where a platform had been raised and draped in cloth of royal purple so that King David could give Henry the buf-

fet of knighthood clearly in all men's sight. Hereford
glanced quickly at the sky and sighed with relief. The day
promised fair, which would make everything pleasant. The
knightly buffet was no joke; Hereford half-expected to be
knocked right off the scaffolding and was just as pleased
that he would not have to land in a mud puddle. He did
not, in the event, actually fall off the platform, but his
head sang for hours and when he undressed that night
there was a huge bruise between his ear and his shoulder
where David's mailed fist had caught him. He heard
Henry laugh as he staggered and shook his head and
stepped back to join his overlord while David knighted fifteen other young men.

"You ought to put on some weight, Roger. You nearly
went off," Henry whispered. He had stood his ground like
a rock when David struck, and although the king had
doubtless tempered his blow to his nephew, it was still a
feat of strength not to have reeled.

"How can I put on weight when you never allow me
time to eat or sleep?" Hereford rejoined, laughing softly. "I
have shed a stone, at least, since I have returned to England."

"That was not because of my affairs," Henry said so
firmly that one might have thought him serious, "that's
lechery."

"Then you should be a wraith."

Henry dug his elbow into Hereford's ribs. "Have some
respect for your betters. Is that the way to talk to the man
to whom you are about to do homage?"

"I am only trying to protect you from the mortal sin of
pride. You should be grateful for my efforts on your be-
half."

"Be quiet, madman, everybody is looking at us. You
have a fine way of saving me anyhow. To preserve me
from the hell-fire for pride, you send me there for lechery."

"It is because I love you so much. At least for that we
will go together."

"Likely enough, but you will get there as fast as I for
the first cause as well as the second. Why not go to hell
with dignity?"

"There's nothing dignified about pride. If your pride

goeth before a fall and you miss your leap because you weigh as much as an ox, I'll have my turn to laugh, and the dignity of your pride will only make it funnier."

Henry chuckled. There was about as much chance of his missing his leap into the saddle of his horse without touching the stirrups as there was of his flying straight up to heaven in a fiery chariot. He had practiced that first trial of knighthood too long and too well to worry. He had no time to reply to Hereford, however, because David was stepping down to make way for his nephew to take his place. The laughter faded from Henry's eyes, and when he mounted the small additional rise that lifted him above the men who would do him homage, his young face was very set. The mobile mouth had thinned to a hard line, the brutal jaw was thrust forward; Henry fully intended to keep every one of these men to the letter of their vows. Kingship was no light matter or empty phrase to him, and so plain was his determination and so strong the force of his presence that a hush fell over the huge crowd gathered to watch the ceremonies.

Hereford, the first in importance, was the first to come forward, kneel, and raise his ungloved hands to his lord. Henry took them in his in a painful grip and the two pairs of eyes, blue and gray, deadly serious, deadly earnest, locked.

"Sire, I enter into your homage and faith and become your man, by mouth and hands, and I swear and promise to keep faith and loyalty to you against all others, and to guard your rights with all my strength."

"We do promise you, Roger, Earl of Hereford, that we and our heirs will guarantee to you the lands held of us, to you and your heirs against every creature with all our power, to hold these lands in peace and quiet."

Henry bent forward slowly and kissed Hereford lingeringly upon the lips. As he straightened, Hereford rose to his feet and they broke the hand grip. The Bishop of Carlisle then came up, holding out to Hereford a magnificent reliquary. The cover, pyramid shape, had golden bas-relief on each of its four faces, depicting the Annunciation, Birth, Crucifixion, and Ascension of Christ. On the panels of front, sides, and back were other scenes from the life on earth of the Son of God. The whole was set with beautifully polished gems, sapphire, emerald, and ruby, so that it flashed and sparkled in the brilliant sunshine of late spring. Hereford laid his hands upon the casket.

"In the name of the Holy Trinity, and in reverence of these sacred relics, I, Roger, Earl of Hereford, swear that I will truly keep the oath I have taken, and always remain faithful to Henry, rightful King of England, my overlord."

The bishop stepped back, and Henry came forward again. He kissed Hereford once more and handed him a gauntlet, for the right hand, of purple-dyed leather, its back completely covered with thick plates of bright-gleaming gold.

"Wear it in honor. Protected by it, strike hard for my cause."

Hereford slipped on the glove, his eyes incandescent with enthusiasm, and curled his hand into a fist. "For Henry, for England," he cried aloud, shaking the glittering glove at heaven.

"Fiat! Fiat!" roared the crowd of assembled nobles, "so be it."

CHAPTER 15

LARGE, SOFT-LOOKING WHITE CLOUDS hung suspended in a peacock-blue sky. No high wind stirred them, nor did any breeze flutter the green leaves of the trees that bordered the garden of Hereford Castle. The sunlight-dappled shade was so still, as was the beautiful woman who sat on the grass in it, that the whole scene might well have been painted. Eventually Elizabeth's hands moved, rolling the top portion of the parchment she was reading so that she could unroll the bottom. The crackle of sound was a violence upon the noon-time hush as was Elizabeth's orange dress upon the grass and the dark bole of the tree against which she leaned, but she neither saw nor heard. Her attention was concentrated upon the letter she was reading with such trembling haste that she had several times to go back and read a portion again.

She lifted her head briefly when she came to the end but unrolled the parchment again and began to read it through once more. Quite apparently part of it had been written in haste and in uncomfortable circumstances, and, no doubt, Roger had given up a brief period of rest to send it to her. Elizabeth was very much disturbed without exactly knowing why. Certainly the news was not bad. The first section of the letter concerned itself with a description of the knighting ceremony and the tourney and other celebrations which followed it. That description was broken off abruptly, as though Roger had been interrupted, and was not resumed, the remainder of the letter being in a cramped and uneven hand which bore evidence to the fact that it had been written on some unsteady surface, perhaps Roger's lap. The tone was entirely different too. They were, after all, to attack York, Roger wrote. He had intended to send only a token force against that city to draw Stephen north, but King David had promised more assistance than they had expected, Chester had urged the move very strongly, and Henry had been eager to engage and show his mettle against the king. If they were successful, they could drive steadily southward while the forces in Gloucestershire turned north and Hugh Bigod pressed westward out of Norfolk.

This sounded excellent, but it was all wrong. It was wrong strategically because Stephen's greatest strength was in the southeast; battle in the north could do him little real harm even if he were defeated unless he were killed or taken prisoner. On the other hand, the ravaging of the northern territories might do Henry's cause serious harm. The northern barons were mostly neutrals in the civil war, largely taken up with their struggles with the Scots. If Henry led a force of Scots against them, they would hate him if he won and despise him if he lost. It was wrong politically, too, because the taking of Stephen and the reduction of the country to misery—a plain result of the strategy described—was not Henry's aim, according to what Roger had told her originally. Eustace was the one who had to be prisoner—Eustace or Maud—so that Stephen who was kind, affectionate, and not strong-minded could be bargained with. For the sake of his wife or child, both of whom he loved passionately, he might well be willing to name Henry his heir before a convocation of the barons or even, for a high enough price, relinquish the throne. He could never be induced to do so to save himself, because although he might be a fool, he was not in the least a coward, and he cared really very little for the welfare of the country at large so that no concern for its ravaging would move him.

Worst of all, though, was the wrongness of the whole letter; it should never have been written. It was not like Roger to write about such matters at all and take the desperate chance of sending a courier abroad with such information, and even less like him to write what he did considering that he had not parted from her on the highest terms of confidence. Elizabeth wrinkled her brow and left off reading to stare into space. If he was driven to write to her to ease his heart, he must have no one he could talk to. If he needed to ease his heart about such matters at all, he must have been very unhappy about the plans indeed, even though the letter itself contained no word of complaint or disapproval. Although Elizabeth could understand that Roger would be dissatisfied with the changes made in his well-thought-out arrangements, she could see no obvious reasons for an oppression of the spirits so strong. Something beyond the surface difficulties was troubling him, but Elizabeth could not guess what, and she was tense and uneasy. Still, to sit and fret could not profit either her or her husband. She went first to her chamber to conceal her letter and change her orange silk bliaut and cream-colored tunic for hardier garments of linen and then to the mews for her hawk. A few hours of hard riding after her merlin was likely to calm her.

Her husband was also riding hard, but he was anything but calmed by it. He and Henry with the men they had personally brought were playing a desperate game of hide-and-go-seek with parties of Stephen's knights sent to ambush them. The attack of York had proved a fiasco, as Hereford had feared. Stephen had been warned well in advance, of course. Roger had planned that, because originally the attack was to be a feint to draw the king north. He had told Henry of that, told David, told Chester—they would not listen. Stephen was dilatory, they replied, he would not arrive in time and the city would be theirs without trouble. He had told them too that Stephen might already be well north of London with forces gathered because of his encounter at Nottingham; to that they replied that they were strong enough to defeat the king whatever forces he brought. Desperately Hereford had cried out—no longer caring whether he offended David or not—that to bring Scots into the northern provinces of England would drive every baron there into Stephen's camp. David had been offended, Chester had laughed, and Henry had lost his temper and called Hereford a coward.

Several days later, Henry had apologized handsomely, but the damage had been done and there was nothing left to do but run. When the size of Stephen's army, ready and waiting for them, had become apparent, as did the truth of Hereford's prediction about the feeling of York-shire men against the Scots, David's forces had melted away. Chester lost his desire for battle, too, when he real-ized that Stephen had arrived in time. In his present mood he had no intention of literally coming to blows with the king. In the recriminations that had flown about before the forces separated, Hereford took no part. He had been warned by God more than once—in Burford, by Chester's vacillation, and by his own constant misgivings. He had chosen his path, in spite of those warnings, and was fol-lowing it, perhaps to his own destruction. Thus far, how-ever, his prayers had been answered for it was no failure of his own strength or courage or planning that was bring-ing disaster upon them. He had no complaint to make.

Strangely, with each encounter which left them more weary, more bloody and battered, and with fewer men, Hereford's spirits rose again. He was neither happy nor confident, nor did he believe he would be again until this affair was over, but he was no longer utterly hopeless ei-ther. Perhaps, he had been thinking, only the hour they had chosen was wrong because surely some power beyond their own strength was preserving them. Time after time they lost their way in that unfamiliar country, and often they found their road again only to see behind them the gleam of shields and spears of a force of Stephen's men large enough to have overwhelmed them. Time after time they encountered bands of Stephen's knights, but those bands were always either unprepared to fight at the mo-ment or small enough to be beaten off.

"There are saints, I have been told, who take care of fools and madmen," Henry grunted after one of these meetings, wiping the blood off his sword. "No doubt, since I qualify under both names, they are watching me with especial tenderness. What I cannot understand is why they are guarding you so carefully, Roger."

"Have I not clung to you through all, my lord?" Here-ford replied with mixed humor and spite. "Does that not qualify me also?"

Henry laughed. Apparently his liege man was com-pletely reconciled to him. Until now he had been rather coolly polite, always a bad sign with Hereford, who usually demonstrated his affection for his overlord with a freedom of speech and manner that often amounted to rudeness.

That was a foul blow. Do you know where the devil we are?"

"Yes, praise Chirst. At least, I think so. If those saints will only attend to us a little longer, we will be on Chester's land some hours after dark."

Eyes narrowing a little, Henry gave his companion an attentive and questioning look. "You believe it safe to stop at Chester?"

"No," Hereford replied flatly. Then, urged by love against conscience, he mitigated the statement. "It is safe to stop nowhere that we may not command the castlefolk to fight. But from Chester on, nearly all the barons are opposed to Stephen, more or less, and will give his troops no aid, comfort, or information. And I know every stone, rill, and twig on every path. If need be, I can lead you through Chester's forests. From there we will be safe. At Hereford we may stop and rest for a day or two."

"Why not stand and defend ourselves? The keep is strong and the people loyal, as I have seen."

"Defend ourselves?" Hereford's eyes widened and his jaw dropped with shock. He studied Henry's face anxiously, but the expression was unreadable. "I have no lust to tear my lands apart without cause. I never knew you to be so fainthearted before. There is an army waiting for me in the south, and thither will I go as fast as I may, not to defend myself but to attack so that Stephen must defend himself. There is no profit in defense. Courage, my lord. Our plans are not awry, for we have done perforce at last what I intended at first. I will lay my head that Eustace will be in the south by the time we come there so that in the end we have lost nothing but a little blood and a few days' time."

"You are true as steel, Roger. Nor am I become so fainthearted as you think. I did but seek to know something, but I have had no answer and so I will ask you outright. Of what are you afraid?"

"Afraid? I?"

"Ay. You have dreams I would not wish to share. Your laughter is stilled except when you remember to try for it, and your spirit is so oppressed that you walk about all that part of the nights which you do not spend tossing and groaning. I have waited long for you to speak of your own will. Now I ask you—what do you know that I do not?"

Henry's eyes held his, and even if he had been able to look away, Hereford was a very poor liar. "I know two things, my lord. One I cannot tell you; the other I will not. Neither, I believe, can have any effect upon what we are about to do."

"What do you mean, you cannot and will not?" Henry's voice was quiet, but a flush began to rise under the freckled tan.

"What I said. If you believe me true, you must believe I would hide nothing from you that I thought could be amended by your knowledge." That was true enough. Chester had yet made no move and was presently no danger to them. Henry could do nothing now except be more angry with him if he knew certainly that Chester was considering changing sides again. Besides Hereford was fairly sure that Henry had a good notion of what was going on without being told. Concerning his personal feeling of futility and frustration, what could he say? Very possibly the warnings concerned him alone or were the fancies of a sick mind. It would be foolish and might be dangerous to infect Henry with the same defeatist ideas.

"I do believe it," Henry was saying. "I am not questioning your loyalty, you idiot, I am offering to share your troubles." He shifted the reins to his left hand and extended his right to Hereford with a warm gesture of sympathy.

It was too much. The struggle to conceal and suppress his fears had gone on too long. Right or wrong, here was a sympathetic ear to listen to him and a high courage to support him. Hereford opened his mouth to unburden himself, lifting his eyes to the horizon so that he would not need to look at Henry and perhaps see his overlord astonished and contemptuous of his weakness.

"Ware? Arms!" he cried instead. A flash of gleaming

metal from behind the trees at a bend in the road had stopped his glance. Once more accident, fate, or a beneficent power had saved them, and by the time they won free, all thought of their previous conversation had passed from their minds.

When the horses could go no further they rested, eating what was left of the food they carried, drinking, and bathing their wounds in a stream. Henry and Hereford talked desultorily, but they were too tired by now to discuss any important subject. They decided only that they would press on into Chester's domain and, without taking the chance of entering any of the keeps wherein they might be trapped, camp for the night on the borders of Chester's forest hunting preserve. Neither of them had been badly hurt, but they were sore with minor cuts and bruises and some of their men were much more seriously injured. Indeed, they had already left many men behind, dead or too badly wounded to travel. A night's rest might save them from losing any more.

Elizabeth's exercise had not had the effect she had hoped for. Although she had spent the entire afternoon galloping over fields and through the woods, resisting with determination the idea that there might be another message from Roger waiting for her, the fatigue brought her no peace of mind. Useless as it was, she continued to worry, going twice to reread what Roger had written because she feared to miss some hidden instruction. No matter how she turned the words, however, she could find nothing. Her unease continued through the night and through the next day, making her temper, never gentle, unendurable. She beat her maids until they cowered at the sight of her, threw things at the menservants, snapped at her mother-in-law, and even slapped Hereford's eldest daughter, of whom she was actually very fond. A moment later she had pulled the startled child, who had hitherto received only the gentlest treatment from her, into her arms and burst into tears.

Lady Hereford who had been growing more and more furious, since Elizabeth had told her only of the contents of the first part of Roger's communication, looked speculatively at her daughter-in-law after that outburst and her subsequent tender fondling of the child and held her tongue. When she was able to catch them alone, she asked Elizabeth's maids certain questions which they could not answer, because their mistress was very secretive about her bodily functions. Lady Hereford remembered that she herself had always been very irritable at the start of each of her pregnancies, and the hope that that was causing Elizabeth's unreasonable behavior permitted her to endure it. In a way this was unfortunate because it denied Elizabeth the outlet of a rousing quarrel which would have been very beneficial to her, but in the end her restlessness served her purposes better.

It was because she could not sleep and was standing by the unshuttered window that she heard the groans of metal against stone as the drawbridge was lowered. For one man alone at this time of night would that bridge go down. Elizabeth ran, snatching up a branch of candles, to wake the servants and then, abandoning the candles for a torch which the wind would not extinguish, went down the stairs and out into the bailey to greet her lord. She did not even see Henry. There was Roger, only Roger, still full-armed even to his helmet, and staggering with weariness. With a cry of thanksgiving she dropped the torch and flung her arms around him.

"Roger, Roger."

"We need food, Elizabeth, and wine, and beds above all."

"The servants are making ready. Are you all right?"

"Yes."

He would say no more, nor did he really eat, although he drank. Thoughtfully, Henry refused the offer of their room for this night and of Elizabeth's services. Lady Hereford, hurriedly awakened, went with him to be sure he would lack nothing, and Elizabeth was left to attend to her husband. She disarmed him and disrobed him herself, greedy to touch him, not having realized until this moment how great her fears for his safety had really been. Her curiosity was eating her up alive, but she could not question a man who showed her a face gray with fatigue, hollow-eyed, and with lines that she had never seen before etched into the flesh. He dozed, sitting on the bed, as she undressed him, and she had to lift his feet and roll him under the covers. Yet when she slipped in beside him, she knew he was not asleep because she could see the gleam of his open eyes.

"Go to sleep, Roger," she whispered finally. "Whatever has befallen, it is over now. You are at home."

Only for him it was not over. It was going to begin again, tomorrow or the next day at the latest. Hereford, incapable of further effort, began to tremble. He felt his wife stiffen beside him and tried to control himself, ashamed of his weakness and thinking that she was revolted by it. His body was beyond control, though, and the attempt to stop it only made the trembling worse. Once again he had misjudged Elizabeth. Her tension was due only to doubt as to what she should do. Was it better to pretend she noticed nothing? Should she try to soothe him? Did he wish to speak or be silent? The minutes passed slowly and he became easier. Elizabeth could now feel him gasping for breath in the intervals between the fits of shivering. It was painful that he would not turn to her for comfort even in this extremity, but Elizabeth's pride had taken so many blows of late that this one scarcely affected her from a selfish point of view at all. She could only think that what Roger was doing must be unendurable to him; it would be better for him to be angry with her than to go on like this, and she turned on her side and put her arms around him.

"What is it, Roger? Please let me help you."

He could not answer, but he pressed himself, cold as ice, against her comforting warmth. For Elizabeth it was enough; her heart pounded so with triumph that she thought he would hear it, and she tightened her arms fiercely and protectively about him. The security of that embrace released Hereford's tears—tears of fury and of shamed pride—and when the storm was over he gave Elizabeth a final token of trust by falling asleep at once. Eventually Elizabeth slept too, but not well, for her husband's every sound or movement woke her, and his sleep, although deep, was not easy. Toward morning she started awake anxiously once more to find that this time Hereford was sleeping no longer.

"Do you feel better, Roger?"

"Yes. I am sorry to have acted the fool last night. I was tired."

Elizabeth caught his eyes and held his gaze steadily. "That is nothing to be sorry for. Any man, even you, may be overburdened. I wish I might be of help—but I do not blame you for mistrusting me. I have given you little reason to confide in my judgment. Only I am so strong and so eager, and there is nothing for me to do or to think of. You know, Roger, I am not used to this life of idleness, and the devil breeds work for idle hands."

"You must be patient, Elizabeth. It has been in my mind to give this keep into your management. It was a mistake for me to think that you would not wish to be troubled with the simple duties of living, but I have no time—" His voice drifted off uncertainly. "So much is happening," he added more firmly. "You must wait until my duties are over—one way or another."

"Will you tell me nothing? Not even what is past? Surely my knowledge of that could do no harm."

"Nay, Elizbeth, I will tell you anything you wish to know. Only there is little enough that will make pleasant hearing for you."

"Were you defeated at York? I knew from your letter that there would be trouble, but—. Wait, let me fetch my salves. You can say what you will while I dress your hurts."

"No," he sighed, "we were not defeated. We never came to blows." He lay quietly allowing her to wash him and rub ointments into the raw spots on his body, wincing now and again but soothed by her attentions. "The worst of it was the running. I do not like to run, and we came in haste and fear, fighting off ambushes all the way from York. Aside from that shame and some men, we lost little. I never planned to try for York—what gain would that be to us?—only to draw Stephen away from his son. This we have accomplished. The profit, if any, is that Henry will listen more closely and trust my judgment better. I knew we could not do it and said so; he called me a coward." Hereford's mouth twisted. "That was sweet hearing on my overlord's lips."

"He was angry, Roger. You yourself told me he will say anything in a rage. No man could mean that of you. There must have been more than that to distress you."

"Ay, there was," Hereford answered bitterly, tired of being pressed for information which he was trying to conceal only to spare her pain. "What will you do, Elizabeth, if your father and I come to blows? To whom will you cling?"

"Oh, my God!" she cried, dropping a pot, which broke and splattered the rug with grease. "He has been firm so long. This is a cruel way to try my loyalty if it be not true."

"If you do not wish to have to make that choice, and you have the skill to bend your father's mind, you had better do so." Hereford was already a little ashamed of the harsh way he had introduced the subject, but an idea had crossed his mind that was an answer to two problems at once. "Elizabeth, setting aside your father's good, are you faithful to me?"

"I would I were a man and could do you homage," she said passionately. "I swear I would fulfill that pledge, letter and spirit. What can a woman do to show her faith?"

"You are more a man than some that bear the name." An odd looked crossed Hereford's face as he contemplated doing something very strange, something that would make him the butt of jest the length and breadth of England if it became known. He was considering, in all seriousness, accepting the oath of homage from Elizabeth. She would hold by that, he believed, against all ties, even those of love, for he mistakenly thought that her pride was stronger than her affection. "Bring me my sword," he said finally, "and my right gauntlet."

Numb with surprise, Elizabeth did as she was told, although she had not the vaguest notion of what was coming next, for the idea that Roger would take up her offer never crossed her mind. It was easier to believe that he wanted the sword to kill her with, for what fault she could not imagine except that possibly the burdens he bore had driven him mad—but why the glove? She was distastefully aware, not of fear, but of little things that did not matter, of the damp stickiness of the leather which a bad cut on

Roger's right forearm had soaked with blood that had not dried, of her bare foot slipping in the grease on the rug, and of the frightful red marks on Roger's alabaster skin as he stood to receive her.

"You have offered to do me homage, Elizabeth. I think enough of your pride, strength, and courage to accept that offer, but before I go further, I bid you think. If you swear to me as a man, I will hold you to your word as a man. I will no longer regard your swerving from your duty to me as a woman's weakness."

This was what Elizabeth had striven for all her life. This was more even that her father's confidence had ever offered her. She should have been overwhelmed with joy and satisfaction at the successful culmination of her struggle for independence. Instead—"What does that mean?" Elizabeth asked, terrified. "Will you have me to wife no longer?"

Momentarily Hereford's expression softened. "Nay, my heart, I love the woman in you too much to abandon it for any cause. I mean that if I ask a man's duty of you, you may not say me nay for a woman's reasons, because you are angry with me for not yielding you some trinket or privilege or because as a husband I have forbidden you some friend or activity. Do you understand?"

"I think so."

"Do you want time to consider? We will rest here one or two more nights. You have a little time."

"No," she answered faintly, "there is nothing to consider. You may have my faith any way you want it. I will be your 'man' as well as your woman."

To an observer the scene might well have had humorous aspects. In the faint grayish light of early dawn, a man, naked as the day he was born, stood above a kneeling woman whose loosened hair flowing to the ground betokened her intimate relationship to him. Yet he spoke to her as to a male vassal, and his mouth when he took and received the kiss of peace was hard, his lips having none of the softness of the lover's. In the end he held out his sword to her—there were holy relics in the pommel, and the hilt formed a cross—and she rose, laid her hands upon it, and swore. Last of all he gave her his bloody glove as a token of the new bond between them, and a final hard kiss. To the participants in the ceremony, however, there was nothing humorous at all in the circumstances. Both were completely in earnest; Hereford as determined to hold his wife to her oath as any other vassal, and Elizabeth, frightened because in the moment of the fulfillment of her ambition she realized that she did not desire this type of relationship with her husband, still determined to strive to her uttermost to live up to this honor so seldom granted to a woman even in private.

"Fiat," Hereford said, then sighed and stepped back to sit down on the bed and draw the covers around himself. "Now, Liza, I have work for you."

"Oh, Roger, wait! I am afraid."

"What?" Surprised for a moment, Hereford laughed and reached out to pull his wife into his arms. "If ever I learn to understand you, I will surely be the wisest of all men. You meddle in my affairs constantly, usually without my knowledge or consent, but when I am about to ask you to do just that, you tremble and grow pale and say you are afraid. Have I ever been so harsh to you or so unreasonable that you should be afraid of me or anything I would ask of you?"

"You were different before. I am not afraid when you are like this, but I know now why Walter fears you and why your men obey you so absolutely."

"A nice case I would be in if I needed to seat all my vassals in my lap and caress them to reassure them that I desire only their good." Hereford's mouth was soft then, his lips sweetly curved. "More especially if I felt toward them as I do to you, nothing would ever be done, for I could never keep my mind upon the work in hand. I always thought it was because women could not bear arms that they were not held in vassalage, but now I see that there are other dangers in the situation." He laughed, amused by the idea of the havoc that would be created if women were generally granted vassalage. "Well, Elizabeth, we always do everything backwards, why stop now. It is growing light, I am in desperate need of time, and I have much to tell you, so—let us make love."

He tipped her back on to the bed and she offered no

resistance. She felt at first no passion or excitement, only a warm joy which made her soft and receptive. Roger must have shared her sensation for he was in no hurry, in spite of his claim that he lacked time. He moved slowly, stopping altogether from time to time to kiss her and fondle her, twisting his body to caress her breasts with his lips and to stroke her thighs. Elizabeth sighed, softly at first, then louder, and when Roger hesitated again she made an impatient movement. A slight frown of concentration marred the previous peace of her expression, but she was as unconscious of that as she was of clutching her husband closer.

"You know, Elizabeth," he said some time later, lying flat on his back and staring at the gathered bed curtains above him, "I once said I should some day make you howl like a bitch in heat—and I have."

Elizabeth shuddered. "What a horrid thing to say."

"But expressive and appropriate." He turned to look at her and even while his eyes misted with tears of tenderness he sought escape from sentiment in laughter. "Did you know too that your skin turns violet when you blush. You look good enough to eat."

"You had better hold your tongue. You will look green, not violet, if I tell what I know about you." Elizabeth was not to be beaten, she would give as good as she got, teasing or loving.

Hereford's eyes opened wide with surprise. "What can you know of me now that you have not always known?"

Elizabeth giggled. "I can say, and with perfect truth, if you go about calling me a bitch in heat, that you are so depraved a wretch that you have taken to going to bed with your vassal. I would love to hear you trying to explain that."

"Bitch," he said fondly, nipping her shoulder, "ungrateful bitch, biting the—the hand that feeds you."

That made her gurgle with laughter again, but her husband was distracted from his love play, looking at the lightening sky, and his mood changed swiftly. He had so much to do and he felt the pressure of time, always. It was not that there was really any hurry any more—except for Henry's natural impatience. Once Henry was safely in

England, theoretically they had all the time in the world to win the throne and actually there was not much urgency, only that caused by the possible discouragement of their allies if the war dragged on too long. When it came to the point, Hereford did not know why he felt he had to rush, felt that if he did not hurry, hurry, everything would fall to pieces. He only knew that he did feel that way, and, being in many ways a simple person, he responded directly by getting out of bed.

Elizabeth did not wish to move and murmured that Roger should drop the curtains. She wanted to remain in the warm dimness, savoring this new total release of physical tension, recalling the piercing pain-pleasure of her new experience. To Roger, of course, the sensation was not at all new and not in the least remarkable. Nonetheless, under ordinary circumstances he would have been happy to lie with her, teasing, caressing, possibly even renewing the pleasure. Instead he turned back quickly.

"Nay, love, I know what you would like, but this is not the hour for it." He smiled kindly, but there was sufficient firmness in his voice to admit of no argument. "Up, vassal, I have work for you."

"Do not give me labor greater than my strength, Roger."

"I know no limit to your strength when you will exert it. I can only give you the task I need you to do. Will the men of your dower lands obey you—even in matters of war?"

"I believe so." Elizabeth was now frowning. Surely Roger could not be mad enough to plan to use her as a fighting captain. It was true she knew a great deal about tactics, and there were women who had donned armor and gone to war, but both her knowledge of tactics and their actions had always been in matters of defense when their husbands were gone. To plan to use her offensively, however, would be so great a blow to his prestige that she could not, not for all the vassalage in the world nor all the love in the world, permit him to carry through such an idea. Very soon it became apparent that that was not Roger's intention, and Elizabeth relaxed and listened attentively.

"I will recall your men from the south, at least the

mounted troops. Unless the fighting and losses have been
heavier than I expected, that will give you near seven
hundred tried men. With that force you should be safe to
travel anywhere. After Henry and I go south, you will ride
north to find your father. We parted with no great love, so
that I cannot tell you exactly where he will be. You must
keep him steady to us, Elizabeth. Or, if not steady, at
least you must keep him from joining Stephen, or, even
more important, from coming south. I care little enough
what he does in the north so long as he does not hinder
our work. Do you understand what I want? Can you do
it?"

"Can I? I do not know. Often I can bend him to my
will, but sometimes I believe the devil enters his soul.
Then no one can move him. It depends a little on what
has taken place since you parted. I will do my best,
Roger, but I tell you this—for all the duty I owe you, and
all the love I bear you, I will not even try to stop him by
force, not my father."

"I do not expect that, nor, I believe, could you make
your men go against him who has so long led them, but I
do expect that you will send me word if you fail to hold
him. Write to Devizes, always. They will know where to
send your message further."

"You would not fight him, would you, Roger?" Elizabeth pleaded.

Hereford set his jaw. "I do not know. I love him also,
Elizabeth, but what I have sworn, I have sworn. If you do
not wish to be ripped apart between us, you had best not
fail. Let me be now, I must write and that is never easy
for me."

After one brief effort to keep Elizabeth away from
Henry, Roger gave up. Henry flirted disgracefully with her
during the few days that they remained, at Hereford, Elizabeth naughtily aiding and abetting him. Nonetheless after Hereford's initial resistance Henry could not succeed in
getting much reaction from him. For one thing, having
conquered his wife's sexual reserve, Roger was much more
sure of her and for another he was fully occupied. Hereford, unable to do two and three things at once, as Henry
could, was preoccupied with military matters and scarcely

saw his overlord, even when they sat side by side, unless he was conferring with him. It was a mark of Henry of Anjou's real brilliance as a leader and Hereford's grim application to duty that they just about kept pace with each other, Henry grasping instantly the possibilities and leaping to the conclusions that Hereford labored hours over. They were now in perfect agreement; Henry had learned that however skilled he was at sizing up terrain and arraying his battle order, Hereford better understood the reliability of the forces and the temper of the people through experience. Tactically Hereford generally bowed to Henry's decisions, but if Hereford said a certain plan of action could not be successful and gave his reasons, Henry did not argue.

Elizabeth's dark, glossy head lifted away from Henry's abruptly as her husband spoke. "We can do no more here, my lord. The next step is to perform what we have planned."

"I thought you wanted to wait until you heard from your brother."

"I did, but Walter is not a reliable correspondent."

Hereford did not say that he also thought Walter was an unreliable ally and, not having heard from him, was most anxious to return to the scene of action personally. He was also disturbed at not having heard from Gloucester. It was possible that after the news of the fiasco at York had reached that squeamish duke, he was again hesitating about committing himself fully to Henry's cause by leaving the court to join the rebel forces. Hereford did not wish to find the city of Gloucester closed against them and said so, proposing that they ride directly there on the morrow. Depending upon the news they were able to obtain in that city, they could move east to Shrivenham or south to Devizes.

Henry shrugged and agreed readily. "Only I am a little tired of this tour of England. When do we see some action?"

"We go for that purpose, my lord, not to tour. If Walter has taken Shrivenham, we should try for Faringdon. That taken, we have the south blocked off from Oxford, which is a favorite stronghold of Eustace. He will not stay long

away when he has the news of what we are about, if he
be not there already. If we are agreed, then, I will go to
give the orders."

"We will not have time to finish our game, Lady Elizabeth," Henry said to her when Hereford was gone. Henry
played chess well, but so did his hostess, and they had
been involved in a very protracted struggle which showed
no sigh of an early termination.

"I am sorry for it, but I will mark the places and then,
when you come again, we may go on."

"You seem less distressed at this parting than at the one
at Chester. Do you have no fears for your husband's
safety?"

"Roger's safety? No, he bears a charmed life." Elizabeth's calm manner and fathomless golden eyes gave no
clue to her inner tremors. It was never safe to display an
emotional attachment which might be turned into a
weapon against one. Presumably there would never be a
reason to fear Henry's knowledge, but Elizabeth firmly believed that the less anyone knew about her, the better off
she would be.

"Does he too believe that?" Henry wondered whether
Elizabeth knew what was troubling her husband. He did
not expect to learn anything from her; indeed, she had not
dropped a single piece of information relative to her husband or herself in all the talk they had shared, but there
was no harm in trying.

"I have no idea. Certainly he never says anything to
show that he worries about himself."

Henry laughed. "Lady Elizabeth, if I asked you what
color hose your husband planned to wear tomorrow,
would you put me off with equally literal truthfulness?"

"No doubt I should, my lord." Warm affection, admiration, and amusement lent additional color to her face and
a leaping brilliance to her eyes. "After all, I should wonder
why you wanted to know—and—not believe you if you told
me. My lord," she added seriously, "it is no distrust of you
that makes me thus. So would I reply to my own father,
who I know loves Roger tenderly." And with more cause,
Henry thought, but did not interrupt her. "It is a woman's
only defense, not to trust."

It was true, however, that Elizabeth was parting with Roger far more easily this time, and doing so even though she now acknowledged that she loved him more than life. In fact she loved him so that she could hardly manage to speak about him or use his name. Every time she thought of her husband these days her bowels stirred and a strange soft pain under her breasts made it very hard to breathe. Her fears for his personal safety were greater under the circumstances, but now she could face those fears with resolution. Several factors contributed to her equanimity. Roger's renewed trust in her had reestablished to a great extent her faith in herself. Her sexual satisfaction, established and repeated so that she had confidence in her ability to give and receive that pleasure at will, removed an immense core of frustration and unhappiness that Elizabeth had not known to exist until its weight was lifted from her soul. Moreover she had discovered that, yielding this, she had gained everything and lost nothing, so that she was sure that the more she gave Roger throughout her life the more he would give her of trust and confidence in return. Most important of all, however, was that she knew she would not need to sit still in fear and ignorance, waiting, waiting.

She was afraid for him, so afraid that after their passion was spent that night she crept back into Roger's arms and kept him awake a full hour with demands to be fondled. It might be the last time, she kept telling herself, fighting sleep, the last time. It might be the last time, and Elizabeth was determined to savor it to the full, but though she feared for Roger she was not afraid of the future any more. If her husband were killed, her heart would be torn apart, but her life would not be broken. She no longer felt weak or defenseless or wondered what would become of her. If God were good and she had conceived a child—Elizabeth stopped at that thought and smiled, she had never considered having Roger's child before, not seriously considered it with pleasure. Well, if she did, she could hold the lands for that child against all comers—of that she was sure. If there was no child, there were many other paths to follow. One thing was certain, however, if Roger was not there to give her orders, she would take them from no one else. To her mind there was not a man in England who was his match, and she would have no other.

On the morning of their separation, the Earl of Hereford seemed more distressed than his wife. He was plainly reluctant to leave the room where Elizabeth had helped him dress and arm, and he paced about giving her detailed instructions about what route to take north and what to do in all possible and impossible situations. Again and again he looked toward the spire of the church in Hereford, bitterly regretting Alan of Evesham's death. One part of him knew that Elizabeth was strong and capable, the other cried out that she was a woman and he loved her and was deliberately sending her into danger.

"For God's sake, Elizabeth, be careful. Be cautious even if caution will make you lose your point. Do not be afraid or ashamed to run away. I will have no word of blame to say to you. Above all, do not fail to send a courier daily—every day, without fail from wherever you are—even if you have nothing to tell me." He lifted her heavy braids and kissed them.

"I will not fail in that, if you desire it, but you should not count too much upon it. Many things may happen to a single rider over the distance that will be between us. You know I will be safe once I find my father, and so many couriers will deplete my men."

"A single man, changing horses, should not take above three to five days to find me, and I will send him back again once he is rested. That will mean that no more than twenty or thirty riders will be needed. I do not wish ever again to feel the terror of not knowing where to look for you. You have no doubts as to what you are to do?"

"No. I am to keep my father in the north and against the king if possible. You—" she hesitated, studying Roger's face. He had aged ten years, no twenty, in the past months and even after several days of rest showed silvery shadows below his cheek bones and mauve-ringed eyes. "You will be careful too, will you not?"

"As careful as duty and honor permit. Our cases are not the same, Elizabeth. Well, that is all, I think. Have courage but not too much, dear heart."

CHAPTER 16

Elizabeth Hereford took one last look at herself in the mirror and smiled at what she saw. Her heavy braids were looped up and pinned as close as possible to her head; the russet homespun tunic and bliaut she wore were nothing like her usual luxurious garments and in no way flattered her dark skin, which looked rather sallow. She removed her earrings and added them to the rest of her jewelry in the coffer before her, then began to tug at her betrothal ring. It resisted her first effort to take it off and Elizabeth desisted, suddenly pushing it back over the knuckle of her finger with an odd sinking sensation. Not that, she would not remove that, ever. She turned the stone in toward her palm and pulled her riding gloves over it. With her hood up, she might easily be taken for a boy of no high degree.

Her last act at Hereford Castle was to seal her note to Roger and give instructions to the messenger. She had said her good-bys to Lady Hereford, Catherine, and Roger's daughters the evening before and would not repeat them now. There was nothing left to do and nothing left to linger for. Without a backward glance or a backward thought, for with Roger gone there was nothing dear enough to bind her to Hereford, Elizabeth mounted her mare in the courtyard and ordered her troop northward.

Knowing her father's habit of indecision, Elizabeth had decided to move as quickly as possible to Yorkshire. It was very likely that Chester was still there, unable to decide whether to make overtures to Stephen or attack his forces. She had already sent out foreriders to Chester Castle who had instructions to meet her near Winsford in case her father had gone home, but she wished to pass well east of Shrewsbury to avoid danger and because the roads were

better in England than in Wales. Roger would approve of
that, she thought with satisfaction, and did not realize
how different her point of view had become since Decem-
ber.

At the moment, however, Hereford had not a single
thought to spare for his wife. He was about ten miles
north of Bristol, vibrantly alive with the expectation of an
early, easy, and unplanned end to the conflict. He and
Henry found, when they arrived at Gloucester, that they
had misjudged Duke William. That gentleman was not at
all perturbed by the setback in the north and the only reason they had not heard from him was that they had
outrun his messengers, who were still seeking them around
York and Chester. Actually they had found William fuming because he had made a little plan of his own that
seemed about to fall through because of their absence. He
had expected them two or three days before—and had his
couriers caught them they would have arrived in time—so
that they could be at Dursley as he had informed Eustace
they would be through a common confidant. Revealed, the
simple plot made Henry and Hereford nod in agreement.

Eustace had arrived in Gloucestershire according to his
father's orders, and William had greeted him and readily
given him the right to ride through the lands to seek for
whatever he would. Then he had dropped the hint into
ears he knew would carry the tale that the prize Eustace
sought was at Dursley. He could not mention it to Eustace
himself, he had murmured, because his father's friends still
faithful to Henry's cause would kill him, and he was
afraid.

"And that is where you should be." Gloucester said in
his silky petulant tones, ignoring the averted eyes of his
listeners who were horrified to hear that a man had made
such an admission to one whom he knew would carry the
tale. Gloucester could barely stop himself from laughing at
them, the proud fools. "We can only hope that you can
beat out his foreriders and spies. Bristol is already raised
in expectation of your coming and a large force ready and
waiting at Almonersbury. Once Eustace is sure you are at
Dursley you need only pretend to flee south to the greater
security of Bristol. My men will not open the keep at

Dursley but will say that you have gone on to Bristol. Eustace, God willing, will follow, young and hotheaded as he is, unless Rannulf of the South Riding can stop him. If you can lead him to Almonersbury—you have him."

"My dear William," Henry praised, flashing his most charming smile, "if we take him so easily—you will not be sorry."

"If I thought I should be, I would not have made the plan, my lord," William replied smoothly. "Nor do I wish to seem inhospitable, but if you intend to be in time, you had better go."

Mounted and riding, Henry asked again, "Is it a trap?" And this time Hereford shrugged in reply, because he could not even guess what was in William's mind.

Nonetheless, suspicious as it sounded, thus far everything had run smoothly. They had waited at Dursley almost until the van of Eustace's force was in sight and then slipped out about midnight with only the small force they had arrived with. They had refused the castellan's offer to augment their troop, partly because they did not wish to carry possible traitors with them, but also because it was possible that Eustace would stay and attack Dursley. In that case they felt that it would be unwise to reduce the number of defenders so much that the keep would be unable to hold out until they could return to protect it. William's spies had warned them well in advance of three separate ambushes set on the southward road and had led them safely around Eustace's men so that they had made contact with the army sent out from Bristol without difficulty. Any moment should bring their pursuers into sight. Hereford stroked the back of his purple and gold gauntlet with the bare fingers of his left hand, an unconscious nervous gesture. Even Henry's tongue was stilled as they listened.

At last there was the dull thunder of hundreds of horses coming at a quick walk. Hereford's breath quickened, his mouth set hard into the cold, merciless smile he wore when fighting, and his eyes brightened to a pale, burning blue as he drew on his left gauntlet, tightened his helm, and fixed his shield. A low-toned order brought William Beauchamp close up behind his master to receive whispered orders which he transmitted.

"Take Eustace." The word passed from mouth to mouth. "It matters not whether we win or lose, so long as the prince be taken. Whoever has him, let him break for Bristol, risking no chance of rescue."

Take Eustace. The sentence was more easily said than the deed done. It was plain from the moment the forces joined battle that Eustace and his men had little trust in their informants. Usually the prince, a brave and hardy knight, fought well to the front of his army. Not so this night. Eustace held back or was held back, surrounded by the best of his men, and obviously the whole troop had been on their guard against just such a surprise as was planned.

The first rush, led by Henry while Hereford held about half the force in reserve, did not demoralize the oncoming men as expected. Eustace's army closed ranks and struck back fiercely. The rear guard, no doubt instructed in advance of what to do in such a case, fanned out at a gallop and, bursting through fields and woods, attacked Henry's flank with determination. Henry's forces wavered and fell back under the impact at first, but the shouts and curses of their leader, who was setting them a brilliant example by hewing down every opponent within his reach, and the knowledge that reinforcements were at hand rallied them. Hereford became more and more nervous, straining his ears to pick out single sounds in that cacophony until his eyes started. Amid the crash of underbrush, the clangor of metal on shield and hauberk, the shrieks and groans of the wounded and dying, and the fierce shouts of encouragement from the captains of both parties, he was terrified that he would miss Henry's voice calling him into action. The only reason he held back at all, once it became apparent that his men would not be used to pursue the fleeing or cut down a last-stand guard around Eustace, was that he knew Henry to be very jealous of any sharing the glory of a victory.

Hereford did not miss the call when it came, but Henry's pride had delayed until almost too late. By the time Roger led his men into the fray, they could prevent Eustace from forcing Henry to retreat, but they could no longer turn the tide into anything less than a major defeat. Much blood was shed before this became apparent to the embattled leaders of both parties, for they were too busy fighting for their own lives to consider the general situation. With the coming of full day, however, the stalemate became obvious. Eustace had the stronger force, had suffered fewer casualties, and had a little advantage in the ground, but Henry's troop was on friendly territory only a few miles from a major stronghold which could resist a far greater army than Eustace's. One more desperate charge was rallied by Henry in a last attempt to take Eustace prisoner, but that young prince defended himself ably and his men made a solid wall around him which even the ferocity of the Angevin could not pierce.

That attack nearly spelled disaster for Henry. His men followed him in a thin wedge through Eustace's line, and, while he tried to break the guard around the prince, his own path of escape was very nearly closed off. Hereford launched himself personally at the group closing in behind his overlord, his vassals following closely and desperately, and they hewed a new opening through which Henry was finally forced to withdraw. That was the end as far as the rebel army was concerned. They had suffered far greater losses than the king's men, and the objective of their struggle was unobtainable. To stay and fight longer was senseless; they could not win, and they could lose all. Obedient to the new orders being shouted from troop to troop, they broke contact and retreated in good order toward Bristol. A brisk rear-guard action was fought while Eustace's men still thought they could turn a retreat into a rout, but Hereford had excellent control over his forces and the prince soon abandoned the pursuit because he had no desire to come any closer to that passionately rebel city.

"He knew," Henry panted furiously, "he knew. He was prepared to meet us. That ambush was no surprise."

"Mayhap." Hereford was depressed, aching from the battering he had taken, "But I think not. Eustace has been under arms for several years now, with his father and alone. Stephen is a fool, but not in matters of war, and taught his son well. He would need to be very foolish indeed to come so far on such information as William's and not guard against attack. The fault is mine, if there is a fault, in being too eager to think all would fall as we desired. I should have known it was too easy."

"Holy Mother, I am sore all over. Can we bring more men out from Bristol and fall upon him again?"

"We can try. You will not find him, I think. Eustace planned to take us at Dursley, which is not specially strong, or hoped to catch us unprepared on the road. He will never attempt Bristol. Stephen did that with the whole army and failed. I suspect he will make the best speed he can back to Oxford now. He has suffered less loss than we, but he still needs time to lick his wounds."

"Curse you, Roger, let us turn and try again then."

"If you will, my lord, but the men are tired, and their hearts, I fear, will fail them."

"It is your heart that fails—"

Hereford turned with blazing eyes. "That is the second time you have called me coward. If I do not suit you, find another who will so readily shed his blood and spend his substance in your cause."

Henry was not angry at Hereford but at the failure of their plans. He controlled his temper with an effort, therefore, not desiring to inflame his equally frustrated companion any further. "Nay, I know it is not your failing. I do but strike out at you because I am enraged and you are dear to me. What is now best to be done?"

Dully, Hereford stared between his horse's ears for a while. Finally he spoke in a dead voice. "I will send to Bath, Devizes, and Shrivenham and urge our men there to take him if possible or at least to harry him. The more men he loses, the better will be our chances of seizing him."

Eustace, as Hereford knew he would, won safely back to Oxford and gave his opponents every reason to regret his escape bitterly. He remained at that stronghold, instead of returning to London, issuing out to raid the countryside often enough to keep both Hereford and Henry continually occupied with protecting what was theirs. Everything they desired to accomplish, such as the taking of Faringdon, hung mid-air while they first raced southward to aid John Fitz Gilbert protect Marlborough, then north again to reinforce Devizes from which they had drawn the troops to aid John. Possibly it was just as well that Hereford was too busy to think, or his courage might well have faltered under the accumulation of failures. Even the news from the north, which at first had been hopeful, began to grow worse.

Elizabeth's couriers arrived with good regularity, seldom failing a day unless Hereford outstripped them. She had accomplished her purpose so well that Chester agreed to attempt a defense of the position Henry's adherents held in Yorkshire. Unfortunately his forces, even augmented by Elizabeth's men, were not sufficient to stop Stephen, who, once aroused to action, was a very adequate warrior. First one and then another stronghold fell; Chester was no man to remain steady in the face of adversity, and soon Elizabeth's letters took on a note of weariness and desperation. She could not hold her father longer, she wrote to her husband one blazing day in July, he would return to Chester. "I have prevailed so far over him," her letter ran, "that he will offer Stephen no truce, nor will he travel south to aid or hinder your efforts. More I cannot do. Not knowing your wishes, I ride to Chester with him and, unless you have further commands for me, I will stay, endeavoring to stiffen his purpose toward your cause. Sealed under my hand on this 12th day of July, Elizabeth Hereford."

Dropping his head into his hands, Hereford stared dully at the earth between his feet. Commands for her, he thought wearily; he wished he had some for his own men which would have some profitable purpose. But the true nightmare had not yet begun, for when Chester left Yorkshire, Stephen too was freed. The king was an exceptionally good-natured man, slow to anger and slow to take any type of action. Once roused, however, he seemed to have been driven insane. He descended upon the south of England, not to fight Henry but to destroy completely the already ravaged land. No restraints at all were placed upon the royal troops; they had license to commit every atrocity and special instructions to scorch the earth. Wherever they arrived, not a hut remained standing, not a blade of the newly reaped or standing crops was permitted to survive, not a beast suitable for work or food escaped destruction. What they could not consume themselves, they heaped together and set aflame. The men and children were slain outright, the women used, then slain. A black horror of burnt hovels and vegetation and putrefying bodies covered the land.

Hereford rode one way, Henry another, but nowhere could they catch the king or bring his troops to stand and fight. They rode through the burning days and sultry, smothering nights of one of the hottest summers England had known in a long time. They rode until Hereford looked like a gaunt wraith with burning, horror-filled eyes and until even Henry's iron limbs twitched and shuddered when he fell off his horse to snatch the unrestful slumber of exhaustion and despair. Hopeless of conciliating or vanquishing Salisbury and John Fitz Gilbert as well as Henry of Anjou and the Earl of Hereford, Stephen had determined to destroy them by starvation, and he was well on his way to accomplishing his purpose.

Roger of Hereford pushed off his helmet and unlaced his mail hood. His golden curls were a muddy brown, so soaked was his hair with filth and sweat, and his face was wet with mingled rivulets of perspiration and unashamed tears. Once more he was too late, and the fields and hamlets around the great keep of Devizes itself were nothing but smoking ruins. He sat and sobbed like a tired child, too hopeless and helpless even to be angry. Within the keep, a half hour later, he found Henry, also sobbing and half hysterical with rage and frustration.

"We were here," he shrieked, "here, right here, yet we saw nothing, heard nothing, until all at once the entire countryside was in flames. I swear by the bloody hands and feet of Christ that we were not above half an hour in arming and issuing forth after them. They melted away like smoke before our very eyes. We combed the countryside; we looked under the very stones seeking them. The devil must be his partner; the devil himself alone could perform such works of evil."

Or God, Hereford thought, sinking into a seat, silent and sick. Stephen was God's anointed king. Had they offended the Almighty by opposing him? Was this their punishment—to starve, to see their lands rot? Henry continued to rave, storming up and down the great hall; Hereford sat silent, possessed by that one horrible thought and incapable of voicing it, studying his dirt encrusted hands as if he could read the future in the streaks and smears of filth.

"My lord." William Beauchamp put a hand on his master's shoulder and shook him gently. He often had to do that these days to attract Hereford's attention, and his heart ached at the dull, lack-luster look of the blue eyes that turned up to his. This will kill him, Beauchamp thought, remembering the vibrantly alive man he used to serve who before this had laughed in the face of every adversity. "Letters, my lord," he said; there was nothing else to say.

"My wife?"

William handed over several brief notes from Elizabeth. Her father was still doing nothing, sulking in his favorite castle, hunting, and complaining to his daughter, but he was possessed, said Elizabeth, of a "black and bitter bile" which boded his attachment to his son-in-law's cause little good. Chester, Elizabeth wrote, must be forced into some action, and she pleaded with Roger to tell her which way to push him to separate him irrevocably from the king lest he leap into action which would do just the opposite. Hereford did not even feel a quiver of emotion as he read. He was too played out, mentally and physically, to feel anything, even his wife's appeal for help. He did not even notice or care what was written between the lines of how Chester's behavior, together with his own bad news or sullen silence, was wearing on Elizabeth's nerves. He merely put the letters aside and reached for the others William still held. At least all was well with his own lands; Stephen had not yet had time to turn his attention to them, and his mother wrote only ordinary news and asked only minor advice about serfs' misdoings and good or bad crops. Thus far he had been spared the blow of personal loss. Apparently Stephen was saving his property for the deathblow to Henry's attempt.

The seals on the last two letters brought a frown to a countenance which previously had been rigid with exhaustion. One was his sister Anne's, the other the Earl of Lincoln's. He tore open Anne's letter first and read hastily. Casting the parchment aside with a low exclamation of irritation he then virtually devoured Lincoln's missive.

"Oh, God," he groaned aloud, "that was all that was needful. I warned him—I warned him."

Startled by a sound from Hereford, whom he had begun to think had lost the power of speech, Henry came away from the window he had been moodily staring out of. "What more can have befallen us?"

"Not us, praise Mary. This blow is mine alone, a personal one. I did not tell you when I spoke to you of Nottingham that I was there because my wife was taken by Peverel. I regained her in a trial by combat with de Caldoet who was Peverel's champion and whom I took prisoner. I yielded him to the Earl of Lincoln for private reasons, warning Lincoln that de Caldoet was a treacherous cur. How he has done it, I know not, but he has wrested several strongholds from Lincoln and turned the city itself against its master."

"Why should you care?" Henry asked impatiently. "From what I hear of Lincoln his vassals are looking for any excuse to turn on him. If Lincoln willingly took de Caldoet and you warned him, it is no problem of yours."

"Lincoln is the father of my sister's husband, and as such has blood claims upon me. My sister Anne is married to his third son, Rannulf. He asks my aid, relying upon that bond, and what is more, here is a letter from my sister, frantic because her husband has answered his father's call to arms—most rightly—and she is with child."

Henry stopped his restless movements and stared at Hereford, his gray eyes narrowing. "Well, do you send him aid?"

"Have I the men?" Hereford asked bitterly. "Can I spare so much as a cook's helper from our task here? I can do no more than write to my mother to squeeze the serfs. Belike she can wring some gold from them to send him, or perhaps I could borrow of Chester for Lincoln is Chester's—. Merciful Christ," Hereford cried suddenly, starting to his feet, and the words carried no blasphemy but a note of prayer and entreaty. He spoke no more aloud, shaking his head in reply to Henry's questions, for he had not yet confided in Henry the tale of Chester's vacillation, but his thoughts continued the sentence. Merciful Christ, perhaps de Caldoet's treachery is the answer to our troubles with Chester. It is true that Lincoln and Chester do not overly love each other, but for this kind of trouble—the revolt of a servitor—I am sure Chester will go to the support of his half brother. Then, if Elizabeth can spur them on, they will not stop with subduing de Caldoet, but will ravage the province. She might even be able to urge them south to attack Nottingham. God willing, such action may draw Stephen north and leave us only Eustace to deal with.

"Roger, I am speaking to you. Would not Lincoln already have appealed to Chester?"

Henry's sharpness jolted Hereford into speech. "Perhaps. I cannot tell. There is no hatred between them, only little love, but Chester takes time to decide things, and even if Lincoln has written he knows that Chester will not act at once, specially to part with money. I am quicker to say yea or nay. You must pardon me, my lord, I must write to Chester, to Elizabeth, and to Lincoln to find out what I can do and what is going forward—oh, yes, and to poor Anne too. Poor child. I can offer her little comfort save my assurances that her husband is doing what is right—and little enough will she care for that."

The sun had set and the moon was high before Hereford was through with his correspondence for by and large the letters were difficult to write. Elizabeth's was the easiest. He gave her flat instructions as to what he wished done and told her the plain unvarnished truth about the seriousness of their situation without any attempt at beautiful words or phrases. She was to drive her father to support Lincoln and even ride north with him if necessary, but under no circumstances was she to take part in the fighting, and, if possible, she was to leave once Chester seemed well involved and return home to Hereford. He was afraid, of course, that if Chester and Lincoln should by some chance be beaten that she would be taken prisoner.

The beautiful words Hereford reserved for his letter to Anne, striving to raise her courage and build her resignation with a combination of sympathy, reason, and praise. That he would not be successful was a foregone conclusion, but he guessed correctly that seeing his hand would be of some comfort to her. Before Hereford started writing to Chester, he sat for some time gently pulling his ear and running his hands through his hair. He needed to relate Lincoln's situation and apply what pressure he could to Chester, without hinting that there could be any benefit to himself other than personal satisfaction. That was not so difficult; what held him back was the struggle with his conscience about whether he should say that he was asking Chester to fight for Lincoln because he was personally occupied with Stephen in the south. Literally, of course, this was true, but to say it was to suggest that he would keep Stephen where he was if he could, which certainly was not true. Hereford sighed and wrote. This war had now made a liar of him also. Storm was right when he said that once you were drowned in the mud it was easier to keep sinking lower. Would there be anything left of him, Hereford wondered, when it was over?

Last of all and most difficult was Hereford's letter to Lincoln, which must contain sympathy and encouragement without any direct promise of aid and certainly without indication that he planned to use his sister's father-in-law as a cat's-paw in his rebellion. If Stephen did ride north to stop Chester, Lincoln would suffer great losses, win, lose, or draw. In spite of his revulsion at his own dishonesty, Hereford saw his last courier ride off with a certain sense of satisfaction. At least he was doing something, attempting to direct events rather then being swept along like a helpless chip of wood on the tide of circumstance. As he returned to the great hall where the exhausted men-at-arms slept strewn over the floor on straw pallets or on the bare rushes alone, Hereford's brain started to operate again. He had been pursuing a vanishing foe for so long that the reality of his effort had become entangled with the hopeless and unending pursuit of the phantoms of his recurring nightmare. If he was not to go mad, Hereford thought suddenly, he must stop this dream action and break free of his sense of inevitable futility because it was plainly leading him to the defeat of exhaustion and starvation which Stephen planned.

Instead of pursuit, hoping to catch the king and defeat him in one large battle, they could try dividing part of their forces into smaller parties that would be stationed in any unravaged areas sure to draw Stephen sooner or later. But not stationed in the keeps, Hereford thought. The uselessness of that method had been proved by the scorching of the area around Devizes. The men would have to make do in the villages, in the very huts of the serfs themselves for to set up camps would be to display their presence and numbers openly. The danger to the troops would be, of course, far greater, since they would have neither the stone walls nor the supplies and armaments of a castle to support them, but that knowledge should make them watch all the more keenly. Furthermore, even if one group was destroyed, the loss would not be serious because the groups would be small. Slowly the idea evolved even further. He and Henry could wait with a reasonably large force in some central place and each fighting group could be supplied with several couriers on fast horses. Perhaps thus, if fighting with the small force delayed Stephen, who would think he could hurt his enemies without danger to himself, they could reach him in time to inflict a punishing defeat upon him. Perhaps not, but at least there would be someone other than the defenseless serfs to protect what crops and land remained to them.

Hereford went to get his long unused charts and, stimulated by the first ray of hope he had seen in weeks, settled down to study them in spite of the late hour and his fatigue. Almost as if his personal feelings had some incalculable effect on external events, matters began to mend for Roger and his overlord. The day after his decision was made, Walter, whom he had not been able to contact for two weeks, turned up at Devizes, bloody, disheveled, with one third of his men dead or incapacitated, but with the heartening report that he had met Stephen's forces by accident moving southwest again and had trounced them soundly.

"Their losses were at least double mine," he reported, his dark eyes flashing with pride, and I swear we would have taken the king himself except that darkness came and they slipped away to one of Henry de Tracy's keeps. Tired and wounded as we were, I dared not follow lest they send out a fresh force from the castle against us."

"God bless you, Walter, you are like a bright fire on a dark winter's night. We have not had such heart-warming news from anyone. Come and have your hurts dressed before you fall into a fever from them."

"You are like an old woman, Roger. I am barely scratched," Walter laughed. "It would be better for us to make haste back to where I left Stephen. My men are weary, but yours are fresh. Come, I am not so worn. I will make shift to show you the way."

Hereford hesitated, partly because he was truly concerned for his brother's welfare and partly because he wanted time to set his own plan into operation. Finally he glanced at Henry, and his overlord nodded eagerly.

"Even if he is already gone, Roger, it will do my heart good to see his men's crops burn for once, and there is always the chance that he will think himself safe and stay to rest. Can we take the keep, think you, Walter?"

"I could not see. It was full dark and I had no lust to come too close. Whatever else he is, Stephen of Blois is a brave man and a fine fighter. Had he not been so firm in leading his men and rallying them, we would have received less hurt and, mayhap, finished them. I do not know that keep, but such things always depend upon how much time you can spend and how many men you can afford to lose."

Henry looked approving. This was his first personal contact with Walter of Hereford, and the young man was certainly showing himself in his best light. From Henry's point of view Walter had advantages over Roger. He did not seem nearly so squeamish or concerned with fine points of honor. Hereford glowed with an inner pride that was very like a father's when his little son shows off successfully for company. Nonetheless, he shepherded Walter away firmly, ignoring his protests. The less chance Walter had of exposing his less endearing characteristics to Henry, the better Hereford would like it.

"Yes, yes," he said, his face breaking into an unaccustomed smile, "I know I am an old woman and anything else you wish to call me, but I will see your wounds washed and salved and see you laid down upon a bed for a few hours' rest while we make ready." Hereford laughed aloud as Walter expressed himself freely about what he called Roger's mother-hen attitude.

"I am no infant that you need lead me away as if to change my wetted hose. In any case, you are a fine one to talk about my needed rest. Have you looked at yourself recently? If Beauchamp had not pointed you out, I would have passed you by. You look like one of my filthier, less reputable mercenaries. Have you given up bathing and changing your clothes? A man could smell you above a pigsty."

"Ay," Hereford replied with half-serious humor, watching Walter's squire and some of the castle women undressing and washing him, "I am mortifying my flesh like some saints in the hope that it will placate the Lord and make him look more kindly upon us. Have you received my messages, Walter?"

"Oh, yes. I was too busy to reply. You know how I love to write."

"Then you know how matters have gone. I was not jesting when I said you brought us the first light we have seen in this darkness for long and long."

Walter looked consideringly at his brother and dismissed his man and the servants with a gesture as he went to lie down. His face was perfectly expressionless as he got into the bed and drew a light coverlet over himself. "If you regret your choice, there is still time to change," he said in a voice too low to carry more than a few feet.

Dumbly Hereford shook his head, then with a quick movement seated himself on the edge of the bed beside Walter. "Nay, good or ill, life or death, I am Henry's man—so I swore and so I will abide." There was a long pause which Walter made no effort to ease. After a while with a slow gesture of infinite tenderness, Roger of Hereford touched his brother's face. "You have sworn nothing, however. My brother, you do not believe me, or do not wish to believe me, but you are very dear to my heart. For all my rage at times, I have never ceased for a moment to love you. I wish you were well out of this. I wish I had never dragged you into my affairs. I curse the weakness that made me lean upon you in the bitterness of the hour in which I lost Alan."

For once Walter did not jerk away from Hereford's caress, but he made no reply that could help his brother. Out of Hereford's influence, he had done good work for Henry's cause solely because he enjoyed what he was doing, unmoved by the promise of reward and title of which Roger had written. Walter coveted only one title in the land—that of the Earl of Hereford—and if he had allowed himself to think of reward and titles at all, he would probably have turned against Hereford. Face to face with the brother whom he adored and hated, he fell prey once more to the tearing love-hate dichotomy and was paralyzed by his emotions. He would do nothing to help Roger out of the dilemma he was obviously struggling with, but he could not just now bring himself to reject the tenderness of the worn wraith of a man sitting beside him.

It was Roger who broke the silence again. "I would like to release you from the promise you made to me, Walter. If you wish to go, I will find some excuse." Roger's voice trembled a little, and he paused to steady it. "Wait until we see what the outcome of this action will be. If we take Stephen, of course, there will be no need for you to withdraw, but if we are beaten—. Whatever comes to me, I would have you safe. Perhaps—"

"Salving your conscience, Roger?" Walter laughed, but in a strained uncomfortable way. "With all your fine talk, you are a selfish brute at best. Do you care what I think and feel? Not a whit. You drag me in and push me out only according to your own need or to ease your own heart. Do you remember our compact? I was to serve you until you had a man to replace me or until *I* wished to break free. Well, you have no man yet and I am not ready. When I wish to go, I will send you word."

Seizing his brother, who was at a considerable physical disadvantage lying down, Hereford kissed him soundly in spite of his struggles, cheeks, forehead, and lips. "You have the foulest tongue in offering a kindness I have ever known in a man, Walter. No doubt you would have to kill me before you could bring yourself to admit you love me." Hereford did not notice Walter's start and naked, if momentary, expression of fear because he was getting up to leave. He would never know how close to the truth his joke was. The only time Walter would love his brother without any other twinge of emotion was when Roger was dead.

"Go to sleep," Hereford said, briefly turning back to tousle Walter's hair and kiss him again. "I will wake you just before we are ready to move."

The relief that Walter's renewed pledge gave Hereford

did not put his mind at peace for any length of time. He was in earnest about freeing Walter from partisanship in the civil war and was very ready to admit that his motives were not solely altruistic or dictated by affection. A good part of his concern was for the safety of his lands and title which might fall forfeit to the king if there was no strong man to defend them and he died a rebel. His youngest brother was still a child, and Chester could not be trusted to extend himself fully for something that was not his. If Walter became the Earl of Hereford, however, Roger was sure no one would wrest a tittle of land from him. The talk they had, moreover, had set his mind working upon another personal problem. It would not be easy for Walter to find a suitable husband for Catherine when this mess was over if they lost. Of course, if he contracted her to one of his partisans—which was all he could do just now—she too might be ruined.

Hereford broached the subject to his brother as they rode southward. "Catherine is your favorite, Walter, and I have long meant to ask you what you think I should do regarding her marriage."

"She is just turned fourteen, you have time sufficient to consider where to bestow her. Why ask me, anyhow? You asked me nothing about Anne's marriage."

"You are older now, for one thing, and particularly tender of Catherine for another. Moreover—" Hereford hesitated, trying to choose words, and then plunged ahead without any effort to gild his bald statement. "Moreover, the fulfillment of the contract will be your burden if this matter ends ill for me, and I know you well enough to understand that you would care little enough for the contract if the man did not suit you."

"You always think so well of me!"

"I have been wrong before; belike I am wrong now, but you asked and I have answered. Instead of quarreling with me, Walter, consider what I have said."

"There is not much to consider, all in all. There are few enough houses equal to ours in this country, so unless you wish to send her into France—." Walter sucked his teeth and shifted a trifle in the saddle to ease his aching body. "Nay," he went on after a few minutes' silence, "the best we may do here is Patric Fitz Gilbert, John's eldest son. The others are second sons, which Catherine could not abide, or Gloucester's boy—faugh! She could not abide that for other reasons."

"Your thought falls in just with mine, and from what I can learn through Elizabeth, Catherine has a lust to an established warrior. I did think that possibly a still older man—"

"Yes, but that would of necessity be a widower, and I can think of none of suitable rank who does not have sons. Do you suppose Catherine could bear her children to be younger sons?"

"I had not thought of that. Well, what do you think, then, should I approach Fitz Gilbert with a definite proposal? I have sounded him out already, and the boy is free and he himself willing."

"If you are set upon contracting her now, I cannot see what else you can do."

Hereford hesitated again, wondering how to introduce the secondary object of this discussion and again decided that he would gain nothing by elaborate words. Walter had a habit of reducing everything to the plainest and most unflattering terms no matter how one tried to coat a bitter pill with honey.

"There is one more advantage in contracting her to Patric now. Under those conditions I believe his father would yield him to me. I like him and I believe he returns my regard. I could use him—"

"To take my place," Walter concluded. "God, you are a singleminded bastard, Roger. I would love to know why you are so anxious to be rid of me. Are my successes putting your light into the shade, brother dear?"

Shaking his head disgustedly, Hereford made no attempt to deny the allegation. It was useless to argue with Walter when he was in this mood. "If that is what you wish to believe, believe it. Have I ever given you reason to doubt my good will towards you? Nay, do not answer. We will but go round and round as always. Whatever I decide to do about Patric, do you agree that he will be suitable for Catherine?"

"Does it matter?"

"I told you yes," Hereford replied sharply, barely controlling his temper. "I am not given to asking advice when

I do not wish for an answer. Will you ignore Catherine's welfare just to anger me?"

"From all I know of him, he is suitable." Walter answered sullenly. "How can I know what sort of husband he will make? Have I ever been married to him?"

"Bah!" was all Hereford could bring himself to reply to that, and he set spurs to his horse to ride back along the line of armed men. Possibly if he had not been in such a debilitated state he would have found Walter's contrariness funny, he often had in the past, but he was too tired and worried now to laugh at even a mild problem.

The keep at Bruton, to which Walter led them, had been razed after the battle of Castle Cary, but Gloucester's disinclination to fight and Henry de Tracy's passionate partisanship for Stephen had allowed de Tracy to rebuild it. Scarcely three miles from Cary, a far larger stronghold, Bruton had been left in peace because it did not seem to pose a threat to anything important, and Hereford judged that it could be reduced by the Cary garrison at will when that became necessary. His judgment as to the weakness of Bruton was correct, it was apparent when they arrived in the early evening, for the keep was taken in a short encounter which cost them little. The bird they sought was flown, of course, or the conflict would have been neither so short nor so easy. In fact it was because Stephen had taken a large part of the able-bodied garrison with him to fill his depleted ranks that made Bruton so specially vulnerable. Even this minor success was important as a morale builder, and a number of valuable prisoners, wounded and left behind, were taken. Their ransoms would be useful to Henry's treasury, and some of them, resentful at being abandoned, responded very well to Henry's disarming manner, genuine kindness, and charming ways.

As Stephen was temporarily quiet, probably reorganizing his somewhat shattered forces, they remained at Bruton, Hereford setting up his new plan of action, Walter recovering from his wounds which were superficial but many, and Henry charming his new converts.

While the south rested, the north began to boil over anew, for Elizabeth too had received a letter from Anne, who was still convinced that she could make Hereford do anything. Elizabeth did not need her husband's instructions to grasp the advantages of embroiling her father in Lincoln's quarrel, although she did not realize that such action might bring Stephen north again. As matters stood, she could see little danger to Chester's welfare if he went to help his half brother. It seemed a private matter, and it would give him something to do which would effectively prevent him from worrying about his future. Elizabeth had not been feeling well, suffering the malaise and depression common to early pregnancy, and, although she had not confessed the cause of her illness, she had been taking full advantage of it as a means to occupy her doting parent's mind. When she received Anne's letter, Chester was sitting beside her in the garden playing chess to divert her, and he watched her eyes fill with tears with deep concern.

"My child, do not weep. Have you bad news about Roger?"

"No," Elizabeth replied rather faintly. The tears had been of empathy and self-pity, for Anne's case and her own were vaguely similar, but Chester's tenderness sent her mind into action. He was malleable now; what she asked he would very likely perform. "The letter is from Roger's sister Anne," she added slowly, seeking the best way of using her information. "She has deep trouble, but it is not that which makes me sad. You know, Papa, when I was taken at Nottingham, your brother helped Roger to free me, and—"

"No, now, Liza dear, it is not good to think of unpleasant things when you are ill."

"I cannot help it, Papa, for the very man that nearly killed Roger and who Roger gave as a prisoner to Uncle William has by some great treachery turned many keeps and the city of Lincoln itself against him. Indeed, I would do as Anne asks and write to Roger to ask that he help Uncle William, but he is so pressed, and things do not go well for him—." Elizabeth had no need to pretend a trembling voice, for she really was frightened by the bad news she had been receiving from her husband.

Chester patted his daughter's hand soothingly. "This must be some disordered freak of your sister-in-law's. I cannot believe that William could be so taken in nor that he would not appeal to me for support. Perhaps we do not always agree upon everything, but the blood of my father runs in his veins and I should surely support him against the revolt of a servant or vassal."

"I hope you are right, Papa," Elizabeth sighed. She had what she wanted without asking, it seemed, for Chester was already willing to help Lincoln if asked.

That afternoon put the point to the proof, since a letter from Lincoln with just such a request did arrive. Elizabeth's preliminary work was not wasted, however, because her father, as usual, began to hesitate, and she had to remind him tactfully of their earlier conversation.

"My love," he replied at last, to her gentle prodding, "do not distress yourself. Of course I will go, but I need time to summon my troops. Come, you shall see that I am in earnest. If you are strong enough we shall pretend that you are still in your old state as a daughter of this house, and you shall help me write the summonses."

She was certainly strong enough for that and agreed with alacrity. As she bent over her parchment, her quill automatically tracing the standard words of summons, her mind was busy with a different problem. The initial meeting between Lincoln and Chester was always difficult. After some time in each other's company they seemed to settle into a fairly workable relationship with only mild and periodic flare-ups, but if some ameliorating influence were not present when they first came together, they might part very rapidly. Elizabeth did not wish to travel halfway across England, but she felt that she must. She had not much spirit or inclination for argument either, but she saw no other way to convince her father rapidly enough that she was complately recovered. The campaign was opened with the flat statement that she would go too because her men were fresh and she wished to show her gratitude for Lincoln's help at Nottingham.

"No, dear," Chester denied gently, stroking his daughter's hair. "You are not well. You will stay here and rest. If you insist, I will take your men, but it will not be needful."

"I am much better, Father. Indeed, I begin to think that perhaps I have not been sick at all, only bored and distressed by all this bad news we have had. Now that there is something to do, I am stronger already."

"I do not doubt that you feel better in the first excitement, but this strength will not last and you will be weaker than ever when it passes. I cannot permit you to take that chance."

"But, Papa, I am not excited. Why should I be? I am only interested."

"That is enough, Elizabeth. I will not take you, so do not tease me. Why, child, can you not see that if you failed midway you would be a terrible danger to me?"

Elizabeth did see it, but she did not think she would fail. There was a chance, of course, that so much riding would make her miscarry, but she thought it too early in her pregnancy to cause her more than a day's delay. The thought distressed her; she wanted very much to bear Roger's child, but she comforted herself with the thought that if God had granted her prayers to have an heir to Roger's land, He would not permit her to lose it. Therefore her father's remark that he had heard enough was very far from the truth. He had not heard even the beginning of the argument. For the next three days Elizabeth reasoned and pleaded; after the receipt of Roger's letter she began to rail. Poor Chester had not a chance. His only reason for objecting to his daughter's company was that he believed her too weak to make the trip with ease, and here she was displaying far more energy in pressing her point than he had in resisting it. In less than a week, before all the men Chester had summoned had assembled, she had won. Another week saw her dressed once again as a boy with somewhat less success. Always voluptuous, Elizabeth's figure was responding quickly to her condition, and now her breasts strained at the russet tunic in such a way as to make clear, even from a distance, her womanhood. She sighed, removed the garments, and reclothed herself in her most sober-colored gown. Even the comfort of riding astride was not worth the chance that someone would notice the change in her body and remark upon it to her father, who, no fool, might put two and two together.

CHAPTER 17

———————————

De Caldoet had been realizing for some time that he had made a serious mistake. Like a cornered rat, however, he bared his teeth at his enemies, unwilling or unable to disgorge what he had swallowed. The mistake lay not in the seizure of the Earl of Lincoln's keeps but in the belief that the city of Lincoln would accept his rule once he had shown them the way to be free of their earl. Without the slightest compunction the rich burghers had turned him out, written a charter for themselves, and sent it with their promises of fealty to the king. The castles de Caldoet had taken, all near the city with the idea that they would reinforce his great prize, were all now virtually useless to him for two reasons. First, whoever held the city of Lincoln could swallow everything in sight of those great, gray stone walls. The burghers, of course, were no threat, but they would not control the military aspect of Lincoln long. Either the king or the earl would win that power, and both were bad for de Caldoet. Second, if the city withheld its truage, he was destitute. Not a mil more could be wrung from the people in and around the castles now his—Lincoln did not leave his people more than a mil and de Caldoet had taken that. The only money in that country was in the purses of the burghers of the city of Lincoln and in the Earl of Lincoln's strongboxes, which were also concealed in the city. Those de Caldoet had been unable to find before he had been ejected—he had been so sure they would be yielded to him too.

Although it was true that the strongboxes were beyond Lincoln's grasp also—thus preventing him from immediately hiring the men he needed to win back his own, Lincoln was not, like de Caldoet, without other resources.

Now de Caldoet could see that even if Lincoln's other vassals, most of whom hated him sincerely, remained neutral, giving excuses for not answering their overlord's summons, time was Lincoln's friend and his enemy. Doubtless time would bring Lincoln's sons to his aid, and his half brother, Chester, and—here de Caldoet's face turned purple with a mixture of rage, hate, and fear—that accursed son-in-law of Chester's, Hereford.

All his troubles had begun with Hereford. Unconsciously de Caldoet's lips lifted in the snarl of a vicious dog as he thought that his life would be a cheap price to pay if he could take Hereford with him. He forgot, distance and rage bolstering his courage, the paralysis of fear that those ice-cold blue eyes could engender in him. He told himself Hereford would be nothing, a frail puppet, without Storm's demoniac presence, and just then he believed it, forgetting also how hard it was to die. It was in that mood he awaited his doom, knowing it was coming, knowing that he should gather his men and run. If he ran, possibly he could find another war lord unscrupulous enough and trusting enough or stupid enough to use him. Still, he could not. Knowing he must lose all if he stayed, still he could not leave land which he now considered his by right of conquest, so strong was his sense of possession and his need for land of his own. Land was the power, the security, the bringer of all good things to him who possessed it. Even gold was nothing in comparison with land, for once spent gold was gone, while the land remained forever, yielding gold, food, and men year after year. He had lost his land through greed for more land and would now probably lose his life because of his greed for land. He knew it, but still he could not go.

Elizabeth swallowed her nausea and smiled sweetly at her uncle. "You must not take too seriously what my father says, Uncle William. You know how he is. He will never believe you are a grown man, just because he knew you when you were a child. He treats me the same way, although I am long since a woman grown—"

"I asked him for help, not advice," Lincoln said heatedly.

Elizabeth raised a deprecating hand. "I know, Uncle, I know. But with elder brothers the two come together. Have patience. You know he means well for you. Indeed, you must forgive me for smiling, but it is the same with my husband and his brother Walter. They never come together but they quarrel; Roger can never learn to let Walter make his own mistakes and live his own life, nor can he resist the urge to tell Walter how much better things would have been had he followed the advice of his elder brother. Let not a few sharp words turn you from great gain."

Lincoln opened his mouth to answer sharply, still angry, and then slowly closed it. He looked with steadily increasing amazement at his niece who was standing demurely before him, hands clasped, eyes lowered, a little pale, but smiling sweetly. The pose should not have been surprising, it was that which all modest and docile women were supposed to assume, but Elizabeth—? Not Elizabeth! Lincoln searched his memory but could find no precedent for this behavior, neither for the physical attitude nor the soft words. Elizabeth would be more likely to offer unpleasant advice of her own than to salve the wounds made by her father's. Then she must want something. But what? Surely he was in no position just now to grant her anything, and, to the best of his knowledge, neither Hereford nor Chester needed anything either. The pause had grown awkward and Elizabeth had flashed a glance at her uncle which told her much. She was well prepared for his next question.

"Very well, my dear niece, I will not fence with you. What do all these sweet words mean? What do you want?"

"You misunderstand me, Uncle William. I desire nothing except your well-doing, my father's and my husband's. I have learned a bitter lesson through my own bad temper and willfulness, and I am most anxious that those faults, even in others, should cause no more trouble."

Elizabeth maintained her manner with some little difficulty now, for she had an almost irresistible temptation to laugh. It was so easy when one knew how. These men, one could mold them like wax—all except Roger. Look at

Lincoln, she thought. Not a spark of anger or resentment
against Chester remained. His whole being would now be
taken up with suspicion of her and with wondering what
she wanted, yet she wanted nothing really, and she had
spoken the truth. Merely because she had not spoken in
her usual manner, Lincoln saw the truth as a lie or a
concealment, and would spend what time he had for
thought planning how to circumvent her nonexistent plots.
Probably, she thought, murmuring some modest answer to
another probing question, he would now run to her father
to ask why she had come. She choked with laughter and
changed it to a cough, thinking what his face would be
like when Chester reported that she had insisted with all
her strength on bringing her men to repay his "kindness"
in helping her husband rescue her. Elizabeth's body curtsied a good-by almost without volition, and her eyes followed Lincoln as he walked away; it would be perfect.
Lincoln's suspicions would set her father worrying, remembering how peculiar her behavior had been, how insistent
she had been about coming, and when they were not
planning some military action they would talk about her
and about what she was after and forget to quarrel.

It was funny, and Elizabeth did smile as she strolled
through the well-tended paths of the garden, but her
pleasure in mischief and management was not what it had
been. The sun beat down and the scents of herbs, rosemary and thyme, rose from the beds beside her. A patch
of shade from a mulberry tree, heavy with the red promise
of ripe, mahogany-colored berries in the autumn, dappled
the path. Beyond that lavender grew in purple spires.
Elizabeth paused, the gentle scent bringing to mind her
gentle friend Leah. Perhaps Leah's was the better path.
Her heart held room only for her family and her friends.
She cared nothing for power and, in spite of her cleverness, desired nothing more than to manage her household
and live in peace with her husband and child. Such an attitude, Elizabeth had always regarded as a mere
weakness, cowardice, a lack of spirit which made a
woman tamely yield to the rule of the men around her.
Now she was not so sure. There came a time, apparently,
when every woman wished to sit with folded hands or

with her sewing and her dreams. Certainly she was not afraid nor weak, she had even accomplished a state of vassalage, yet looking at her feelings honestly she wished she had not; peace was what she desired.

What Elizabeth had to face, however, were plans for war. It was true that Lincoln and Chester both continued to regard her a little queerly, which made her choke with laughter from time to time, but she had seven hundred good fighting men at her orders, and it was necessary for her to agree with their plans. Elizabeth made no objection to anything her father and uncle suggested. They were long experienced in this type of fighting and she listened only to be sure that her men would not be used for any particularly dangerous activity. Beyond that she had little enough interest in precisely how they managed their attack.

As it happened, Elizabeth's faith in their skill was justified, for de Caldoet's gains were swept away before the strength of the few vassals who responded to Lincoln's call, the small forces his sons brought, and the substantial army which came with Chester and Elizabeth. The last keep to fall was that which sheltered de Caldoet himself, but it fell in the end, no help coming from the city of Lincoln to which he sent in his extremity a reminder of what he had done for them and a desperate appeal. The great gates, ironhard oak, remained shut. The burghers had no intention of helping de Caldoet, although they preferred him as a neighbor sufficiently to send several anxious and urgent messages to Stephen reporting the fact that Chester was ravaging Lincolnshire and threatening the city itself with siege and destruction.

De Caldoet was dragged finally, screaming curses, and still struggling, from the mass of dead men he had first slaughtered and then hidden behind. By right he should have suffered the same fate as his brother, he should have been hanged, but when Elizabeth and Chester indifferently cast their votes for that end, Lincoln slammed his fist down upon the table before him.

"No! Grant him confession and send him to God? No! With such an easy end, who would not dare to try the same. What has he lost—a man without family, without honor? The shame can be nothing to him. I say it is too easy."

"Brother, be calm. I care nothing what you do with him. He has done me no hurt. Whatever you say, I will agree to and Elizabeth also, doubtless."

Terrified to the borders of insanity, de Caldoet struggled for a moment more fiercely and then fell quiet. Strangely, he did not look either at Chester or Lincoln but at Elizabeth, whom he associated with her husband. He made no attempt to plead for mercy, but in the pause in which Lincoln was obviously considering the most painful and lingering death he could demand, the doomed man began to laugh weirdly.

"Confession? You need not worry. Confession will not save me, but it will not save you, Lady Hereford, or your accursed husband either. The longer it takes me to die, the longer I will have to call on the master I have served so well. So faithful have I been, surely Satan will grant my one wish. I will come back, I swear it by the Evil One Himself. I will come back and foul the fruit of your womb and destroy Roger, Earl of Hereford."

Elizabeth turned livid, speechless. Instinctively Lincoln thrust his shoulder before her, as if his bulk could shield her from the curse, and Chester took his rigid daughter into his arms.

"You need not die at all, de Caldoet," Lincoln said, his voice shaking. "I cannot think of an end fit for such as you. Take him out," he snarled to his men, "and lop off his right hand. Cut off his ears and his nose, and his hangars, and brand him as a thief and a runaway serf. See that he does *not* die. Then turn him loose."

"No!" de Caldoet shrieked. "No! Let me die and I will recall my curses. Let me die and I will pray for you and her, even for Hereford, with my dying breath." But the men were already dragging him away.

Elizabeth drew herself upright. "Satan is a notably ungrateful master," she managed to say steadily with an attempt at lightness. "We must hope that he will fulfill his promise in his usual way—by ignoring it." A brief shudder passed through her body. "God, what an evil thing it is! Mayhap we should have destroyed it altogether."

"We have destroyed it," Lincoln replied. "Without a right hand, he cannot wield a sword or defend himself. No honest man in the land will even give alms to a man so marked, and not even a band of outlaws will harbor him. What good is he to them who cannot fight or work or spy?"

Regaining complete control of herself Elizabeth apparently dismissed de Caldoet with an impatient gesture. "Yes. No doubt you are right. What is much more important is what we are next to do. It is true, Uncle William, that your keeps are your own again, but their condition makes it beyond hope that they will yield you anything this year. As long as the city of Lincoln holds against you, then, you are in bad case."

"Those fat burghers. I will roast them over a slow fire and watch the fat drip off and then eat them like roast suckling pigs."

"Ay," Chester put in wryly, "if you can get at them. Elizabeth is right. While they hold your strongboxes we are somewhat pressed for money—that campaign in the north sucked me nearly dry, and Hereford is in the same case. If those pigs hold firm against us, I do not believe we have a force strong enough to take the town. We need money to buy more men."

Lincoln growled and bit his nails. "For money, there is another way. Why should I waste my substance on lessoning them? Look you, hard by is Tuxford whose master holds by Stephen. You have no love for him. We may refill your coffers and mine—which is only right, since it is his fault yours are empty and his promised support of those rebellious hogs of mine that has given them courage to withstand me."

Chester hesitated somewhat because he was still not decided upon his future course, but his half brother's persuasion was hard to resist. Especially when Lincoln pointed out how easy the taking of that previously peaceful keep would be and that it would serve the double purpose of terrifying one of his own recalcitrant vassals who counted on his unwillingness to cross the lands of Tuxford, Chester began to waver. By the time they had dined and been well fortified with reasonably good wine, Elizabeth could see that her influence would scarcely be necessary to prod her father into action. If they were successful in this first raid, her men would not be needed much longer either, and she would be able to move south as Roger had ordered.

Hereford looked up from the letter which recounted this information with a faint sense of satisfaction. He would feel much easier when Elizabeth was safe behind the stone walls of Hereford Castle. Less and less as the days passed and the rains of late summer gave way to the golden days and nipping nights of autumn, did he like the idea of her being out in the open.

"Your wife is a most faithful correspondent," Henry said indolently, shifting his body so that another portion of it would be toasted by the fire.

"Yes. She writes that all progresses as we would desire. Lincoln having regained his own now proposes to swallow what is Stephen's, as I supposed, and Chester has agreed to help him and share the profits."

Henry's mouth hardened somewhat. "I suppose I am glad enough of their help now, but what I am to do in the future with that pair, I know not."

Gilding gleamed briefly as Hereford slowly rotated an elegant shoe, his eyes following the movement of the light on the toe and instep. The weeks of quiet they had enjoyed since Walter had given Stephen something to think about had permitted Hereford to return to his normal sartorial magnificence. That had been a mistake, however, for the brilliant, gemlike colors, the gold and silver embroidery, the furs and jewels only made more noticeable the change in the man so adorned. Rest had not improved Hereford's appearance much, although he was now perfectly clean, but that was possibly because he had taken no real rest. A sense of urgency so extreme possessed him now that sitting still, even when there was nothing he could possibly do, was a torment. He knew, somehow he knew that time for something was drawing to a close. With a carefully controlled slowness, Hereford rotated his foot in the other direction. His hands resting on the arms of his chair quivered constantly although almost imperceptibly because of their tenseness.

"I know not either," he replied to Henry in a slightly bored voice. "But I can give you the comfort that they are no true-loving pair. You look too far ahead. If Stephen responds to this by turning north, as I hope, where shall we strike?"

There was a long pause as Henry pretended to consider while he really watched his companion. Nothing about the rigid control Hereford was exercising over himself, from the flat, bored tone of voice to the careful, slow movements, was lost. Henry had seen plenty of men pushed to their breaking points and knew the signs well, but week after week Roger of Hereford did not break, and as far as Henry knew there was nothing serious enough weighing upon him to account for his condition.

"Roger, how long have you been under arms?"

"Eight months, one week, and three days. Do you want to know the hours?"

"It is too long. Oh, be quiet, Roger, your answer alone shows it is too long. What man, except he be overworn and thinking overmuch of his home counts the days and hours he has been absent from it. You need rest—real rest, not this idling on tenterhooks waiting to attack or be attacked. Look you, Eustace is in the east battling Bigod. Stephen is likely, as you say, to turn northward again. I think you should go home for a few weeks, even a month or more. This is a good time for it, and I can summon you if there is a sudden need."

"I cannot deny that the rest would be welcome," Hereford replied in the measured tone which was more unnatural to him than a scream. "Mayhap there is reason to what you say. I—"

"You will not desert me entirely?" Henry said, half laughing, and then as Hereford's face whitened still further, "Nay, Roger, it was but a jest. If you abode with me when all went ill, why should you part company when everything promises well for us? I will make no more bad jokes. Go home and—"

"No!" Hereford leapt to his feet and began to pace the hall nervously. "No. Do not tempt me, my lord." He shuddered and came up to lay a hand on Henry's shoulder. "The devil himself must have put our parting into your mind, and some good angel made you say I should not desert you. No, by God, even at your urging, I will not yield to that dream—"

"What dream, Roger? Of what do you dream?"

Hereford passed his hand over his face, hesitating, and then said slowly in a shaking voice, "Of desertion, but by whom and of whom I do not know. The dream is ever the same—a great battle and through the fighting there is a—a feeling of joy, of success within the grasp of my hand. Then suddenly I am alone, riding through a strange, ravaged countryside with the feeling of failure and despair heavy upon me, but I do not feel like myself, I feel strange and distant as though, perhaps, it is not my body but my spirit which rides so. And all the time that I ride a voice calls, perhaps within me, perhaps to me, 'Do not go—do not go now.' But still I ride on and I know that I am alone, all alone, with no other human thing ever to come near me, and it is because I have deserted someone—or have been deserted—I do not know—"

"Only that?"

With an impatient gesture Hereford turned away and began to pace again. "How can I say what feeling oppresses me. What—. Nonsense, Henry," he added suddenly with a slightly shaken laugh, coming back and sitting down. "It is nothing to do with us, I am sure. I have always had such dreams—ever since my father died I have dreamt of being too late or making some mistake which has cost me and those I love dear. I feel lighter already for having spoken of it. I tell you," he said forcefully, as Henry stared at the fire with a troubled frown, "it is all nonsense. This talk can profit neither of us. We would spend our time better planning what move next to make."

"You say nonsense, yet you believe it enough to refuse to go home—. Roger—"

"I do not believe in tempting fate when it is not necessary." Hereford replied firmly in a much more natural tone of impatience. "Besides, it is mad to abandon such an opportunity to make great gains. If Stephen takes his army north—and belike the fool will take those vassals from the south who are still under arms with him north also—he will leave this area virtually naked of protection. What idiots we would be to take such a time to rest."

"Ay, that is true." Henry's natural optimism was already shaking off the uneasy superstitious fears Roger's tale had engendered in him. "What we should do is bid Gloucester to join us and strike hard."

"Good. Where?"

"Bridport."

"Why Bridport? Why not Faringdon?"

"Because a good port in our hands is always valuable and because I have had some strong indication that the castellan of the keep that guards the port is not all unfriendly to us. If we make a strong enough show of force before the gates, I am told, he will open to us without battle."

"But Henry de Tracy—"

"That is the rub. We must prove to Bridport that we are stronger than de Tracy, and how to bring him to battle is more than I know. The man is wily as a fox, and very few of his keeps are weak as Bruton. Particularly near the coast he has taken pains to make them nearly impregnable. I doubt that we could take anything near enough to Bridport to make an impression without great loss of time and men, and—"

"Never mind that now. Let us take one step forward at a time." Action, any action was so necessary to Hereford that even sensible planning paled into insignificance before his need. "For this we need Gloucester so that much depends upon his willingness. Let us go to him—we are doing nothing here anyway. I will lay you a small wager that he will think of a way to tempt de Tracy out. In such matters he is very keen."

Hereford would have lost that wager, although Duke William fulfilled every other expectation. When they arrived they were welcomed with knowing smiles, and William confirmed positively what they had only surmised, that Stephen had gathered his forces and already turned north.

"How do you know?"

"Ah, my lord, that would take too long to explain," William said smoothly, "but you may be assured that I am right. I know. I am so sure that I will offer, before you ask, to summon my vassals and join you in the field." His eyes wandered from Henry to Hereford. "Roger, my dear boy, you do not look at all well. I will be very cross with our dear overlord if he is pressing you too hard. To furrow such a brow with care is almost too great a price to pay—even for a crown. I would not treat you so."

"If Stephen of Blois is already gone northward," Henry said hurriedly, nobly casting himself into the breach he saw opening, "we had better set ourselves at once to the task of readying our own men. There is no time to lose."

"Certainly. My clerks have a list of the vassals whose military service is due and you may have it at once. But really, my concern is for the Earl of Hereford. You are with him constantly and perhaps have not noticed how pale and thin—"

"Do not concern yourself for me, William. However I look, I am no delicate flowerlet."

Gloucester restrained himself with a mighty effort from laughing. It was true that he had once approached Hereford with the idea of winning him sexually because of his beauty and his delicate appearance. He was far too clever a man, however, to need more than a slight hint that his attentions were unwelcome. It was just because Hereford reacted so violently that Gloucester could not deny himself the pleasure of tormenting him.

"But you will be ill if you continue to drive yourself," William murmured dulcetly. "Come, I will show you to a quiet room."

"I am never ill," Hereford snapped edgily.

"A good meal and a fresh wench would do him more good than quiet," Henry interposed, digging his elbows surreptitiously but painfully into Hereford's ribs. "The only trouble with Roger is that he is like a hound, straining so eagerly at the leash in his desire for the hunt that he is near strangled. If you would improve his state, give him work so that he will cease from fretting at doing nothing. Give Hereford those lists, William," Henry said, taking Gloucester by the arm in a caressing manner and turning the full force of the charm he had inherited from his father upon him, "and come with me. He will have the benefit of a task that calls for little effort and will yet occupy his mind, and I need the benefit of your advice upon certain matters."

The interest of such an appeal was, of course, far too great to resist just to annoy Hereford. William went with Henry, hoping to learn something new but perfectly willing to listen to anything the young man said, and Henry kept him interested by applying to him for information on the various prisoners taken at Bruton and for advice on how to treat those who seemed ready to join him. Hereford sighed with relief. William always revolted him, but usually he could control his natural recoil. He laughed a little wryly, promising himself not to snap so irritably in the future. After all, the man could scarcely ravish him against his will. Nonetheless, the small additional distraction in his present state of nervous irritation made him careless. After ordering the scribes to write the summonses and writing some of the more important ones himself, Hereford scrawled a note to Elizabeth warning her of Stephen's move and urging her to make all reasonable speed consonant with her safety to return to Hereford Castle. Just as he was about to address this, he was interrupted for what seemed like the twentieth time by the need to settle a minor dispute about the division of spoils and the distribution of supplies. Cursing his men roundly, he sent them about their business, seized what he thought was his letter to Elizabeth to direct it and hand it to a waiting courier.

"With all haste possible to my wife, and enjoin her by mouth that I bid her heed most strictly what I wrote herein."

"Yes, my lord. Shall I return with her reply?"

"There will be no need for an immediate reply if she is able to obey my orders. If not, she will direct you or another. Make haste—and bid her make all possible haste also."

Some twenty-four hours later the exhausted rider gasped out his message—when Hereford said to make haste his men were prone to kill horses in an effort to obey him—and Elizabeth broke her husband's seal in a trembling hurry. What she read made her open her eyes to their fullest extent in blank amazement. Without salutation or address, in a hand that was obviously not Roger's, the letter she received was a formal summons for her to appear at Gloucester to perform her military duties to her over-lord.

"Is this for me? You are sure there is no mistake?"

"My lord gave me the letter with his own hand, madam, and bid me tell you that you should strictly obey his orders and that with all possible haste."

"But—" It was ridiculous to question the courier further for he could plainly tell her no more. Elizabeth bit back what she had been about to say and dismissed him with a gesture. What in the world, she wondered, had gotten into Roger? Surely however pressed for time he was he could have written a line in his own hand, and she was not, af-ter all, a military vassal. The only thing she could think of was that things were so bad that he was afraid to describe them for fear of the letter falling into enemy hands and guessed that she would understand what he meant by his unusual proceedings. Whatever the explanation, it be-hooved her to go to him at once, for surely he must be in an extremity of need to summon her in such a way. Eliza-beth hurriedly sought out her chief vassal and gave orders which would start them on their way south immediately.

"Now, madam? Through this hostile country?"

Elizabeth's heart quailed. Those words were almost identical with what Alan of Evesham had said before they started for Castle Corby and, indeed, it was the same country—a little north—through which they would ride. Her resolution did not falter long, however.

"Yes, through the night also. My husband and your liege lord has great need of us. We are too strong a force to be lightly taken. Do not be so fainthearted. Shall I don armor and protect you? Are you not shamed that a mere woman should need to urge you to your duty? Fie, is this man-hood?"

"As you say, madam. All shall be as you order," the grizzled warrior said hastily, before his mistress could get her tongue well warmed. As Elizabeth turned away to find her father, he shook his head. "Mere woman," he mumbled, "mere woman. God save me from being on the opposing side if she ever should have cause to lead a force in battle. Her father is a milkmaid compared with his mere daughter." He went to summon the men and order the packing for the long ride. "Woman," he muttered under his breath again, "devil is more like, and the only one who is worse is that husband of hers who is not only madder than she, but can make the craziest things seem like an ordinary matter."

Chester was somewhat harder to convince than her vassal, and Elizabeth did not dare show him her letter for fear he would think Roger had gone mad. Chester, of course, knew nothing of the ceremony of homage she had gone through and would see no sense in the summons at all. She prevailed at last, naturally, because there was nothing her father could do to hold her short of imprisoning her. She was, after all, her own mistress, and the men would obey her orders. The only reason she argued and pleaded at all was that she loved him and did not wish to part from him on bad terms.

"Dear Father, I must go if Roger needs me, you know I must. More particularly since you do not need me any longer. Lincoln's vassals have at last heeded his call, you have men and money sufficient—"

"Elizabeth, I am not trying to hold you here. Of course you must go to your husband. But through the night? His need could not be so great as that."

"I do not know," Elizabeth replied softly, but with frightened eyes. "It is not like him to call me so urgently. My men have almost completed their time of service and I know he planned that I should return to Hereford when I left you. Yet his letter urges haste and his messenger brought orders from his own lips more straitly urging haste. I dare not delay even an hour more than necessary."

"Mayhap if necessity presses so hard it would be well for me to come also?"

"He would have asked if he desired that. But I thank you for your kindness, Father. Do you hold yourself in readiness for a day or two. If I find that the case is desperate, I will send you word."

"Very well, Elizabeth." Chester drew his daughter close and kissed her fondly. "You were ever one to go your own way. Whatever happens, I will help you, my love. Do not fail to send me word, one way or another."

That evening Elizabeth's courage nearly failed her. A slight drizzle was falling and the light was failing just as it had that March when she was taken. Her vassals, like Alan, also asked more than once whether they should stop, and Elizabeth, again feeling that to go back was more dangerous than to go forward and stopping most dangerous of all, again urged them onward with barbed words. It was only externals that were smiliar, however, and Elizabeth comforted herself with that knowledge. Her troop this time was almost strong enough to fight off an army and her travel was for far different reasons. The outcome of her journey was also quite different, and despite the trepidation of her vassals they arrived toward evening in sight of the great walled city of Gloucester. Elizabeth looked long and searchingly at the terrain, sighed, and motioned her men forward again. At least Gloucester was not under siege. She was shaking with fatigue by the time she dismounted but still in full possession of her wits and her nerves and prepared for anything. Anything, that is, except what greeted her, which was a husband whose eyes blazed and whose face was positively distorted by fury.

"What in the name of the unholy are you doing here? What does this mean?" he roared, and then giving her no time to reply, "What disordered freak has taken possession of you now?"

"But Roger—" Elizabeth expostulated with starting eyes.

"God, oh, God, how did I ever come to marry such a madwoman! Can nothing restrain you from following your own willful path to our mutual disaster?"

"God curse you, Roger, shut your mouth," Elizabeth shrieked, her higher-pitched voice overriding his at last. "My willful path!" She fumbled in the purse which hung from her belt. Extracting the parchment upon which his last message had been written, she threw it into his face. "There, there are your own orders which brought me here. Do you really think I would ride two feet of my own free will to be with you?"

Tired and shaken as she was, Elizabeth could not help

being amused at the comical expression of chagrin which overspread her husband's countenance as he read the summons. It did not last long, however, for he became angry again almost immediately.

"That is ridiculous, Elizabeth, and you know it. You are no idiot—or perhaps you are if you did not realize that this summons could not possibly be meant for you."

"So I thought, my lord," she replied with a deadly sweetness of tone that should have warned Hereford what was coming. "And I asked the messenger if there was not a mistake." Elizabeth paused, her golden eyes going fiercer and fiercer. "But he replied to me that you had given him that letter with your own dear, careful hands and that with your own sweet, clever lips you had added a verbal message that I must straitly obey what was in the letter, and with all haste." Her words had come quicker and quicker, louder and louder until in the end she was screaming.

If Roger's previous expression had been comical, the dismay that now covered his face was ludicrous. He remembered only too well having given that message and he knew what an effort Elizabeth must have made to arrive so soon. But now she was beyond laughter, and before he could find his voice she had flounced out of the hall calling for the vassal who usually transmitted her orders to the men. That gentleman, however, had been present at the foregoing scene and deliberately made himself scarce because he knew what Elizabeth's temper was. Undoubtedly if she caught him within the next half hour or so they would be ordered to ride out again. Possibly if he could avoid her for a while, her husband could calm her down; he devoutly hoped so for they had already been thirty-six hours in the saddle, barring the stops they had made to feed and rest the horses.

Roger caught his wife in the passage and, failing to hold her with words, pinned her physically against the wall. She struggled only for a moment, telling herself that useless struggles were undignified, but really being only too anxious to accept his explanation. He was not explaining, however, he was laughing.

"Good God, Elizabeth," he gasped finally, gazing with

tear-filled eyes into his wife's rigid face. "I have not laughed like that since we parted. You are always the best thing in the world for me."

"I am very happy that I can afford you amusement, if I have failed in my intention of bringing you needed help," she replied coldly, but with a slightly suspicious quiver in her own voice.

"It is not you at whom I am laughing, Elizabeth, and you know it, so stop pretending you do not think it is funny too. Lord, what an ass I must have looked reading that silly summons. I must have picked up the wrong letter, but how I can have done so—well, it is too late to worry about that now. My poor darling, you must be half dead. It is less than three days since I sent that message out."

"Looked an ass," Elizabeth said trenchantly, "you are an ass."

"I am anything you like, my love, if you will forgive me." Roger laughed again, suddenly, learning forward against his wife. "My God, I wonder who got the letter I sent to you? Which of Gloucester's vassals did I address as 'dear love' and tell that I kissed his gentle hands and slender feet."

"Roger, you did not!" Elizabeth was convulsed, thinking of the stunned amazement of some hard-bitten, battle-scarred veteran as he consumed that piece of information.

"The letter must have gone to someone," Roger gasped, and they clung together, laughing. He sobered finally. "In truth it might have been less of a jest if you came to harm. Come, you must not stand here. Will you go up to Lady Gloucester's solar or would you prefer my room?"

"I am in no fit temper to listen to Isabel's whining just now, Roger."

"Very well," he said a little doubtfully, "but I am afraid you will freeze. I chose the north tower of the old keep and the hearth smokes so badly that I have done without a fire. Still—if that is what you desire—"

"You can stop hemming and hawing, Roger. If you have a woman there, just go and tell her to get out. I can sit in the hall for a few minutes."

Hereford leaned forward again and kissed his wife on

the lips with great tenderness. "There is no one there now." He made no claim of having been faithful, which Elizabeth, quite reasonably, would not have believed anyway, but explained that his retreat was from Gloucester whose attentions he could no longer bear with civility nor reject with impunity in the manner he would like. He then busied himself so completely in giving orders for her comfort that his wife had no time to observe him until washed, scented, and beautifully gowned she relaxed on the bed and gestured him to her.

"Come here, Roger, I have something to tell you."

"And I have many things to tell you," Hereford answered obtusely, sitting down on the bed. "It is a little over three months since I spoke with you. So much has happened that I could not write about."

What little light came into the room from the arrow slits and from the candles near the bed fell full upon his face and Elizabeth, who had glanced lovingly up at him, found that what she had been about to say had better be delayed. This was no time, she realized, to introduce any new emotion, even of joy, to her husband's mind. He looked like a thread so finely drawn that the slightest pressure would snap it.

CHAPTER 18

THE SOUND OF THE WIND rustling the dry leaves of late
October came clearly to Roger of Hereford as he lay
awake in the rough cot in his tent. Beside him Elizabeth's
even breathing both soothed and surprised him. The thick,
curling blond lashes dropped over his eyes, bluer and
brighter than ever in his thin, tired face, as he wondered
for the thousandth time how he had been cozened into
bringing her with him. Bringing a woman to the very edge
of battle—it was crazy, and it certainly had not been his
wish to bring her. No, that was not completely true; he
had desired it although he knew it to be wrong, and because he had desired it he had yielded to Henry's urging
and Gloucester's. He could not understand a bit why they
did urge that Elizabeth remain with them. They did not
need her men, and her presence in her present temper was
certainly no social pleasure.

Hereford stirred and the cot creaked protestingly. In her
sleep Elizabeth turned and reached out to touch him.
Her hand was cold, and Hereford pulled the covers
higher over her shoulders. He kept her hand in his,
rubbing it gently as if to warm it but in reality clinging to
her. When he held her, he did not feel himself drifting
away from everything helplessly, he did not feel overwhelmed by the onrush of events. Elizabeth was his haven
and his anchor in the violent tempests which were battering his life—not a quiet haven certainly, for she was fre-
quently cross as two sticks, but a safe one. Whether they
loved, or laughed, or fought, he came away from each encounter with her better able to deal with himself and
others. She did not calm him or relax him—Hereford with
eyes still closed smiled ruefully at the idea because he so

often left Elizabeth so enraged that he shook—somehow, she gave him strength. She slept heavily, exhaustedly, and yet they had done nothing that day that could tire her physically. With a sudden revelation, Hereford thought— I eat her; that is why she is so tired and pale.

Tomorrow would bring an end to the situation, both its good aspects and its bad. The terms of service of Elizabeth's vassals were over now, and their last duty would be to see her safely home to Hereford. And, Roger thought, he had better concentrate on how to draw Henry de Tracy out of his holes and forget about Elizabeth. Away from him she would have a chance to recruit her strength. They had been encamped before Bridport for a week now with no result. It was true that they were living off the fat of the land, for no opposition had been offered to their raiding parties and the summer-fattened cattle and garnered crops had supplied their tables plentifully. There was even some plunder from small keeps and a small town here and there, but they were no nearer to the opening of Bridport. De Tracy would not fight so large a force with Hereford as its leader, and Bridport would not open its gates to them as long as de Tracy had his full strength and they could not openly demonstrate their ability to beat him.

"Move over, Roger, I wish to get in with you." Hereford started awake, not realizing that he had been mumbling and tossing in an uneasy sleep. "I am cold," Elizabeth explained, and her husband was too dazed to wonder why, if that was her reason, her body was so warm. He accepted gratefully the discomfort of being cramped for the brief heaven of relaxation which came with her embrace, and then slept without dreaming.

"Be sure," Hereford was saying to his wife a few moments before she left the next morning, "to follow exactly the route I have outlined. It is somewhat longer, of course, but this way you will never be more than a few miles from a friendly keep. The men I have assigned as foreriders are experienced, so if they even suspect trouble, do as they say."

"I am not a fool, Roger, and you have said all this before. I know, I know, if de Tracy takes me you will be ruined and I know he will be watching. I will take every precaution."

She stepped back out of the way as a scarred and branded serf, apparently some low hanger-on of the troops, staggered in bearing a load of firewood. Neither Hereford nor his wife glanced at the creature, and the truth is that they would not have recognized him if they had. Without ears or nose and after eight weeks of near starvation, de Caldoet was no longer anything resembling a human being. As if the place was empty, which to his way of thinking it was, Hereford took his wife into his arms. He kissed her long, lifting his lips from hers only to kiss her eyes and her cheeks and return to her lips.

"God bless you, Elizabeth, and God keep you, my dear love. Do not be angry because my fondness makes me urge you so often to caution. You are so dear to me, and I blame myself that I have allowed you to be in this dangerous place. God knows what would become of me if harm came to you through my folly."

"Do not fret yourself, Roger. I will be safe and I will take care." Elizabeth not only yielded to her husband's embrace but returned it cordially. She was immeasurably grateful that he had noticed nothing of the change in her body and that she had resisted the urge to tell him of her pregnancy. He was in a considerably better state of mind than when she arrived, but plainly the less worry he had the better off he would be. "For Heaven's sake, do not worry about me when you should be thinking of other matters. You are so near a great success and one which may lead to still greater victories. Do not permit yourself to be distracted by fears for me or"—she pressed herself still closer against him and lowered her voice—"or any other considerations. You can only do what you think is right, Roger. Who knows whether dreams are not sent as temptations to turn us from the true path."

De Caldoet, watching and listening while he pretended to fumble about making a fire was just barely sane enough to prevent himself from laughing aloud. When his mutilations had been half-healed he had been cast out upon the road. The horror of what he had endured before his wounds had been totally healed and he was quick enough to steal a loaf or fowl here and there was such that his memory had blanked it out completely. And even when his mind had returned to him in some degree, it was not a whole mind. There remained in it no more than an animal cunning which enabled him to remain alive and the fixed idea that he must destroy the Earl of Hereford who had done him some great injury—although he was no longer sure and did not care what that injury was. It had taken him six interminable weeks to win his way south to Hereford's army, a week more of cringing and begging before he had been allowed to exchange the filthiest and most menial tasks for a mouthful of leftovers, and still another week to find out where the Earl of Hereford camped. There was some advantage in being less than a beast, de Caldoet soon found, for no one ever paid the slightest attention to him except to kick him if he were in the way. It was easy to pick up a load of wood and bear it into Hereford's tent. His squire, who would have stopped and questioned almost anyone else, did no more than glance briefly at his excrement-clotted, louse-infested, rag-clad body before he returned his attention to cleaning and paring his nails. Even Hereford and his wife regarded him so little that they made love before him and did not notice how long he was puttering about.

All of this struck de Caldoet as funny because he knew he was more dangerous to the earl than de Tracy's whole army. Even funnier was listening to Hereford and his wife worry about the future. De Caldoet alone knew that Hereford had no future. In a few minutes, as soon as Elizabeth stepped out, Hereford would die. Die, with his sins upon him, without time for confession, prayer or even the last rites. A momentary doubt that Hereford would go out with his wife shook de Caldoet, but another quick look reassured him that the earl was not dressed. True, the squire would come in to dress him as soon as Elizabeth left, but all de Caldoet needed was a few seconds. A quick thrust with the stolen knife he was fingering with his left hand, and all would be over.

They kissed once more, clinging, Elizabeth with closed eyes to hold back her tears. And then, to conceal the drops she could not restrain, she turned very swiftly and went out without further farewell. William started to rise, but Elizabeth stopped him with a gesture as she wiped away the tears. She would go in again and say farewell smiling. Roger should not have the burden of her fear to bear; above all she must seem confident at this time.

"Roger!" she screamed from the doorway, and Hereford turned and flung up an arm.

He was guarding automatically against a right-handed blow so that his arm struck nothing, but the twist of his body spoiled de Caldoet's aim. The knife slashed a long cut in his upper arm and sank only a little way into his shoulder instead of piercing his heart before Hereford's instinctive reactions disarmed and overthrew his greatly weakened enemy. By then William had bounded in, sword drawn, and Hereford, pressing his robe against the gushing wound gasped at him to hold his hand.

"Stop, William. I want to know who sent this creature and why I was to be slain. Hold him."

"Roger," Elizabeth faltered, and Hereford moved toward her quickly because she had turned a fine shade of green.

"All right, Elizabeth," he said, letting go of his bleeding arm to support her, "I am not hurt. Sit down."

"It is not that," she breathed, sinking onto a stool, "but I do not think anyone sent him." However she felt, it was important for her husband to know that. For him to add a dread of assassination to everything else would really destroy him. She had been staring steadily at the wretch William had at sword's point and recognition had come to her. "It is de Caldoet. He said he would come back and destroy you; he told me so."

"Impossible!"

"No, do you not remember what I wrote to you? Ask him."

That, however was plainly useless. With the failure of the one plan that had anchored his mind to reality, de Caldoet's sanity had crumpled to nothing. He gibbered and wept uttering incoherent sounds and making bestial, senseless gestures. When William spoke to him and prodded him with the sword, he collapsed on the ground and fouled himself from fear.

"Oh, God," Elizabeth got out, her voice shaking, "in mercy, Roger, destroy him." When she glanced up, however, she forgot de Caldoet. Hereford had gone parchment-white and blood was staining the fingers of the hand with which he was unconsciously clutching his wounded arm. "You are hurt!" she cried. "Let me stanch that blood."

Abstractedly Hereford allowed himself to be attended to, seeming dazed. He roused himself only once to countermand sharply an order given by Elizabeth to call for help and to tell William to gag and bind de Caldoet and then go and sit ouside as if nothing had happened but to keep everyone out. For the rest of the time he sat, staring at nothing, barely wincing as Elizabeth washed and bound his arm and shoulder.

"Lie down, Roger," she said finally. The wound was not serious, but she was worried by how much shaken her husband seemed. "You are not badly hurt, dear. You will feel better when you have rested."

Hereford suddenly began to laugh in a singularly ugly fashion. "You are wrong, Elizabeth. I am very badly hurt indeed. Worse than that—I am dead."

"No, no!" Elizabeth cried, sinking to her knees and taking Hereford's hand in hers. "No, love, you are not. In a few hours you will be much better. Rest now, do not talk so wildly."

"I tell you I am dead," Hereford replied irritably. "Dead. What could be better? It is the answer to our present troubles. God bless the man—de Caldoet, if you say it is he. He has been more help to me than all my friends."

Elizabeth wished she were dead herself; dead, blind, deaf, anything at all before she had come to see the day when her husband's courage broke and he seized on such an excuse to run away. "Roger, please," she began to sob, "be a man. Do not let your courage fail. This cannot be the first time you have faced an assassin's knife. What ails you to turn lily-livered for a scratch?" She would say anything. Possibly if her words were cruel enough they would sting him into resistance.

A pair of exceedingly surprised blue eyes met hers.

"What ails me? What ails you to speak such words to me?" Hereford asked in a stunned voice.

"Praise Christ, praise Mary," Elizabeth whispered, "he was but mad for a moment. It is passed." She dashed the tears from her eyes and summoned a smile. "Nothing ails me. I think you were a little dazed by the shock. You spoke so wildly for a moment about being dead—"

"I tell you I *am* dead. I must be. Nay, Elizabeth, do not look like that. Can you not see that thus we may trick de Tracy out of his keep?"

That last sentence sounded all right, but the beginning—"No, I do not see anything, but that is not surprising because you have fairly frightened me out of my wits," Elizabeth replied with asperity. "If you are not out of yours, would you mind explaining?"

"You should understand without explaining." Hereford was impatient. "You are leaving with about seven hundred men, right? Well, why cannot we make that seem as if our whole force is breaking up? I thought of that before, but could think of no reason for it which de Tracy would believe. Now I have the reason."

"What reason?" Elizabeth regarded her husband with a fascinated but suspicious eye.

"I have told you three or four times. I must be dead."

"Roger!"

"Elizabeth, if you would only stop thinking that I have suddenly gone as mad as that—" Hereford gestured with his head, "or turned into a bloodless and spineless coward in five minutes—and what reason I have ever given you to suspect me of that I know not—you would have no difficulty in understanding me. If I have been assassinated, my vassals and the mercenaries I pay would have no further interest in this conflict. Right?"

Elizabeth nodded. The irritation of her husband's tone and the clarity of his gaze having convinced her that he was perfectly in his right mind.

"Very well. We need, then, to spread the word that I am dead. Of course, Henry, Gloucester, my brother, and my chief vassals will need to know the truth, but for the others it is better that they believe the lie. Then you will leave carrying with you my coffin—"

"No, Roger!"

"This is no time for superstition."

Looking at her husband, Elizabeth knew that she, Gloucester, and Henry had all been wrong. Roger's fears, whatever they were, would never break him. Whatever demons pursued him could kill him by wearing out his physical strength, but no mental or spiritual torture could destroy his emotional endurance. While he lived, his spirit would not fail. In the very moment in which he bid her cast away superstition, he was grappling with his own terror and bearing it down. That was the struggle which had whitened his face and clouded his eyes, but he had emerged triumphant from it as he would from all those of the future. Content at last, with nothing to fear for but her husband's physical safety, Elizabeth bowed her head in submission.

"Very well, Roger. I will do whatever you command."

"Good." He raised his voice. "William!" The squire appeared on the instant, sword drawn. "Put that up and listen closely. We are going to pretend that that creature succeeded in his attempt. Never mind why, it will all come clear later, just do as I order. Kill him now and unbind him and be sure to get yourself well bloodied. Then run at once to my lord Henry and to Gloucester crying aloud for all to hear that an attempt has been made upon me, but see that none enter here except those lords, my brother, and the chief of my vassals."

Five minutes later four white-faced nobles burst into Hereford's tent to be met by a bloody vision who smiled cheerfully and signaled silence urgently. Low-voiced, Elizabeth explained as Hereford had directed her since he did not wish to take the chance that the crowd rapidly gathering about the tent would hear his voice. A few minutes more brought the sound of lamentation to those anxiously waiting outside. Henry, still white enough with shock to enforce the idea that Hereford was indeed dead, ordered a guard set about the tent, ostensibly to protect Elizabeth, and further ordered a coffin to be hastily constructed.

By the early afternoon the sad cortege, bearing the coffin containing the body of de Caldoet in place of Hereford, was ready to leave and Roger of Hereford's vassals were showing signs of breaking camp. The entire army was becoming restless and disordered, as if Hereford's death had broken its purpose and discipline. Plainly the men were in no condition to fight. A few weaker ones even broke away; some carried the tale to de Tracy and sought sanctuary in his keeps. His spies told the same story as those deserters and de Tracy watched more closely, readying his men. Meanwhile, Henry was working like a beast of burden, endeavoring to spread his forces so that they would seem to be breaking up purposelessly and yet be close enough together to fall upon de Tracy if he should be tempted to attack. He needed to see the leader of each small group also and hearten them without disclosing the truth. It was to the credit of his forceful personality that the men regained confidence, promising readily to move as they were directed and to fight with courage. Not nearly as truthful as Hereford, Henry hinted broadly that de Tracy had a hand in the assassination for the purpose of disorganizing them and placing them at a disadvantage. He urged boldness in revenge to prove that they were not men to be trifled with. Generally such an approach went a long way to stiffening the purpose of even those war lords who were not personally attached to Hereford. No man liked to think that such a deed could be carried off with impunity. Assuredly they would help draw de Tracy out and destroy him, they told Henry, and he hurried away to convince another group.

A large group had to follow Elizabeth's men also, so that she would be protected in case de Tracy decided to test the truth by a look into the coffin. Walter of Hereford was the most logical person to undertake that duty, and the force he commanded was used to concealment and lightning dashes from one place to another. Walter was most willing to go. In a short but blazing interview with his puzzled brother, Walter terminated his service to Hereford with this last duty.

"I will see her safe out of this country, Roger, but I am through with you. I will not return."

"As you wish, Walter. I do not believe that we will need your men, and this is a good a time as another, but why are you so angry? Whatever have I done now?"

That question was unanswerable because Walter had recognized at last that he could no longer bear the constant conflict between gladness and sorrow, hope and fear, which close contact with Roger brought him. He also could struggle no longer against being eaten alive by his overwhelming brother; he must yield and be absorbed by Roger's protective and enveloping affection or run away. When he had heard the news that Roger was dead, he had thought he would die himself, so fierce was the pang of grief which tore him. Only moments later, however, seeing his brother slightly damaged but obviously very far from dead or even the danger of dying, Walter was fit to finish him himself, so great was his regret for the lands, titles, and independence which seemed to have been snatched once more from his grasp.

"I simply cannot stand you," he choked in reply to Hereford's question. "You have done nothing wrong. You never do, perfect as you are. Still, I do not deserve to be so near such perfection. You make me sick, and I can bear it no longer."

Hereford raised his beautifully arched brows in surprise and hurt and shrugged. "Very well. What will you do now?"

"None of your affair."

That stung too. Biting his lips and flushing as he controlled his temper, Hereford replied briefly, "True. Do you need money?"

"No. Oh, curse you, Roger, I know you say things like that to shame me and I fall into your snare each time. I will do nothing. I will go back to Shrivenham, which I won for myself. I need nothing from you."

Satisfied, Hereford kissed his protesting brother good-by with profound relief. Walter was extremely useful in a fight but too unpredictable for comfort at other times. In his present nervous state, Hereford could only be grateful that he would not need to worry about what Walter would do next, at least in his immediate vicinity. There was nothing to do now but to be smuggled into Henry's tent and then rest until de Tracy made up his mind.

The fruits of that decision became apparent early two mornings later when de Tracy, having spent the intervening time gathering his forces, descended upon the half-empty camp. Hereford, ready armed in the tent, listened with satisfaction as his men shouted in well-simulated fear and surprise and apparently retreated in disorder, drawing de Tracy through the camp into the open field. Behind that field in the surrounding low hills, Henry lay with the large proportion of the mounted troops. Hereford's men, barely protecting themselves, broke right and left for the patches of woodland which separated the cultivated fields. It looked like a complete rout, but before de Tracy could deploy to follow them, the Angevin's battle cry sounded and down from the hills came Henry with the mercenary troops and Gloucester's vassals. Meanwhile Hereford had mounted and was waiting for his own vassals, who knew he was still alive, to circle round through the woods into camp again. More horses and men, most of which had been concealed in the tents, were waiting, so that it was not half an hour longer before Hereford was able to fling himself upon de Tracy's rear.

"Hereford!" Henry shouted above the sounds of battle as the colors of his friend and vassal appeared on the field, "Hereford lives. It was a trick to draw our enemy. Have courage, help is at hand." And Hereford's own clear voice calling his fighting motto and urging on his men gave proof to the words.

If more proof had been needed, the quick Arab steed, so much lighter and faster than the larger horses of the other mounted men, darting forward in the fray and the swift stroke and recover which wrought such havoc among his enemies would have identified Hereford. Temporarily relieved by his activity of his sense of futility, the young earl was enjoying himself, as he always enjoyed fighting, in spite of the fact that he was living dangerously. His squires had been sent on with Elizabeth, of course, to give more credence to the tale of his death, and, although his vassals were very faithful—their devotion being at least half terror that if Hereford died Walter would inherit—there was no man specifically detailed or trained to protect his back. It needed training to keep up with Hereford in battle, too, because he was not given to mowing down his opponents in a straight line. Instead he rode to and fro across the lines of battle, choosing any place where his men seemed hard-pressed to fling himself forward personally and give them heart.

A pocket bulged the line of fighting men, and Hereford spurred his horse toward it, crying his usual "A *moi*" to his desperately following vassals. He found himself face to face at the peak of the bulge with Henry de Tracy himself.

"Treachor!" de Tracy cried. "Liar! What could not be achieved with honor you seek in the filth of lies."

"Coward!" Hereford replied, his eyes glittering under the shading headband of his helmet. "Rats must be cornered before they will fight."

De Tracy's reply to that was a blow which made the wound de Caldoet had given Hereford bleed again. The earl gasped with pain and thrust forward, but de Tracy's shield sent the blade sideways. Hereford grimaced but disengaged so quickly that de Tracy could not guard against the slashing return. Blood welled from a gash in his exposed thigh and he brought his sword across to cover. Again the return was too swift for him, Hereford's blade rising in an arc that would have cut the tendons in his right arm had the edge landed true. Unfortunately the sword point, the distance being misjudged by half an inch, barely caught de Tracy's shield, and only the flat of the weapon hit. Still the blow was numbing enough to knock de Tracy's sword from his hand. With a cry of triumph, Hereford lifted his weapon high over his head to give it enough force in the downward swing to cleave helmet and skull. The lift, however, took time and de Tracy, as experienced and skilled as his opponent, had a moment's time in which to snatch his mace from his saddlebow and swing it in one smooth motion. Hereford lifted his shield, but his arm was stiff and painful and this time he was not quick enough. The spiked, lead-weighted iron ball, large as a man's head, came straight across at his temple in the same instant that de Tracy's squire, seeking to protect his master, thrust his sword between them and stabbed Hereford's horse in the throat. Horse and man crashed to the earth. De Tracy, whose mace was useless for such work, called to his men to dispatch the fallen earl and spurred forward, more anxious to escape from a field where his defeat was a foregone conclusion than to win the hollow victory of killing Hereford himself.

The men were no more eager to die in a hopeless cause than their master. Some followed him directly without a glance at Hereford, who was struggling to his feet; some hesitated fractionally and would, perhaps, have done his bidding, but it was too late. Hereford's vassals had closed a wall of steel around him. The closest swung himself off his horse, and Hereford gasped, "Sir Thomas, I will not forget," as he leapt into the saddle in his stead. The service was one which each vassal owed his overlord, but since in a battle a man in mail on foot was at a very great disadvantage, the yielding of a horse was a service often overlooked.

"After them!" Hereford called, suiting the action to the word. "Let them not go scatheless from the field. Slayer of horses, turn and fight."

De Tracy was too wily to allow an insult to turn him, however, and he now had a good start on Hereford. The earl pulled up, signaling the men who had followed him to continue the pursuit. It would, of course, be better if they had taken de Tracy, but they had already accomplished their purpose and inflicted a punishing defeat upon him. There could be no doubt that Bridport would open to them now, and the destruction of better than half of de Tracy's force, which was what Hereford estimated, would greatly inhibit his ability to raid in the area for some time. Almost casually, Hereford knocked a fleeing man-at-arms from his horse and caught the mount. He looped the reins around his saddle pommel and moved forward again into the field, seeking Sir Thomas. He would not, if he could prevent it, allow a faithful vassal to die so that he could win a little more honor by destroying a few more enemies. It was dreadful work, for Hereford was fighting his way forward against a stream of men escaping through the break de Tracy had made in the encircling forces. To the left Henry was stiving mightily to close the gap, but desperation gives superhuman strength and the tide of fleeing men could not be stemmed. By the time he found Sir Thomas, Hereford was bleeding like the prover-

bial stuck pig, and the hand he extended to his vassal to
help him up trembled with fatigue. For him, however, it
was the wholesome fatigue of martial exercise instead of
the deadly tiredness of too much "chewing on his own
guts." He spoke cheerfully to his muddied and bloodied
man, and they both returned to the fighting, knowing the
end was not far and that there would be warm baths,
clean robes, and soft beds waiting for them that night.

The expectation was more than fulfilled, for Bridport
not only opened its gates without further ado but also its
kitchens, wine cellars, and brothels. When the men had
slept off the initial exhaustion of killing, gathered up their
wounded, and buried their dead, they turned to making
merry over their success, and their leaders joined them
with wholehearted enthusiasm. For Hereford it was a
triple celebration. Of course he was pleased by their victory, even priding himself, with a certain amount of truth,
on the fact that his cleverness had brought it about, but
he had other causes for being joyful. Word was waiting
for him when he came off the field that Elizabeth was
safe at Bristol, that Walter had ridden eastward in a
slightly better humor than that in which he had left the
field before Bridport, and that the coffin had been broken
up and burned. That coffin had weighed on Hereford's
spirits, although he could deal easily enough with a recog-
nizable fear such as that, because no matter how simple it
was to tell Elizabeth to cast out superstition it was not
such an easy thing to do. To build your coffin before a
battle was tantamount to putting yourself to death—said
the old wives' tales—yet here he was alive, hardly hurt,
and victorious.

Already flushed with drink, Hereford laughed wildly,
lifted his goblet again, and returned to the sport of
shredding the clothes off an all-too-willing wench with the
point of his sword. It was a mad scene altogether, the two
great hearths blazing with fire, the remainder of the flickering light supplied by the resinous torches along the walls
which also filled the huge hall with smoke. Above the ca-
rousing men, the blackened rafters could not be seen
through the murky dark, but the shouts and laughter
mixed with the beat of drum, the rattle of tambourine, the

wail of the flutes, and the trill of the harps, echoed down
from them. At the high table Henry, with Gloucester and
Hereford on either side, made merry, applying every
ounce of his immense energy to enjoying himself in the
same way that he applied it to fighting or planning when
necessary. Lacking his strength and ability, many of the
men at the long tables which lined the sides of the hall
had given up. Some lay across the boards, their faces and
clothes stained with wine and food, some lay underneath,
and the dogs nuzzled under them seeking the garbage
that was thrown into the rushes. Some, however, still sat
more or less upright watching the jugglers, acrobats, and
dancing girls perform. It was from this group of enter-
tainers that Hereford had picked his wench, her flashing
dark eyes and loose, oiled hair having caught his attention. A gold coin flipped upward and caught once or twice
had drawn her closer and closer, followed by an elderly
man who played the flute which he held in one hand
while he rattled a tambourine with the other.

"Up," Hereford laughed, and the girl leapt nimbly on
the table. Hereford threw the coin, which she caught with
practiced skill as she whirled about, and drew his sword.
At that a swift expression of fear crossed her face—some of
the lords were unbelievably cruel and could get pleasure
only from inflicting pain—but it was replaced just as
swiftly by laughter as he used the weapon to sweep the
table clear of food and drink. "Dance!" he cried, making
a low, slow swipe at her legs.

Laughing, the girl leapt over the blade; laughing, Hereford wielded it more quickly and still more quickly. The
bells on the dancer's ankles tinkled, her swinging skirts exposed lovely, dark-shining legs, her hair flew wide, now
and again striking the faces of the watching men. Suddenly Hereford lifted and twisted his newly sharpened
weapon and a whole section of the girl's skirt drifted
slowly to the floor. Henry roared his appreciation, pushing
aside the woman he was holding to see more clearly, and
Gloucester put down his drink to watch with avid eyes.

"I'll lay you ten golden pounds that you cannot strip her
naked thus without marking her skin," Henry wagered.

"Done," Hereford agreed.

"You cannot do it, Roger. You are three parts drunk and your eye is out for such fine work. Moreover that longsword is no weapon for stripping women. Hedge—take your poniard." That was Gloucester, soberer than the others and thinking it a shame to slash such a pretty wench.

The girl had stopped, and stood trembling through this exchange, and her father had come forward. He dared not protest, not when their lordships were obviously hot with wine, but he was drawn forward irresistibly. It was at that point that Hereford had lifted and drained his goblet again.

"Dance," he said to the girl, "quick." and then focusing on her for a moment so that her terror penetrated to him, he smiled gently. "Have no fear, I will not hurt you. Dance."

He did not hurt her, and as her confidence grew and more and more of her body was exposed without a prick she abandoned herself to the rhythm, hypnotized by her own movements and by the flashing blade. She did not even realize when Hereford won his wager and the last rag dropped from her, but continued to dance, the uncertain light gleaming on her fresh body, her high immature breasts and her rich rounded thighs moist with her exertion. A sensuous smile curved Hereford's mouth as he drank, watched, and drank more. Eventually the girl dropped and Hereford caught her. With his free hand he fumbled in his purse and drew two more golden coins which he flung to the father.

"My lord," the man cried, knowing when it was safe to speak, "she is a maid."

Hereford shook his head at that and laughed. "Then you are fortunate in having a gentleman to pluck the bud." He was too wise, even drunk, to be taken, and besides, he was too drunk to care what the girl was. Vaguely he thought that he would give her a few coins more or one of the many gold chains which decked his garments if it were true. Some days later he remembered that and wondered whether she had been a virgin and whether he had suitably rewarded her, but he could not recall what had happened, and it was a very unimportant incident in the rush of events which followed.

These events were introduced in the most horrible way possible, by a hand roughly shaking a sore shoulder and a voice which pierced a much sorer head. "Roger, wake up!"

"Go away," Hereford replied thickly, burying his head in the down pillows.

"Don't be a fool, Roger. Wake up. Devizes is under siege."

Jerked upright by an involuntary reaction of his muscles, Hereford gasped, "What?" and then gagged as the excruciating pain in his head really gripped him.

"I have had word, not ten minutes since." Henry was mercilessly pressing a parchment into his hand, and Hereford, controlling his nausea with a mighty effort, took it. Try as he would, however, the words would not come into focus until he closed one eye and turned his head sideways to squint at the message. There could be no doubt about it. The short, frantic note was more than an appeal, it was a demand for help, immediate help. Hereford dropped the letter and seized his aching head in both hands, groaning.

"Pull yourself together," Henry said sharply, and then laughed in spite of his rage as Hereford painfully looked up at him.

The brilliant sunlight was a torment, but there was some comfort in Henry's own haggard countenance which gave evidence of a discomfort similar to his own. "Wine," was all he found himself capable of mumbling and Henry, too impatient to call for a servant, brought it with his own hands. A few moments after that had gone down Hereford, wincing but rational, bent to pick up the letter again. That nearly brought disaster, and a cold sweat covered him as he fought to keep the wine down.

"The hand looks like the castellan's scribe, but—. Who brought the message?"

"What can it matter?"

"For God's sake, keep your voice down, you are killing me. It matters because it may well be a trap. To draw us out of here in force, leaving our prize unprotected—to draw us along the shortest best-known route to Devizes so that we may be ambushed—"

"Nay, Harry Fortesque brought it—do you doubt him?"

"No. What says he?"

"Eustace!"

"I thought Hugh Bigod was keeping him busy."

"Plainly he is not. Make ready, Roger. Fortesque tells me it is a really desperate attempt on the keep. They have every variety of siege engine and a huge force. Eustace recks no cost this time. He says he will take Devizes or die."

"How came Fortesque through the lines?"

"Ask him yourself! Do I look as if I spared the time for useless questions?"

Certainly he did not. Henry's powerful body was naked beneath a hastily corded robe, his feet bare in the rushes on the cold stone. He looked sick and angry, his gray eyes cold as granite. Devizes and Wallingford were the two keeps most fanatically devoted to his cause. Not once since 1135 had they wavered in their allegiance, and thus far no attack, no matter how vicious, had even threatened to overthrow their great strength. So many years had passed since Stephen had even cast an eye in their direction that Henry had blithely left only a token force to defend the castles when he summoned the men for the taking of Bridport, and Hereford, usually more cautious because of previous bitter experience, had agreed without a protest to this folly. It was useless to cry over spilt milk now; haste was essential, but haste with safety.

"Listen, Henry—"

"What ails you? Will you speak more of treachery? We cannot take the chance of losing Devizes even if this is a trap. We must go—now! By God's bright eyes, I will go alone if you will not."

Hereford stifled another groan. "Yes, yes, we must go, I agree, but listen. It would be madness to leave this place as naked as we left Devizes. Dare we trust him who opened without protest to you after he had sworn to Stephen? Gloucester cares nothing for Devizes and—as you know—will not fight. Let him stay here. I warrant you he will be happy enough to do so."

"Nonsense. We need his men."

"Ay. So go smile at him and wheedle him. Let him bid

his vassals obey you until their service be finished or until he calls them elsewhere. Some may stay here, together with the wounded who anyway cannot ride far or be of use in heavy fighting although they may well be able to help defend this place at need."

"That is good sense." Henry's face became slightly less rigid. It was a plan he approved of in all aspects—for the present need and for the possibility of impressing Gloucester's vassals sufficiently so that they might lean to his side if a quarrel ever arose between himself and their master. Hereford was not ignorant of this and, although he did not entirely approve of Henry's ways, felt that the need outweighed any consideration he owed Gloucester. Let Gloucester be more active and see to his own vassals, Hereford thought, I am not above keeping mine on a tight rein.

"Meanwhile," Roger said, his complexion turning grayish green as he got out of bed and the movement initiated a new wave of nausea and head-throbbing, "I will see what can be done about rousing the men." He managed a wry smile. "No light task if, as I know well is true, the better part of them is no merrier than myself."

Whatever the weight of the task, it was done. In spite of their rebellious murmurings both lordly vassals and common men-at-arms dragged themselves into their clothing and armor and onto their horses. It was fortunate that a long ride faced them before it would be necessary to engage in fighting, for a more wretched army would be hard to find. The two leaders alone seemed capable of doing anything more than moaning and clinging to their mounts. Cursing and cajoling the men had cleared Hereford's head, although it still ached abominably and his stomach still occasionally heaved. Henry, on the contrary, seemed in fine fettle, for he had thrown off the effects of overindulgence with the same resilience that he threw off fatigue or depression. He was tense and eager, anxious to rescue the only home he had in England from the results of his own error. It was well indeed that they had not delayed an instant, well that they had ridden through the night, well that Henry had protested taking any rest except a brief two-hour stop to feed and water the horses and take some nourishment themselves when they were only a few miles from Devizes. The long ride had cleared the men's hangovers, the rest and food restored their vigor so that when they came in sight of the keep they were prepared to throw themselves upon its attackers immediately. And they were not a moment too soon. Fortesque had spoken no more than the truth. Indeed, for an agonized few moments both Henry and Hereford thought they were too late.

Smoke rose from fires through the keep where the Greek fire cast over the walls by giant catapults had set outbuildings ablaze. The moat had been filled in several places with earth and brush so that two giant *beffrois*, towers constructed of timber and covered with rawhide, could be rolled up to the walls permitting Eustace's foot soldiers to scale that height perfectly protected and attack the defenders. Great trenchbuts, three of the largest they had ever seen, hurled huge stones at the walls, which were already breached in one place, and although the immense oaken gates still held, they were obviously being shaken by the blows of the battering ram.

The vision of the destruction already accomplished had almost convinced Henry that the keep had fallen, and he flew into such a rage that even Hereford, who had seen his ungovernable temper many times before and had a temper of his own, was startled. He too thought the keep was taken and briefly wondered whether it would be necessary to restrain Henry by force from throwing his life away in a hysterical, disorganized attempt to regain it at one stroke. A moment's longer observation, however, showed that only the outer walls were breached and even these were being defended. Shrieks of agony rose from time to time from the attackers as cartwheels soaked in pitch and set aflame were tossed down into their midst. Wherever scaling ladders went up, they were cast back again, large stones being rolled off the walls onto those attempting to mount them. Again and again, too, a whole section of wall would be cleared as huge cauldrons of pitch or boiling oil were raised by willing hands and poured down. The *beffrois* were not making much progress either, for the catapults and trenchbuts of

Devizes had been drawn into position against them and were firing stones or very large arrows with deadly regularity.

"Steady," Hereford said, clutching Henry's arm, his voice trembling a little with relief, "the keep is still ours. How best may we fall upon them?"

Henry grunted sullenly in reply. He had also seen the situation. Now his eyes ranged over as much of the field as was visible, hard and calculating. "It would be better if we had time to send riders around and discover if their full force is here or if more lie outside of our vision—but there is no time. Look, Hereford, while we are watching their spirits or maybe their numbers fail. The defense grows weaker; they are preparing to abandon the outer wall."

"I am not blind. Quick. I will fall upon those at the breach, you take the parties by the gate and towers."

"Accursed litter of accursed parents! When I lay my hands upon him, I will tear him limb from limb. I will return him to his father piece by piece—"

"Let us fight, not talk."

Henry made another effort to control himself. "Wait, I will have their camp too. I swear, not a man will go from this place alive, except he be naked and on foot. Let Gloucester's vassals fall upon the camp." He turned to call orders, ending with, "Kill them—man and boy—whoever is in the camp. Cut the horses loose or slay them also. What cannot be taken or guarded—burn. They will not fall upon my keeps again, I swear it."

"Keep your eyes also upon our flanks," Hereford said more quietly and collectedly. "If a force should seek to fall upon us from either side, stop them, or give us warning. I do not wish to sup of the same soup that we fed de Tracy." Hereford was anxious not to lose Devizes, but he was less emotionally involved than Henry, also anxious not to blunder any further, and less set on complete destruction of the opposing force.

Understanding being readily established, the men settled their gear firmly and rode forward, ready massed for attack but as quietly as possible. The closer they could come to the keep before the attackers noticed them, the more surely the pincers would close and the fewer would escape their swords. If no great force was hidden by the bulk of Devizes their situation was good, except for the fact that they were already battle-weary, strained, and tired from their merrymaking and their long ride.

In the quiet period which followed as they rode slowly closer, free of the tension and anxiety of their hurried travel, Hereford suddenly realized that he felt none of the satisfaction he should for arriving in time, none of the joy of battle which should be rising in him at this moment. He shifted his shield nervously to a more secure position and winced slightly because his left shoulder and arm still bothered him. He was not considering it, but subconsciously he knew that his whole body was sore and that he would not be quick as usual. His mouth went dry and his breath became uneven as he looked around the smoke-filled, burnt-out landscape. Why, he thought, this is the place of my dream. I did not recognize it because I have never seen Devizes under attack. He began to shake with the terrible desire to set spurs to his horse and charge. A terrible feeling of waste, of having delayed too long in seizing life, possessed him. Henry raised a hand, and the arbalists moved forward, the pikemen and other soldiers with them to make a wall of protection with their shields for the bowmen.

In the eons that intervened between the moment of the first flight of arrows which fell on the unsuspecting backs of Eustace's men and the one in which Henry cried the charge. Hereford at last looked straight into the eyes of his specter. This was the battle, there would be no more waiting. If the dream was true, he would die, and whatever else happened, he would now know the best or the worst. Now, too, it seemed that nothing would ever equal the torment of restraint he endured waiting for Henry's order to charge to release him for that revelation.

Relief came at last in the cry that ordered the attack. Eustace's men had seen them and turned at bay, but clearly above their shouts and curses came the cries of welcome and relief from the exhausted defenders within the walls. Hereford was unconscious of both. Forewarned that he had come face to face with his destiny, he was conscious only of the greatest feeling of freedom he had ever known. It did not matter, he realized, what he did now, for his end and the end of this battle and of all things was foreordained. Until he clapped spurs to his horse in the charge, his free will might have altered matters. He might still have turned tail and chosen life and shame; now he had made his choice. Armed by the knowledge that all things were in the hands of God, Hereford fought like a wild thing that had abandoned hope. In a very short time the breach was closed, not with stone but with the corpses of Eustace's dead men piled one upon the other—a grim joke—and Hereford set out to find Eustace himself. In this he was unsuccessful, but he left a swath of dead and dying in the ranks of his enemies wherever he sought and passed such that the sight of his banner alone was sufficient to turn a retreat into a rout.

Henry had even greater success. He split his forces so that he could attack the men attempting to roll the *beffrois* into position, but so well had the anchors done their work that he found almost no resistance. It was then only a labor of minutes to seize several kegs prepared for making Greek fire, coat the timbers of the *beffrois* with this mixture, and set it ablaze. Henry had a moment's regret for the destruction of siege engines so useful and difficult to construct, but he had not the men to leave to guard them and could not chance their falling into enemy hands again if the battle should turn against them. His next objective, the troop assailing the gates, gave somewhat more satisfaction to his enraged spirit, for they fought valiantly and stubbornly. Their case was hopeless, however, for Henry's forces outnumbered them, and the defenders of Devizes now readily opened the gates which previously they had fought desperately to keep closed to pour out and aid their rescuers. To them Henry left the destruction of the shattered remnants of Eustace's troop and, calling his own men, set off to find the prince.

He missed Eustace by bare moments, for the young man had been trying courageously to rally his men in spite of the protests of his older and wiser vassals who recognized a major defeat when they saw it. Rannulf of the South Riding it was who saved the prince from death or capture at the last possible moment. A deeply embittered

man, whom his contemporaries said had reverence for neither king nor God, swung a mailed fist the size of a ham
and with the strength of a mule's kick against Eustace's
temple. Mouthing obscenities on the nature and intelligence of the king he served and his son also, he lifted
Eustace's inanimate form across his saddle bow and fled,
his vassals, Eustace's, and the pitiful remnants of a once-
proud army following as best as they could. Henry saw
the band of flying men across the plain, but the prince's
banner was not among those displayed. He did dispatch a
troop to pursue and take them if possible, or to give him
news of where they went if they could not be caught, but
this was done more in the spirit of efficiency in eliminating
his enemies than in any expectation of their carrying with
them a great prize. It was not until he had searched and
searched round Devizes, meeting Roger engaged in the
same search, and through the enemy camp, that he recognized the perfidy that had been practiced. He should have
flown into another rage, but he did not. In the flush of his
second major victory in arms in a week, he was merely
contemptuous of a man so afraid that he would strike his
colors and hide himself among his vassals.

Those men who had the strength and the desire for it,
continued to pursue stragglers of Eustace's force through
the afternoon and night of that bloody day. The major
porportion of the army, however, staggered in through the
battered but welcoming gates of Devizes and collapsed.
Among these were Hereford and his overlord who, having
heartily embraced and danced, caroling, around the hall,
found when their breath gave out that they were fit for
nothing—not even celebration.

CHAPTER 19

————◆————

HEREFORD WOKE in the dawn of another day with first a feeling of blissful relaxation and lack of responsibility and then surprise at the fact that he was still completely clad in mail. The events of the past day, swiftly returning to memory, explained his condition, and he lay quietly smiling into the dimness of the room, realizing that some-one must have carried him to bed after he dropped into the ruses of the hall. Decidedly, he thought, his sense of freedom and release welling up until he believed he would burst with joy, the dream was a false temptation, as Eliza-beth had suggested, or he had overridden his fate, for his uneasiness was gone. He remembered too, his smile going a little grim, that Eustace was trapped in Faringdon. The end was in sight, clearly and unmistakably now, because Faringdon was ringed about by castles, smaller it was true, but stuffed and garnished for war and filled with fresh fighting men loyal to Henry. His breathing deepened with the first sensation of truly unalloyed enthusiasm he had had since Gaunt had offered him this task. Henry, he knew, had issued orders already to the surrounding keeps to send out men to besiege Faringdon. After a day or two to rest—with no celebrating in between, Hereford thought wryly—they would go out and take Faringdon. That would be amusing, in a way, for they would assail Faringdon with many of the siege engines Eustace had brought to destroy Devizes. The fact that they would not need to spend time constructing these giving them a substantial additional advantage.

He stretched outward and then clasped his hands to flex the muscles in the back of his neck. This action brought to his attention the fact that he was stained with dried blood. With a grimace of mild distaste, Hereford bellowed for his servants to order a bath. It was cold and he would freeze, but freezing was better than remaining filthy, even though the blood was largely that of his enemies and he was honorably bespattered. It was not so cold, after all, thought the earl, luxuriating in the hot, scented water and watching the leaping flames in the hearth. He stiffened momentarily as the door opened, for he was totally defenseless, and de Caldoet's attempt on him was still close enough in time to make him cautious. It was only Henry, however, and Hereford relaxed, stretching out a wet but welcoming hand.

"A good monring to you, my lord, a lovely, bright, blessed morning."

"Mayhap to you, but to the rest of the world it rains." The voice Henry replied in was strange and strained, but wrapped in his own peace, Hereford did not notice.

"Well then," he said, irrepressibly cheerful, "it is a good, fruitful rain that will moisten the winter planting."

Henry fidgeted about the room, picking up Roger's clothing, handling his gear and his weapons, and scuffing at the rushes on the floor. Hereford was inured to this restless behavior and paid no attention, scrubbing himself thoroughly and accepting a large, soft cloth with which to wrap and dry himself.

"Have you news from Faringdon?"

Hereford mildly hoped not because he wanted to linger in pleasant inactivity for a while. All sense of fear and urgency had left him, and he was slightly reluctant to bring his mind to bear upon another campaign. Only slightly, however, because, though he was in a mood for easy idleness, he was also buoyantly prepared to don his mail and fight with his old eager joy, his keenness undulled by vague shadows. No more than why the fears had come did Hereford know why they were gone. He knew only that he had met his crisis in a few moments on the field before Devizes and passed through it.

"Faringdon? No—I have no word from there. Roger—"

That time Hereford could not miss the uneasiness in his overlord's voice. He turned quickly toward Henry with a natural concern for what he felt would be bad news, but with no foreboding of disaster. "Well?" he was still smiling slightly. "What unforeseen event has overtaken us now? Has Eustace escaped? Is Stephen at our gates?"

"I am returning to France as soon as I can reach the shore and as soon as the winds favor my crossing."

There was a dead silence in the room, broken by the faint hissing of the flames in the hearth. The smile still lingered on Hereford's lips, but now without meaning, for the blue eyes had gone dark and empty. A sharp explosion and a shower of sparks that escaped onto the rushes caused an instinctive physical reaction in Hereford who jumped back.

"I suppose I heard you aright?" His voice was flat and careful. "Just like that—no reason. You are bored with the game we have played?"

"Roger, in the merciful name of Christ, do not torment me. You cannot think I have desired this—not at this time when within our very grasp is—"

"Then do not go—who is there who can make you do so?—and we can forget you ever mentioned it."

The eyes, gray and blue, locked and fought, but the gray did not give way. Stubborn and decisive, Henry held on. He was sad and a little reluctant to do this, but his conflict had raged through the night and his decision was unshakable.

"I have had word from my father that I am to come home at once. The letter must have arrived shortly after we left for Gloucester, but there seemed no urgency in it and it was not sent on. Then the siege—"

A faint flutter of hope fought for life in Hereford. "Ay. No doubt he heard how all things seemed to conspire against our effort. That is reasonable—to recall you from a defeated cause. But now—. Write and tell him how we have prospered. There is no longer need for his caution."

The little hope died stillborn as Henry shook his head. "Would I have troubled you for such a matter, Roger? Nay, he wants me for a far different purpose. There is a rumor—well, it is more than that—that the Queen of France, she whose dower lands are greater than King Louis' inheritance, the Lady Eleanor, wishes to shed her husband and take a new spouse. Apparently there has been trouble between them for years and my father has slyly watched this. On this Crusade—it takes a sanctified fool like Louis to go on Crusade and let his kingdom fall into ruins around him—they seem to have come to a parting of the ways. Pope Eugenius pacified Louis, but the Lady Eleanor seems to have remained secretly of the same mind. My father thinks she might have me, if she should find me to her taste."

"Do you mean to tell me that Louis and Eleanor are divorced? I will not believe it. We have little news here, but something of that note would not pass us."

"Of course not. I told you Louis is reconciled with her through Eugenius' mediation, but the lady—"

"They are still married then?"

"Yes, of—"

"Then where is your haste? Let the lady shed him. It is indecent to hang about like a vulture waiting for the last breath to be taken. Besides, she will be more like to look with favor on the King of England than upon the heir of Geoffrey of Anjou."

"Roger, this is senseless. I have spent the night going over and over this matter from every point of view. You can suggest nothing to me that I have not already brought forth and looked at. Plainly it is this. She must make her decision, and the man must be ready and waiting before she sheds Louis. How long do you think she will remain unwed? If she will have me, I must be ready to snatch her up the moment the decree comes to her hand. Most important of all is that she see me and decide on *me*. Doubtless the lady will not marry beneath her, but she has been married too long to a monk. My father believes that I—who am plainly not in the least monkish, indeed some say I am wholly given over to the lusts of the flesh— can tempt her to take the final step by my person, not by my titles or expectations." Henry's face hardened, the brutal lower jaw thrusting forward. "I can be King of England any time, Roger, for my claim to the throne is just and must be recognized in the end. Do not mistake me, I mean to have it all—all. But to be Eleanor of Aquitaine's husband—. Roger, if she takes me I will be master of all of western France when my father dies, all western France, a good part of the south of France, and England too, for England will fall into my hand like a ripe plum when that power is behind me." Henry's voice trembled with eagerness, his eyes incandescent with the lust for power.

Hereford looked down at his naked body, at the long sicle-shaped scar he had taken at Faringdon, the ugly red line of knotted flesh on his thigh—that too he had taken in Henry's cause in Normandy. He fingered the still suppurating wound de Caldoet had given him and noted with eyes which were beautiful, limpid, empty blanks the myriad cuts and bruises he had received in the last battles.

"Do not go. Do not go now."

Those words were instinctive, born of shock and disbelief. Hereford had never planned to say them, had not even thought them. What he wished to do was to offer a lucid plan for taking Faringdon quickly, although he knew that no matter how soon Eustace fell into their hands the negotiations would drag on for months. As soon as the words were out, however, he lost all desire to speak further. He recognized those words, just as he recognized the choked, strangled voice which uttered them as his own, just as he had recognized the burnt-out fields around Devizes as the place of his dream the day before. Night after weary night for eight long months he had heard those words, that voice, and he had been frozen in the same agonizing sense of futility and loss thinking that the words were addressed to him. He had in truth found his dream and it was false because his nightmare fear was that he had deserted the cause. Still he was wrong, too, because the dream had been an honest warning and was true. Hereford closed his eyes, which suddenly felt dry and scratchy because he had not blinked for so long. The only desertion which in all that time had not haunted him—had not, indeed, crossed his mind—that which he had made no attempt to guard against, naturally enough, and could not guard against, had destroyed in a moment the work of— "Three years. Three bitter years have I cast away, God help me."

"Nay, Roger. You are dearer to my heart than almost any living man. If I gain great good, what you ask thereof, you shall have. God knows, I am not overgenerous, but what you ask of me you shall have, if it is in my power to give without harm to myself. Never say you have lost your labor. I shall not forget it, nor you."

"I labored that England might have a king who would save her from being daily rent asunder, and all I have done is tear that bleeding body further." Hereford's voice was quiet, defeated. He had no intention of reproaching Henry nor, for that matter, was he blaming himself. He was merely stating the facts as he saw them, yielding without further struggle to what he recognized was ordained from the beginning.

"England will have such a king, you need not fear me. Let me but achieve this woman and I will be able to sweep all before me in one quick, clean stroke. You will lead that army also, Roger. Not one drop will be taken from your cup. Besides, there need be no waste of effort. Take Eustace and hold him for warranty of Stephen's good behavior. You can—"

"No. I will not hold that young man in chains for who knows how many years. A fool he may be, but he is brave and courteous and, I believe, well meaning."

"Was it well meaning to put this land to fire and the sword?"

Hereford raised his eyes, and even empty as they were they held Henry's again. "Who drove him to it? In my memory Stephen has always been the mildest and most merciful of men, and his son follows his way. Mayhap we have driven him to madness." This time the Angevin's eyes dropped. He had tasted Stephen's mercy himself, and Roger knew it. "I will fight no more, my lord, except to guard what is mine."

"Will you turn to Stephen now, desert me, Roger, and dishonor your oath?"

"Nay, my lord, you desert me. Nor will I dishonor my oath—even though I now know what other men's oaths are worth. I am your man—for good or ill. If you return and you call me to arms, I will come and fight for you, but I will plan no more and strive beyond the letter of my word no more. I will lead no more lost causes."

"Roger, I pray you, do not speak as if all is ended."

Henry's genuinely affectionate heart was wrung by this dearest of vassal's pain. He embraced the resistless shoulders. "Come back to France with me. I will spare a week longer so that we can fetch your wife from Hereford in safety. Come, I pray you. Lady Elizabeth will love the court at Paris and you will have great sport watching me go secretly a-wooing."

Dumbly Hereford shook his head.

"I cannot help it, Roger," Henry cried at last. "Do not blame me for what I cannot help. You must see—"

"Do not distress yourself, Harry." Henry tightened his embrace at Hereford's use of the affectionate diminutive of his name. "I do not blame you, nor myself, for all things are done by God's will and are in God's hands. I do not understand, but doubtless there is Divine reason for this. I cannot go to France. I am tired—tired beyond believing—and my lands cry out for me. I will go home."

There was more talk, Henry urging Hereford to come to him later, at any time, promising earnestly and in good faith to give or send anything in his power to help his friend, but nothing more of note passed between them. They parted a day later, sadly and reluctantly, but fondly. Gloucester's vassals were dismissed to their master's service once more and Hereford spent a week more at Devizes making sure that their gains would not be lost again, sending instructions to abandon the siege at Faringdon and finally terminating his own vassals' service. He noted wryly that it was a year, exactly a year to the day when, in the pale sunlight of November, he turned his horse's head toward Hereford and began the lonely ride home. Thus he arrived, unheralded and unexpected, followed only by his small household guard, at the gates of Hereford Castle in the afternoon of the first day of the third week of November. He was two days earlier in time in arriving home than he had been a year before, but ages older in feeling. The town, the sloping, winding road up to the gates, the people running out to greet him, all unchanged, brought back vividly the memory of his emotion at that time. The violent conflict between his concealed fear of incapability and his wild desire and enthusiasm for the task, the shadow of the coming defeat, already forming in his mind, the soaring hopes of brilliant success, great power, and, best of all, a peaceful land, all these stirred in his memory. But quietly, everything was quiet now and far away. Even the shouts of the serfs and townfolk that startled his horse into shying sounded small and distant. Hereford smiled gently, opened his purse, and tossed coins. A great peace prevaded him, a great, cold, quiet peace, like death.

Elizabeth, informed of her husband's imminent arrival by a lookout from the gate tower, seized a cloak and ran hurriedly to the courtyard to greet him. The last she had heard had been a jubilant message by word of mouth recounting the victory over de Tracy and the taking of Bridport, but there had not been the slightest indication that Hereford intended to return home. The retainers who had crowded around their lord made way for Elizabeth, and Hereford, perceiving her, dismounted to kiss her hand and then her lips. He was smiling pleasantly and she could plainly see he was well and unhurt; nonetheless, the touch of those lips cold with a greeting that contained nothing more than courtesy turned pleasure to fear.

"What is wrong, Roger? What has happened?"

"A very great deal, my dear, but let me come in and shed my mail. There is no need for haste. I am home for good, Elizabeth."

"For good!" Elizabeth was chilled through and not by the cold breeze that whipped her cloak about. She saw now that Roger's eyes, although turned in her direction and apparently seeing her, were not truly focused upon her. So she had been wrong and his spirit had been broken—but by what? Why? He offered his hand in the court gesture with which a gentleman invited a lady of his acquaintance, but not close acquaintance, to walk.

"Yes, for good," he replied mildly, and then, smiling, "unless of course I am forced to defend my own property against attack. I can still do that. Otherwise, I am a gentleman of leisure. It is too cold for you here, Elizabeth, you are trembling."

She was, in truth, but not with cold. "Have you left Henry, Roger?" It was horrible, she thought, as she asked. Horrible that her voice should be so steady and unconcerned, horrible that she should place her hand upon

Roger's and allow him to lead her formally up the stairs and into the hall of the manor house, horrible that he should smile, then laugh gaily as he replied.

"No, indeed. He left me. Really, there is no need to discuss the matter, for it is quite final. Ah, mother, and my darling Catherine."

He released Elizabeth to embrace his mother and sister, and she remained where he left her, listening, stunned and unbelieving, to his proper questions about their well-being since he had seen them last. He must have broken and run, she thought, and Henry had sent him away because he was useless, and now he was mad. He looked a little mad, as if there were a wall between him and the rest of the world and he was trying to look through it and speak through it, even though what he said and did were perfectly sane. He turned from his mother and sister only to fondle his daughters briefly, say how pretty they had grown, ask about what they had learned since he left them, and laugh at their innocent answers and pleasure at his inquiries. Then he retreated to the bedroom to wash, lay aside his armor and weapons, and dress in the luxurious, fur-trimmed robes of a gentleman who had no expectation of any hurried call to any duty. Emerging shortly, with no indication in face or manner that he wished to avoid company, Hereford devoted the intervening hours before suppertime to a discussion of Catherine's affairs. He told of the arrangements made with John Fitz Gilbert for Catherine's marriage to his son Patric and explained his reasons for that choice. He was perfectly good-humored, jesting lightly in his usual way as he calmed his sister's transports and seriously set himself to reason away his mother's objections.

At no time did he ignore or slight Elizabeth. He included her in every phase of the discussion, even pointedly asking her opinion and her backing for some of his remarks. He was unfailingly courteous, painfully polite—as polite as he would have been to a stranger.

At one point in the evening Elizabeth decided she could bear no more. Unwilling to come to grips with Roger and expose his shame to the rest of his family, she claimed weariness and suggested retiring to bed. Lady Hereford and Catherine were instantly solicitous, Roger plainly surprised both by their concern and by Elizabeth's confession of fatigue. His surprise, however, was nothing to what was mirrored in the expressions of his sister and mother when he let her go.

"Do you not go with your wife, Roger?"

"Go with her? Why? Oh," Hereford laughed, misconstruing completely his mother's thought, "it is true that I have been several weeks away from her bed, but, after all, if she is eager, waiting will make her more eager, and if she is weary, it is kindness in me to let her rest before I tire her further."

"Roger!" Lady Hereford protested. Perhaps she did not like her daughter-in-law even now, but what was right was right. "A woman more than five months gone with her first child deserves more consideration than you are showing her."

"Five—what?" Hereford blinked and shook his head as if he had been hit. The room receded infinitely and then, all at once, became his hall, his own familiar hall, not some immense cold place of tiny spots of brilliant color filled with little people he didn't really know and little sounds all very far away.

"Did she not tell you?"

"No," Hereford got out. "No, she—good God, she must have thought—." Hereford cut that off. His mother, of course, did not know he had taken Elizabeth as a vassal, and, to his mind, it was none of her business, but he felt then that his wife had concealed her pregnancy because she considered that a "woman's reason" for not performing the duties he had ordered.

"But Roger, could you not see—. She is swollen with it already. Surely you are not such a fool that your eyes did not tell you she was with child."

"Fool—I am ten times a fool about everything. No, I did not see anything. I have been so taken up with—other matters."

"What matters? Roger, what have you been doing? What—"

"Not now. Besides, it is not a woman's affair." He stood up almost reluctantly, thinking how angry Elizabeth would be and that he had no more strength left to use in calming her. "I had better go to her."

Elizabeth was not yet in bed. Her maids were brushing her long black hair, but Hereford dismissed them with a gesture and took the brush into his own hand. She did not turn to face him; if she saw those eyes fixed on some infinitely distant point again, she knew she would not be able to control herself enough to help him. For a while he brushed in silence, long, strong strokes that made the hair crackle and rise to follow the brush. The scent of her hair came to him and suddenly he dropped the brush and lifted an armful of the shining black mass to bury his face in it.

"Why did you keep this—Elizabeth, are you with child?"

The voice was different and Elizabeth would have turned, but Roger held her hair. "Yes."

"Why did you not tell me?"

"I—do not be angry, Roger. Somehow the time was never right. When I first knew, I had just received your orders to travel north with my father, and then, somehow, I could never find the right words for a letter. I started to tell you in Gloucester, but—but you were so overburdened already, and I did not wish you to have any further cause for concern."

"Elizabeth! You might have done yourself some hurt with all that riding."

He did not sound angry now. "Oh, no. I am very strong, and your heir, if it be an heir, is safe."

"I do not care for that." At that instant it was no lie, for Elizabeth's voluptuous curves, in spite of the thickened waist and coarsening lines of the body, were more desirable than ever. He had been thinking only of her, not of the child.

Now she pulled her hair from his grip and turned. "I am not sure I care either. Roger, in God's name, tell me what has happened. You cannot say to me that Henry has left you and nothing else. Why? Did you quarrel with him? Did you suffer some great defeat?" That was as close as she could come to her fear that he had, in his madness,

committed some act of great cowardice. "What will become of us? What will become of this poor child?"

Hereford's face contorted with pain, for the peace of rejection of all feeling which he had made for himself had
been broken by his fierce pleasure at hearing of his wife's
condition. He was fond of children, attached to his natural
daughters even though he had never cared much for their
mothers, but he was surprised by the violent surge of protective emotion which tore him in reply to Elizabeth's
questions. Still he could not bear to face squarely that agony of frustration and futility he had experienced in
Devizes, and he turned away, fighting to retain his distant
peace. Now too there was Elizabeth's frustrated ambition
to face. He could hear her before she spoke, the bitter
questioning of why he had done no more to keep Henry,
why he had refused to capture Eustace and take the
power into his own hands.

"Is not the earldom of Hereford sufficient to satisfy your
ambition for your child?"

"If it be held with honor, more than enough. What
have you done, Roger, that you are ashamed to tell me
of?"

That turned him toward her, and the horror and terror
of her expression betrayed what she had been thinking.
"Why do you always think the worst of me?"

"I do not. I do not. But what other reason can you have
to refuse to speak?"

"None of import to you," he lashed out bitterly. "Only
the pain it costs me to recount in my own mind and to
my ears with my own voice the blood and substance I have
lost, the wasted years of battle and bloodshed—. He left
me, left his land and his word, left me to court a woman
and gain a rich dower." His voice broke and he covered
his face with his hands. It was too late for peace, the dam
he had built to keep back his grief and disappointment,
his rebellion in the face of God's will to the idea that
Henry would desert his given oath to seize a richer prize,
was broken.

"Oh Roger, Roger." Elizabeth ran to him and took him
in her arms. "So long as our honor is not smirched, so long
as you have done nothing of which to be ashamed, I do

not care." There was a moment's pause, and Hereford dropped his head so that his cheek rested against Elizabeth's hair. "Nay," she continued, surprising her husband by the note of fierce joy in her voice, "I do not care. I am glad. Glad, do you hear. Let them kill each other and burn each other. Let Satan gobble up all this accursed land. Only let us live in peace and be together. My husband," she put up a hand to stroke his hair, "my beloved husband, go no more to war. Stay and give me the comfort of your presence."

They stood a while longer, Hereford's tears wetting his wife's cheek and hair. Finally Elizabeth broke their embrace gently. "Let us go to bed, Roger. I will ask you nothing, ever. Forget and be at peace."

In the intimate dark behind the bed curtains, clasped again in Elizabeth's warm embrace, Hereford found his tongue and also an urgent need to unburden himself. Haltingly at first, and then more easily, he began to explain what had happened, not the events, although he did describe those, but what had happened to him. He spoke at last of his early and increasing foreboding of preordained failure and its cause, of the freezing terror of his dream, of his release from that fear, and of the culmination of victory in the final loss of all he had striven for.

"Storm said that Stephen was God's anointed king and that it was wrong to try to wrest that power from him, but that man must do what he thought right. He said that it was possible that I would be God's instrument to change this land's destiny. Well, I was not. Still, though, I must bow to the Infinite Wisdom, and though I was warned so many times, I must believe that Henry is the rightful king of this realm. No better, in some ways mayhap even worse, than the man who is before him, but still the rightful king."

"You cannot know, Roger. Mayhap you have changed the destiny of this land. Have you ever seen Stephen display the energy and determination he has shown in this last half year? Perhaps God used you to create the miracle of making Stephen a better king. I too believe Henry is the rightful heir to the throne, but now I think it is plain that he must come to it in peace. If Stephen can bring quiet to England by better management, and Henry follows him under the crown, then you have succeeded, not failed, and succeeded without the sin of wresting the crown from the king by force."

Hereford did not reply to that. He did not believe Stephen could change, but he thought wearily that if the great barons could be welded together they, themselves could bring quiet to England. After a while he sighed deeply and slid his hand down to Elizabeth's swelling abdomen. Under his hand the child quickened, and Hereford felt the faint flutter of life. A smile, uncertain at first and then gladder and more sure, illumined his face.

"I doubt you are right, but yet, there are other ways to achieve the same end. Christ is merciful and the Father just and good. It must be so. Do you feel the child, Elizabeth? I cannot tell you why, but that little life makes my heart sing. I will not give up. I will but rest a little until I am less weary and then I will tell Henry that I will make my peace with Stephen—unless he should call me to arms again, which I have promised—and strive still, but in different ways to make a better land."

"Roger," Elizabeth said softly, reaching under her pillow, "now we are at peace, give me leave to return this to you." He took the glove which was the symbol of her vassalage with a slight stiffening of surprise and apprehension, but she continued speaking before he could question. "There was never need for it. Whatever you commanded, I have done for love. I never thought once of that oath. You have taught me many things, Roger. I do not desire to rule the world, nor even you. I wish only to be a woman and live in peace."

There was only one way to thank her and accept that sacrifice which was no sacrifice. Later, smiling but a little regretfully, Hereford said, "Does that mean you will rail at me no more, Liza my love?"

And Elizabeth laughed and kissed him, and replied, "You have taken all the covers from me, you clumsy clod, and I am freezing. You are an oaf, and a dolt, and have no notion of how to treat a woman properly."

"Have I not?" her husband answered, drawing her back into his embrace. "Then I will have to practice."